AFTER THE GOLDEN AGE

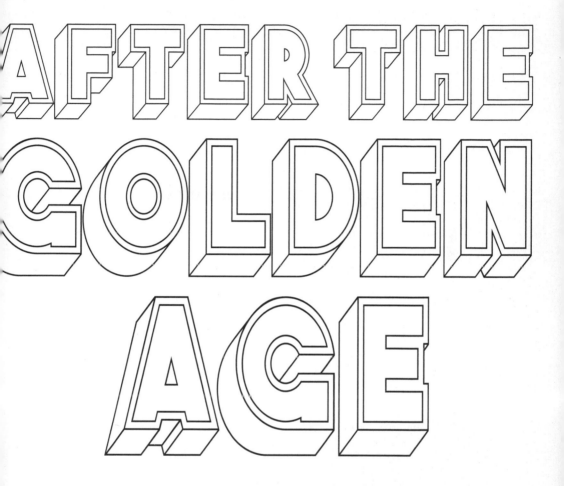

AFTER THE GOLDEN AGE

CARRIE VAUGHN

TOR®

A TOM DOHERTY ASSOCIATES BOOK • NEW YORK

AFTER THE GOLDEN AGE

Copyright © 2011 by Carrie Vaughn, LLC

Edited by David G. Hartwell

A Tor Book
Published by Tom Doherty Associates, LLC
175 Fifth Avenue
New York, NY 10010

www.tor-forge.com

Tor® is a registered trademark of Tom Doherty Associates, LLC.

Library of Congress Cataloging-in-Publication Data

Vaughn, Carrie.
  After the Golden Age / Carrie Vaughn.—1st ed.
   p. cm.
  "A Tom Doherty Associates book."
  ISBN 978-0-7653-2555-6
  I. Title.
  PS3622.A9475A68 2011
  813'.6—dc22

                                    2010036541

First Edition: April 2011

Printed in the United States of America

0 9 8 7 6 5 4 3 2 1

To Max,
who introduced me to the Silver and Golden Ages,
and who always shares his comics

AFTER THE GOLDEN AGE

ONE

CELIA took the late bus home, riding along with other young workaholic professionals, the odd student, and late-shift retail clerks. A quiet, working bunch, cogs and wheels that kept Commerce City running.

Only a block away from the office, the person in the seat behind her leaned forward and spoke in her ear:

"Get off at the next stop."

She hadn't noticed him before. He was ordinary; in his thirties, he had a rugged, stubbled face, and wore jeans and a button-up shirt. He looked like he belonged. With a lift to his brow, he glared at her over the back of the plastic seat and raised the handgun from his lap. Without moving his gaze, he pushed the stop call button by the window.

Damn, not again.

Her heart pounded hard—with anger. Not fear, she reminded herself. Her fists clenched, her face a mask, she stood. She could hardly move her legs, wanting only to turn and throttle the bastard for interrupting her evening.

He stood with her, following a step behind as she moved forward toward the door. He could stop her before she called to the driver for help. And what could the driver do, but stand aside as her kidnapper waved the gun at him?

She was still two miles from home. She could try to run—in pumps and a dress suit. Right. Really, she only had to run far enough away to duck into a corner and call 9-1-1. Or her parents.

9-1-1. That was what she'd do.

She didn't dig in the pocket of her attaché for her phone. Did nothing that would give away her plan. She stepped off the bus, onto the sidewalk. Her kidnapper disembarked right behind her.

"Turn right. Walk five steps."

She turned right. Her muscles tensed, ready—

The bus pulled away. She prepared to launch herself into a run.

A sedan stopped at the curb. Two men jumped out of the back, and the kidnapper from the bus grabbed her arm. The three surrounded her and spirited her into the car, which rolled away in seconds.

They'd planned this, hadn't they?

In the backseat, one of the men tied her hands in front of her with nylon cord. The other pressed a gun to her ribs.

The one from the bus sat on the passenger side of the front seat and looked back at her.

"You're Warren and Suzanne West's daughter."

Not like this was news.

"What will the Olympiad do to keep you safe?"

"You'll have to ask them," she said.

"I will." He grinned, a self-satisfied, cat-with-the-canary grin that she recognized from a half-dozen two-bit hoodlums who thought they'd done something clever, that they'd figured out how to corner the Olympiad. As if no one else had tried this before.

"What are you going to do with me?" She said it perfunctorily. It was a way to make conversation. Maybe distract him.

His grin widened. "We're going to send your parents a message. With the Destructor out of the picture, the city's wide open for a new gang to move in. The Olympiad is going to stay out of our way, or you get hurt."

He really was stupid enough to tell her his plan. Amateurs.

Wasn't much she could do until he'd sent the message and the

Olympiad learned what had happened. She'd leave the hard work to them. She always did.

Then, of course, they blindfolded her so she couldn't keep track of their route. By the time they stopped, she had no idea where they were. Someplace west, by the docks maybe. The air smelled of concrete and industry.

A stooge on each arm pulled her out of the car and guided her down a corridor. They must have parked inside a building. Her feet stepped on tile, and the walls felt close. Finally, they pushed her into a hard wooden chair and tied her wrists to its arms.

The blindfold came off. Before her, a video camera was mounted on a tripod.

The man from the bus stood next to the camera. She smirked at him, and his frown deepened. He'd probably expected her to be frightened, crying and begging him to let her go. Giving him that power of fear over her.

She had already been as frightened as she was ever likely to be in her life. This guy was nothing.

"Read this." He lifted a piece of paper with large writing.

She just wanted to go home. Have some hot cocoa and cookies. Supper had been microwave ramen and her stomach was growling. The blindfold had messed up her short red hair, making it itch, and she couldn't reach up to scratch it. Irrationally, she thought of her parents, and her anger began to turn toward them. If it wasn't for them and what they were . . .

Thinking like that had gotten her in trouble before. She focused on her captor. This was *his* fault.

She skimmed over the text, groaned. They couldn't even be a little creative. "Are you kidding?"

"Just read it."

In a frustrated monotone, she did as she was told.

"I'm Celia West, and I'm being held in an undisclosed location. If the Olympiad has not responded to their demands in six hours, my captors cannot guarantee my safety—"

"Wait. Stop."

She glared an inquiry.

"Couldn't you sound . . . you know . . . Scared or something?"

"Sorry. But you know I've done this before. This isn't exactly new to me."

"*We're* different."

"They all say that."

"Shut up. Finish reading."

She raised her brow. He waved her on.

She said, "If you really want to scare everyone you'd cut off one of my fingers and send it to them. Of course, then you'd *really* piss them off. That whole nonlethal force thing might not apply then."

He stepped forward, fists clenched, like he might actually hit her. "Unless you really want me to do something like that, just stick to the script. I know what I'm doing."

"Whatever you say." She read out the usual list of demands: the Olympiad was to leave Commerce City and not interfere with the actions of the Baxter Gang— "Baxter Gang?" she added in a disbelieving aside, then shook her head and continued. They'd let her go when the Baxter Gang had the run of the city. They'd send another video in six hours to show just how mean they could be, etcetera.

The plan must have sounded so good on paper.

She made a point of not looking at the men with guns who seemed to fill the room. In truth there were only five. Even so, if she did anything more aggressive than mock the man she assumed was Baxter, they just might shoot her.

There was a time when even that wouldn't have bothered her. She remembered. She drew on that now. Don't reveal anything to them. No weakness.

She didn't want to die. What an oddly pleasing thought.

Finally, she reached the end of the script and Baxter shut off the recorder. He popped the memory card out of the camera, gave her a final glare, and left the room. The men with the guns remained.

All she could do was wait.

*   *   *

How it usually worked: the kidnappers sent the video to the police. The police delivered it to the Olympiad. The kidnappers expected Warren and Suzanne West to be despondent over the imminent danger toward their only child and to cave in to their every demand.

What the kidnappers never understood was that Celia West was expendable.

She'd understood that early on. When it came to choosing between her own safety or the safety of Commerce City, the city always won. She understood that, and usually even believed it herself.

She thought she might try to sleep. She'd been losing lots, with the late nights at the office. Leaning back in the chair, she breathed deeply, closed her eyes, and tried to relax. Unfortunately, relaxing in a hard-backed chair you were tied to was difficult at best. Though she imagined her falling asleep in the midst of her own kidnapping would annoy Baxter, which made her want to do it even more. But she was sweating inside her jacket and wanted to fidget.

All the breathing and attempts at relaxation did was keep her heart from racing, which was enough. She could meet the gazes of the gun-toting stooges in the room and not give in to blind panic.

Eventually, Baxter returned to the room. He eyed her warily, but didn't approach, didn't speak. He broke his minions into shifts, sending one of them for fast food. The food returned a half hour later, and they sat around a table to eat. Her stomach rumbled at the smell of cheap hamburgers. She hadn't eaten, and she needed to use a restroom.

Just breathe. She'd had to wait longer than this before. Her watch said that only three hours had passed. It was just now midnight. She had a couple more hours at least. More dramatic that way.

She might say a dozen things to aggravate Baxter. She figured she could annoy him enough to get him to come over and hit her. That was the bored, self-destructive teenager of yore talking. And a little bit of revenge. If she ended up with a big black eye, things would go so much more badly for him later on.

Then, the waiting ended.

—Celia, are you there?—

It was odd, an inner whisper that felt like a thought, but which came from outside. Rather like how a psychotic must feel, listening to the voices. This one was understated, with a British accent. She'd felt Dr. Mentis's telepathic reach before. She couldn't respond in kind, not with such articulate, well-formed thoughts. Instead, she filled her mind with a *yes*, knowing he'd read it there. Along with a little bit of, *It's about time.*

—I'm going to put the room to sleep. I'm afraid I can't pick and choose. You'll feel a little dizzy, then pass out. I wanted to warn you.—

She kept herself from nodding. Mustn't let the erstwhile arch-villains of Commerce City know anything was happening.

The guard by the door blacked out first. He shook his head, as if trying to stay awake, swayed a little, and pitched over sideways, dropping his gun. Startled, his compatriots looked over.

"Bill? Hey, Bill!"

Two at the table keeled over next. Then one standing by his chair. Baxter stood and stared at them, looking from one to another with growing urgency. Her vision was swimming. Squinting to focus, she braced, waiting, wanting it to be over.

Baxter looked at her, his eyes widening. "You. What's happening? You know, I know you know—"

He stepped forward, arm outstretched. Then he blinked, stopped, gave a shudder—

She thought she smelled sage.

—Sleep—

C elia?"

The world was black and lurching. If she opened her eyes, she'd find herself on the deck of a sailing ship.

"Celia, time to wake up." A cool hand pressed her cheek.

She opened her eyes, and the light stabbed to life a headache that ran from her temples to the back of her neck.

"Ow," she said and covered her face with her hands.

"There you are. Good morning."

She was lying on the floor. Dr. Arthur Mentis knelt beside her, his brown trench coat spread around him, his smile wry. The cavalry, finally. Now she could relax.

He put an arm around her shoulders and helped her sit up. The headache shifted and pounded in another direction. She had to hold her head. On the bright side, members of the Baxter Gang were all writhing around on the floor, groaning, while the police picked them up and dragged them away.

"Sorry about the headache," he said. "It'll go away in a couple of hours."

"That's okay," she said softly, to not jostle herself. "I think I used to be better at this hostage thing."

"Are you joking? That ransom video was a riot. Even Warren laughed."

She raised her brow, disbelieving.

"Will you be all right for the next few minutes?" he said.

"Yeah."

He gave her shoulder a comforting squeeze and left her propped against the wall while he helped with cleanup. As the police collected and removed the gang members, Mentis looked each of them in the eyes, reading their minds, learning what he could from them. They wouldn't even know what was happening.

The wall around the door was scorched, streaked black with soot, and the door itself had disappeared. Spark must have had to blast it open. The room smelled toasted with that particular flavor Celia had always associated with Spark's flames: baking chocolate. Celia was surprised to find the scent comforting.

Her mother entered the room a moment later.

Suzanne West—Spark—was beautiful, marvelously svelte in her form-fitted skin suit, black with flame-colored accents. Her red hair swept thick and luxurious down her back. She moved with energy and purpose.

She paused, looked around, and found Celia. "Celia!"

This was just like old times, nearly. Suzanne crouched beside her, gripped Celia's shoulders, and pursed her face like she might cry.

Celia sighed and put her arms around her mother. Suzanne hugged back tightly. "Hi, Mom."

"Oh Celia, are you all right?"

"Headache. But yeah. Did you guys find my bag? I had notes from work in it."

"I don't know. We'll look. I was so worried—did they hurt you? Are you okay?"

"I'm fine." She tried to stand, but the headache made her vision splotchy. The floor was nice and stable.

"Don't try to move; paramedics are on the way."

"I don't need paramedics. I just want to go home."

Suzanne sighed with frustration. "I really wish you'd come live at the plaza. It's so much safer—"

Celia shook her head. "No way. Uh-uh."

"This sort of thing wouldn't happen—"

"Mom, they picked me off the bus on the way home from work. I can't not leave home."

"What were you doing riding the bus?"

"I don't have a car."

"Celia, if you need a car we can—"

Headache or no, she wasn't sitting still to listen to this. Bracing against the wall, she got her feet under her and managed to push herself up. Suzanne reached for her, but Celia shrugged her away. "I'm *fine*."

She hated being like this. She felt sixteen years old, all over again.

"Why won't you let us help you?"

The question wasn't about this, the rescue from the kidnapping, the arm to get her off the floor. It was the big question.

Celia focused on the wall, which didn't make her dizzy. "I haven't taken a cent from you in years; I'm not going to start now."

"If it'll keep you from getting assaulted like this—"

"Well, I wouldn't get assaulted like this if I weren't your daughter, would I?"

If she'd said that to her father, he would have lost his temper, broken a chair or punched through the wall with a glance, and stalked out of the room. Her mother, on the other hand . . . Suzanne's lips pursed, and her eyes reddened like she was about to cry. Instantly Celia felt guilty, but she couldn't take it back, and she couldn't apologize, because it was true.

"Everything all right?" Mentis had returned. He stood, hands in the pockets of his trench coat, and looked between the two of them inquiringly. He was in his thirties, with brown hair grown slightly shaggy and a pale, searching face. The Olympiad had been active for over ten years already when he joined, as a student at the university medical school. Despite his younger age, he carried around with him this maddening, ancient air of wisdom.

Celia and her mother stared at one another. Mentis, the telepath, must have seen a frothing mass of pent-up frustrations and unspoken thoughts. They couldn't hide from him like they could from each other.

Nevertheless, Celia said, "Fine. I'd just like to go home and sleep off this hangover."

"Right," Mentis said. He held out her attaché case, unopened and none the worse for wear. "I think this is yours. We found it in Baxter's car."

"Thanks."

He turned to Suzanne. "We should move on. Captain and the Bullet have cleaned up the bank robberies, but two branches of the gang are still at large."

Celia paused. "What's happening?"

"This was more than a simple kidnapping," Mentis said. "It was a distraction. Baxter's people launched attacks all over the city. He wanted to see how much he could get away with while we were busy rescuing you."

If Baxter could have held her indefinitely, moving from place to place, keeping one step ahead of the Olympiad, he might have run them ragged.

They'd taken the time to rescue her.

"Detective? Could you see that Miss West arrives home safely?"

Mentis called to a young man in a suit and overcoat standing near the doorway. One of the detectives on the case, he held a notepad and pencil, jotting notes as Baxter's men were escorted out. The cop looked at Mentis and nodded.

She suppressed a vague feeling of abandonment, that she could have died, and now Mentis and her mother were just leaving her alone. But she remembered: the city was more important. And Celia was always saying she could take care of herself, wasn't she?

—*You'll be fine. I have faith in you.*—Mentis's smile was wry, and Celia nodded in acknowledgment.

"Thanks," she said. "For coming after me. Tell Dad I said hi."

Suzanne crossed her arms. "You could call once in a while."

He could call me. "Maybe I will." She managed a smile for her mother and a last wave at Mentis before leaving.

The cop escorted her out of the building. "I'm Detective Paulson. Mark Paulson." Endearingly, he offered his hand, and she shook it.

"Celia West."

"Yeah, I know."

A few awkward, silent minutes brought them to the curb and a swarm of police cars, lights flashing a fireworks display on the street. A half-dozen men were occupied keeping reporters and news cameras behind a line of caution tape. A couple of hero groupies were there as well—the creator of a low-end gossip website dedicated to the city's heroes, another guy holding up a big poster declaring: CAPTAIN OLYMPUS: OUR ALIEN SAVIOR. There were always a few lurking around every time something like this happened. Instinctively, Celia looked away and hunched her shoulders, trying to duck into her collar.

Paulson brought her to an unmarked sedan. They might actually get away without the reporters noticing. Opening the passenger side door, he helped her in.

While he situated himself and started the car, she said, "Paulson. Any relation to Mayor Paulson?"

He developed a funny little half smile. "I'm his son."

That was where she'd seen that jawline before. And the flop of dark hair. The mayor's hair had gone handsomely salt and pepper in his middle age. Mark's still shone.

"Ah," she said, grinning. "Then you know all about it. I shouldn't pry—but he wanted you to go into politics, didn't he?"

"Not quite. He wanted me to be a lawyer, then go into politics. I got the law degree. Then, well . . ." He shrugged, his glance taking in the car and the flashing lights behind them. "Then I decided I wanted to be on the front lines rather than the rearguard. Make sure no one gets off on a technicality because they weren't read their rights."

"Cool," she said.

"What about you? I mean, your parents—" He let out an awestruck sigh. And who wouldn't, after meeting Spark? "They want you to go into . . . the family business, I guess it is?"

"Oh, they certainly did. Nature had different ideas, though. I'm the offspring of Commerce City's greatest superhumans, and the most exciting thing I ever did was win a silver medal in a high-school swim meet." Good thing she could look back on it now and laugh.

She still had that medal sitting on her dresser.

"It must have been amazing, growing up with them."

"Yeah, you could say that." The strength of her sarcasm invited no further questions.

Finally, they arrived at her apartment building. Detective Paulson insisted on walking her to her front door, as if one of the Baxter Gang splinters would leap out of the shadows and snatch her up. She had to admit, twice in a night would be embarrassing.

"Thanks for taking me home," she said, once her door was unlocked. "I know you've got better things to do."

"Not at all," he said. "Maybe I could do it again sometime."

Though he turned away before she could read the expression on his face, she thought he was smiling. She watched him until he turned the corner.

Closing the door behind her, she shook her head. She'd imagined it. Her head was still foggy.

Later, she sat in bed, drinking a cup of chamomile tea and watching the news. All the city's "independent law-enforcement agents" were out in force, quelling the riot of criminal activity. Typhoon created floods to incapacitate a group of bank robbers. Breezeway swept them off their feet with gusts of air. Even the telekinetic Mind-masher and his on-again, off-again lover, Earth Mother, were out and about. Block Buster Senior and Junior were as usual directing their brute-force mode of combat toward a trio of vandals holed up in an abandoned convenience store. The two superhumans were taking the building apart, concrete block by concrete block, until it formed an impromptu jail. Block Buster Senior used to be just Block Buster until a couple of years ago, when Junior showed up. Anyone could tell he wasn't much more than a kid under the mask and skin-suit uniform. Lots of people speculated if the two were actually father and son as their names suggested, or if they instead had a mentor/apprentice relationship. Whatever their story, Celia thought they took a little too much joy in inflicting property damage.

And if they *were* father and son—how had Junior managed to inherit his father's power? Why him and not her?

Most of the coverage focused on the beloved Olympiad, who'd been protecting Commerce City for twenty-five years now. One of the stations had exclusive footage of Captain Olympus and the Bullet, the fourth member of the Olympiad, tearing open the warehouse that held the Baxter Gang's main headquarters.

The camera could only follow the Bullet's progress by tracking a whirlwind that traveled from one end of the building to the other, tossing masked gunmen aside in a storm of dust and debris. Guns flew from their hands and spiraled upward, shattering with the force of movement. It was all the Bullet, Robbie Denton, moving faster than the eye could see, disrupting one enemy attack after another in mere seconds.

Captain Olympus—the Golden Thunderbolt, most powerful man in the world—wore black and gold, and tore down walls with his will. He stood before his target, braced, arms outstretched, and created a hammer of force that crumpled half the building.

Celia's hands started shaking. The warehouse district was across town. He wasn't anywhere near here. The news reporter on the scene raved on and on about the spectacular scene, the malevolence of the criminals, the courage of the Olympiad.

She found the remote and turned off the TV.

TWO

THIS was the kind of story that made up West family lore:

When Warren West was six years old, he fell. This wasn't a stumble and a skinned knee, a crash on a bike, or a roll down the stairs, any of which most kids had suffered by his age. No, this was a fall out of a tree—from the top of a twenty-foot tall oak in City Park. He'd landed on a bent elbow, which should have shattered his arm at the very least. A fall like that should have killed him. But Warren walked away with no injuries. He didn't even cry. Then, his parents realized he had never skinned his knees or elbows, scratched himself, or gotten a bruise of any kind. He'd only ever cried when he was tired, hungry, or didn't get what he wanted.

There was something special about Warren.

Celia's parents went to high school together at the Elmwood Academy, Commerce City's premier private school, where Celia herself had gone until she dropped out, earning her GED instead. Warren and Suzanne knew *of* each other all along—Warren watched Suzanne first. Suzanne was hard to miss with her bright red hair, which she wore long and rippling. Warren was captain of the football team, son of Commerce City's wealthiest businessman, and Suzanne thought he was a snob. So she wasn't thrilled when, while standing at her locker one day, Warren propped his hand on the locker next to her's and gave her a jock smile.

She had a trick she used on guys who came on too strong. She'd touch his hand, give him eyes like she was coming on right back— then really turn on the heat. Within seconds he'd get the hint, usually leaping away with some sort of squeal as her power scorched him.

But Warren just stood there and took it. Her saccharine smile fell, and his eyes got wide. He held her hand and his flesh didn't burn. He could take the heat.

After that, they taught each other, tested each other, learned to use their powers for more than high-school games. Together, they made a vow: to use their powers for good. Together, they could change the world.

"Come in, Celia."

Celia entered the office of the elder Kurchanski. Kurchanski was a year from retirement, except that he'd said that every year for the last three, as long as Celia had been with the firm Smith and Kurchanski, Certified Public Accountants. The senior partner's office had a core of respectability. It had at one point been designed to impress clients: corner windows, leather executive chairs, a vast walnut desk, plush carpeting, wood-paneled walls, and real ferns living in brass pots on the bookshelves between bound tomes of tax law stretching back for decades. No one had bound copies of tax law anymore—everyone subscribed to online databases. But Kurchanski collected the volumes and used them to provide atmosphere. The room had long ago developed a lived-in atmosphere; a newspaper lay discarded over a chair arm, a coat lay slung over the back, and paperwork covered the desk.

He'd called her to his office first thing this morning.

"Do you know the District Attorney's office has hired the firm to work on the Simon Sito prosecution?" He didn't look up from the papers on his desk. His was the only office in the firm without a computer.

"Yes, sir," she said calmly, belying the sinking feeling in her gut. It wasn't a surprise. Smith and Kurchanski was a pioneer in the field of forensic accounting and had worked with the DA before. The case against Simon Sito—aka the Destructor—was possibly the most extensive criminal prosecution in Commerce City's history.

But surely the firm didn't have to involve her in it.

"DA Bronson has specifically requested that you be assigned to work on the case."

She was the firm's youngest CPA. She was inexperienced, definitely, but more than that she was far too personally involved. Conflict of interest? Kurchanski had no idea.

She was too desperate to keep the nervous waver out of her voice. "That isn't a good idea. He knows that isn't a good idea, doesn't he?"

He finally looked at her as he leaned back in his chair. "I'd have thought you'd jump at a chance to work on this."

She wanted to stay as far away from it as possible, for so many reasons. "I'd just as soon keep those memories buried. Not to mention the possible conflict of interest. The firm has plenty of impartial accountants—why would the DA even ask for me?"

"I imagine your connections make for good press."

The daughter of Captain Olympus helping to prosecute the Olympiad's greatest adversary? Good press, indeed.

Could she get out of this? How much vacation time did she have saved?

"Celia, if you're really adamant about not taking this case, I'll tell the DA no. But I'm sure he has a good reason for asking for you, and I'm sure you can handle it. I have to confess, I can't ignore the publicity this will generate for the firm. As a favor to me, will you take the case?"

Put like that, she couldn't refuse. "All right, sir."

"Thank you. I knew we could count on you."

She left his office wondering what her parents would think of this.

*　*　*

After all the news from last night, Analise insisted they have lunch together.

Celia met Analise by accident four years ago. On a bright spring day, Celia was climbing the steps to the university library, a bag of books weighing her down. Ahead, the door slammed open and a woman stormed out as if the building were on fire. Celia didn't see any smoke or hear any alarms. The woman, about Celia's age, brown-skinned, cornrow braids tied back with a bandana, seemed to not even notice her on the stairs. She plowed into Celia, who stumbled back against the metal railing and managed to grab it before she fell.

The woman bounced away in the other direction, dropping the loose books she carried. She barked some complaint as she retrieved them.

Celia knew her. Roughly, distantly. She didn't realize it until she saw that snarl, the determined line of her jaw—the expression of a warrior frustrated in her task. If the woman were wearing a sleek blue mask, she'd be unmistakable.

"Typhoon," she said.

The woman halted mid-stride and turned to Celia. The simmering anger in her dark eyes made her even more recognizable as the superhuman crime fighter. She marched toward Celia, who stood her ground, trapped as she was against the railing. The woman, Typhoon, clearly wasn't going to let her escape.

"You're joking, right?" she said.

"No, actually," Celia said, smiling weakly. "You know, I expected you to laugh at me and then rush off, so I'd stand here wondering if I'd made a mistake. But that look on your face right now—I'm pretty sure I'm right."

Celia shouldn't have said anything. She should have convinced herself she was seeing things and let it go. Typhoon, even in her civilian guise, looked angry enough to do damage. But Celia had stood up to Captain Olympus. This was nothing.

"How?" the woman said softly. "How do you know you're right?"

Blushing, Celia squirmed inside her jacket. The woman was

looking at her like she was part of some conspiracy, some criminal mastermind in the midst of a nefarious plot. Paranoia seemed to be an inherent part of the crime-fighting lifestyle.

It was like finding another member of a secret club; Celia had to show that she knew the handshake.

"I sort of grew up learning to recognize people under their masks. I guess I have a knack for it. I'm Celia West." She offered her hand.

The woman's eyes grew wide. "*The* Celia West? Damn, I guess you would have a knack for it. Look, there's a freighter sinking in the harbor so I have to run. But we're going to talk later, okay? I'll call you."

"Yeah, sure," Celia said, but the woman had already started running across the quad.

The call came at 10:00 P.M., and at eleven they were at Pee Wee's, the all-night coffee shop near campus, trading war stories. Her name was Analise Baker. Celia liked her. She was brash and outspoken, impulsive and generous—the kind of personality that might lead one to become a vigilante crime fighter.

She had no problem asking the questions that everyone was thinking, but few ever found the courage to voice. "God, you're the daughter of West Corp's CEO; what the hell are you doing *here*? Shouldn't you have a limo and a penthouse somewhere?"

"I wanted to get away from that for a while." As if she might actually go back to it someday.

"So what was it like? You had half the Olympiad as parents—what was it like growing up with them?"

It sucked like a starving lamprey. But no one wanted to hear that. She had a well-practiced answer. "It was interesting. Really, though, they tried to keep me out of things as much as possible."

Which wasn't all that possible, in the end. But Analise stared back with stars in her eyes and let out a sigh.

Celia kept her mouth shut. Let them imagine whatever they wanted. It was all water under the bridge.

* * *

can't *believe* you're working today," Analise had gushed on the phone. "Couldn't you call in sick or something?"

"I prefer things get back to normal as quickly as possible." That was always how she'd handled it when she was younger. Pretend like nothing had happened. Pretend like you didn't need to be coddled. Pretend like you weren't helpless.

Celia relented to being ranted at in person at Analise's favorite diner, a block from the building that housed Smith and Kurchanski.

Analise, it seemed, *had* called in sick after last night's excitement. She was waiting for Celia in a corner booth, and she'd already ordered salads for them both.

"Tell me all about it. Tell me everything," she said, before Celia had even sat. Analise was hipper than Celia. Her hair, braided in cornrows, was pulled back in a ponytail. She dressed like she was still in college, in jeans and faded concert T-shirt for an old punk band. She worked at an independent record store, of course, lived in a not-so-great part of town, and yet was never afraid to walk home after dark. Her round brown eyes sparkled.

"Don't you read the papers?" Celia said. She was sure Analise had, but that didn't matter. She told the story, again, and she had to admit, with Analise as an eager audience the episode sounded much more adventurous than it had felt.

When she got to the part where Mentis incapacitated the room, Analise shivered. "You can actually feel him in your mind? Ugh. That guy makes me nervous."

"He's not so bad. For someone who can read minds, he's really nonjudgmental. You know; you've met him."

"Briefly," she said. "Professionally. And I kept my distance. Besides, I'm incredibly jealous. He always gets much better press than I do. I mean, look at this." Her voice dropped in volume.

She pulled a rolled-up paper out of her backpack and spread it out on the table, facing Celia. *The Commerce Eye*, the city's tabloid rag. The headline blared: "Typhoon and Breezeway: On Again?"

Celia didn't know for certain, but she was sure Analise kept a scrapbook of these headlines. "You know better than to read that crap."

"They've spent months inventing this whole sordid affair, and then just because we both show up at the same place at the same time and happen to do a little tag-teaming, they think there's something going on. Like I would ever go out with that jerk." A blurry photo showed the city's two hippest superhuman fighters: Breezeway was a tall, lithe man wearing a silver skin suit and a mask, hovering a dozen feet above the ground as he surveyed a tidal wave rising from a fountain, where Typhoon stood. She also went masked, and wore a blue costume of shimmering silk, but some of her features remained clear: dark skin, and a cascade of braided hair.

"You could call them and complain," Celia said.

"What, and validate everything they've said? No. I'm just venting, you know that." She rolled up the newspaper and started to put it back in her bag.

"Wait, can I see that again?" Celia gestured for her to hand over the paper. Analise spread the tabloid back on the table.

The previous night's activities and the photo of Typhoon and Breezeway had preempted another headline, shoving it to a strip along the bottom: "Mayor's Superhighway Plan: Genius or Madness?" A thumbnail photo showed gray-haired Anthony Paulson smiling at the camera. Mention of the mayor made her think of Detective Mark Paulson, of course. She hadn't told Analise *which* handsome police detective had escorted her home.

"What is it? Oh—is Paulson on about that again? You know the historic preservation people'll never let him get away with it. It'll take an earthquake to level half the city before they let anything get torn down."

Part of Paulson's platform for the last election featured a "revitalization" plan. He wanted to build a multilane ring highway circumscribing the city, to facilitate commerce and to attract business. The usual buzzwords. The trouble was, a number of existing neighborhoods would have to be demolished to accommodate the highway. Many argued, convincingly, that an essential character of Commerce City would be lost if it turned into yet another un-gainly urban sprawl surrounded by cookie-cutter bedroom com-munities.

"That's not really what I was thinking of," Celia said absently, refolding the paper and handing it back to Analise. Could she still date Mark if she hadn't voted for his father?

Celia's lunch hour was almost finished, and the dishes were cleared away, when Analise asked, "You're really okay after what happened? You don't seem shaken up at all."

"Yeah. Remember, this is like kidnapping number"—she actu-ally had to stop and count—"seven for me. It's been a couple years since the last. I was probably due for it."

"That's really messed up. That you can even think like that."

"It's either that or spend the rest of my life in therapy."

"You could probably use some. Therapy, I mean. You're always complaining about your parents, that their reputation is always get-ting in your way. Why don't you leave town? You could change your name, start a new life somewhere."

She'd always told herself she shouldn't have to give up her iden-tity for them. "I like it here. What would I do without coffee at Pee Wee's? I guess I keep thinking I can make a place for myself. I keep thinking someday people will just forget about me. Stop try-ing to kidnap me." Every kid wanted to get out of their parents' shadow. Her problem was, for her that shadow was just so *big*.

Analise huffed self-righteously. "Your folks should have retired when their cover was blown."

Not that it would have helped. Then, people would have used her to try to draw them out of retirement. Or try to ransom her. Warren West was still one of the richest men in town.

"Just remember you said that, if it ever happens to you."

THREE

ELIA put her hands on her hips and surveyed the computer
printouts, financial statements, and depositions spread across
the table in the conference room. "I think you've got him on a
dozen counts at least. Insider trading, money laundering, tax evasion, mail fraud. You *did* get warrants?"

DA Kevin Bronson patted his suit's breast pocket. "Oh yeah.
Three different judges signed 'em. I'm not taking any chances with
the Destructor."

Celia let out a sigh. "Good."

"Don't worry. This one's personal for all of us."

To think, for all the Destructor's megalomania, his fantastical
plans of annihilation and mayhem, his unending vows to rule the
world and the Olympiad's failure to bring him to justice, it was the
accountants who were finally going to lock the key to his jail cell.
Celia West, CPA. She had to admit, it felt pretty good.

"We haven't identified all his assets," the DA continued. "I'll
need you to track them down."

The materials filled banker's boxes. Usually, these cases involved
a file folder. But the Destructor was a big case. She paged through
some of the records. They went back years, decades. Sito's entire
history was laid out here, in bits and pieces and bank statements.

Fascinating stuff, to her at least. Which was why she had this job. She resisted an urge to rub her hands together and cackle.

Celia and Bronson carefully organized and labeled every possible shred of evidence that might have a bearing on the trial. Bronson already knew that Sito planned to plead insanity. It was a dangerous defense: the very nature of his crimes—calculating, methodical, and ambitious—spoke the coldest brand of criminal sanity. Celia could help show that. Even so, no matter what the verdict, with enough evidence to show he was a danger to himself and others—mainly others—the judge could order him locked so deep inside Elroy Asylum he'd never dig his way out.

They had almost finished when Bronson paused and checked the door to make sure it was closed. He stood with his hands clasped behind his back and studied her.

"Did Kurchanski tell you that I requested you for this case?"

"Yes, he did."

"Do you know why?"

She shrugged. "Good press. Because of my parents. Get the whole West clan on board."

"Is that a problem?"

Time to be professional and swallow her angst. "If you aren't worried about a conflict of interest, then it's not a problem."

"Good. Because I was hoping you could give me a little more insight into Sito than what we can tell from the records."

A sinking feeling struck her stomach. His statement wasn't casual, it was leading. His gaze focused on her like she was a defendant on the witness stand—like she was guilty and he knew it.

"My parents would probably be better for that."

"You used to work for Sito, didn't you?" he said, like he might have commented on the weather.

A familiar, icy anger crawled up her spine. She built up the walls of her life and people like him, like Baxter, kept knocking holes in them.

Everyone knew about the kidnapping. When she was sixteen, the Destructor stole her right off the street and unmasked her parents' identities. That made all the papers, every news outlet, in three-inch headlines, lurid color photos, and TV movies of the week. But no one outside the members of the Olympiad, the Chief of Police, and Sito himself knew that a year later, she'd gone over to the Destructor's side. Her supreme act of teenage rebellion had been buried and hidden from all public view, a fact that she was grateful for every day of her life.

Bronson had no right to shine a light on that part of her past.

She spoke softly. If she did more than whisper, her voice would come out in a scream. "Those records are supposed to be sealed." Juvenile records. She'd been seventeen. Just barely, they were juvenile records.

"I opened them," he said coldly. "Oh, don't worry, they're still officially sealed. I won't whisper this to anyone. But you realize that if it weren't for your parents' influence, you'd be in prison now."

She'd fought this battle already. She wasn't supposed to have to fight it again. "It was Stockholm Syndrome. Ask Dr. Mentis, he made the diagnosis, it's all in the file." She shook her head, a steady denial. "I've worked very hard to put that behind me."

"I know, I know." He was suddenly gentle, a whiplash change of mood that left her more unbalanced than a continued attack would have. "I'm not trying to dredge up old business. I just want you to know that you can talk to me. If you have any insights, if there's anything you can tell me that will help with the case, I need to know."

Stay calm. Pragmatically, she couldn't blame him. If he thought she had information, he was obligated to pursue that. On the other hand, she couldn't help but wonder who had nudged him toward that file, or if he'd been clever enough to wonder why the Wests' daughter had a sealed juvenile record.

"Tell me about Sito," he said. "Anything at all. What's he like? How does he work?"

She sighed at the memories.

She'd felt so grown up, so sexy and wicked, standing at the De-structor's side as he prepared to destroy the city yet again. Looking back on it, though, she must not have really believed that he'd succeed. He'd never succeeded before. She must have believed the Olympiad would stop him, like they always did, and she wouldn't be forced into some sort of moral quandary—stop the Destructor and save them, or turn evil for real. Even so, she'd never planned for what she would do after the smoke cleared, one way or the other.

Part of her must have believed that she'd die in the crossfire. Maybe Captain Olympus would have wept apologies and regrets over her bloodied body.

It happened on the top floor of the only skyscraper in Commerce City taller than West Plaza. Such a clever bit of symbolism.

"Soon, now, this city will be reduced to ashes," the Destructor said calmly, his hand poised over the remote detonation switch.

The sound of crashing glass interrupted the preparations. Ten guards raised their machine guns, aiming for the windows where three members of the Olympiad burst through with their powered gliders. The guards were professional muscle at the top of their game, the best in the business, loyal to the power and charisma of the Destructor. But such men were never a match for the Olympiad.

Spark swept a third of the room with a wall of fire. Guns melted and men shrieked, scrambling away as their hands scorched. Another third of them blinked and found their weapons simply missing, there one moment and gone the next. Then, the Bullet stood by the broken window and dropped their rifles one by one, sending them tumbling a hundred stories to the pavement below.

Captain Olympus, the Golden Thunderbolt, was force itself. He pushed with his mind and his hands, and guards flew back, their rifles tumbling away, knocked unconscious by the hero's will alone.

Far from being surprised by the invasion, the Destructor, ensconced behind his computers and control systems, regarded the scene with a frown of mild disgust. Once again, the Olympiad had escaped from the trap he had set to keep them away from here.

Only three of them were here. There should have been four.

Spark, a striking woman with flame-red hair, stared at the Destructor on his control dais and cried, "Celia!"

Pretty, petulant, a young woman stood next to the Destructor. Wearing all black and too much makeup, she was the kind of trophy that added to a man's prestige. Who wouldn't feel more powerful with such a creature hanging on his every whim and word as Celia did?

"Celia, stand with me, my dear," the Destructor said, beckoning the girl closer.

She did so, putting her hand on the Destructor's shoulder, glaring at the woman who'd spoken her name.

Olympus said, "Celia. I didn't want to believe it. I didn't want to find you here."

"Deal with it," she said, pouting, her jaw taut with anger.

The Destructor put his hand over the girl's. Olympus flinched. "She came to me of her own free will, Captain. Not like the last time."

"Celia," Olympus said, trembling with suppressed fury. "Get down from there. I don't want to hurt you, but I will."

The girl made an indignant huff. "It's a little late for that."

"What in God's name are you talking about?"

"You said I was useless! You said I embarrass you!"

This was the first time in her life Celia West had ever dared yell at her father.

Olympus clenched a fist and started for the dais. Spark—his wife—grabbed his arm. "Don't," she said.

"*He* appreciates me," Celia said, nodding toward the Destructor.

"But he doesn't, don't you see? He's only using you to get to us!"

The Destructor showed a thin, appreciative smile.

Celia, perhaps because of the short skirt and too much makeup, looked even younger as her eyes shone with tears. "You just can't admit that I don't need you. I never needed you."

So much of the Captain's power came from his anger. So often he clung to that anger when he couldn't see another solution. "You're no child of mine. No child of mine would do this to me."

Standing, the Destructor put his arm around Celia's waist. "This is all very entertaining, but it distracts from the purpose at hand. You're too late, Captain. I will still bomb this city to oblivion, and you can't stop me."

Then the Captain smiled. "Really?"

The Destructor hated that smile. It usually preceded unexpected complications. Nevertheless, he had to move forward. He picked up his remote and pushed the detonator button.

The three of the Olympiad stood side by side, arms crossed, watching him expectantly.

The closed-circuit screens showing a dozen views of the city didn't change. The bombs didn't go off. Somehow, the Olympiad had stopped them. Once again, the Destructor's elegant plan was crumbling to pieces.

The elevator door slid open, and a man wearing a well-tailored suit and a trench coat strolled into the room. The fourth member of the Olympiad, the young Doctor Mentis.

"Found your bombs, if that's what you're wondering," he said amiably in a clipped British accent.

And this was why, no matter how perfect his plans were, they always included an escape route. The Destructor pressed another button. A trapdoor opened behind him, where a chute led to his rocket pod. "This is when I leave you all."

He brushed the girl away and turned to the door.

She grabbed his arm. "Take me with you."

"The pod only holds one."

"But I thought—"

"My dear, your father was right. I only kept you because of the pain it would cause him. Now, good-bye."

He shouldered her out of his way and disappeared down the chute. Celia, stumbling on her heeled sandals, fell off the dais and sprawled on the floor.

The building's sprinkler system finally reacted to Spark's flames and burst into action, raining down on them all. After the Destructor's sudden departure, the only sound was water hitting the floor.

"Dammit," the Bullet said, kicking a puddle. "I *hate* when he does that."

Mentis joined them. "But the city is safe once again. It's good enough for me."

The Golden Thunderbolt's grimace showed nothing but contempt for Celia. "You could have stopped him! You didn't know we'd defused the bombs, you thought he was really bombing the city, and you just stood there, you didn't even try to stop him! What the hell were you *thinking*? The only thing left is to lock you away. I don't know what else to do with you."

Celia only cried. Hugging her knees, she turned her face away. Her makeup was smearing, black streaks streaming from her eyes.

Captain Olympus growled. The sound grew into a shout. He punched his fist into the air in front of him—and twenty feet away, the Destructor's control station folded, the steel crumpling like tin foil. Celia screamed and shuffled crablike from the mess.

Arms bent now, the Captain stalked toward her, his face rigid with anger, as if he still faced the Destructor.

Despite the water from the sprinklers, a wall of fire roared up from the floor in front of the Captain. Spark, across the room, guided the flames with her outstretched hands. Tongues of flame licked at Olympus, and heat radiated throughout the room.

"Warren!" Spark shouted.

The flames didn't hurt Olympus, but they stopped him. He looked at Suzanne. At last, his shoulders sagged and his arms hung loose. Spark let the flames burn out, dropping a few last embers as they died.

Spark—Suzanne—started to run to Celia's side. "Celia—"

"Don't touch me!" the girl screamed, scooting away. "Get away from me!" The shout broke down to uncontrollable sobbing.

"God, what are we going to do with her?" Warren muttered.

Mentis put his hands in the pockets of his coat. "Warren, if you want my professional opinion, Celia is not evil. She isn't even bad, really. She's only trying to find her own way in the world, and is doing it by getting as far away from you as she possibly can. Let her alone for a time. There's nothing else you can do, at least not anymore."

"When, Arthur? When could I have stopped this?"

Mentis's lips thinned. Flatly, he said, "Ten years ago, when she worshipped the ground you walked on and you didn't have the time of day for her. Sorry."

In the end, Celia let Mentis and Robbie approach her. They got her out of the building and took her home, leaving Suzanne and Warren to clean up after the Destructor's gang. She'd run away from home two months before to join the Destructor. After, she obtained legal emancipation and struck out on her own.

The next time her father spoke to her was when she graduated from college.

It seemed like a long time ago, now. If she threw Bronson a bone, maybe he'd leave her be. Let her do her job. Forget about the whole thing.

"He's charismatic, but you already know that. He draws people to him, uses them. He's selfish, morally blind. It's like people aren't real to him. They're just tools, or obstacles. You'll have to remember that when he talks about other people he's not really talking about people. And you have to understand that he doesn't want to conquer, take over the city, or the world, or any of those things. He's the Destructor for a reason. He just wants to destroy. He wants to see the world burned to ash."

"Why?"

"I couldn't say. It was a long time ago and I didn't really pay attention."

Some people theorized that he was an alien criminal who took human form and came to Earth to wreak havoc. She could believe it. There'd been so little about him that was human.

"Why did you join him?"

The file called it Stockholm Syndrome, when a kidnapping victim began to sympathize with her abductor. That was true enough, as far as it went. That was the reason that kept her out of jail. But everyone who knew the truth of the matter, knew the whole truth. No reason Bronson shouldn't as well.

"I did it to piss off my parents," she said.

"Most kids just take up smoking."

"Yeah, well. Smoking'll kill you."

They had just locked the evidence cabinet and left the conference room when one of Bronson's aides rushed down the hallway from the lobby. "Mr. Bronson! He's here—it's him. He wants to see you, he wouldn't wait—"

"Who? Who's here?"

"Captain Olympus!"

Celia's stomach froze, and she glanced around, looking for a place to hide. Too late, he came through the far door, dressed in his uniform, a black-and-gold skin suit that showed every inch of his supertoned muscles. A crowd of office workers trailed after him, pressing forward to catch a glimpse, grinning with wonder, eyes wide with awe. So, this was all going to happen with an audience. Great.

Square-jawed, frowning magnificently, Olympus pushed past the aide and stared down DA Bronson. "Is it true? You've filed charges against him?"

Bronson donned a vacant, smiling mask—his politician expression. "Captain Olympus! Thanks so much for coming! What can I do for you?"

Celia kept to the back, hoping Bronson would hide her.

"If the rumors are true, and you've pressed charges without consulting the Olympiad—"

"We had the warrants, we had to act quickly—"

"I'm not sure you understand the gravity of this. He wouldn't let himself get caught with evidence you could use. He always destroys his plans, his devices, his associates never talk . . . Celia?" Olympus squinted, peering around Bronson. "Celia, what are you doing here?"

Bronson stepped aside, looking back and forth between them.

Captain Olympus, leader of the crime-fighting Olympiad,

beloved protector of the city—Warren West, her father—put his hands on his hips and waited for her answer.

"I'm working with the DA's office as a consultant in forensic accounting."

"A what?"

She closed her eyes and sighed. He still didn't want to admit it. The daughter of the greatest crime fighter Commerce City had ever known had become an accountant, and Warren West still hadn't reconciled himself to the shame of it.

Bronson stepped forward. *My hero,* Celia thought. "Captain, we have the evidence this time. We seized the records of his clandestine financial empire. Tax evasion, fraud—all of it is good in court. He's in custody without bail at the maximum security wing of the Elroy Asylum. He isn't breaking out this time."

Captain Olympus hardly seemed able to take his gaze from Celia. At last, he looked at Bronson in acknowledgment of what he had said. "Tax evasion? This man tried to destroy the city I don't know how many times and you're charging him with *tax evasion?*"

"Anything to lock him up," Bronson said calmly.

He clenched his jaw—a bad sign. "I don't believe . . . Was this your idea?" He pointed at Celia.

Enough was enough. "Dad, please. I'm helping sort through the records. It's part of my job."

"*Forensic* accounting? I've never *heard* of such a thing."

She tried to sound calm and reasonable. "We can prosecute the Destructor within the structure of the legal system. Isn't that the important thing?"

"The legal system . . . I've got half a mind to head over to the Asylum and finish him myself—"

Bronson raised his hands. "Please don't do that, sir. I'll need you to testify in the trial, all right, Captain?"

Olympus glared. Bronson may have had the authority to stand up to the superhero, but Celia knew that glare. It had terrified her as a child, and, well, it still terrified her.

His lips thinned, his eyes narrowed. "Wait 'til your mother hears about this."

Celia slumped against the nearest wall and closed her eyes. She couldn't win with him. She just couldn't.

Olympus turned to stalk out of the room, but the admiring crowd blocked the way. Everyone in the room held their breath a moment: what would Olympus do? But even from the back, Celia recognized him settling into his public persona, squaring his shoulders and taking a deep breath. The crowd before him sighed, seemingly as one.

A woman in a gray dress suit stepped forward, tentative. "Sir? You probably don't remember this but about fifteen years ago you saved a school bus from falling off a bridge? I was on that bus, and I . . . I just wanted to thank you." Her voice cracked and tears fell.

Kindly, Captain Olympus touched her shoulder. "No thanks needed. It's what I do."

Then a flurry of voices rose up, and people stuck their hands out, and Olympus shook them all as he pressed forward through the crowd. People applauded as he finally left the room.

And that was Captain Olympus, Celia thought with a tired sigh.

Meanwhile, Bronson stared at Celia. "You didn't tell him you were working on the case?"

"I try not to talk to him at all if I can help it." It was a perfect end to the afternoon, really.

"Huh. Wild."

Yeah, every kid dreamed of having Captain Olympus as a father. They had no idea.

FOUR

S HE called Bronson to make sure Captain Olympus wasn't going to be at the prosecution team's strategy meeting. If he had been, she would have called in sick. She didn't care about her career enough to go through that.

She walked into the conference room, harried because the bus was late. The place was packed. Every branch of law enforcement in town wanted a piece of the Destructor, and they'd all sent people here to make sure they got it. Cops, detectives, the mayor's office, the DA's office. Detective Paulson was there and gave her a friendly smile that made her knees go a little shaky. He looked taller in daylight, when her vision wasn't swimming.

Stacks of paper filled the table and flow charts were pinned to the walls: photographs, diagrams, copies marked EXHIBIT A, EXHIBIT B, and so on. And no Captain Olympus.

But Dr. Mentis was there. Her stomach did a flip, responding to that self-conscious twinge she felt whenever she encountered any members of the Olympiad. Even him.

He caught her eye and nodded. Made no move to approach her, to berate her, or to tell her how her family was doing. Her nervousness eased. She could always count on him to give her the space she needed.

Of all of them, Mentis had a clear idea of what her childhood had been like. Telepath that he was and all.

The room's ventilation system couldn't keep up with the mass of body heat. People fanned themselves with photocopied handouts, but managed to keep their tempers in check. Their intensity was palpable, though. Bronson left no loose ends, demanded that every shred of evidence be brought to light. When Celia's turn came to stand and plot out the details of Sito's nefarious accounting practices, her anxiety went away. She had to make it clear to these people exactly what the evidence entailed, so they could coordinate and ensure there were no holes in the prosecution.

Arthur Mentis was heading up the psychological evaluation. Unflappable, he spoke of his belief that Sito was perfectly sane. He'd already been declared competent to stand trial, and the various crimes of which he was accused were proof of his own rationality. No irrational madman planned fraud so assiduously as he had.

It felt like a conference of generals, like they were preparing for battle. Even Celia felt the excitement of it—ready to move forward with the plan, happy to be part of a team. God, teamwork. What would her father say?

When the meeting broke up, people drifted off or gathered in small groups to talk. As she was repacking her attaché case, Mentis moved around the table toward her.

"Celia. It's good to see you."

She had to take his word for it. He never let emotions get the better of him, which made up for the overexcitableness of the rest of the Olympiad. It also made him irritatingly hard to read.

"Hi." Her returning smile, she discovered, was genuine.

"I have to admit, I was a little surprised when I heard you were working with the DA. Does Bronson know you have, ah . . . a bit of history with this case?"

She wryly pursed her lips. "He knows. He unsealed the records. He got the idea that I have some sort of privileged insight into the case because of it."

"Hm. A bit presumptuous of him. Let me know if he gives you trouble and I'll see what I can do."

"Thanks."

He walked alongside her as they left the room. When they reached the elevator, he asked, "Are you hungry? May I take you to lunch?"

"So you can get the full report of what I've been doing to take back to Mom and Dad?"

"Suzanne does complain that you never call."

"But I do!"

He looked at her sidelong, disbelieving. She slouched. "Right. There's a deli on the corner, about a block down. That okay?"

"Lead on."

The place was run-down, with a scarred tile floor, forty-year-old chrome and formica chairs and tables, and flickering fluorescent lights. But they seasoned their own pastrami and made a killer egg salad. Celia had a turkey sandwich big enough to provide tomorrow's lunch as well. Arthur ordered onion soup and tea.

She said, "Last week Dad stormed into the DA's office and threatened to walk into Elroy Asylum and murder Sito himself. He sort of freaked when he saw me there."

"Yes, I heard about that."

"Oh yeah? What did *he* say about it?"

He shrugged, said offhandedly, "Couldn't seem to understand why you were bothering to get involved."

"I think he's convinced himself I'm going to jinx the case." As if she weren't capable of sabotaging the prosecution on purpose, if she wanted to.

He chuckled. "You know how he is. No one could possibly be as right and justified as he is."

"And Mom wonders why I never call home."

He sat back in his chair, regarding her a moment. "So. How are you doing?"

Blushing a little, she picked part of the crust off her sandwich. "You just ask that out of politeness. You already know." She smiled, to let him know it was a joke, that she was just teasing him. But then again, he already knew.

He held his cup of hot tea in both hands and studied her like he was regarding a painting: intent, academic. "I believe this is the happiest I've ever seen you."

Her first thought was, that if this was happy it left a lot to be desired. But honestly, she couldn't argue. She had her troubles—but they were *hers*. "I'm doing all right. What about you? You happy these days?"

"Reasonably contented, as ever."

"You ever get tired of it?"

"Of what?"

She realized the ambiguousness of the question. There was a lot to get tired of. "The vigilante hero gig," she said finally.

"I don't have much choice in the matter. It's who I am."

She winced, her face puckering with a strange-tasting thought. Arthur waited patiently while she formed the words and finally asked, "Do any of us have any choice about who we are?"

"People have been debating that question for ages. No definitive answer, I'm afraid. Although, if I may be so bold, you seem to have made a choice. There was a time when your life might have gone differently."

Not likely. Her choices had been determined by her failures. She was here, now, because this was the only life she seemed to be good at. She shook her head. "If I'd had a choice, I think I would have chosen to be a superhuman. That would have made everything easier."

"If you say so."

FIVE

CELIA had to deal with trouble before she even reached the courtroom. She'd expected reporters, cops, fans, and groupies. The CAPTAIN OLYMPUS: OUR ALIEN SAVIOR sign was back. But she also had to face Breezeway, who had stationed himself outside the courthouse to keep watch. Some people seemed to think the Destructor would summon zeppelins from the sky to rescue him.

Lithe and brash, Breezeway was Celia's age. He had a showy silver uniform, complete with mask. Sinking on a breath of air, he landed on the steps in front of her. And the crowd went wild. Cameras flashed around him.

"Hiya, cutie," he said to Celia.

Be polite, Celia reminded herself. The press had all their cameras rolling and snapping out here. She had to reflect well on the firm.

"Hi." Be curt without snubbing. That was the trick.

"Always the cold shoulder with you," he continued, like this was some kind of show. "What's a guy have to do to get you to smile? Save your life or something? 'Cause I could do that—"

"And I'm sure I'd be grateful, but I wouldn't be smiling."

"Aw, come on, Celia. I think you do have a superpower—you're immune to charm."

"Breezeway . . . you almost dropped me off a roof."

"Hey, that was years ago. It was joke. I wasn't really—"

She went around him and climbed the steps. Laughing, Breeze-way launched himself skyward.

The judge barred cameras from the proceedings, under much protest from the media. It seemed like every reporter in town was here to cover the trial. Add to that the massive prosecution team, dozens of witnesses, and an army of law enforcement officers, there was barely room to move in the gallery. No one seemed concerned with the fire code today.

To the side of the bench, standing with the bailiff's crew, was the Olympiad, in all their four-color glory, though in recent years they had dispensed with masks. The Captain stood tall, his arms crossed, frowning, ready to deal with whatever trick the De-structor had planned for the morning. To his right, Spark, hands on hips, thick hair rippling in the light, surveyed the courtroom. To his left, the Bullet, short and compact, bronze skin, salt-and-pepper hair, leaned on the wall with practiced nonchalance. That was a ruse, of course.

Dr. Mentis was the only one of them who didn't wear a skin-suit uniform. Until all their identities were revealed, no one even knew he was a member of the Olympiad. He was their ace in the hole. As always, he wore a suit and coat, seemingly old-fashioned, an eccentric academic out of place in the real world. One looked at him and never knew what to expect. He was easy to underestimate.

The courtroom was restless. Every moment Sito didn't appear left more time for people to imagine what was going wrong, how he was escaping, what disaster was about to befall. Nothing went as planned where the Destructor was concerned. The proceedings were already a half hour late starting. And this was just a prelimi-nary hearing, for him to enter his plea. What would the actual trial be like?

A door at the side of the courtroom opened. Half the people in the room stood, craning their necks for a view into the holding area, wanting to be the first to see the great villain.

He appeared small, old. Anyone would walk right by him on

the street, or maybe smile to themselves at the memories he evoked of their own aged grandfathers, who taught them how to fish or brought candy at Christmas. He was harmless, they would think.

Celia stayed in her seat, staring at her hands. She didn't want to be here, didn't want to see him. In the second row, she was too close to the front. She should have sat farther back.

A squad of police officers escorted him. It seemed absurd, a dozen men in full riot gear surrounding a bent, pale figure, who shuffled because of the manacles chained to his hands and feet. Yet, the cops were tense, wary, and all held Tasers ready.

They hurried him past the Olympiad, who stood like stone guardians. Simon Sito appeared not to notice them.

His defense team—and they were his, bought and paid for—wearing tailored suits, looking intent and sinister, shepherded him to their table. He seemed hunched, trembling almost. Only wisps of his hair were left.

Then a gap opened in his protective circle. As if drawn by some vague instinct, he turned, looked through that gap, saw her, and stared.

She let her gaze be caught by him.

He smiled, and in any other situation the expression might have seemed kind. Celia saw only malice.

"Celia, how good to see you again. You're looking well."

The voice crawled into her gut and inspired nausea. She shouldn't have come, she shouldn't have—

Captain Olympus started to move forward, but Spark held him back with a hand on his arm.

Celia didn't move, didn't speak. Calm. Stay as cold and unremarkable as ice.

Then he was gone, his circle of handlers closing in around him. Sito gazed ahead and didn't look back at her again.

The bailiff stepped forward. "All rise for the Honorable Judge Berkley."

Celia had to unlace her fingers. She hadn't realized she'd been squeezing her hands tightly together.

The judge, a middle-aged woman with graying hair and stylish wire-frame glasses, sat at the bench.

The rest of Sito's courtroom appearance was blessedly dull. He didn't speak again, not even to his lawyers, who entered a plea of not guilty by reason of insanity, as expected.

The judge announced when jury selection would begin, set trial dates, demanded that everyone behave themselves in the meantime. Then, the cops led Sito away, back to whatever hole they were keeping him in.

The room seemed to refill with air as soon as he was gone, and everyone breathed a sigh of relief.

Celia felt like she'd been holding her breath the entire hour Sito was in the courtroom.

As soon as the judge disappeared to her chambers, reporters accosted Celia, pressing close and trapping her against the row of seats. Faces and digital recorders formed a bristling wall in front of her.

They seemed to speak with one voice. "Ms. West! Ms. West! Why did the Destructor talk to you? What did he say? Ms. West, do you have any idea why the Destructor singled you out?"

Calm. If she could face down the Destructor, she could face down them.

"He's just trying to get a rise out of people," she said. "No other comment."

"Ms. West!"

She was shocked and grateful—shocked that she was grateful—when the Olympiad swept her up and escorted her away from the journalistic horde. Mentis appeared on one side of her, Spark on the other, and the Captain and the Bullet broke through the crowd and herded them back.

Everyone stepped aside when Captain Olympus appeared.

"Conference room. This way," Bronson said, nodding over his shoulder.

By then, the reporters were shouting at all of them, but they'd all had experience ignoring the press. They left the courtroom without a backward glance.

—*Better?*—

"Yeah, thanks," Celia said, and her mother glanced at her, questioning. Chuckling to herself, Celia had to shake her head.

Once safe in the privacy of Bronson's conference room, which was windowless and annoyingly devoid of chairs, the Captain began pacing the length of the longest wall.

"He had no business talking to you," he muttered. He glanced at Celia and frowned. "Mentis, why'd he do it? What did he mean by it?"

"Haven't a clue. I've never been able to read him. That hasn't changed," the telepath said.

"You must have made quite an impression on him. At some point," Bronson said to her.

She had to take a calming breath before speaking. "It's the same old story. He's using me to get to them."

"We know," Spark said.

"I am definitely not putting you on the stand. Not after that."

Good, Celia thought. She was a bit panicked that Bronson had ever considered calling her to testify.

Bronson thanked the heroes for being there, for giving their stamp of approval to the proceedings. Maybe now the media would stop asking why the Olympiad didn't take justice into its own hands. The heroes were servants of the city. Not its judge and jury.

The meeting broke up after that. She was happy enough to leave Bronson's posthearing war council. The hallway had finally cleared out, and she could navigate it in peace. Almost.

"Ms. West. Celia. I mean . . . Hi." Detective Mark Paulson came from the back of the courtroom to intercept her. He had the best aw-shucks grin she'd seen in weeks.

She tried to look encouraging. "Detective, hello. What can I do for you?"

"Well, see, as a matter of fact . . . I've got a couple of tickets to the symphony fund-raiser on Friday. I know this isn't a good time, but I don't know when I'm going to see you again—"

"You could call."

"I don't have your number."

"You're a detective and you couldn't dig up my phone number?" He was starting to blush. She felt like she was wearing an awfully silly smile in response. "Or you could ask for it."

"So," he said. "How about it?"

"My number?"

He sighed. "Yeah. And the symphony."

"I think I'd like that. It's formal, right?"

"Right."

"So I should get a dress?"

"Right." He smiled with what looked like relief. "Can I pick you up at six?"

"Sounds great."

"Okay."

"Okay."

He tugged at the edges of his coat as he sauntered out of the room.

Wow. A real grown-up date. That was almost easy. Even the idea of looking for an evening gown before Friday didn't seem so scary.

"What was that all about?" said a sly voice near her shoulder.

Celia turned to her mother. "I'm going on a date."

"With Detective Paulson?" That was her father, standing by Spark and scowling.

"Yeah, with Detective Paulson," Celia said.

All four of them were there now. Mom beamed. Robbie, her surrogate uncle, looked like he wanted to ruffle her hair and crack a joke. Arthur seemed thoughtful, like he always did. Then there was the Captain, who appeared annoyed. He'd worn the same sour, frowning expression before every date she'd ever gone on.

Time to get out of here. "I'll see you guys later."

Feeling intensely smug, she strolled out of the courthouse, swinging her attaché case.

*   *   *

She'd been kidnapped the first time when she was sixteen.

She got the call at home, at the West Plaza penthouse. Back then, no one knew that the top floor served as the headquarters of the Olympiad.

Celia knew, but if she told anyone, who would believe her?

She was doing math homework at the kitchen table when the phone rang. Sighing with frustration—she was actually starting to understand trigonometry and was annoyed at being interrupted—she answered, expecting that it was her mother asking her to start fixing supper, or a friend inviting her to a movie or party that she wouldn't be allowed to go to.

"Hello?"

"Celia! Thank God! I need your help, come to City Park right now—"

"Dad?" She pressed the phone closer to her ear, as if that would make his voice come through clearer. He'd never sounded like this, harried and desperate. It was enough to make her panic. "What's wrong?"

"I can't explain. I need your help, please hurry!"

What could *she* possibly do to help? But there must be something, or he wouldn't have called. He must be in trouble, him and Mom both. Maybe this was her chance. He was trusting her. She wouldn't let him down.

"Yes, yes, I'll hurry. City Park?"

"By the fountain."

"Okay, Dad. I'm on my way." She hung up the phone before hearing his response.

It was only four blocks away. She could reach it by bike in a few minutes. She hoped that was fast enough; he must have known she wouldn't have another way to travel. Maybe he'd called her as a last resort. That would mean that *all* of the Olympiad was in trouble.

Security let her keep her bike behind the desk in the lobby. The guard on duty, an older guy named Damon, called a friendly greeting to her as she hauled it toward the doors, but she didn't have time to respond. Her heart was racing. God, this was just like some kind of secret mission. Was this what her parents felt every time the Olympiad's alarm rang?

She still couldn't think what her father was doing calling her with a mission. He'd call the city dog catchers before he called her. Nevertheless, he'd called, and he'd said he needed her. That was enough.

On her way to the park, she ran two red lights and didn't look back at the noise of screeching tires as cars barely missed hitting her. It didn't really occur to her that her chance at completing a mission for the Olympiad would be utterly destroyed if she were creamed by a garbage truck. She just had to get to the park before it was too late.

Racing from the sidewalk to the park's main bike path, she swerved to avoid a jogger, cut across the grass, and swooped down to the cobblestone pad circling the park's central fountain.

No one was there.

Water arced and danced away from a trio of art-deco lily-shaped spouts, splashing into the marble pool below. A couple of pigeons strutted around, searching for invisible bread crumbs. Celia stopped, got off her bike, and let it fall to the ground.

"Dad?" She looked around. Not so much as a jogger or dog walker was in sight.

She heard a hiss and felt a sting in her shoulder. Wincing in pain, she grabbed for it, thinking to find a hell of a monster mosquito. Instead, she pulled out a dart.

She stared at it a moment, a silver pellet with an inch-long needle—terrifyingly long—lying in her hand. A wave of dizziness crashed against her skull, only because she realized what had happened.

The tranquilizer took effect a second later, and she dropped to her knees.

Her limbs went numb, her nerves died, her muscles escaped her control, and she fell. Her eyes remained open, and her mind raced in a futile panic. Lying on her back, staring up, she saw the old man approach. Two black-suited guards flanked him. He wore charcoal gray.

He had a fringe of thin white hair and smiled a grandfather's smile down at her.

He held up a mini tape recorder and pressed the button. "Celia! Thank God! I need your help—"

Her father's voice, synthesized.

With gentle fingers he pressed her eyelids closed, and his men carried her away.

At some point she gratefully fell into unconsciousness. Didn't dream. Regretted waking up, which she knew she was doing when she heard a voice.

"You have your mother's hair, don't you?"

She opened her eyes and jerked back at the sight of the old man bending over her. Or tried to jerk back. She'd regained control of her muscles, but she was in a dentist's-type chair, nylon straps securing her arms and legs in place. Even her head was restrained. She felt tired, weak, but nothing hurt. Except her knotted stomach.

"And your father's eyes," he said. "Lovely."

The room was dark. She squinted, trying to see. A row of computer banks stood along one wall. They gave off a blue-white glow and a faint hum of cooling fans.

"What else do you have of theirs? Spark's fire, the Captain's strength? A bit of telekinesis perhaps. The ability to fly, or to see through solid walls. No? Nothing? How disappointing."

She glared at him, her face contorting in a grimace. It wasn't any of his business.

But he knew that her parents were the Olympiad.

Had she said anything, done anything to reveal their identity? No, of course not. He'd taken her because he already knew who they were. But when she disappeared the police would think it was a simple kidnapping of the daughter of a wealthy businessman for ransom. They'd be expecting a ransom note. She wondered if they would get one.

She didn't think so. This didn't seem right. A "simple" kidnapping involved warehouses and car trunks, not tranquilizer darts and computer labs. What this room reminded her of most was the Olympiad's command center, gleaming and sinister.

The man reached out, and she drew away as much as she was able, wincing. "Oh, shh, shh there," he said, like he might calm an animal. He ran his finger along her chin. He had a look in his eyes, intense and clinical, like a child who took pleasure in breaking his toys to see what made them work. He would gladly use people, but he didn't need any of them.

She managed to whisper, "What are you going to do with me?"

"Well. I'm going to send you back to your parents. After I've made a few adjustments to your pretty little mind. A childish sort of revenge, I admit. Enjoyable nonetheless."

"Who are you?" she said, though in her gut she already knew.

"Can't you guess? I'm the Destructor."

Screaming at this point would be so undignified. She swallowed back any noise into her too-tight throat.

She prayed. *Dr. Mentis, I'm here, please look for me, please help me.* The telepath had only been with the Olympiad a year, but she liked him. He didn't brush her off just because she didn't have any powers. He didn't treat her like a kid. Surely he would hear her.

The Destructor leaned on the chair, an arm on either side of her waist, and stared down at her with a look of such vicious longing she wanted to vomit. Tears welled in her eyes, which she squeezed shut. She had to be brave. She'd be brave, and she'd get out of this.

"It would be so easy to break you. Such a young, innocent thing—a blank slate. I could write anything on you." He let his body lean close to her, brought his face to her shirt and inhaled deeply through his nose, smelling her. She could feel his breath through her shirt, on her breasts, then on her throat.

"No. Please, no." Her tears streamed steadily now. She knew what this was, knew she didn't want it to happen. Not like this.

If only she were strong. If only she had her mother's power, her father's strength. Such a disappointment, as he'd said.

He straightened his arms, pushing away from her, and she gasped a sigh of relief. "Hush, my dear. I'm not so gauche as that."

Moving to the head of the chair, he reached for an equipment stand. In moments, he was pasting electrodes to her scalp, burying them in her red hair, pressing them to her skin.

She'd almost prefer the other. At least she knew what was happening, then. She bit her lips closed and refused to cry anymore.

He'd secured over a dozen of the electrodes, then pulled a device mounted on a jointed arm to the side of the chair. Made of steel and glass, it looked like a gun, a long nose with narrow rings of wires and disks protruding from a complicated mechanism. The Destructor studied it, making adjustments, then aimed the point of it at her forehead.

He went to the computer banks. "I call this process Psychostasis. A freezing of the mind. You won't feel anything, I promise. You'll start to forget, and you won't even notice that you're forgetting. You'll go on without a care in the world. And when you've forgotten enough, then we'll stop. It only becomes really dangerous if your heart forgets to beat. But I won't let that happen." He smiled at her over his shoulder.

No, no, no—her thoughts narrowed to that simple, desperate pleading. If she thought hard enough, maybe she could make it happen. Maybe she could give herself powers through sheer will.

No, she couldn't, because then she'd have had powers a long time ago.

"Doctor! Something's happening outside!" A man wearing a black suit ran into the room.

The Destructor paused, frowned. "I don't want to be disturbed."

"But I think it's the Olympiad!"

She couldn't see the villain's expression, but his voice turned cold and determined. "Never mind. I only need a few moments."

He turned back to his computer. A vibration passed along her skin, like the hum of a voice close to her ear.

"No," she whispered, crying. Only a minute, she only had to hold on for one more minute. Don't forget, never forget.

A fireball roiled through the doorway, tossing aside the Destructor's goon, who rolled to the protective cover of a computer console.

The Destructor frowned and stepped back.

"Mentis! She's in here!" Her mother's voice, ringing clear.

A wall of flame erupted, a shield between Spark and Celia, and the Destructor and his computers. In the next moment, Dr. Mentis was beside her, holding her face, looking into her eyes.

"Celia, can you hear me?"

"Yes," she said, because she couldn't nod.

More than hear him, she could feel him prodding in the corners of her mind, like an extra voice, a thought that wasn't hers, a dream that she didn't know the origin of. An odd smell of sage filled her nose. She couldn't stop it or respond—she didn't have that power. But she didn't struggle. Whatever the Destructor had done to her, Mentis would find it and fix it.

He must have been satisfied with what he found in her mind, because he grabbed the wires, all of them together, and tore them away. Her hair and skin ripped; she braced and didn't cry out. Calmly and methodically, he pulled loose all the straps, then put her arms over his shoulders.

"Hold on," he said. "Close your eyes."

He lifted her out of the chair. She clung to him, pressing her face to his shoulder as he carried her away. Her thoughts filled with panic and gratitude, and Mentis didn't let go until she was safely inside the Olympiad's hovership.

Safe. She was safe now.

The Destructor escaped, like he always did. He always planned a back door for himself. Despite his disappearance, he wasn't finished inflicting damage this time. The headlines in the newspapers the next day said it all: "The Olympiad, Unmasked! Commerce City Socialites Warren and Suzanne West Don't Deny It! They Are Captain Olympus and Spark!" The anonymous tips the paper had received included completely verifiable photographs. Their secret identities were ruined.

And their daughter was fair game.

S EVERAL mornings after Sito's preliminary hearing, Celia entered the maddeningly serene lobby of the Greenbriar Convalescent Home, a long-term mental health care facility. The carpet was plush, sound-absorbing, and the walls were a calming shade of blue. Soft, inoffensive music played. The place was aggressively calm. She hurried to the receptionist's desk.

"Hi, I'm Celia West. I have an appointment with Ian Miller in accounting."

The receptionist was a young woman with a gentle demeanor and a voice that could talk people down from rooftops. "Yes, he's expecting you. His office is just around the corner."

Celia followed the directions and soon found herself seated before the desk of Ian Miller, Greenbriar's head of accounts receivable. He sat rigid in his chair, leaning toward the desk, picking up one item after another and rearranging them: stapler, pencil, file folder.

"You're here about the Sito case?" he said.

She considered him a moment, then nodded.

"You know our records don't go back that far. Not the accounting records, at any rate."

One might think she was investigating him directly.

Before donning his criminal persona as the Destructor and beginning his reign of terror, Simon Sito had spent over a decade at the Greenbriar mental hospital. By all accounts he had suffered a severe nervous breakdown as a result of his job as a research scientist. The records during this time were hazy, as if he suddenly appeared at the hospital one day. All her leads into his past ended there. The rest had been lost, or buried.

"I'm trying to find out how he paid for his stay here," she said. "Did he have insurance? Who was the insurance with? Is there anyone alive from that time who might be able to help me?"

"I really don't know. Our personnel files don't even go back that far."

"Do you have anything that does go back that far?"

He nodded, quick and birdlike. "The medical records. Our doctors use them for research data. Anonymously, of course."

It was something. "Could I take a look at those, do you think?"

"Do you have a warrant?"

The people who asked that watched too much television.

She pulled a business-size envelope from her attaché case and handed it over. DA Bronson had written it up and had it approved especially for her.

Most of the trails she followed in her line of work were very well hidden, but recent. Phony bank accounts, fraudulent expense reports, laundered income—the records showing the truth about where the money came from and where it went still existed.

Thirty years was a long time for such records to stick around. She couldn't hope to be lucky enough to find a canceled check showing the account number that held Sito's original fortune. But if she was lucky, she'd find some thread to follow, however tenuous.

Miller let her into a musty basement room that held the hospital's archives: rows and rows of shelves crammed with medical records in brown pasteboard folders. The place was lit by bare bulbs clipped to the ceiling's naked boards, and smelled of fermented dust.

After fifteen minutes of searching the Ss, Miller pulled Sito's thick and yellowed file off the shelf. He left her alone with it at a desk in a cubbyhole of a room off the main accounting office.

Nothing to do but start at the front and work her way back.

Sito had been released from the hospital, declared fully recovered and capable of resuming a place as a productive member of society. An experimental treatment involving electroshock therapy had been declared a resounding success. On the contrary, it had been what pushed Sito over the edge—unhinged the part of his mind that held any sort of conscience or moral scruples. He'd fooled them all, told the doctors what they wanted to hear, and behaved how they needed him to behave in order to declare him sane. Who could tell? Maybe he really had been sane when he left. Maybe he hadn't been planning his campaign of destruction while still under the care of the hospital's psychiatrists. No one would ever know. The doctor who signed his release had died in the first onslaught, the inelegant but effective firebombing of a medical conference at the university.

Every page under that top one was a catalog of treatments, medications, lengthy reports, and professional musings about this man and what had triggered his debilitating depression. Sito became something of a pet project among the hospital's doctors. The nurses and orderlies reported that he never gave them any trouble.

With growing anticipation, Celia neared the beginning of the file, the pages that would, she hoped, tell her why Sito had ended up here in the first place, who had admitted him, and how the bills got paid. An insurance ID number, that was all she wanted.

A knock sounded on the frame of the door, which Celia had left open. Startled, she looked up and avoided heaving a frustrated sigh.

A young man in a white lab coat leaned on the door frame. He wore a vaguely predatory expression, staring at her like he might leap at her. She contemplated retreating into a corner.

"Are you Celia West?" he said. His eyes gleamed.

"Yes. And you are—"

He took that as his invitation to rush in, hand extended for her to shake. She did so, confusedly. "I'm Gerald Ivers. Doctor Gerald Ivers. Miller told me you were here."

Great, she thought. The question was, Why had Miller told anyone she was here? "Can I help you with something?"

He pulled a spare chair from a corner over to her desk and sat on it, right at the edge, leaning forward eagerly. He could strangle her if he wanted. Or she could strangle him.

"I just—well, this is going to sound crazy. But you're *the* Celia West? The daughter of Captain Olympus and Spark?"

Just shoot me now . . . She managed a thin smile. "I'm Warren and Suzanne West's daughter, yes."

"Can I ask you a few questions? Let me back up a little. I'm very interested in the psychology of superhuman crime fighters. I've written several articles on the subject—I could get copies for you, if you're interested. You might have a particular insight into this area of study. Purely anecdotal, of course."

He regarded her, brow raised like he expected her to launch into a personal chat about her parents then and there.

"I'm probably not the best person to ask," she said. "I'm a little too close to the joke, as it were."

"You think what your parents do is a joke?"

The last thing she wanted was to have *herself* psychoanalyzed. "No, of course not. But you should know that I left home on not very good terms when I was seventeen. It wasn't the best environment to grow up in."

If he'd whipped out a notepad and started writing, as he looked like he wanted to do, she'd have snatched it out of his hands and beat him with it. But he just stared attentively.

"No, I suppose not. But your perspective on the topic is unique, you have to admit. Why do you think your parents do what they do? Why do any of the city's crime fighters don costumes and risk their lives?"

He probably wouldn't go away if she just told him to. If she did that, he'd probably get all kinds of warped ideas about her bitter attitude being a defense mechanism that stemmed from the trauma of growing up in the uncertainty of a household of superhuman vigilantes.

Not that she'd ever thought about this before or anything.

She said, "I think most of them believe their powers are a gift. That because of it they have some kind of destiny, a responsibility to protect those weaker than themselves. It's a calling."

"I can't help but wonder if there's more to it than that. Look at the Hawk—I've studied his case extensively, and he wasn't superhuman. He had no powers. What drove him to fight crime? Especially under the guise of a costumed persona?"

The Hawk. The original vigilante. He appeared on the scene in Commerce City forty years ago, disappeared twenty years later— after secretly placing a note on the then mayor's desk that read, "I retire." Every five years or so a new book came out discussing his case, speculating on his psychology, and guessing who he might have been, really. Worse than the debate about who wrote Shakespeare's plays. The evidence was just as sketchy. What intrigued people most about him: he'd had no powers. Perfectly normal, mortal. Everyman.

"Maybe some of them get a rush out of it."

"But if that were the case, why did the Hawk just retire? In studies of people who participate in extreme sports, their activities come to resemble an addiction. They rarely stop until they're incapacitated or killed. I have an idea that it's the same with the vigilante crime fighters."

She might worry about her father getting killed, except he was the indestructible Captain Olympus and the point seemed moot. He looked after her mother and the others. They'd all had scrapes, sure. But they'd come through, every time.

He continued. "Do your parents ever talk about retiring? Do they show any sign of it?"

None at all. But she didn't think that was Ivers's business.

"Doctor, have you ever talked to any of the city's superhumans?"

His lips pressed into a line. "I'm treating Barry Quinn currently."

Barry Quinn, also known as Plasma. His affinity for electricity made him immune to electric shock. In fact, when he absorbed enough of a charge, he could throw back bolts of lightning at any chosen target. A human capacitor. He'd spent a couple of years as a celebrated hero, made the front pages of the papers. He was also a paranoid schizophrenic who believed his medication dampened his powers. It had only been a matter of time before he ended up here. Mentis had consulted on the case originally. He'd passed along a summary, and an unhopeful prognosis.

"How is that going?"

He started to say something, then shook his head. "Doctor-patient confidentiality. I really can't say. On the other hand, there's your father. Successful, healthy—he's been at this for a quarter of a century."

Her father, healthy? To her credit, she didn't laugh. "You should talk to him yourself."

His eyes went round; he looked stricken. "But how would I find him? How would I contact him? Vigilante crime fighters don't exactly have phone numbers."

"His identity's been known for years. The number for West Corp's central offices is listed. You could set up an appointment with my dad's secretary."

"I suppose . . . I hadn't really considered . . . I can see you're busy, Ms. West. I ought to leave you to it. Thanks for your time." He retreated, backing out of the room as he stammered his excuses.

If she wanted to give the guy a heart attack, she could ask Arthur Mentis or Analise to give *him* a call.

She finally reached the first entry in Simon Sito's medical file. This was a five-page report detailing a laboratory accident that had precipitated Sito's nervous breakdown. At least, Celia assumed the report detailed the accident. Great swaths of it were blacked out, censored by government order. Sito had been working on government research. None of this was new information. She might be inclined to assume that Sito had been cared for by a government or military pension. But that wouldn't have paid for a stay at a place like Greenbriar. He'd have been placed at Elroy or some other public or military hospital.

According to the report, or what was left of it, Sito hadn't been physically injured. The project wasn't of a kind that could cause physical injury. Instead, the failure of the project had unbalanced him. That was why he'd been placed in a psychiatric ward. The hospital bills had been paid by a trust fund set up on his behalf—the source of the fund wasn't listed.

The information that had been blacked out involved the substance of the experiment—what exactly Sito and the research team had been trying to accomplish—and the other parties involved. There was another party involved. Sito was working for a private lab, and that lab was under contract to the government. That lab had probably provided Sito's trust fund.

The censors had left her one scrap of information. They had been most concerned with people, with the research, anything that could be used to figure out what Sito had been working on. But they'd left her the name of the building where the lab had been located: Leyden Industrial Park. That was enough of a scrap to keep her moving.

In the meantime, she had a date to get ready for.

SEVEN

CELIA felt like the belle of the ball, strolling into the lobby of the symphony hall on the arm of Detective Paulson. He wore a dark suit with a band-collar silk shirt, smelled pleasantly of aftershave, and had not a hair out of place. He was slickly handsome, in an international spy kind of way.

She wore a strapless black cocktail dress accented with a silk shawl, beaded midnight blue and silver that shimmered and changed color when she moved, and carried a clutch too tiny for anything but a couple of condoms and cab fare home, because you just never knew. She wore her short hair fashionably ruffled, and had silver dangling earrings.

The two of them turned heads when they passed by. Celia wasn't used to people paying attention to her for any other reason than her being at the center of some disaster. It was a nice change. Mark liberated a couple of glasses of champagne from the tray of a passing waiter and gave one to her with a slight bow. Grinning, Celia toasted him.

The evening had a theme: Italian villa at twilight. Fake marble pillars draped with ivy had been set up in the corners, and strings of white lights decorated lattice arches under which people could sit on carved benches next to neoclassical statues. The gathered company was a who's-who of Commerce City's elite, politicians and businesspeople, actors and sports figures, all eager to show themselves great patrons of the arts. They were a mass of designer gowns and tuxedos, expensive perfumes and jewelry. Mark had revealed that he'd gotten his tickets for the gala from his father.

A string quartet played Vivaldi. As part of the fund-raiser's draw, the musicians played rare Stradivarius instruments, the best in the world, brought together for the first time to play in concert. They were worth millions. Celia honestly couldn't tell the difference. Beautiful music was beautiful music.

She still felt like she didn't belong. She could have, if she'd wanted to, once upon a time. This was the kind of thing her parents had done during their young socialite days.

"This is pretty swank, isn't it?" Mark said.

"Sure is. I feel like a million bucks."

"Wait a minute—aren't you the heir to the West fortune? You *are* a million bucks."

She masked her grimace by sipping her champagne. "Maybe, on paper. I kind of try to ignore that. I have a nice, normal job, and a nice, normal apartment."

"And then some joker kidnaps you off the midtown bus."

She shrugged. "I try to ignore that, too."

He huffed, looking like he was about to counter with some pragmatic quip that might have come from her parents, when they were interrupted.

"Mark! You actually made it. There's hope for you yet."

Striding toward them, flanked by ever-present aides, reporters, and sycophants, was Mayor Anthony Paulson. He was tall—as tall as Mark, even—with a rugged, weathered face and thick salt-and-pepper hair. He was a charismatic force, his smile wide and genuine.

"Hi, Dad." Father and son shook hands, firmly and warmly, clearly happy to see each other.

Mayor Paulson looked expectantly at her.

"Dad, this is Celia West. Celia, my father: Mayor Anthony Paulson."

Celia braced for the wide-eyed flash of recognition that usually accompanied these introductions. Then the awe, the hesitation, and the impossibility of being treated normally.

It didn't happen. Paulson offered his hand; she placed hers in it and they shook politely. "Ms. West, it's a pleasure."

"Likewise, sir." She smiled, secretly relieved. She was going to have a good time this evening after all.

"Please, call me Tony." The mayor glanced conspiratorially at his son. "I don't believe it. You not only found someone who'll be seen in public with you, but she's lovely and charming as well. Good work."

The group chuckled politely. Mark smiled an apology at her, but at the same time he seemed pleased with the approval. He stayed protectively close to her through the introductions his father insisted on making, showing off his son to the people he wanted to show off to. Mark needed a date, she realized, to be acceptable to his father in this setting. An accessory to increase his status, like an expensive watch. She was nearly flattered that she qualified as a trophy date. At least, she couldn't be angry.

This was what it'd be like to be a politician's wife, she thought vaguely. To have a life in the public eye. Might not be so bad. Then again . . .

Tony Paulson looked back to his entourage, searching for some-one. He finally found her and had to coax her forward. "Andrea? Andrea, come meet Mark's date."

Andrea Paulson, the mayor's wife and Mark's mother, didn't look much like she wanted to be here. She held a half-empty glass of champagne and still managed to cross her arms. In her designer gown, sparkling black and silver, and perfect hair, she blended into the crowd. She gave Celia a tight-lipped smile.

"Nice to meet you." She turned to her husband. "Tony, I still have the headache, I'll just have one of the boys drive me home—"

"Not now, Andrea. I need you here."

Both of them were speaking through their teeth. Andrea turned her back on her husband and walked away. She always looked happier in the campaign photos.

Mark let out a breath he'd been holding. "I think after eight years in office she's a little tired of this."

"She's fine," Mayor Paulson said. His smile had turned static. "Another glass of champagne and she'll be all smiles, you know how she is. So Mark, have you thought about my offer?"

"I told you, Dad. I'm happy where I am."

The mayor provided the explanation. "I've got a place in my office all wrapped up with his name on it—Legal Affairs Administrator. It's a short step from there to the DA's office. You'll be after my job in no time!" He beamed.

"He thinks I want his job," Mark said in an aside to Celia.

The light in the mayor's eyes dimmed. "You might listen to me for once. I'm only trying to help."

This must have been a long-running argument. Celia's heart went out to Mark. She was actually encouraged that this sort of thing went on in other families. She said, "I'm sure Mark appreciates it."

That diffused the tension that had begun to mount, which was good, because Celia didn't know what she'd do if Mark stalked away, as his mother had done, and left her there alone.

"He'll come around." The mayor winked at Celia.

Tony Paulson returned his attention to his entourage of personalities, all of whom pretended not to notice that Andrea had left, or that they'd narrowly avoided a family squabble.

"Your father's a bit of a force," Celia said, grateful when Mark guided her away.

"Yeah, I haven't decided yet if he's like that because he's the mayor, or if he's the mayor because he's like that."

"It's tough being in that kind of shadow."

"Tell me about it. I guess you could, couldn't you?"

"Only thing you can do is make a break and move on."

"Easier said than done."

In the end, it hadn't been that hard at all. She'd stayed away from her parents for four years during college. Built a life for herself that had nothing to do with them. Pretended to be some other Celia West. Worked two jobs—bookkeeping in the evenings and shelving at the university library on weekends—to pay her tuition and expenses, and it had all been worth it. She'd even started swimming again, able to do so without dwelling on old disappointments.

The time for speech-making arrived. She lingered with Mark in the back of the hall, growing pleasantly tipsy on her third glass of champagne, leaning on him, and drawing stories out of him— amusing anecdotes about the mayor from his childhood, harrowing tales of his years on the police force. Not so many of them. He'd only made detective six months ago and was young for the rank. He tried to turn the conversation back on her. Deftly, she avoided his questions. It didn't seem right, telling amusing stories about Captain Olympus from her childhood. *He was going to throw me off the roof to see if I could fly. . . .*

The first speech came from the symphony's musical director, profusely thanking everyone for their support and subtly digging for more donations. Next, the mayor stepped up to the podium. He went on about the city's cultural heritage, managing to work in some stumping appropriate for the venue. She was fuzzily not paying attention.

At least, she wasn't paying attention to the podium. Movement at the edges of the hall caught her notice. The crowd of socialites and symphony patrons stood in the center of the foyer, faces turned attentively to the front. But here and there, a half-dozen people wearing catering staff uniforms moved purposefully along the walls.

One of them drew a handgun from under his apron.

Celia's hand clenched on Mark's arm.

He glanced sharply at her. "What—"

He didn't have time to ask. A hand closed around her throat and hauled her away from him. The steel nose of a gun pressed against her temple. She dropped her champagne glass, which shattered.

An irrational part of her complained, *Not tonight, of all nights.*

In moments, it was over. A couple of women screamed. A large space, in which Celia and her captor formed the center, cleared. Mayor Paulson's voice demanded over the PA, "What is this?"

The other gunmen surrounded the string quartet and their priceless instruments.

"Nobody move, nobody make a sound, or she gets it!" shouted her captor. He held her in a headlock, pinning her against his body. She gripped his arm for balance, and couldn't move without his assistance. "Hand over the instruments!"

Before the musicians could comply, the assailants took them out of their hands. The cello player started to resist; he held both hands on the cello's neck and glared. Celia's captor made a noise and gestured with the gun for emphasis. The cellist let go.

She was insurance. Somebody might launch into heroics at the risk of destroying a chunk of wood and string. But not when someone had a gun pointed at her head.

Not for a minute did she believe that their choice of hostage was random.

With the instruments taken captive, the gang made its way to the back of the hall and the service entrance. The leader dragged Celia along. They weren't going to let her go.

Mark broke from the stricken crowd to intercept the gang. Celia had no idea what he thought he could do. Flash his badge and intimidate them? He ought to know better than that.

He said, "Let her go. Take me instead."

"Mark, no!" said the mayor, still speaking into his microphone. *That'd* lose him points in the polls, she bet.

Mark continued. "Don't hurt her. I'll do anything you ask, just don't hurt her."

God, it was touching. If only he had a clue. "Mark, don't," she said. "It'll be okay. I'm used to this." *I'm a pro by now.*

"Please," Mark said, ignoring her.

"Okay," the gunman said. Celia groaned to herself.

Still dragging her alongside, he inched over to Mark to make the switch. He wasn't going to take chances, and he wasn't going to take his gun off both of them. She sincerely hoped Mark didn't have some kind of rough-and-tumble police kung-fu trick planned. She liked him, but she didn't trust him to rescue her.

In one movement, the gunman shoved her away and trained his weapon at Mark, who held his hands up and stayed still. Celia hugged her shawl tight around her shoulders and met Mark's gaze as the gunman grabbed his arm, pushed the gun to his neck, and hauled him away. He seemed calm and determined. Very heroic.

The moment they were all gone, the room burst into motion and conversation. A hundred cell phones came out of clutches and jacket pockets. The first violinist burst into tears. Celia closed her eyes, hugged herself, and sighed. She needed another drink; she'd suddenly sobered up.

"Ms. West! My God, are you all right?" The mayor, cutting through the crowd like an arrow, strode toward her. Mrs. Paulson flanked him, looking interested for the first time all evening. Paulson touched Celia's arm and studied her like he expected her to faint.

"Yes. Except for Mark being an idiot."

"I can't argue with that," Andrea Paulson said.

Sternly, Paulson said, "He probably saved your life."

That was how everyone was going to read the situation, she realized. Handsome young cop puts his life on the line. "I'd have been okay."

"You're taking this very well."

"I've done it before. Several times."

There it was, that look of morbid curiosity, though to his credit the mayor repressed it quickly. Mrs. Paulson wasn't so circumspect. She gaped. "You're *that* Celia West?"

Celia looked away, repressing a wry smile. "I'm assuming the police are after them already?"

"They should have the block surrounded by now," Mayor Paulson said. "If you'll excuse me, I have business. Obviously. One of my people can take you home. Andrea, you should go home, too."

"No, I'm staying until Mark is safe."

"Fine." He pointed at an aide, then continued on, his entourage trailing in a wake behind him. Andrea went with him. Celia let them go. She'd done the polite thing and left her cell phone at home, but now she needed to make a call.

The mayor had left her staring up at a bulky, bodyguard-looking man in a suit, who stared back, expressionless. He gave the impression that he'd pick her up and sling her over his shoulder if she argued.

She tried anyway. "I think I can make my own way home. I appreciate the thought, though."

"I think the mayor would prefer that I see you safely home."

He was probably one who prided himself on following orders. Not quite clever enough for her to be able to talk into letting her go. Too bad she didn't want to go home just yet.

"Then do you mind if I go find a phone to call my folks? Tell them I'm okay? If they hear there's been a kidnapping, they'll assume it was me who was kidnapped and I don't want them to worry."

He considered a moment, nodded coolly, and followed her to the coat-check desk. She asked the clerk there if she could use the phone.

She dialed, the phone rang; a stern, accusing voice answered. "This is a secure line, how did you get this number?"

The bodyguard watched her, listening in, she assumed. She turned her back to him and spoke softly. "Hi, Robbie. It's Celia."

His tone changed from suspicious to amiable. Off guard duty and talking to a friend, now. "Oh, hey, kid! What's wrong?"

Such a vote of confidence. "You guys hear anything about an attack at the symphony tonight?"

"Yeah. We're monitoring. The police say they have it under control."

Surprised, her brow furrowed. The situation didn't *look* under control. She hunkered closer to the phone. "Really? Because the attackers took Mark Paulson hostage."

Robbie hesitated a moment, then said, "Detective Paulson? Not you?" There was a laugh behind the voice. She supposed it sounded funny on his end.

"They took me first. Then Mark decided he had to be a hero."

"That must be a nice switch."

"I'd have preferred it if they'd taken me. I wouldn't do something brave and stupid that would get me killed. My first real date in months and he gets kidnapped right off my arm."

"Aw, kid, I'm sorry." He sounded genuinely sympathetic.

"Can you let me know if you hear anything? I'm getting to like the guy and I'd hate for something to happen to him."

"Will do. I'll pass on the news about Paulson. The cops didn't tell us that part."

Which was weird. Mayor's son gets kidnapped and the cops didn't mention it? They probably wanted to save Mark themselves and get brownie points with the mayor, rather than letting the Olympiad have all the glory, again.

"Thanks."

She gave the phone back to the coat-check clerk. The bodyguard was still lurking nearby. Had to be a way around him. Maybe if she didn't hate being chaperoned so much she wouldn't get kidnapped. Go live at West Plaza like her mother wanted.

For a moment she thought about claiming that she needed to use the restroom, then sneaking out the window, or an emergency exit, or—

On the other hand, this could save her cab fare.

She turned to him and smiled. "All right. I'm ready."

The police were interviewing everyone in the place; they weren't letting anyone leave until they'd recorded contact information and followed every lead. Celia's chaperone cut right through the chaos and left the symphony hall in minutes.

He drove her in an unmarked government sedan. She gave him an address that wasn't her apartment, and helpfully offered directions when they neared the location.

"Here," she said finally. "You can let me out here."

The guy leaned forward to peer through the windshield. "You live at the police station?"

"No, but thanks for the ride anyway. Bye!" She hopped out of the car and darted up the building's steps before he could argue. She wondered what he'd tell Paulson.

She walked through the front doors and the smell of the tired, ancient, sweaty waiting room hit her. It had been a while, and she hadn't missed it at all.

The place buzzed with far more than the usual late-night police station energy. The evening round of drunks and prostitutes had stalled out in the lobby, waiting on plastic chairs until someone remembered that they'd been arrested. The front desk was missing its clerk. Behind the desk, in the back, voices shouted, phones rang, uniformed people scurried back and forth with files in hand and cell phones stuck to ears.

A large, booming man appeared in a doorway and called out. "All right, people, I'm looking for black-market contacts. They won't be able to unload these things in the open, so we need to go to ground. If I see another auction house phone number on the fact list I'm going punch somebody!"

That was Chief Gene Appleton. Head of the force for ten years. Fifteen years as a cop before that. Celia smiled. If Appleton was knocking heads, things couldn't be too bad. She'd always liked him. He never talked down to her.

The liking wasn't mutual, at least not as of seven or so years ago. He'd sealed her juvenile record personally. If he saw Celia here he'd be livid. She slunk away to lean on a wall.

A girl sat in the chair next to her. Magenta hair, black plastic miniskirt, and fishnet shirt over a green bra. She looked about fifteen. Might have been seventeen. Her sullen air made her seem young.

"What's going on?" Celia asked her.

The girl looked her up and down. Celia wasn't dressed for the lobby of a police station at eleven P.M., but leaning on the wall, arms crossed, gazing vaguely out, she acted like she belonged. Made all the difference.

"Dunno. Something big went down."

"Big. Like Destructor big? Like Olympiad showing up big?"

She shrugged. "Dunno. Heard that a cop got hurt."

Celia's stomach lurched. She had to remind herself this was only street gossip. Didn't mean anything. She looked toward the back offices, working herself up to go and ask someone.

The front door opened, ringing the old-fashioned brass bell that no one had the heart to take down. In walked Mark Paulson, his collar unbuttoned and his jacket hanging from his hand.

Celia pushed off from the wall. "Mark!"

His tired eyes brightened. "Celia! What are you doing here?"

In a couple of strides they met, gripping each other's arms. Not an embrace—they needed to look at each other.

"I wanted to be here in case there was news."

"Paulson! God, Paulson, what the hell happened?" Appleton stormed around the front desk, his gaze piercing like bullets.

The detective shrugged. "They just let me go. Dumped me out of their car down the block."

Appleton noticed Celia, even though she'd stepped aside. "You. What the hell are *you* doing here?"

"I was worried about Mark. Nice to see you again, Chief."

"Huh. Right."

Mark put his arm protectively around her shoulders. Appleton took in the gesture and gave his head a frustrated shake. "Whatever. You." He pointed at Mark. "In the back. Tell me what happened."

"I'd like to take my date home first, sir."

"Call her a cab."

Mark glared at him.

As much as she enjoyed the scene, she recognized when she'd been shown the door.

"I'll be okay," she said. "I'll call my own cab."

"Celia . . . are you sure you'll be okay? It's no trouble, I'd really like to make sure you get home safely."

Her giddy feeling was relief. Mark was back safely. He hadn't been killed in her place. The kidnappers had just . . . let him go. Whatever the reason, she wasn't going to argue. All was well with the world. So what if the relief fed into other things?

She stood on tiptoe and pulled his head closer, so she could whisper in his ear. "Don't think that just because you took me home you'd be getting any gratitude sex for being all brave."

He drew away and looked properly shocked, blushing, his tongue stumbling over denials. Finally, he noticed that she was grinning. He was a cop; she'd have to train a sense of humor into him.

She kissed him. A nice, cinematic kiss on the lips, warm and tingling, lasting a half-dozen heartbeats. Enough time for him to react and close his arms around her. The officers and staff who'd gathered in the lobby at Mark's return cheered and catcalled. Even the drunks and hookers cheered. Appleton didn't cheer.

"I'll see you later," she said.

Mark took a breath. "Right. Yeah. Good."

She separated herself from him, readjusted her shawl, and made a calm, smooth exit.

Out on the sidewalk, she let herself giggle. Damn, that had been fun.

EIGHT

MAYOR Paulson made a public statement the next day at noon. Mark called her at home to tell her about it.

"Celia, turn on the news."

"What? Why?"

"Dad just gave a statement about last night."

She grabbed the remote, turned on the TV, and curled up on the sofa.

A perfectly manicured reporter at a news anchor desk read off the teleprompter. "—scene a half hour ago at City Hall."

The picture switched to the marble-lined foyer of City Hall. The camera turned to a podium as Anthony Paulson, flanked by assistants, emerged from a door behind it. Celia recognized some of the flunkies from the concert. Cameras flashed and reporters clustered forward. The mayor, his face set in grim lines, waved them back.

After a moment, he received the silence he needed.

"Ladies and gentlemen, thank you for coming on such short notice. In light of recent attacks and the proliferation of organized criminal elements bent on ruin and anarchy, I am announcing the creation of a task force to deal with these elements. I will hire a hundred new police officers to patrol our streets. Some people will say that I'm overreacting, that I'm taking last night's theft of price-less musical instruments from the symphony gala personally be-cause it also involved the kidnapping of my son Mark. My answer to them is yes, of course I'm taking it personally. As well I should. Every crime committed against a citizen of Commerce City is com-mitted against *someone's* son or daughter. Someone takes each of those crimes personally. It is my sworn duty to protect the safety of every law-abiding man, woman, and child in this city, and so I must take every crime personally.

"And I must apologize for a certain laxness in fulfilling that duty. It has become clear that for too long we have depended on outside, independent forces to defend us. However, it seems that unless those forces are faced with an adversary of the Destructor's magnitude, they simply can't be bothered. I will not be taking questions at this time. Thank you for your attention." He turned and slipped back through the door, followed by his swarm.

"Celia, are you still there?"

Celia had held the phone to her ear silently while watching. When the announcement ended, she had to repeat to herself what the mayor had just said. What she *thought* he'd just said.

"Yeah, Mark. I talked to Robbie last night and he said the cops told them to stay out of it."

"Robbie?"

"The Bullet. I don't know where your dad got his information, but the Olympiad didn't help last night because the cops asked them not to. I'll bet the other vigilantes didn't even know about the theft—they don't have the level of access the Olympiad does."

"Are you sure?"

"About Robbie? Why would he lie to me? If it was a miscom-munication, then it probably ought to get cleared up before some-thing comes along that the cops can't handle."

"You don't have a whole lot of faith in the cops, do you?"

Whoops. There went her foot into her mouth.

She took a deep breath. "I'm sorry. That's not what I meant."

"Look. We're both biased on this. I'll find out who told the Olympiad what about what happened, okay? You're right, it was probably a miscommunication and nobody needs to take it personally."

She was about to argue that she wasn't taking it personally, then decided against it. "That'd be really cool. Thanks. Wait a minute—Dad's on. My dad, I mean."

The anchorwoman said, "We asked Warren West, better known as Captain Olympus of the crime-fighting Olympiad, for his response to the mayor's comments, a veiled accusation that the Olympiad and other crime fighters have failed to make Commerce City safer."

The image wobbled after the frame switched to the camera view of a roving reporter. They were in the lobby of West Plaza, focused on Warren West's back. Celia turned the volume up.

A male reporter chased after him. "Mr. West? Mr. West! What is your response to the mayor's comments?"

Warren turned on him, glaring. His shoulders were bunched, his fists clenched. He was on the verge of losing his temper. Celia recognized the signs. Then he glanced at the camera and let out a breath and straightened. He had *some* consideration for his public image, and was able to speak calmly and with heart.

"After more than twenty years of serving this city, is that the kind of gratitude we've earned? All I can say is we don't need the mayor's good opinion to do what's right. No more questions, thank you."

He stalked off, reporters scattering in his wake.

The anchorwoman popped back on screen. "The masked vigilante Breezeway was less offended about the mayor's conference."

The image switched to show Breezeway. The reporter had found him—or maybe he'd found the reporter—scaring up wind storms for kite flyers at City Park. A bevy of laughing children crowded behind him after he landed—quite the PR coup.

He shrugged in response to the reporter's question. "He has to look like he's doing *something* to keep the polls happy."

Celia had never liked that guy. He was a loose cannon. A couple of other scenes followed, sound bites from Mind-masher and Earth Mother. She wondered if they'd flash an interview with Analise next, but Typhoon didn't seem to be out and about this afternoon.

"Celia?" It was Mark on the phone again. "Are you still there?"

"Yeah. Hey, I'm glad you called. We should have dinner or something soon. To make up for last night."

"I could sure use a hello like the good-bye I got from you."

Oh yeah. Definitely a keeper.

When she finally hung up, the phone flashed a message waiting light at her. It was Analise, practically screaming: "What happened last night? Don't try to tell me you weren't there because I know you were. And you didn't call me? Why didn't I hear about this? My supreme deductive reasoning powers tell me that this Mark Paulson guy is the cop who took you home after the last time. Am I right? There's a picture of you making eyes at him on page three of the *Eye*. Girl, you guys look *hot*. You have to—" The message timed out there.

Monday morning, she was back in the office researching the Leyden Industrial Park, the next strand in the web that was Sito's life.

The current phone book and city title records had no listings for a Leyden Industrial Park, which meant the name had changed sometime during the last fifty years, or the place didn't exist anymore. An address would have helped, but the censored Greenbriar file hadn't been that generous. She'd have to head to City Hall or the library and hope they had historical street plans or title information going back that far.

She also made time for a little independent research, looking into valuations of Stradivarius instruments. It wasn't exactly a straightforward endeavor. The average thief would never be able to unload one on the black market. Most of the instruments were well known within the communities that would pay the most for them. Their histories, characteristics, ownership, were all recorded in detail. They even had nicknames. It would be like trying to sell someone's child. Someone's *famous* child. Not that criminals hadn't tried that, too.

If the thieves had a private buyer lined up, one who didn't care about the niceties of law, no one would ever see those instruments again.

So why had they taken a hostage if they were just going to let him go? Once they were out of the building, they didn't need the human shield anymore—they could have released him immediately. Except they hadn't originally taken any hostage, they'd wanted *her*. Which meant they'd wanted to get at the Olympiad. If they'd kept her as a hostage, her parents might not have listened when the cops asked them to stay out of it. Maybe that was why they'd let Mark go. He was the wrong bait.

The hubris, putting herself at the middle of this.

She had dinner with Mark Saturday night. Just dinner. She was becoming so conservative. Really, though, she had enjoyed the chance to talk to him when they weren't in a courtroom or a kidnapping scene.

Appleton had grilled him about the Stradivarius Brothers, as the press had named the gang, most of Friday night and into Saturday. He'd given descriptions of his captors to the sketch artist and profiling software; the department was still trying to find matches with the mug shots on file. He'd spent the entire time in their car, which never went more than a mile from the symphony hall and the police station, and points in between. The Stradivarius instruments had been in a different car. Not much to go on, as far as tracking the instruments was concerned. He hadn't gotten a look at the plates of either car.

He had heard part of a phone conversation. The driver of the car called someone to ask what to do, since the plan had gone awry.

"The guy he was talking to was yelling so loud I could hear him. He said, 'You were supposed to get the girl.' Then the driver said, 'The mayor's son ought to be just as good.' But the answer was no. Then they dropped me off. I thought you'd want to know."

They'd been after her, and she wasn't willing to call two kid-napping attempts in as many weeks a coincidence.

Mark came over to her place Monday evening with carry-out Chinese. She dumped lo mein onto plates and poured hot-and-sour soup into bowls while he leaned on the doorway to the kitchen, watching.

"I asked around about who talked to the Olympiad Friday night. All anyone knows is the order came from upstairs, from higher up than Appleton. Probably the Commissioner. Nobody was too up-set about it; you know we've never really gotten along with those guys."

Because the Olympiad kept making them look bad. . . . "But there was an order. I wish your dad wouldn't go around saying it was *their* fault they weren't there."

"It would have been like them to just show up. Why didn't they?"

Because they hadn't known there was a kidnapping involved and there were lives at stake. She didn't want to argue with him. "Who knows? I can't explain them."

"Can't you?"

"You may have noticed, I've spent the whole of my adult life putting distance between them and me."

"Yeah, I've noticed."

As they ate, she watched Mark across the table. Broad shoul-dered, frowning, his eyes alight, animated and resolute, an ideal poster boy for the city's police force. He looked ready to leap to the rescue of a damsel in distress, willing to save the city from what-ever dangers befell it. Another crusading hero, in his own way.

She ought to kick him out right now, before it was too late.

"You look all serious all of a sudden."

"Sorry." She smiled and glanced away.

The table was small enough that he was able to reach across and touch her face, a light brush of fingertips across her cheek. Quell-ing a smile, he drew his hand away. *Too late.*

He helped her clear away the dishes, and he stood too close, so that she could feel the heat of his body. She let her arm brush his as she reached for a towel. After drying her hands, she twined her arms around his waist. He was kissing her before he brought his hands to her shoulders.

She was hot and bothered, unthinking, and let it happen. Watched herself pull off his shirt, press her hands to his bare chest, and give a sigh of satisfaction.

She needed, she decided, to be held in his arms.

NINE

"CELIA. It's your father. Your mother would really like you to come over for dinner. She thinks it'd be a good idea for us to get together, when it isn't the middle of a crisis. And . . . I guess I think it'd be a good idea, too. Call back."

Celia stared at the telephone for an astounded moment. She couldn't remember her father ever calling her at home. She couldn't remember him ever calling her *at all*. Suzanne, yes—as soon as Celia had given her a number she called every week.

Mom put him up to this. She'd probably held her blowtorch finger up to his skull to make him call. He wouldn't have had to; she'd have just scorched him a little. But he'd swallowed his pride enough to call her.

How could she say no?

"Jury selection's taking forever. I'm not surprised. Who hasn't heard of the Destructor? The guy published a best-selling autobiography, for crying out loud. Who knows when the trial is actually going to *start*." Suzanne chatted amiably.

The scene was incongruously domestic. Suzanne, who stood at the stove testing a piece of fettuccine, wore jeans and a sweater, over-size and baggy, exactly the opposite of Spark's uniform. She was a good cook. Celia hated to admit she was looking forward to her mother's marinara, which she hadn't tasted in years.

The pasta conventionally boiled away in a pot on the stove. The saucepan with the marinara sat on a cold burner. Suzanne held her hand against the outside of the pot. *That* was what glowed red-hot. She used her power to heat the pot and simmer the sauce. She'd always done it that way, saying she could control the temperature exactly and not let it scorch that way. Celia had been in grade school before she realized that not everyone's mother made marinara by holding the saucepan in her hands.

Suzanne also made an excellent crème brulée—by hand, so to speak.

Warren, Captain Olympus himself, leaned back against the counter, arms crossed, watching his wife. He wore a blue oxford shirt, khakis, and had bare feet. "I could take care of the problem in a minute. None of this would even be an issue."

Suzanne threw him a glare. "And have you up on murder charges? I don't think so."

"It'd be worth it."

She retrieved a spoon, dipped it in the sauce, and held it to his mouth. "How's this?"

He leaned forward and tasted, licked his lips, looked thoughtful. "Hm. Perfect."

"You always say that," Suzanne said, frowning. Warren grinned and kissed her forehead.

Celia sat at the kitchen table. She'd asked about three times if she could help. The table had already been set when she got to her parents' penthouse, and Suzanne insisted she didn't need anything. Her parents could have afforded a dozen live-in maids, cooks, butlers, whatever. They didn't have any help, though, apart from someone who came to clean once a week. Suzanne had always set the table herself.

Celia couldn't remember the last time they'd all been together like this, at home, in civilian clothes, quiet and relaxed. She bit her lip.

Warren looked at her. "What are you smiling at?"

She chose to interpret his tone as casual. Ten years ago, she would have taken the words as a personal attack. "I'm thinking you may have a point. What's a few years in jail if it keeps Sito from hurting anyone ever again? Heck, I might do it myself."

"You see?" Warren said to Suzanne.

Her mother frowned at her. "Don't encourage him. And you— don't encourage *her*."

The pasta finished cooking, the sauce finished simmering, Suzanne let Celia serve the salad, and they sat down to eat. Celia didn't even mind that they couldn't find anything to talk about except work. Really, work was what any normal family talked about around the dinner table, wasn't it?

"Bronson's not going to make you testify, is he?" Suzanne asked.

"No. That is, he'd better not. I wouldn't want to have to say something that would cause trouble." This was treading on very touchy ground. More than anything, she didn't want her father to start in on the subject. "I'm just there to do my job. It isn't about me, and Bronson knows that. He'll keep me out of the spotlight."

Warren nodded like he approved, and Celia sighed.

Celia traced the bottom of her wineglass, fidgeting. "This is nice. Thanks for having me over. Maybe next time you could come over to my place. It isn't fancy or anything, and I can't cook, not like this, so you might get pizza delivery—"

"I'd like that," Suzanne said. "We both would. Just let us know a time and we'll be there."

Maybe this would be easier than Celia thought. Maybe it wasn't too late to have a decent family life. Her parents had never seen her apartment. The idea made her a little giddy, a little nervous, like getting ready for a test. She'd have to *clean*. "Okay," she said.

Suzanne said, "Maybe we could make it a weekly thing. We're all so busy, but if we had a scheduled time we wouldn't go for six months without seeing each other. Robbie and Arthur could come over. And Celia, if you ever want to bring someone along, that'd be all right. I'd really like to meet your friends. Or if there's someone, you know, special." She shyly lowered her gaze to the piece of pasta she'd been twirling on her fork for the last minute.

Celia had to repeat to herself, *She means well, she means well.* But the thought of bringing Mark—or any guy—here gave her a mild panic attack. *My parents, the superhuman crime fighters. And what do you do, son? Stockbroker? You don't say . . .*

"Maybe."

"Detective Paulson seems nice." Suzanne eyed Celia.

"He is."

Her father huffed. "His father's a—"

"Warren . . ." Suzanne gave him *the look*.

"I'm just saying Celia needs to watch her back. Who knows what they're up to."

Suzanne said, "You shouldn't judge people by their fathers."

Amen, Celia thought. "It's okay. He's never liked anyone I've dated." Warren was about to say something; a red flush was creeping into his features.

Klaxons wailed. And wasn't that a blast from the past, the Olympiad alarm system sounding in the middle of dinner?

Warren dropped his fork and leaped from the table. Suzanne hesitated, looking at Celia apologetically.

"Don't worry. I'll let myself out and lock up. You guys be careful."

Her mother smiled, squeezed her hand, and followed her husband to the Olympiad control room.

Ten minutes later the penthouse trembled for a moment as the jumpjet launched from its rooftop hangar. Celia's wineglass chimed, rattling against a piece of silverware. She grabbed it to hold it still.

She finished eating, though her heart wasn't in it. Not with two half-eaten meals staring at her. Leftovers in this house were never a problem, though. Suzanne just waved her hand at them—instant hot meal.

Her parents had remodeled the kitchen since she moved out. They'd traded the slate tile floor for hardwood, the black lacquer cabinets for oak, and the stainless steel appliances for off-white. They were mellowing in their old age.

The Tupperware was still in the cupboard next to the dishwasher. Celia packaged the leftovers and found room for them in the fridge, ran the dishwasher, rinsed out the wineglasses, and took a nostalgic swing around the place.

An entire floor of Celia's apartment building would fit inside the West penthouse. More than half of that was taken up by the Olympiad's base of operations. That still left a spacious home that had been featured in *City Living Magazine*, back when the Wests were still just the Wests, socialites and heirs to a mercantile fortune. Floor-to-ceiling windows made up one wall of the great room—living room and rec room on one end, dining room on another. It was like having a gymnasium in your house. The carpet was soft and newly cleaned, not a speck of dust or a wrinkle anywhere. The place hardly looked lived in. Her parents probably didn't spend much time here anymore. It had been a while since they had a kid losing popcorn down the sides of the cushions on the leather sofa while she watched videos.

Visitors never noticed the décor at first. They always went to the windows, which looked over the city: a grid of streetlights, a mosaic of buildings stretching out to the distance, to a black band that was the river and harbor. A faint noise—the hum of car engines, an occasional siren or barking horn—could be heard despite the thick glass. A person could feel like a god, standing up here, gazing over a world that seemed smaller—like a picture, or a model. They might feel like they owned it all. *Wonderful view,* people always said.

She'd learned her way around Commerce City by staring out these windows, naming the streets, identifying the buildings, labeling the green swath that was City Park and the university beyond it. She always knew where she was by looking up and spotting the glowing blue West Corp sign with its crescent moon logo attached to the skyscraper's side.

A hallway past the living room led to a suite of offices where Warren ran the family business. Around one more corner were the bedrooms: the master suite and half a dozen guest suites. And her room. Curious, Celia continued on and opened the door.

Inside were her four-poster bed, oak dresser, a couple of toy chests, bookshelves, all the same as when she'd left. Someone had taken down the heavy metal band posters that had decorated the place when she'd last lived here and repainted. But if she looked in the closet they'd probably be there, rolled up and waiting.

She'd left so quickly, without a backward glance. She hadn't been given a chance to grow out of the teenager she'd been. Instead, she'd had to smash that teenager utterly and try to build something decent to replace her. In doing so, she'd burned a lot of bridges. She wondered: Had she ever been expected to work for her father—in the business, not as part of the Olympiad—and that somehow got lost amid the disappointment of learning she was a perfectly average model of Homo sapiens? Did West Corp need another accountant? Although working in a company as the daughter of the owner wouldn't be any different than living in a city as the daughter of its premier superhero.

She wasn't going to complain. She was lucky to be alive.

The cab that she'd called was waiting for her by the time she reached the lobby of West Plaza. That was how huge the damn thing was. *Heir to the West fortune.* She ignored the label, because she honestly didn't believe it. She hadn't seen her parents' will. They hadn't offered to show it to her, and she hadn't asked. She really didn't think her father would leave a cent to his traitorous, mundane daughter.

"Celia? Celia West? Is that you?"

She turned, startled. The security man at the front desk of the lobby had called to her. He was a different guy than had been here when she arrived. The shift must have changed. He was older, but still lean and fit; he wore the dark blue uniform well. Probably a retired cop. Then she brightened and found a smile.

"It's Damon, isn't it?" she said, walking over to the desk.

Damon Parks, he'd worked the desk here since forever. He must have had to unlock the door of the building for her a hundred times, during her rebellious phase when she insisted on coming home past curfew. He'd never said a word of reproof. He'd just given her a half-smiling, half-reprimanding look, and called up to her parents.

Now, he beamed. "I wasn't sure you'd remember me. It's been a while."

"Of course I remember you. How are you?"

He shrugged. "Can't complain. But you—look at you, all grown up. Back visiting your folks?"

"Yes."

"First time, isn't it? Since you left."

"I guess we all decided it was time."

"That's good. I'm glad."

The cab honked its horn, so Celia waved a farewell and turned to the door.

Another piece of the old life fell into place, but at a slightly different angle, or with a subtle change in color. Like the redecorated kitchen. All she had to do was go away for a few years, and she came back to a world that looked a little friendlier than it had before. That was all it took.

TEN

ELIA was riding the bus to Smith and Kurchanski when one of Bronson's lackeys called her cell.

"Bronson wants you here right away."

"Why? What happened?" Jury selection had been a complicated, contentious process—the lawyers faced not just the problem of finding jurors who didn't have a strong opinion about Simon Sito, but of finding ones not likely to be intimidated by the presence of the Destructor in the courtroom. It was over now, a jury had been seated, and the trial was due to start. Celia worried that something had happened to stall that.

"He wouldn't say, he just said he wants to see you immediately. When can you get here?"

She looked at her watch, looked out the window to the route the bus was taking. She was going the wrong way. "Give me half an hour."

"You can't get here sooner?" The guy sounded like he was having a seizure. Bronson probably held him personally responsible for not being able to teleport her to his office instantly.

She hung up on him, then called work to tell them she'd be late.

Exactly a half hour later, she knocked on the door of Bronson's office.

"Who is it?" His voice was rough, exhausted.

"Celia West."

"Get in here, close the door." She did so, shutting it quietly behind her, not willing to let go of the doorknob. She wanted to be able to escape.

"Look at this." Bronson, sitting behind his desk, offered her a sheet of paper.

She stepped forward to take the page from him, moving softly, gently, as if that would calm Bronson and make whatever was wrong less terrible. "What is it?"

"The witnesses the defense wants to call. Read it over."

The page held a list of about a dozen names, in alphabetical order. Mostly doctors, testifying to Sito's insanity. The very last name, though, was Celia West.

She flushed, her cheeks burning. She felt like she was going to faint. Or throw up. She set the page down and dropped her arms to her sides, so Bronson wouldn't see her hands shake.

"Why would they do that?" she said. "What could they possibly—"

"Come on, you know. They're going to discredit you, that's what this is about. Discredit every piece of evidence you've touched by blowing your story wide open."

"They can't, the record's sealed—" Her voice was shaking, and she wished it wouldn't.

"They can. Yeah, it's sealed, but you can bet Sito told his lawyers all about you. All they have to do is bring it up. Even if the testimony gets thrown out, it's still there. What was it you said? They're using you to get to your parents."

Mechanically, she shook her head. She'd leave town. She'd go into hiding. Get Dr. Mentis to induce a coma so she'd sleep through the whole trial—"I can't do it, I can't get up there and let them do this."

"I've already lodged a complaint. That's why we get to look at all this stuff beforehand. You were one of Sito's more prominent victims. That was what made the papers, and no judge would expect you to face that guy in court. But I thought you should get a heads-up. If this leaks to the press at all, someone else will dig up your record like I did. Consider yourself warned."

She couldn't be Celia West without that record, without her parents, without the publicity. She should have figured that out by now. "Thank you."

White-faced, still shaking, she left and tried to have a normal day.

By midday, someone had leaked the defense's witness list. It came out in special news flashes all afternoon.

Everyone had an opinion about it. Most of the opinions expressed outrage that the defense would stoop so low. The thought was the defense was going to use what Sito had done to Celia as yet more evidence of his insanity. But they didn't know the truth.

Mark and Analise, in separate phone calls, told her that no judge would make her testify.

"They can't do it," Mark said with inspiring vehemence. "That's ludicrous. If anything, you should be testifying for the prosecution. Why isn't Bronson putting you on the stand?"

She couldn't tell him. She just kept saying, "I don't know," and sounding scared. He threatened to rush to her office and take her home then and there, but she talked him out of it. He promised to bring her Thai food for supper instead.

When Analise offered to bring her supper, Celia had to turn her down. "Mark's bringing food."

"Hm, good for him. Wait a minute, he's a cop. Can't he make the judge keep you from testifying or something?"

"I don't think it works like that. The DA's already filed a protest. That's all we can do."

"They'll listen to him, right?"

Wrong. All the defense had to do was present evidence that Celia wasn't the squeaky-clean victim everybody thought she was, and the judge wouldn't be able to wait to haul her onto the stand. But she couldn't tell Analise that any more than she could tell Mark.

"I don't know." Feigned ignorance made a hell of a shield to hide behind.

She received her subpoena by courier that afternoon.

She felt grateful that she had work to bury herself in. City Hall had deeds and street plans going back far enough to track down Leyden Park. This was the part of her job she liked, hunting down the elusive clues, tracking her quarry, and pouncing on the target. Since she didn't have superpowers, she had to settle for battling evil from behind a desk.

The Leyden Park building still existed, but it was vacant. It was located in an industrial neighborhood northeast of town, an area populated by oil refineries and chemical plants. A wasteland. No one would notice an empty warehouse building there. Demolishing it wasn't worth the expense, since the demand for the land it was on was low. At least until now. The site was marked as one of the areas Mayor Paulson's superhighway would pass through. His office had recently ordered surveys of the land.

Based on the date, the building had apparently been abandoned, written off as a capital loss and donated to the city, shortly after the accident that had put Sito in the hospital. All Celia had to do was find the original deed, and the original owner who'd hired Sito and sponsored the failed experiment. Never mind that the original deed seemed to be missing.

Celia went to the clerk and recorder's office and talked to the front-line assistant. The woman looked harried, and Celia tried to be polite.

"I'm trying to trace an original title deed for the DA's office. It's for this property." At least she'd been able to track down the address.

"Have you checked with records?"

"I just came from there. The information seems to be missing, and they thought you might have some other ideas."

The woman heaved a long-suffering sigh. "It's probably misfiled. Which means we may never find it . . . unless you feel like cleaning out the place?"

Celia liked digging for information, but not that much. "What about the property tax records? Even if we can't find the deed, we should be able to find out who was paying property tax on the building back then, right?"

The woman brightened. "I think I can help you with that."

In a back corner of the office sat an ancient microfiche machine and a row of filing cabinets. The woman chatted as she opened drawers and scanned file-folder tabs. "They put everything on microfiche about twenty years ago. Now they want everything on computer. Because no one can find the time or energy to transfer the microfiche to digital files, we have to keep both. You're lucky you're not trying to find something that got entered during the transition. Then, it could be anywhere."

Celia waited patiently, but she tapped her foot.

The clerk thumbed through one of the file folders, then thumbed through again. "Hm. It should be right here—"

It was enough to make Celia think that someone had taken the data, that someone was hiding something.

"Oh, here it is!" The clerk pulled a folder from a file bin on top of the cabinet, near the machines. "Someone else was looking at it and didn't get around to putting it back. Ah, that's why."

She showed Celia the label on the file folder, which read CITY URBAN RENEWAL. "That building of yours must be in one of the areas they want to put the highway through. The mayor's people are in here all the time looking up property assessments. I'll find your building in a minute."

She sat down at the reader with a sheet of microfilm and started searching. While grateful for the clerk's helpfulness, Celia almost offered to work the machine herself; bringing the little squares of film into focus was taking forever.

"There it is," the woman finally said. She pressed a button, and the machine's printer whirred and spat out a sheet of paper. The clerk handed the page over proudly.

Celia studied it. She had to read it three times, convinced her eyes weren't focusing right. There was the right property, Leyden Industrial Park, and the right address, and this was the data for the year that Sito's accident had happened. Everything was right.

West Corp had paid the site's property tax for that year.

ELEVEN

THIRTY laps. She could swim thirty laps without thinking about it. It would wear her out enough to make sure she slept well that night without exhausting her. Then she wouldn't lie awake dreading impending testimony that was still a week away, at least.

She was going to be swimming a lot of laps in the foreseeable future.

By the end of the session, she had the pool to herself, which was nice. The only noises were hers, and if she didn't see anyone spitting she could pretend like the water really was clean.

The lifeguard had stepped away for a moment. He knew her as a regular, knew she wasn't likely to suddenly drown, and must have taken the opportunity for a break while no one else was around. She could pretend she had the whole *building* to herself.

When she found the locker room empty as well, her neck prickled. Closing wasn't for another three hours. She'd have heard any announcements in that regard over the PA. She pulled her towel tightly around her, skipping the showers, and going straight to the lockers. She could shower at home. She wanted to get out of here.

Three men in ski masks were waiting for her, standing by the bank of bright orange lockers, terribly out of place. She didn't scream, didn't panic. Just turned around and walked out again.

A fourth man blocked the passage that led to the pool.

This is not happening. Even worse than getting kidnapped was getting kidnapped soaking wet, wearing only a swimsuit.

The men closed in, moving toward her from either side. Two of them held handguns. She hadn't noticed the weapons at first; they were black and blended in with the gloves and jackets.

She looked for anything that might double as a weapon. The hand dryers were heavy enough to clock someone, but were bolted to the wall. She could break the mirror, use a shard as a knife. And what would she use to break the mirror, her elbow? Action-hero Celia?

If they just wanted to kill her, they'd have shot her already and it would have only taken one of them. She just had to take a deep breath and wait for rescue. Again.

The subtle, gurgling noise was barely noticeable—it might have been a shower left running. But the kidnapper in front of her took a step, and his boot splashed. He was standing in an inch of water. It lapped over Celia's toes, and was pouring in faster. The floor outside the row of shower stalls had a drain in it. The locker area had two more drains. Water started backing up from all of them.

"Come on!" the one in the front said, grabbing her arm.

By then, the water was ankle deep and still rising. No longer just covering the floor, it flowed toward them, in opposition to the law of gravity.

The kidnappers crowded her out of the women's locker room, to the pool annex, and toward the door to the men's locker room. That must have been how they snuck in here, and how they planned on spiriting her away.

A tidal wave, a wall of water, rose up from the swimming pool and fell toward them. It might have had a mind of its own, the way it homed in on them.

In fact, Celia was sure it did. Typhoon.

She turned her back to the wave and hunched over, not hoping to keep her feet but trying to protect herself. It slammed into her— and it slammed into the kidnappers. They screamed, she noted.

She thought she hit the wall. She hit *something*, then she was floundering, splashing across the cement of the pool deck, which scraped her up as she tumbled.

The water carried her toward the pool, then set her down at the edge as it spilled away, over the side, back where it came from. The four kidnappers ended up dunked in the middle; every time they tried to swim for the edge, a wave surged over them. The surface of the water churned and thrashed, like the ocean in a storm, and they were using all their effort to keep their heads clear.

Typhoon leaned on the wall near the annex by the locker rooms, arms crossed, admiring her handiwork with a satisfied glare. Her suit shone with condensation, her mask was slick and gleaming, and her hair was swept back, like an extension of her costume. Celia only recognized Analise because she knew what to look for.

Celia stayed sitting on the pool deck, catching her breath, and glowering. Good thing she'd still been wet when this happened. It would have been just her luck to have dried off and dressed, *then* gotten picked up by one of Typhoon's waves.

"You okay?" Typhoon said. Her tone was cautious.

Celia supposed she expected a thank you. It had been too much to hope for, to get out of here without talking to anyone.

She said, "How is it I always get caught in whatever offensive you guys use to take out the bad guys?"

"Nonlethal force. You don't have to be too careful about bystanders." She shrugged. "And you always seem to be standing in front of the target."

"They *put* me there."

"Kinda dumb of them, trying to kidnap you at a swimming pool," she said.

"Not really. They knew to find me here. You're the only one who could have soaked them like that, and what are the odds you would have been within easy range to get here and—"

What were the odds, indeed? The familiar hint of anger crawled through her heart and tightened her gut. "You've been watching me. Following me."

Typhoon looked like she was going to deny it—she set her jaw in a scowl and returned Celia's glare. But she waited too long to say anything.

Finally, she said, "We all have. We've been taking turns."

Celia's voice caught, and she had to swallow the lump in her throat before trying again. "Why didn't you tell me? Why didn't anyone tell me you were . . . were *babysitting* me?"

"It wasn't babysitting. You were bait. We were hoping they'd try for you again, and we could catch them. If you knew, you'd have acted differently. Word might have gotten out, and they might not have tried."

The four in the pool looked caught, to say the least. There was her hidden talent. Celia West: Bait Girl. Hostage Lass. The Captive Wonder.

The police arrived then, right on schedule, a dozen of them stomping out of the locker rooms, guns out and pointed at the would-be kidnappers.

Of course, Mark was with them. How could he not be? She didn't want him here. She didn't want him to see her angry.

Before any well-meaning officers could try to help her, she got to her feet. Her towel was gone—probably a sodden mess washed up in a corner somewhere. Never mind. She'd stand under the wall dryer if she had to.

"Celia!" Mark called and ran to her. She took a deep breath and was calm by the time her counting reached seven. "Are you all right?"

"I'm fine," she said, her voice flat. "Just a little shaken up."

He held her arms, studied her, then kissed her forehead. She let him, but her skin crawled. She just wanted to get out of here.

"Are you sure?"

"Yeah, I'm fine. Really. I'm sorry, I'm not thinking straight." She tried a brave smile. He was trying to be nice. Being very gentlemanly, really.

The surface of the water had settled; the kidnappers dog-paddled awkwardly to the ladder, and the cops fished them out. Typhoon gave Mark a haphazard salute.

"I'm out of here, boys. 'Til next time." She ducked out through the locker room. She'd be out of the building and out of her costume in minutes.

"She sure got here quick," Mark said.

"They've been following me. My parents, the other supers—they thought this would happen again."

"You don't sound happy about it."

"I'm . . . never mind."

"Give me ten minutes. I'll drive you home."

Then he'd want to stay with her. She had to think of a way to tell him no without hurting his feelings.

She found a dry towel, dried off, and changed while Mark arrested the kidnappers. She finished before him, and went to wait in the front lobby of the rec center.

Meeting Arthur Mentis on the way in was almost the last straw. Presumably he was here to scan the kidnappers before they could get their thoughts in order. He saw her; she couldn't hide. Not that he had to see her to *see* her.

She turned her back to him, as if that would make him disappear, or hide her thoughts from him.

"Don't worry. I'll leave you alone," he said, continuing through the lobby to the pool area.

Almost, she called out to him. Almost, she begged him to wait. She could tell him how she was feeling; he'd understand.

But he kept walking, and she kept her mouth shut.

Mark brought her dinner to her place. It took three hours to convince him to leave. He couldn't understand that what she most wanted—the best way to handle days like these—was to get back to normal as quickly as possible. No coddling, no special treatment. Just normal. Was it so hard?

TWELVE

CELIA was back at work the next day. She started in on the first thing in her in-box that didn't involve the Sito case.

The receptionist buzzed her at noon. "Celia, you have a visitor."

She wasn't expecting anyone. Maybe it was Mark, still showering her with concern. But he always called first. She braced herself for a surprise.

Arthur Mentis waited in the lobby.

"Hi," she said bluntly, before mentally shaking herself into a more polite frame. But she couldn't think of a polite way to ask, *What are you doing here?*

"I thought you might like some lunch," he said. "I was in the neighborhood."

He might very well have been. "You always seem to know exactly when I'm ready to break for lunch."

"Logic," he said. "It's noon. You aren't implying something nefarious, are you?"

"It's your babysitting shift, isn't it?"

He chuckled. "Yes, actually. But what better way to keep an eye on you?"

If it had been anyone else, her mother or Robbie or even

Analise, she'd have grumbled and ranted about how they couldn't leave her alone, and didn't they trust her, and couldn't they show a little respect. But with Arthur, she had to laugh.

They went to the Italian place in the building's ground floor.

They sat, exchanged pleasantries. Her parents were fine. He'd convinced them not to call right away after the latest kidnapping, for which she expressed her gratitude.

"Do you want to talk about it? You seemed rather upset yesterday."

At least he waited until the breadsticks were out before asking. "Are you asking as a psychologist or as a friend?"

"Which do you prefer?"

Psychologist implied she needed counseling, that something was wrong with her. While that very well may have been true, she'd been doing pretty well lately—she thought—and preferred to maintain the illusion. "Friend, I suppose. It wasn't the kidnapping that upset me. It was finding out about the surveillance. That you guys have been keeping tabs on me, in secret."

"Typhoon told you?"

"I confronted her. She showed up too quickly. I just want to be left alone, to take care of myself—but I can't do that, evidently. Not when it seems like half the town's crooks are after me. I guess I need superhuman bodyguards. I hate that I can't get away from that part of my past. I'll never get away. I'm not making choices about my life, it's all just . . . trapping me. No matter what I do. I've worked so hard—"

"What else?"

What else indeed? What *wasn't* there? "Sito's defense called me to testify. I think they want to use me to discredit the prosecution. Bronson's trying to get me out of it, but it doesn't look good. It's all going to come out." She wanted to pretend it didn't bother her so much, but thinking about it made her either want to break a chair or burst into tears. She tried to clamp down on the feelings. But around Arthur, why bother? So she seethed, quietly.

"Would you like me to do something about it?"

"Like what—change the defense attorney's mind for him? Mess with the judge?" She said this last in a whisper.

He didn't react. He never reacted. She might have asked him to pass the sugar, as concerned as he seemed. He'd do it, too, she realized. If she asked.

"Could you?" she said. "I mean, I know you could. But would you? It's not right, you know."

He shrugged. "There's right and then there's right. You don't deserve to get raked over the coals for this."

As he said, there was right and then there was right.

"No, I guess not. But if I don't want you guys around at all, I can't come running to you for help when I want it. It'll be okay. I'll get through it."

He smiled thinly. "I knew you'd say that. And what if the record does come out? You were a rebellious kid who made a mistake. Most of the people in that courtroom have made mistakes. Any witness the defense calls, Bronson can cross-examine. No matter what they make you say, Bronson can clean it up. I'll coach him. I made the temporary insanity diagnosis not to keep you out of jail, but because it was true. In rebelling against your parents, you identified with their enemy, and it was totally irrational. You weren't in your right mind. Here's the ultimate proof: After that incident, what did you do? Did you get in trouble again? Did you spiral down into a life of crime and mayhem? Did you return to Sito's clutches? No. You disappeared for four years, and it was the best possible thing you could have done. You came back from college a different person. You were more confident, you could take care of yourself, and you no longer depended on your parents for your identity. You simply aren't the same person."

"You can see all that because you're telepathic."

He huffed. "Anyone with eyes can see you're a decent human being."

"Even Dad?"

"If he ever actually *looked* at you, he'd see it. But he's a man who's very good at seeing what he wants to see."

Mentis always knew the right thing to say. Didn't make her any happier about the situation.

"I don't want my personal history made a spectacle."

"No. But we all make sacrifices for the cause of justice. This might be yours."

Second place. She'd won *second place* in the 200-meter freestyle. That was in the medals. She'd never done that well, and had never been so proud. It was the pinnacle of her freshman year in high school. Maybe even her whole life. She could actually do something right.

There was a ceremony, and she stood on the podium. The medal hung weighty and solid around her neck. It wasn't *really* silver, but some kind of alloy plated silver. It didn't matter. She held it in her hand. It *meant* something. It had to mean something. Mom cheered for her from the stands. Dad wasn't there because he had to work. Mom had apologized for him, and Celia said she understood.

Back home after the meet, Celia found her father in his office and showed him the silver medal. He gave her a tight-lipped smile and ruffled her hair. "Good job. Maybe next time you'll win." He turned back to his work without another word.

She had expected something . . . more. A cheer, a hug. She wanted him to be as happy as she was. But she wasn't the champion, and anything less wasn't enough.

Next time. Why bother?

She stayed up past midnight that night watching TV in the living room, lying flat on the sofa. She flipped channels. Two hundred of them on the satellite TV, minus the ones her parents had blocked. She wore her silver medal over her pajamas.

Then, Suzanne's voice carried from down the hallway, growing closer. "You let them get the better of you. You underestimated them."

Celia used the remote to quickly shut off the TV and huddled flat on the sofa, hiding in the shadow behind the arm. She hadn't expected her parents to make an appearance in this part of the house tonight. They were working. Not the day job working, but *working* working, as she thought of it, when they donned their costumes and saved the city.

"They surprised me more like—"

"They shot at you and you just stood there, man," said Robbie Denton, aka the Bullet. Captain Olympus was getting dressed down by *both* of them. Huh.

"Warren, you can't take chances like that. I know the mission is important, but you can't . . . *waste* yourself on two-bit robberies."

Warren said, "Robbie was backing me up. At least, you were *supposed* to be."

"Hey, the plan had me watching the back exit."

"And it's not like I can get hurt—"

Suzanne said, "That's not the point! There are other ways of getting hurt than getting shot. This . . . this *stranger* knows all of our secrets now."

If the Olympiad was arguing, it meant something had gone wrong. The trio passed by the living room, reaching the open kitchen.

"What are we going to do about him?" Suzanne said, her voice softer now.

Celia wondered who they were talking about.

"I think we should invite him onto the team," Warren said.

"No, we don't know anything about him—"

"Not to mention he's inexperienced," Robbie added. "He's just a kid. Heck, does he even shave yet?"

Warren said, "Having him on the team would give him a stake in keeping our secret."

"But how can we trust him?"

"He helped us, Suzanne. He didn't have to, he could have let those gunmen surround me. Instead, he just knocked them all out without lifting a finger."

"That kind of power frightens me," she said.

What had happened? Someone with powers had discovered their secret identities, obviously, but how? Celia remained perfectly still, listening.

Then the voice of a stranger said, "This is when you try to convince me to use my powers for good, rather than for cheating at poker. Although it's lucky I was cheating at poker, or I never would have been in a position to help you." He had a crisp British accent, calm in tone, maybe even a little amused.

After a moment's pause, her father grumbled, "I was doing fine by myself."

"Fifteen against one says otherwise," the stranger said.

"We told you to stay in the command room," Robbie said, threateningly.

The stranger replied, offhandedly, "I can tell what you're saying about me from a hundred feet away, I might as well be here so I can defend myself."

Celia lay there, clutching her swimming medal, her heart racing. She desperately wanted to jump up, run out to the kitchen, and demand to know what had happened, who the stranger was, and was Dad okay—

"You know you have an eavesdropper?" the stranger said. "Next room over."

Celia held her breath—she hadn't made a sound. Who was this guy? Did he have amplified hearing and sense her heartbeat? Could he smell her?

After a pause, her parents both said, with an air of frustration, "Celia."

Her mother's soft footsteps approached the area where the kitchen opened into the living room. "Celia? Why aren't you in bed?"

She hesitated. Maybe she could pretend she wasn't here, that the stranger was wrong. But all Suzanne had to do was enter the room and look at the sofa. Celia answered, "I wanted to watch TV."

"Why don't you come on out?"

Celia stared at the darkened ceiling. "I don't want to."

"Well, come out anyway. I don't want you sneaking off with only half the story."

Sighing heavily, Celia lurched off the sofa and prepared to trudge to her mother. She tucked the medal under her nightshirt. As soon as she appeared, Suzanne put her arm around Celia's shoulder and guided her to the kitchen.

Her father stood near the table, arms crossed, glaring at the world in general. Robbie leaned against the wall nearby, looking equally sullen. They'd focused their attention on a man she'd never seen before. He stood at the end of the hallway, his hands tucked in the pockets of his brown trench coat, open to show a dress shirt unbuttoned at the collar. He had pale hair, ruffled back from a long face. His gaze was piercing. He studied her calmly.

"This is our daughter Celia. Celia, this is Arthur Mentis."

"Hello," he said.

She didn't say anything. Just glared. He quirked a smile, like he understood her mistrust.

He looked at Suzanne. "She knows? Your secret identities, everything?"

Suzanne said, "We didn't see a point in keeping it secret. She'd find out eventually."

"She was supposed to join us one day," Warren said, his voice flat.

Supposed to. No one expected that to happen now.

"Then you don't have any particular . . . talents, I take it?" he said to her. That he spoke directly to her, and not through one of her parents, surprised her. He looked a lot younger than them, but he wasn't intimidated by them, which made her warm to him.

That didn't mean she had to answer him, especially when her father's tone had made the answer obvious. "So what do you do?" she said, frowning.

"I spend my free time cheating at poker to pay for medical school. Not quite as glamorous as being the Olympiad. But there you are."

"He's a telepath," Suzanne said.

Celia flushed, her cheeks burning. She suddenly felt naked—all her thoughts and frustrations, he could see them all. He could see that at this moment, she wasn't particularly fond of her parents, and she certainly wasn't interested in being nice to him. He must think she was awful.

"Then he knows about you guys," she said.

"We're working out what to do about that," her mother said.

"Is everything going to be okay?"

"Everything'll be fine. Don't worry about it. Go on to bed, okay?"

Mentis said, "It's hardly fair, asking her not to worry when you've exposed her to your world. How could she not worry? She's been worrying her whole life."

"It's not really any of your business, now, is it?" Warren said, glaring.

But that was it exactly, she'd been worried her whole life. Worried, scared, frustrated, embarrassed, disappointed. . . .

"Go on," Suzanne said, patting Celia's shoulder. "We'll see you in the morning, all right?"

Celia approached the hallway obliquely, keeping as far away from the stranger as she could. He appeared to not pay any attention to her.

She had moved past him when he said, "Congratulations on the silver medal."

Celia was startled into politeness. "Thanks."

Then, she ran down the hall to her room.

THIRTEEN

MARK and Arthur both told her what they'd learned from the poolside kidnappers. They weren't part of the so-called Strad Brothers, the group that masterminded the heist at the symphony gala. They were, however, working for the Strad Brothers. Criminal subcontractors, which would have been laughable if Celia hadn't seen that kind of organization in action. It hinted at a larger conspiracy. The details were murky. They'd only been instructed to take Celia West alive. A new conspiracy, with her at the center?

The evening news didn't mention her, thankfully. They had a bigger story. She and Mark lounged on her sofa, watching.

The pretty anchorwoman read her cue seriously. "Our top story, a robbery has taken place at the Commerce City Botanical Gardens. The perpetrators are believed to be the same group of thieves that stole four priceless Stradivarius instruments from the symphony gala last week."

Celia turned the volume up.

"The thieves' target this time? Three prize-winning koi. Because of their breeding potential, these koi were estimated to be worth tens of thousands of dollars."

Mark huffed. "*Fish?* You've got to be kidding me."

"Witnesses say the thieves took the fish from the Garden's Japanese pond, an ornamental landscape that forms the central attraction of the Garden's collection. Apparently, the fish were taken alive. Garden officials expressed some hope that they could be recovered in the same condition."

They should be so lucky. This gang obviously knew what it was doing and chose its targets carefully: unusual, high-ticket items that would be impossible to unload on the conventional marketplace.

"They're making a statement, not robbing for money," she said.

"That means there's a pattern. It makes them easier to catch."

Both robberies coincided with her kidnapping attempts—just like her kidnapping off the bus coincided with a city-wide crime spree. She didn't think she rated classification as a valuable cultural artifact. But in all three cases, she'd provided a distraction. Law enforcement and the supers had been looking at her, not at any robberies.

Until the Strad Brothers were caught, this was likely to happen again.

Now that she knew what to look for, she could spot her bodyguards. The next day, gazing upward, she caught a glimpse of Breezeway jumping from one building to the next, across the street from where she waited for the bus. He had a good view of her and all the streets around her. She almost waved hello.

Back in college, Celia had taken perverse delight in walking across campus alone in the middle of the night. As a freshman she'd gotten tired of the women's groups and security activists insisting that no girl should ever venture forth into the darkness without a can of mace and a uniformed cop escorting her. That reeked of regressive Victorian thinking. Celia made a point of walking alone, with enough of a badass attitude that no one ever approached her.

One night, a breeze kicked up autumn leaves as she marched from the library to her dorm, half a mile away. It was a nice night for a walk. Her peasant skirt swished around her legs, her oversize cotton tunic was cozy. In another month the air would be too cold for comfort.

Or in another hour it would be too cold. The breeze turned into a gust, a harbinger of a storm. It whipped her hair into her face, she had to hold her skirt down, and she started leaning into the wind to walk.

Across the street, the trees weren't blowing at all.

Her feet slipped, and she yelped. Cushioned by a whirlwind pounding around her, she floated a few feet off the ground. Her backpack slipped off her shoulder. She flailed her arms; it felt almost like swimming. The pocket of wind held her like a hand. Thank God she was wearing tights; her skirt tossed around her hips.

From above her, a man floated down, arms outstretched, riding the breeze like it was a surfboard. He wore the unmistakable sleek costume of a superhuman vigilante—or villain. A strip of silk ran along the insides of his arms, down his torso, rippling like sails. He wore a mask on the top part of his face. His frame was thin— barely postadolescent. He had overgrown brown hair and a shit-eating grin.

Celia struggled, but she only flopped like a fish out of water.

"You're Celia West?" he said, calmly hovering before her.

"Who the hell are you?"

"Hm," he murmured, like he was all macho or something. "I expected you to be more . . ."

"More *what?*"

"I don't know. More *something.*"

"What do you want with me?"

"You're going to tell me how to join the Olympiad."

She rolled her eyes. This was the most dangerous type out there: smart enough to track her down, and stupid enough to think she was worth something. Eager enough to want to save the world— but not a clue as to what he was trying to save. To him it was all one supercharged cinematic adventure.

"You think I know how? I can't help you."

"But Captain Olympus is your father."

And she hadn't spoken to him in a couple of years now. "We don't get along. Now put me down and go send a résumé to West Corp."

He pursed his lips thoughtfully for a moment, then gave his head a decisive shake. "No. I'm too close. Can't back down. If I bring you to them, they'll see what I can do. They'll have to take me."

Stretching forward, he swooped toward her and scooped her up. Cradling her in his arms, he soared up, over the campus, toward downtown. They weaved around buildings like they were trees in some immense forest, the streets dwindling beneath them.

He could fly. Easily, like he was taking a stroll across town. He used the wind somehow; a swell of air carried them along. She might have been impressed, if she hadn't been so pissed off and scared. She clung to him, because if she struggled now and he let go, she'd drop a couple hundred feet to the ground.

He aimed his flight toward West Plaza. The glowing blue logo shone as a beacon.

Cruising along one side of the tower, he flew up, straightened, and gracefully touched down on the helipad, feet first. He set her down beside him. She stumbled; her legs were shaking. She wanted to run away, but she couldn't.

The service door by the helipad opened and the Bullet jogged onto the roof, no doubt called by the West Plaza alarm system. He took in the scene, glancing at the masked guy, then at Celia, and back.

"What's going on?" Robbie said, half-directing the question to Celia.

"The Bullet, just who I want to see," the stranger said. "I want to join the Olympiad."

Robbie rounded his shoulders and crossed his arms, donning an annoyed frown. "What makes you think we have any openings?"

"You'll take me." He nodded, clenched his fists. "You'll take me, or I'll drop her."

The wind snatched Celia off her feet again, wrenching a shriek out of her. She tried to clamp her mouth shut, wanting to be brave and quiet so she wouldn't distract Robbie. But the handlike breeze scooped her up and carried her over the edge of the building. She hung there, suspended, a hundred stories over cold pavement, nothing between her and the ground. Her scream was blood-curdling. *Don't look down, don't look down . . .*

The stranger reached toward her, guiding the power that kept her aloft. *Please don't distract him,* she prayed at Robbie. *Please.*

He looked at Robbie. "What do you say?"

"I say you're going about this all wrong."

"Get Captain Olympus and Spark up here. I bet they won't have any hesitation."

Robbie's arms uncrossed, his gaze narrowed. "I wouldn't make that bet if I were you."

"I mean it! I'll drop her!"

Mouth clenched closed, she stared up at a stark, washed-out sky. *Please, please, please—*

The Bullet disappeared.

Another wind came out of nowhere and smacked into her gut, knocking the breath from her. It heaved her in another direction, snatching her from the stranger's grip and dragging her back to the roof.

When she opened her eyes, she was standing on solid roof and leaning against Robbie, whose arm held her around her middle. The Bullet had run so fast, he'd dashed into the air itself, using his own special talent to fly, grabbed her, and carried her to safety. Her lungs heaved, trying to catch a breath.

"You okay, kid?" he whispered.

She could only nod. When he let her go, she managed to stay standing, for which she was grateful.

He turned to the stranger, who backed away a couple of steps. "You want to talk about this now? What made you think that dangling his daughter off the roof would convince the Captain to trust you enough to bring you onto the team?"

The Bullet was being far nicer than Celia would have been.

The stranger shook his head, still backing away, glancing over his shoulder to judge his distance from the edge, which didn't add anything to his impressiveness. "I had to make them—you—listen!"

Robbie stepped toward him, hastening the other's retreat. "I'm listening now. So, you have any other talents besides summoning winds and kidnapping girls? Come on, I'm listening."

He sputtered for a moment, like he wanted to say something. Then, he jumped. He'd reached the edge, and rather than stay put, he threw himself over it. A wind picked him up and carried him off. He flew away, his body stretched out flat and streamlined.

"We're going to have to keep track of that one," Robbie said, hands on hips. He looked at Celia. "You really okay?"

She'd found her breath and voice by then. "Yeah, I think so. Thanks for the save."

"No problem. You should come inside, get warmed up. You look like you could use a drink."

"Only if it's bourbon."

"I was thinking hot cocoa."

"I think I just want to go home."

He hesitated, and she braced, because it probably meant an argument. When she said home, he was probably thinking of something different than she was.

"You haven't been back here in months." Actually, it was years. "Your folks should be getting back any minute now, and I'll never hear the end of it if I let you leave without seeing them."

"I'd prefer it if they didn't know I was here at all."

He gestured with a thumb over his shoulders. "Security cameras. I can't hide the footage." Uncle Robbie, always siding with her parents.

"Robbie, please. I need to get back to campus." She started toward the roof door.

"How are you going to get back at this hour?"

"The late bus."

"Celia!" That pleading tone in the voice always stopped her, even now. "I guess I don't understand it. You were born with all this." He gestured to encompass the West Plaza building. "You could have had the best of everything. How many people would kill to have all this? And you just throw it all away?"

Robbie had come from the east side, the not-so-great part of town, the son of a machinist and a hairdresser. He hadn't gone to the Elmwood Academy like Warren and Suzanne had. Instead, he'd graduated from P.S. 12. He'd have gone to college on a track scholarship—if he hadn't been kicked out of the sport for cheating because of his powers. Then he'd met Captain Olympus and Spark, and found another outlet.

"You ever get tired of it?" she asked. "Being on Dad's payroll for doing stuff like this? Keeping up the vigilante gig? You ever wonder what would have happened if you hadn't joined the Olympiad? Just gone on, gotten a normal job, had a normal life?"

"Normal isn't an option for folks like me. We are what we are."

"Well. I've got a chance to try normal for a little while. So that's what I'm doing." She made a broad shrug, dismissing the topic.

His short-cropped hair was more gray than black now. She couldn't recall when that had happened.

"You are one stubborn kid," he said.

She hugged herself and looked away.

"At least take your folks' limo. It'll be warm, and it'll get you right to your doorstep."

And it would have something to drink in the minibar. "Okay."

"I'll call down to the garage for you."

"Thanks."

Together, they went through the door, to the foyer of the penthouse, to the elevator. She stepped in and punched the button for the parking garage.

He held his hand over the door to keep it from closing. "It's normal to call your parents once in a while, you know. They miss you, Celia. Do you think you could at least come home for Christmas this year?"

She shook her head before he'd even finished. "I'm not ready. I'm sorry, but I'm not ready."

"Will you ever be?"

She couldn't explain it to him, that it really was getting better, that being on her own—out of the middle of the madness that was her parents' double lives—had brought the world into focus for her. She looked in the mirror now and saw herself. A little more time, and she'd start to see the road before her, and it wouldn't seem so murky.

"Yeah, I will. I think. But it's going to take time. I'm sorry. Tell them I'm sorry." It was the first time she'd ever apologized or expressed sympathy, even indirectly.

She touched his hand, squeezed it, pushed it away from the door, and held his gaze until the doors closed.

Breezeway was something of a lone wolf. His getting involved meant the superhumans had been in conference, which meant they thought this was serious. She was almost flattered, but she couldn't help but feel like they were wasting their time. She wasn't the target. She wasn't where they'd strike again, not really. She was a red herring.

Once on the bus, she called her mother's cell phone.

"Celia, what's wrong?"

"Why does everyone always assume something's wrong when I call?"

"Because you never call unless something's wrong."

"That's not true."

"Celia—"

Okay. It was true. "I'm sorry, Mom. I just think you guys should call off the surveillance on me."

"No. Absolutely not. In case you haven't noticed, the Strad Brothers tried to kidnap you during both their robberies. They'll try again."

"I know, that's just it. They're using me as a distraction. While you guys are busy worrying about me, they get away with another robbery."

"I'll worry about you over a fish any day of the week. Celia, this is serious, it's not like we're following you around on a high-school date."

Except that they would be following her on dates, the next time she and Mark went out. Hell, Mark was probably in on it.

No need to get paranoid or anything.

"I think your resources would be better spent tracking them down than trying to protect me. You heard what Arthur said, they want me alive. Even if they managed to catch me, I'd be safe. Hell, I might even learn something that could bring them down."

"Don't get any ideas. You're not trained for that kind of mission."

She wasn't trained for any kind of mission, except auditing income statements. "Don't worry, I won't." She was starting to sound surly. She needed to wrap this up before she said something she'd regret later.

Suzanne said, "We'll stop the surveillance on one condition: you come back to live at West Plaza, where we can keep an eye on you."

She didn't even have to hesitate. "No, Mom, I can't do that."

"You didn't even think about it."

"Hey, Mom? My stop's coming up, I really have to go—"

"You're not still riding the bus, are you?"

"I'll talk to you later, okay? Say hi to Dad for me."

She clicked off the phone.

FOURTEEN

EST Corp's connection to the Leyden Industrial Park hit awfully close to home. She had the next key to the puzzle, and she could keep going—if she could get access to West Corp's files. If she did, she could find out if Sito had been working for West Corp, and if West Corp had compensated Sito well enough to pay for Greenbriar. She could maybe even find out what Sito had been doing when he had his initial breakdown.

And if she learned all those answers, what was she going to tell Bronson about it? Not to mention her parents.

Jacob West, her grandfather, had headed the corporation then. Her father hadn't been born yet. No one could have known back then what Sito would become. It didn't mean anything. Unless the tabloids got hold of the information, of course.

She made good on her offer to have her parents over for dinner.

Her mother fussed, still worried about Celia after the latest kidnapping attempt. Suzanne wanted to cook for her—in her own kitchen no less—but Celia managed to put her foot down. She ordered pizza to be delivered, as she'd threatened, but Suzanne seemed relieved that Celia wasn't actually going to do any work.

Her father, on the other hand, was in a snit. "It has to be the Destructor masterminding this. We know these hits are all connected. Only the Destructor is capable of organizing a citywide spree."

"He's under suicide watch at the Elroy Asylum," Suzanne said. "He can't organize a crime spree under those conditions."

"He'd find a way."

Celia toyed with a leftover crust of pizza. Something didn't ring true about that. The targets of the robberies were too odd. The kidnapping attempts were too haphazard. Like it was all some kind of distraction, a means rather than an end.

"I don't think it's the Destructor," she said.

"Why?" Warren demanded.

"It's not his MO. The Destructor would have pinned the flayed koi to the mayor's desk. He'd have sent the Stradivariuses back to the symphony in splinters."

He said, "Is that a fact?"

"It's a hypothesis."

A few moments of silence passed before Suzanne said, "She's right, Warren. This isn't how Sito operated."

"Then there's someone else," he said. "A new mastermind."

Suzanne considered, her brow furrowed. Celia used the pause in conversation to start clearing the table. She wasn't thinking about the Destructor or masterminds—the less she thought about such topics the happier she was. Instead, she'd spent most of the evening trying to figure out how to ask her father for a favor.

The pause lengthened, and she decided to take the chance.

"Dad, do you know anything about a building West Corp owned about fifty years ago? It's in the northeast industrial district. It used to be called the Leyden Industrial Park."

He shook his head. "I don't know. That long ago, it would have been one of my father's projects."

"Do you think West Corp still has the records on it?"

"Probably. We never throw anything away."

"He got that from his father," Suzanne said.

"Do you think I could have a look?" She held her breath.

"What's your interest?"

It wasn't an accusation. Just a natural question. She had to remember that. "I stumbled across it at work. The building came up with West Corp's name attached to it. I got curious, but I'm having trouble finding records from that far back. I thought it couldn't hurt to ask you."

Suzanne watched Warren with as much focus as Celia did; her mother might have been holding her breath as well.

Warren took a drink of water. "Just curious?"

"Yeah."

"No conflict of interest—you wanting to dig up something that'll come back to bite the company later."

Of all the . . . "It's fifty-year-old data. It should be completely irrelevant."

"Then why is it important to you?"

Whatever she said, she refused to bring up Sito and feed her father's paranoid fantasies. Even if those fantasies might be correct. . . . Softly, she said, "I didn't think it would be that big a deal."

"Come on, now I'm curious. What's so interesting about this building?"

"I won't know that until I find those records, will I?"

Warren glared. He broke walls with that glare. "It's not like you've ever taken an interest in the company before."

"You don't trust me, do you? I can see the wheels in your brain inventing some plot that I must be hatching—"

"Oh, give me a break!"

"Warren—" Suzanne said, her voice a warning.

"If it's so harmless, then tell me how you found out about this building."

"It came up at work—"

"So now you're using personal connections for professional gain."

"You'd do the same thing!"

"I wouldn't have to!"

"Warren! Celia! Both of you, sit down!"

Celia and her father were glowering at each other across the table. The temperature in the room was rising.

Warren didn't sit down. Instead, he clenched his fists, and smashed one of them into the table. The wood laminate split, all the way through, across the entire length. The surface held together by mere splinters. The soda cans they'd been drinking from tipped over and spilled. Celia jumped back, her heart racing, and didn't have the wits to even grab a towel. Suzanne just crossed her arms and frowned.

Warren marched out of the apartment. It was a small blessing that he didn't slam the front door behind him.

Slowly, Celia returned to her seat. She sat on her hands, but they wouldn't stop shaking. Her face was shaking. Every nerve in her body was shaking.

Suzanne ran her hands through her hair. "And here I was thinking this was going well."

"I'm sorry, Mom." She sounded small, like a little girl. But her voice was shaking, too, and she had to either talk small or scream.

"Celia, why can't you just—" Suzanne sighed, once again leaving Celia unclear as to what she hadn't done, or ought to do, or couldn't do. She went over to Celia, put a hand on her shoulder. "It's not your fault. I ought to go after him. Make sure he doesn't get into any trouble."

He wasn't getting into trouble. They'd have heard it, if he was.

"I'll get you a new table," her mother said. "We could go shopping for one together."

"I was going to replace it soon anyway. I think." Celia shook her head. Feeling exhausted and perfunctory, she said, "Thanks for coming over."

"He'll calm down eventually. Then we just have to wait for the next time it happens." She shrugged, smiling wryly. "You're still coming over next week, yes?"

"Sure."

Suzanne left, and Celia threw away the rest of the pizza.

* * *

Just when she'd had enough of parents, Mayor Paulson invited her and Mark to dinner. She almost broke it off with Mark right there.

Was there such a thing as too normal?

Mark drove. "I think Dad feels like he needs to make up for the symphony disaster."

"That wasn't his fault."

"No, but in some ways he thinks he's responsible for everything that happens in the city. Like he ought to be able to fix every little problem."

That sounded hearteningly familiar. She wondered, Had the mayor ever met her father in person? They might actually get along.

She started blathering. "I have to warn you, I'm really not ready for you to meet my parents. Not like this, the nice-dinner-at-home thing. I mean, yeah, you already met my mom, but that wasn't really my mom, you know? That was Spark, and—" She realized how bad this must sound. "It's not you, it's just they can be difficult, and I still don't get along with them too well." She could see it now: Dad loses his temper and smashes the table to pieces, Mark's police instincts take over and he draws the gun he keeps in a shoulder holster, Dad sees the gun and throws Mark out the window. . . .

"It's okay. I'll meet them when the time's right. Hopefully someday when they're not, you know . . . being the Olympiad."

They were always the Olympiad. Sometimes Celia was sure the mundane sides of them were the disguise. That *she* was part of the disguise.

They pulled up in front of the mayor's mansion, which stood at the west end of a fifty-acre city park. A valet took charge of the car. Mark was in college when his father was first elected mayor. He'd never lived here.

The Paulsons must have been waiting for them, because the front door opened, held by a butler, as soon as they reached the top of the landing. They then launched into the sort of domestic scene Celia had only ever seen on TV commercials during the holidays. The mayor—Mark's father, in this context, Celia reminded herself— greeted them expansively, arms open as if to close them in a bear hug. He shook Celia's hand in both of his own, then clapped his son on the shoulder, grinning madly all the while. They might have been already married and returning home from their honeymoon, the way he carried on. How desperate was he to see his son married off? *What have I gotten myself into?*

"Come in, come in! Good to see you again, Celia, you're looking very well. Haven't scared her off yet, Mark?" His enthusiastic demeanor always played well on television. In person, it was nearly overwhelming.

Behind Anthony Paulson, waiting quietly in the foyer for her turn, stood Andrea Paulson, hands folded in front of her, smiling graciously. She wore an expensive dress suit in a feminine, non-threatening rose color. Evidently, she was much more comfortable on her home turf. Downright tranquilized compared to their last meeting. She must have been having a bad night at the symphony.

Andrea caught Celia watching her and strode forward hand extended. "Celia, I'm so happy to see you again."

Celia shook the woman's hand. Her smile was beginning to feel rather stricken. Andrea turned to her son next and stood on tiptoe so he could kiss her cheek.

"Shall we have a seat in the parlor? Dinner will be in just a few minutes."

The four of them retired to an honest-to-God parlor. It had plush Persian carpets on hardwood floors, antique furniture in rich woods and velvet upholstery. Each painting on the wall had its own display lamp. The whole mansion was the real deal, a Victorian edifice built by an early industrialist and donated to the city. The ground floor, with its wide foyer, opulent sitting rooms, and formal dining room, were often used for city receptions and ceremonies. The West Plaza penthouse looked almost homey in comparison.

Mayor Paulson settled at the edge of a regal wing-backed chair and said, "Celia, Mark tells me you're working with the DA's office on the Sito prosecution?" He waited expectantly for an answer. She'd hoped she could sit back on the chintz sofa and watch the

Paulson family dynamic, smiling and nodding politely now and then.

"Yes, I am."

"That's quite a coup for him, I imagine. It's like having a stamp of approval from the whole West family. Looks great in the papers."

If he'd only seen that altercation with her father outside Bronson's office. She smiled demurely. "I'm just trying to do my job as well as I can."

"For which the city thanks you. This trial may be the most important one we've ever seen."

God, he was on all the time. Was that the trick of politics, that you had to actually *mean* all the earnest things you said? Celia couldn't change the subject by complimenting Mrs. Paulson on the clever and tasty hors d'oeuvres set out for them. The mansion's cook had made them.

How would she have turned out if her parents had raised her in *this* kind of environment?

"Thank you, sir."

Mark, bless him, caught the rebound. "So, Mom, you getting to play much tennis? Mom plays tennis," he said in an aside to Celia. Andrea might have been one of the paintings, her smile was so fixed. She kept her gaze on her husband while she rattled on about tennis at the country club.

Dinner arrived, finally. Celia could relax as the conversation turned more banal.

That didn't last, though.

Paulson, jovial, said, "I keep expecting to find a note on my desk one of these days announcing the Olympiad's retirement—just like the Hawk did. How long have they been at this? Twenty, twenty-five years? The Hawk didn't last that long."

Celia smiled politely, as if acknowledging an old joke, and offered no reply. He couldn't have waited until after dessert to bring up the Olympiad.

"I remember them at their peak. God, they were amazing."

Celia could imagine what her father would say to that. He'd

punch through a wall and say, *How's that for peak?* And Spark might not even stop him.

He kept talking at her. "You must wish that they'd give up the double life. You must worry about them."

Her polite smile turned wry. "They're big kids. They can take care of themselves."

"Of course. I'm only curious. They say they're defending my city—I want to understand them."

His city? What was it with people claiming the city?

"There's not much to understand. They're using their talents the way they see fit." Was she actually defending them? She glanced at Mark. *Get me out of this . . .*

Mark shifted in his chair, calling attention to himself. "Celia can't be expected to speak for the Olympiad, Dad."

"No, no, of course not. My apologies. But Mark . . . let me run a thought by you. I've been wondering if our police forces have gotten soft." Understandably, Mark straightened in preparation of some vehement denial. His father waved him down. "Now, no offense, this certainly is no reflection on you personally. With a criminal like the Destructor, who was so far out of reach of what any normal law enforcement agency could handle, of course I can see how they might come to depend on the Olympiad, who were a bit better equipped to face opposition like that. But these recent crime sprees—they're perfectly ordinary crimes. They're fully within the ability of any law enforcement agency. I chastised the Olympiad for not getting involved—but after giving the issue some thought, I don't see that they, or any of the city's superhuman crime fighters, should involve themselves. They're simply not needed."

Celia was getting to practice her polite face. "I always thought that maybe they could work together. With law enforcement."

Paulson offered a thin, condescending smile. "If it hasn't happened by now, it never will."

"Sir, I'd hate to think you invited me here because you thought I'd take this conversation back to my parents and throw a little kerosene on the feud you all are having."

"Feud?" Paulson said.

"Ah, dessert's here!" Andrea Paulson announced brightly. "Celia, I hope you like chocolate."

Dessert was chocolate raspberry torte. Brilliant. It almost made up for Mayor Paulson.

As the house staff cleared dishes away, Andrea stood—abruptly, almost rudely, if it had been anyone else's table.

"Celia, would you like a tour of the upstairs? That's one of my jobs—giving tours. We have some really wonderful paintings that don't get seen much."

Mark gave an encouraging smile, and Paulson didn't seem inclined to accompany them. All that made the offer attractive.

"Sure," Celia said.

The second floor was as impressive as the first. Andrea and her husband lived on the third floor, so even here wasn't much evidence that this was an actual home. They occasionally hosted dignitaries in the guest rooms, or held charity concerts in the music room.

Andrea gushed about the house, the history, and her husband. "Tony is *so* dedicated. He gives so much of himself. He truly is the most generous man I've ever met. Don't you think? I hope Mark follows in his footsteps."

"He seems to be," Celia offered. "Being a cop's a tough job."

"Hm, yes. Normally in this situation I suppose I'd ask you to tell me about *your* family. But I think they're in the news even more than Tony. It must have been so interesting for you growing up. I hope this isn't prying too much, but I'm terribly curious—"

Celia smiled inwardly and waited for the inevitable question: *What was it like having Captain Olympus and Spark as parents? Isn't Captain Olympus wonderful?*

Instead, Andrea Paulson asked, "Do you ever worry?"

She shrugged. "I suppose. I worry about them getting hurt. Growing up I was always a little scared until they came home—"

Andrea gave a tiny, impatient shake of her head. "Don't we all worry about that sort of thing? I mean, do you worry about yourself? It's my understanding that your parents' powers might be passed on genetically. Now, I understand *you* didn't inherit anything like that. But do you worry that your children might inherit some of their more . . . unusual qualities?"

If you marry my son, will my grandchildren be mutant freaks? Celia could have used a cup of tea, a cup of coffee—any kind of social crutch to occupy her hands and keep her from reaching out and breaking something. As it was, she had to use willpower. Not her best attribute.

"Honestly, Mrs. Paulson, it's not something I've ever thought about." *And thank you so much for adding that to my list of anxieties.* "I figure I'll cross that bridge when I get to it."

"Of course, you're young yet." She offered the polished smile of a politician's wife. Paulson had probably married her for that smile. "I was simply curious. Really, I don't suppose anyone can help but wonder . . . what was it like having Captain Olympus as a father?"

The ride home with Mark started awkwardly. Mark clutched the steering wheel, Celia leaned on the passenger-side door, head propped on her hand, feeling surly. He kept glancing at her, stealing quick looks out of the corner of his eye when he wasn't driving through intersections. She waited for him to say something; he seemed on the verge of it, if he could just take a deep enough breath.

It was endearing. It didn't matter who you were or who your parents were, they'd always embarrass you.

Mark pressed back against the seat and smirked. "That was a disaster, wasn't it?"

"Oh, I don't know. If it had been my father, he might have broken a few walls."

"Not really," he said. "You always say he's like that . . . but you're exaggerating, right? He always seems so together."

"Sure," she drawled, and decided then and there that she would never, ever take Mark to dinner with her parents. "Hey—did your mom seem okay?"

"What do you mean?"

"She was just so different than she was when I met her at the symphony. I guess I'm wondering which is more like the real her."

"She did seem a little perky, didn't she?"

"You tell me."

He shrugged, resettling himself against the seat. "I don't know. I don't think she's ever been real happy with Dad in politics. I remember, the first time he ran for mayor, she'd have a glass of wine before the publicity photos. It was the only way she could relax."

"She must have had a glass of wine before we showed up, because she looked like a publicity photo all night."

Mark didn't respond, and by the time they got back to her place, she had no intention of mentioning his parents again.

FIFTEEN

THE prosecution's case dragged on for two weeks. For all his fire and brimstone behind the scenes, Bronson was solid and methodical in the courtroom, not taking any chances with speculation or questionable evidence. The financial evidence was plain, the witnesses primed and well spoken. Every objection Sito's lawyers made was overruled.

Warren and Suzanne West testified, along with Robbie Denton and Arthur Mentis. The first three wore street clothes—respectable trousers and jackets for the men, Suzanne in a conservative tweed dress suit. For that day, they were their alter egos, citizens of Commerce City who'd seen the extraordinary and come to tell about it. Arthur wore what he always wore, his suit and coat, looking studious and watchful, his thin smile hinting that he knew the dirt on everyone in the room. Even the judge looked at him askance.

The four members of the Olympiad were the last witnesses Bronson called. With them, he finished presenting his case, as if the presence of those who had fought the Destructor for so long were all the argument he needed.

Sito's lawyers surprised them all by refusing to cross-examine any of them.

It would have been an easy enough thing to raise questions

about the Olympiad's motives, to suggest that the rivalry between the two sides had degenerated into a personal feud and had nothing to do with justice or the law. That their persecution had driven Sito to insanity. But they didn't.

They were saving their questions for Celia.

Do you swear to tell the truth, the whole truth, and nothing but the truth, so help you God?"

She had to repeat her "I swear" because she'd spoken too softly the first time. Her hand was shaking on the Bible. She settled into the witness stand and when she finally looked up, she spotted Arthur Mentis sitting in the row directly behind DA Bronson. He nodded, smiled, and she felt better. He'd never let her get hurt. If things got really bad, he'd get her out of this somehow.

Defense Attorney Ronald Malone was slick and unyielding, like a steel wall. He wasn't that big, probably not much taller than Celia, but he had a way of trapping her gaze, and shifting to hold it again when she tried to look away, even standing at his table a half-dozen paces away.

His first questions were mundane, or seemed mundane, public knowledge that anyone in the courtroom could have learned. She still felt like she was giving away secrets. He was only warming her up for the hard questions.

Then came an odd one that made her think.

"Ms. West, when did you learn that your parents, Warren and Suzanne West, are the superhuman crime fighters Captain Olympus and Spark?"

"I don't know. I think I always knew. They never tried to hide it from me."

How could they? From the time she was born, they studied her for signs that she had inherited some kind of superhuman legacy. To think, most parents were happy with ten fingers and ten toes.

"Then their skills, their reputation, were a part of your life from a very early age?"

Bronson stood. "Objection! Supposition."

"Sustained," the judge said.

Celia blinked, relieved. She didn't want to answer any questions that resembled, *What was it like having Captain Olympus as a father?*

It didn't matter. He'd set her up nicely already.

"One might argue that like your parents, you're in a particularly unique position to judge the defendant's mental state at the time of his crimes."

"I'm not a psychologist—"

Malone raised his hand in a placating gesture. "I'll only ask you to make observations about Mr. Sito's behavior. You were the subject of one his more spectacular adventures, yes?"

That was an interesting way of putting it. "He kidnapped me when I was sixteen."

"And the purpose of this kidnapping?"

"What do you mean?" she asked.

"Did he hold you for ransom? Use you to get something?"

She shook her head. "No. He just wanted to . . . inflict damage."

"So there was no rational reason for him to kidnap you. His motivations could be said to reflect a disturbed mental state."

They weren't here to prove Sito guilty. No one was denying his crimes. Malone only had to prove that Sito had been out of his mind.

"He seemed calculating enough at the time," she said.

"Then let's turn to another event." He dropped the bomb, and knowing it was coming didn't make it easier. "Isn't it true that you were employed by Mr. Sito's organization eight years ago?" A polite way of saying, *Weren't you his criminal henchman?*

Muffled gasps filtered through the courtroom. People whispered to one another, reporters scribbled on notepads, and the courtroom artist worked frantically. She was vaguely aware of members of the jury leaning forward to better hear her answer.

"Yes," she said, meeting his gaze.

"You joined voluntarily?"

"Yes, at the time. I was—"

He cut her off before she could elaborate. "And you belonged to it for how long?"

"About two months."

"Once again, do you think it made any rational sense for Sito to take you into his organization, knowing the trouble it would likely cause him?"

She swallowed the lump in her throat. "I can't speak to that, sir. I wasn't exactly in my right mind myself."

"I'd like to submit that Mr. Sito's actions in regards to Ms. West speak toward an unstable state of mind, a personality more interested in chaos than in reason. His insanity compelled him to make unwise choices. If I may ask just a couple more questions."

Please, Celia thought. It couldn't get much worse.

"Do you regret that time you spent in Mr. Sito's employ?"

He would undermine her involvement in the case. Every piece of evidence she'd touched would be tainted now. It didn't matter what she said, how she answered. She could only be honest, because she had nothing to hide, right?

"Yes," she said. "I do."

"And how would you describe your feelings for Mr. Sito now?"

Burning, mind-numbing rage? "Dislike."

Smiling, Sito watched her, his cuffed hands clasped before him, fingers tapping together. *Don't look at him, look at Arthur.*

Arthur Mentis's expression was neutral. Nonjudgmental. She just had to hang in there.

"Not resentment? Or even outright hatred?"

"Objection! Leading the witness." Bronson, saving her again.

"Sustained."

"Ms. West, wouldn't you say your involvement with the prosecution's case is a clear conflict of interest? That your attitude toward Mr. Sito is personal, not professional?"

"Objection!"

"Sustained."

"Why are you assisting with this case?"

"It's part of my job. I'm a forensic accountant with the firm of

Smith and Kurchanski, which has a history of working with the DA's office."

"Did it ever occur to you to have yourself removed from the case because of a possible conflict of interest?"

"Yes. DA Bronson believed the conflict of interest didn't exist."

"Did he know about your prior involvement with Sito when he brought you in to work on this case?"

Her voice fell again. "Yes."

"No further questions, your honor."

Now that it was over, it didn't seem so bad. She breathed a sigh of relief. It could have been worse.

"Does the prosecution wish to cross-examine?"

"Yes, your honor. Ms. West? You underwent psychiatric evaluation immediately following the two months that Mr. Malone referred to, is this correct?"

"Yes."

"And what was the conclusion of the evaluation?"

She took a deep breath. She hoped those reporters were still paying attention. She and Bronson had crafted this answer. "That I had acted irrationally, that I suffered from a variety of traumatic stress disorders related to both the uncertainty of my parents' lifestyle and the kidnapping by the defendant that I suffered the year before."

"In fact, the conclusion was that you suffered temporary insanity and could not be held accountable for your actions."

"Yes."

"Could you tell me briefly what you've been doing in the eight years since then?"

"I went to college. I earned an MBA, passed the CPA exam on the first try, was hired on at Smith and Kurchanski, and I've been working there for two and a half years. I have an apartment in the west downtown area. I live quietly."

"Would you say that in that time, your actions have been influenced either by hatred of or identification with Mr. Sito or his organization?"

She hesitated. In an indirect sense, Sito had influenced her entire life. Her parents wouldn't have become who they were without Sito, and she wouldn't have become who she was without that.

But Mentis was right. The last eight years were her own. "No."

"Thank you, no further questions."

The judge turned to the defense. "Mr. Malone?"

"No further questions."

"Ms. West, you are dismissed."

"Thank you," she whispered.

She kept her chin up, her eyes up as she walked back to her seat. Bronson flashed her a smile. She felt exhausted.

"You look like you've run a marathon," Mentis said as she sat beside him.

"I need a drink," she said.

After another hour, the judge finally called a recess for lunch. Reporters mobbed Celia. She only heard a fraction of their questions.

"—how did your parents react when—feelings toward the Destructor—why a secret for so long—affect your job—affect the trial—"

She was afraid to say anything that would undermine what she'd already said under oath. Teenage rebellion wasn't normally considered a form of temporary insanity.

Arthur stepped in for her. "I've known Celia for ten years, and I can assure you I have the utmost confidence in her."

They escaped to Bronson's conference room.

"They're going to bring up that first day of the hearing, when he talked to me and no one could figure out why," she said. "They're going to think there's still a connection."

Helpfully, Bronson burst in then. "It's all irrelevant, I think we convinced the jury of that. You did great, Celia, just great. Hey, Rudy—" He went off to harass an assistant.

Mentis handed her a cup. Coffee, not bourbon, alas. She said, "I'm never going to get away from all this, am I? Even if my record never came out, it would always be something else. Why aren't I a better citizen, why don't I do more, why aren't I more like them?" He didn't respond; merely waited, calmly, for her to spill her thoughts. It was easy to do; he already knew what she was going to say, didn't he? "People tell me how great it must have been, growing up with Captain Olympus and Spark for parents." She shook her head.

"Overrated, you think?"

"Everyone is so amazed by them, so awestruck. To be able to move so fast you can fly, to create fire from your bare hands, to knock down walls, to have the power of gods . . . but I grew up with it. It wasn't special to me, it was just normal. It was Mom and Dad. I don't see what everyone else sees. I wish I could, sometimes." She looked at the ceiling, then scrubbed at her eyes to keep tears from starting. Stress. It was just stress.

"I'll tell you something," Arthur said. "Until a certain age, everyone thinks their parents are heroes. Then they grow up a little, start to understand a little more of the world, and they realize their parents are just people. It destroys them, just a little bit. But it's part of becoming an adult. Everyone goes through it. You, on the other hand—your parents really *are* heroes, at least to everyone else. It's a bit remarkable, really. You never went through that disappointment of finding out your parents are just people."

Except they were just people—she saw the side of them that no one else did, the bickering over supper and cooking pasta at the stove. She was the only one who understood that they were just people—that was where her frustration lay.

Arthur smiled his impenetrable smile.

Celia answered it with a wry grin of her own. "Are you psycho-analyzing me again?"

"Would I do such a thing?" He turned on his heel and left the room.

Mom arrived to check on her. Dad wasn't there. He'd already left. Celia didn't ask why. Mom would say "work," and then Celia would have to ask what kind of work—West Corp work or the other work—and she didn't really want to know. Suzanne offered her a ride home and Celia accepted because her mother had driven herself—her own car, not the limo, which was awfully conspicuous. She didn't want anyone noticing her right now.

Mark was waiting in the corridor that led to the courthouse's back door. He was leaning on the wall, arms crossed, shoulders hunched sullenly.

Something's happened, Celia thought.

Straightening, he moved to the middle of the corridor, blocking their path, and stared at her.

"Hi, Mark."

He didn't say anything. Just glared hard at her, like he could peel back skin and see what was underneath, or become a telepath through sheer willpower. Yeah, something had happened, all right. And it was all centered on her.

"What's wrong?" she said, unable to keep a neutral tone. Her muscles had clenched defensively.

"Why didn't you tell me?" His voice was tight, like he was holding back anger, keeping his temper in check. Like she was.

Suzanne remained a step behind Celia, watching.

"Tell you what?" she said, with willful ignorance.

"What you said in there. About you and the Destructor." Like he could barely say the words.

She stared at him. "What exactly was I supposed to say?"

"You should have told me."

"Why? I don't tell anyone. Before now I could count on my hands the number of people who knew about it. It was a long time ago." Mark was just standing there, seething. She couldn't tell what he was thinking. "You're angry," Celia said, trying to prompt a response.

"Of course I am! This is like finding out you're . . . you're—" Evidently, he couldn't think what it was like. "I mean, you're with the Destructor—"

"Was," Celia pointed out. "*Was* with him. Briefly."

"That isn't some petty shoplifting rap on a juvenile record. I—" He glanced at Suzanne and closed his mouth. "I'll call you later."

He shouldered past them, keeping space between himself and Celia as he did.

"Mark!" She called after him, mostly as a matter of form, even though she knew he wasn't going to turn around. He had principles and he liked to stand by them.

She sighed tiredly.

Her mother put a hand on her shoulder. "He'll come around," she said. "He's had a shock, that's all. He'll understand after he's cooled off."

"Are you sure you want him to come to dinner?"

Smiling wryly, Suzanne hooked her arm around Celia's and guided her out to the car.

The Commerce Eye came out with a special evening edition: "Daughter of the Olympiad Turned Against Her Family!" it read in huge, decadent lettering. In a flash, in a sentence, the last eight years disappeared. Nothing good she'd done in her adult life mattered. How depressing.

After her mother dropped her off at her apartment, it started raining. Sheets of rain beat against the kitchen window. Across the street, the sky was throwing a lovely pink and orange sunset against the windows. But outside her windows, and only her windows, rain.

She opened the window in the living room, popped the screen out of the frame, and leaned out.

"Do you want to come in and talk, or are you just going to keep flinging water at me?" she shouted at the roof.

A moment later, a figure rappelled down the wall. In seconds, Typhoon reached the window and slipped inside. Celia closed the window behind her.

She was in costume, dripping water on the carpet. The rain kept on outside, an echo of the dour mood Typhoon projected with her frown. She pulled off the mask, and it was Analise, glaring at her as if Celia had just kicked her dog.

"Is it true?"

Celia rolled her eyes. "If I were going to lie under oath, do you think it would be about *that*? Yes, it's true."

Analise's face puckered, and the bottom dropped from Celia's stomach. *My God—she's going to cry.*

Sure enough, her voice cracked. "How—how could you?"

Why could no one understand this? Couldn't anyone see the despair she'd felt at the time? The utter hopelessness, the utter failure she'd been at making anything of herself. That was it exactly, in a way Celia had never looked at before—she'd been trying to see just how bad it could really get, when she joined the Destructor.

When she didn't say anything, Analise continued. "How could you do it? Look at who your parents are: Captain Olympus and Spark! You had that legacy, a birthright that some of us would kill for, and you spat on it!"

"I didn't have a legacy," Celia said quietly. "Put yourself in my shoes, Analise. Your parents are the greatest superhumans Commerce City has ever known, but you . . . you can't even ride a bicycle straight. You can't win a swim meet. You can't fly, or read minds, or tell the future, or pyrokinetically manipulate pasta sauce. And your parents can't hide their disappointment. Tell me: What do you do then?"

Analise stared back at her, and Celia could tell she didn't understand, because her expression didn't change. Didn't soften. She didn't look away, or let the tears fall. Instead, her mouth hardened. She'd looked at the poolside kidnappers that way.

"That's no excuse. Not for siding with the Destructor."

"Maybe if I'd been able to create tidal waves and make rain fall, it would have been different. I don't know why I didn't inherit any of my parents' powers. I don't know why I turned out so . . . so—" Dull. Boring. Badly. "I was a stupid teenager. Please tell me you're not going to judge me based on that."

Crossing her arms, a wound-up bundle of nerves, Analise started pacing. Celia wondered if she should get her a towel, so she'd stop soaking the carpet.

Analise said, "What else can I do? I'm seeing you in a whole new light. You have that, that *evil* in you—"

"Oh please—"

"And you threw it in your parents' faces!"

"Can we leave them out of it?"

"You don't understand what they mean to the rest of us. Look, I'm sorry you don't have any powers. I can't explain it. Hell, I don't know why I can do what I can do. I have normal parents, and when I discovered my . . . my talent, I thought it was the end of the world. I thought I'd get locked away like some lunatic, or turn into a psycho vigilante like Barry Quinn. But there was something else—I wanted to make it something good. Your parents showed me how to do that. They let me think of this, not as something that happened to me, but as something I could use. As a gift. Without them, I don't know where I'd be."

"Well, you see where I am with them."

"You can't blame your past on them, Celia."

"Aren't I the one who said to leave them out of it? How many times do I have to say it: I've spent the last eight years trying to make up for one mistake, and the only message I'm getting is, that isn't possible. Yesterday I was a respectable upstanding citizen, and today, suddenly, I'm dirt. Mark won't talk to me, the papers brand me a criminal—what the hell happened?"

Analise pursed her lips, looking thoughtful. For a moment Celia thought she was getting through to her, that she wouldn't lose both her and Mark. Then she said, "How do I know you won't do something like that again? You don't get along with your parents any better now than you did then . . . so how do I not you're not still like that? That you're not still working with the Destructor? That you didn't get put on this case on purpose, that—"

"Analise," Celia said as calmly as she could. "That's crazy."

"Is it?"

Celia realized that nothing she said would help, because no one trusted her. Even Analise, her best friend, suddenly assumed that every word was a lie.

"Yes, it is," Celia said, for as much good as it would do.

At first Analise hesitated, like she was about to decide that she trusted Celia after all. Then she moved back to the window.

"I need to go think. I'm sorry." She put her mask on and gripped the dangling rope.

"Analise, don't you dare run away from me!"

But she was already gone, climbing up the rope, her specially designed gloves gripping despite the wet. A few minutes later, the clouds broke, and the last rays of sunset shone in.

SIXTEEN

THE Trial of the Century, the newspapers called it. Like the Storm of the Century. They seemed to happen every ten or twenty years. The last Trial of the Century had been when she was a little girl, involving a husband-and-wife bank robber team that specialized in hacking ATM machines. They were noteworthy because they would make out in front of the security cameras. The Kissing Crooks. Bank robbery soft core porn. Celia hadn't been allowed to watch the trial coverage.

The next day, the front page of the city's so-called respectable newspaper, the *Commerce City Banner*, featured her picture, snapped by an intrepid photographer as she left the courtroom. A close-up, framed by bodies in dark suits, mostly people from the DA's office who all left in a crowd; she was the only one with features visible: brick-red hair, short and tousled, eyes squinting a little in the light, looking ahead, lips pulled in a frown. Her mother should have been nearby, but she'd been cropped out of the image. Artistic license or something.

Her story rated a sidebar, so maybe she hadn't quite graduated from the position of footnote to the Trial of the Century. She wouldn't mind staying a footnote. "West Heiress's Dark Past," read the headline, with a sub-header, "Who is Celia West?" Lots of unanswered questions peppered that article, since the records were sealed and she wasn't commenting. Some people, including Bronson, had given quotes vowing that they trusted her, for which she was grateful.

But other quotes—from politicians, gossip columnists, college professors whom she barely remembered—observed how reclusive she was, that she was estranged from her parents, that she hadn't done anything to follow in their footsteps, and what was she hiding, anyway? Those interviews sounded so much more exciting.

A half-dozen reporters were waiting in the lobby of the building where Smith and Kurchanski had its offices. Celia tightened her grip on her attaché and quickened her pace, as if preparing to run a literal gauntlet. Like a pack of jackals, they spotted her and moved across the granite floor to intercept, striding from different directions to trap her. *And so, separated from the herd, the gazelle stumbles . . .*

She would have gotten away if she hadn't had to stop for the elevator.

The reporters swarmed around her.

"Ms. West! Could I ask you a couple of questions?"

"I really don't have time—"

"Are you working on the Sito trial out of revenge?

The elevator mechanism groaned softly.

"Did you have any contact with the Destructor after those two months you were with him?"

"What *exactly* was the nature of your relationship with the Destructor?"

Oh, she'd been waiting for that one. The stories people must be making up about *that*. Ignore them, just ignore them.

"How long did it take for your parents to forgive you?"

They haven't, she thought.

They kept asking because they knew, eventually, she'd break. It was easy to ignore the difficult, personal, prurient, questions. The one with the easy answer startled her into answering.

A woman with a blond bob and rimless glasses caught her gaze and asked, "What did you do for the Destructor? Malone said you joined him. But what did you do for him?"

Celia smiled bitterly. "Nothing. I didn't do anything. I was seventeen, I was stupid, I ran away from home, and he took me in and kept me around because it drove my parents crazy."

Finally, the elevator door opened. She stepped inside and spread her arms across the door, blocking any of them from following her. She wasn't big or intimidating; they might have just pushed past her. But she glared. "If you could please leave me alone, I'm late for work."

They blinked, startled for a moment, and hesitated, which gave the doors time to close on them. As the elevator rose, Celia leaned against the wall and sighed.

Mary, the receptionist, caught her as she entered the offices. "Celia? Kurchanski Senior wanted to see you as soon as you came in."

"Okay." Did Mary's smile seem a little stiff? Was her expression fearful?

She went to Kurchanski's office before taking off her coat or setting down her bag. The door was ajar; she knocked on the frame and carefully pushed it open enough to stick her head in.

"Mr. Kurchanski? It's Celia. Mary said you wanted to see me."

"Ms. West, yes, come in." He was leaning back in his leather desk chair, reading an accounting trade magazine. He set the magazine aside and rested his hands on the desk. "The Sito trial's been very interesting, hasn't it?"

That sinking feeling was the other shoe dropping, right down the middle of her gut.

"Yes, sir. It is."

"You testified yesterday. I read a transcript."

She gritted her teeth and waited.

"The District Attorney may not have a problem with you being so personally involved. But I have the firm to think about, and its reputation. This isn't easy to say, but I'd like you to take some time off. You're a hard worker and I have a great deal of respect for you. But we've already had too many questions."

Questions like, aren't you worried, can she be trusted, how could she possibly be a good person with that on her record. It was fine, being the daughter of vigilante heroes. But any association with a notorious criminal mastermind? Forget it. A black mark like that never went away.

He continued. "It would be better for all of us. Until this blows over."

If she could stay numb, she'd be fine. She always stayed numb until she could walk away and explode in peace. "Sure. I understand. Mr. Kurchanski?"

"Yes?"

"Am I being fired, or just . . . laid off?"

"You're taking a leave of absence. Until this blows over."

And if it didn't? Would she get a call asking her not to come back, ever? "Until this blows over. If it blows over."

"I'm sorry."

"Don't be. Thanks for telling me in person."

She was glad she didn't have to get her coat and bag. All she had to do was turn around and walk right back out. She ignored her coworkers staring after her. Or, tried to.

What the hell, she needed a vacation anyway.

She swam sixty laps. Counted every one. Each number made a rhythm in her brain, beating in time to her strokes through the water. As long as she counted, she didn't think about anything else.

In college, she'd gone back to swimming, her one successful childhood sport, because the water was soft and uplifting. Caressing. Made her feel like another creature, other than flesh. Today, she wanted to be tired. She wanted to be able to sleep without thinking.

She could hit the water as much as she wanted without consequence.

You've reached the offices of District Attorney Kevin Bronson. Please leave a message."

"Hi, DA Bronson? It's Celia West. I've just been laid off my job. Or given a leave of absence. Whatever. That probably means I'm pulled from the case. I thought you should know."

She called Mark next. He told her he'd call, but he hadn't yet, which was why she thought he'd be sure to pick up. But the ringing rolled over to voice mail.

"Mark, I don't know if you're ready to talk to me. I don't know if there's anything I can say. But I wanted to let you know I've been laid off my job over this. I could use a friend right now. Bye." Now, was he busy or avoiding her? She might never learn.

She spent all afternoon watching TV, dressed in flannel pajamas, eating ice cream out of the carton. She had a bubble bath scheduled for five o'clock, and then planned to order Chinese delivery at seven.

She watched the news to hear what they said about her. Conspiracy theorists had put out the notion that she was still working for Sito, that she was trying to sabotage the prosecution's case from the inside. She found that one on the conservative talk show that aired after lunch. She supposed a lot of people were thinking that. Otherwise, she'd still be at work, and Mark and Analise would still be talking to her. Her father would let her look at the West Corp archives.

If she were lucky, maybe another bomb would drop at the trial and people would forget about her.

After the bath, during the evening news, the phone rang. The tone sent her heart racing, and she jumped a foot from her seat and floundered for the phone. "Yes?"

"It's me." Mark. If she could get him to feel guilty for dissing her maybe he'd bring her supper.

"Hey, hi. How are you? I mean, I'm glad you called. Thanks."

He was silent. For a moment, she thought the connection had cut out. All she heard was a faint hiss. Then, he drew a breath. "How are you doing?"

Besides losing my job, and my best friend yelling at me, and my boyfriend not talking to me? "Bad. What do you expect?"

"With that kind of skeleton in your closet, you shouldn't be surprised."

Of course not. That was why the records had been sealed and she'd kept it secret. "Mark, I really wish you wouldn't judge me based on something that happened when I was a kid."

"What else am I supposed to do? It's . . . weird, it's not right. The Destructor is evil, and you *wanted* that . . . Are you telling me you're a totally different person now?"

She kept her breathing calm so that she could speak clearly, nicely, without shouting. "Actually, I'm a lot different. I've worked hard to make myself different. I wasn't a happy person then."

"Just answer one question for me. The Destructor. Were you his . . ." He paused, grappling for words. "Did you sleep with him?"

The assumption lay between the lines of every news report she'd seen today. It was the question that no matter how much she denied it, no one would ever believe her. Her father hadn't believed her, not even after she let Mentis into her mind, let him see whether or not she was lying. She'd let him broadcast her thoughts to the world if it would do any good.

"No, I didn't. He wasn't interested."

"Wasn't interested? Does that mean you *tried*?"

She'd been seventeen, fond of miniskirts and too much makeup, fascinated by her own burgeoning sexuality and the ways it could be used. How did she explain that to a thirty-year-old police detective who'd already branded her a criminal?

He was angry at himself, she realized. Angry at himself for falling for someone with a past like hers. He hadn't seen it, and maybe he thought he should have.

"Mark, I've been trying for years to redeem myself. I guess I'm not there yet. But give me a chance, please." She shouldn't have to beg. Damn him for making her beg.

"It's just . . . it's hard, looking at you now. Knowing what you did."

She lost it. "I made a mistake! I *know* I made a mistake! Everybody makes mistakes! What do I have to do to make it up? Adopt a kitten? Crucify myself on my parents' doorstep? What? Just tell me and I'll do it. Tell me what you want me to do!"

"This really is all about your parents, isn't it? You really do hate them."

"Have you even been *listening* to me? Why can't anyone talk to me without talking about *them*?" She kept getting louder.

Which might have been why he hung up on her.

She threw the phone. It hit the wall by the kitchen, chirped, and thumped to the floor.

If she could, she would go back in time and warn her seventeen-year-old self:

A mistake like this, you'll never get away from it. It will mark you, brand you. A petty crime is one thing, but joining the Destructor? You? Don't you know what this is going to do to your future?

The trouble was, the seventeen-year-old always replied, *What makes you think I have a future?*

She couldn't remember what that had been like, wanting to seek out Sito, wanting to join him. Rather, she didn't want to. She'd been a different person eight years ago. But the memories were still there.

She'd only put one foot inside the entrance of the eastside bar when a man with greasy hair and a scuffed leather coat put his arm in front of her, stopping her.

"Hey, baby, I'll take you home. I got the cash."

"I'm not a hooker," Celia stated, frowning. He could possibly be forgiven for making the mistake. She didn't even know if it was a mistake. She wasn't for sale to him, and that was what mattered. She wore a short-short leather miniskirt, black stockings, high-heeled sandals, and a lace camisole. Clothing bought in secret and hidden at the bottom of her dresser drawer. Someday, she'd always told herself, she'd put on the outfit, walk out of the penthouse, turn into someone no one would recognize, and never look back.

She hunched inside her bomber jacket, glaring up with narrowed eyes. Something about her manner made the guy back off, even though she was half his size. If he'd wanted to press the point, there wasn't much she could do.

It was all about attitude.

The smell overwhelmed her. Sour beer, sweat, the press of bodies. The place was popular. Tough-looking guys crowded around a pair of pool tables. No music played, only the rumble of voices talking low, punctuated by a few barks of laughter and a few calls for the waitress. This was a place to do business. That was why the guy had stopped her. There were other women around, dressed a lot like her. More vinyl, maybe, and more hairspray. Older women, worn around the edges.

She'd had to do research to find this place, looking through newspaper articles and public record arrest and investigation reports. She'd told the guys at the police station she was doing a report for school on law enforcement, and since she was Celia West, they ruffled her hair and said how proud her folks must be that she was following in their footsteps.

It was all worth it, because she found out that one of the Destructor's informants set up shop at this bar. He was one of the guys who recruited for jobs, served as eyes and ears on the street. He might have been one of the guys who helped lure her to the park and the Destructor's clutches last year. Whatever. Didn't matter. He'd know how to get in touch with the Destructor.

Again, attitude got her through the bar to the back room. Gazes followed her, sizing her up, judging her, but no one stopped her. She walked with a purpose, and they could see that. They were supposed to assume she belonged there.

The back room held four booths. In one, a couple of bored-looking women—innocuously dressed in jeans and blouses, compared to some of the other outfits in the bar—sat quietly, tracing their fingers through the moisture on filled tumblers. Small groups of two or three people sat at the others, bodies hunched over tables. The volume of voices was lower here, the talk more urgent.

In the farthest table to the right, a blond man, middle-aged, with a weathered face and slicked-back hair, seemed to be lecturing a couple of younger men who sat across from him. He pointed his finger at them, raised his brow, and the men shrank back. Middle-management of the crime world dressing down hired muscle.

Keeping to the wall, Celia made her way to that side of the room. She stared at him until he looked up, and she caught his gaze. Polite at heart, she stood across from his booth, just out of earshot, and waited for him to finish his business.

He waved the two heavies away. They looked her up and down as they passed by, but she ignored them.

She moved to the booth, but didn't sit down. She wanted to be taller than him; she would have been lost sitting in the big vinyl seat. Her hip touched the table as she turned to him.

"Are you Ares?"

He smiled a wide, fake, cattish smile. "What can I do for you, honey?"

"I want to see the Destructor," she said.

His smile froze, like he hadn't heard her or didn't believe her. "What makes you think I can help you do that?"

"You hire his goons. I need to talk to him. You can pass on the message."

Finally, the smile fell. He put his elbows on the table. "I don't know what you think you're doing. I don't know what your story is, but you don't want to mess with that. You look like a sweet kid, so why don't you just go home?"

"Tell the Destructor his favorite hostage wants to see him." Her face felt numb, impassive. No expression.

Ares straightened. Celia felt a little surge of pride, because he obviously didn't know what to do with her. She'd said the right thing. She could handle herself. Let them underestimate her, and she'd walk all over them.

"I'll pass on the message," he said finally. "Have a seat. I'll send over a soda for you."

"I'll have a scotch," she said.

"I don't think so." Grinning, he stood up, smoothed his cream-colored jacket, and went through a door at the side of the room.

Sitting in the booth, she closed her eyes and took a deep breath. She could do this. She had to do this.

An hour later, Celia was still there, a glass of soda in front of her, untouched, the ice melting. Ares came through the same side door. She spotted him as soon as it opened.

He put a hand on the table in front of her. "There's a car waiting for you around back. It'll take you to him."

Without a word, she brushed past him and left. She felt his gaze staring after her and had to smile a little. Let him wonder who she was.

The car was a chauffeured Cadillac. The formally dressed driver held the door open for her, closed it behind her, then climbed behind the wheel and pulled out of the alley into the nighttime streets. She settled back against the leather seat. The back windows were tinted to the point of being opaque, preventing her from marking their route.

Too late to back out now. That was okay. This was going to go fine.

Eventually, the car tilted, slanting forward as it traveled down a ramp. They seemed to continue downward for a very long time. For all their efforts, the Olympiad hadn't found the Destructor's most recent headquarters. She could go back and tell them: underground. Far underground.

She could never go back.

After parking, the driver let her out into a dimly lit garage-type structure and escorted her through a door. Again, only a few dim lights showed the way. The Destructor either wanted to create as creepy an effect as possible, or save on electricity bills.

He probably pirated his power off the grid anyway.

The corridor ended in a wide doorway. The driver gestured her through, staying behind.

Ahead, an old man sat at a vast mahogany table. It was the only furniture or decoration in a slate-colored room. His hair was thinned to nothing, and he peered through a pair of wire-rimmed glasses. A half-dozen computer monitors sat on the desk at regular intervals. He spent a little time at each of them, in no particular order: he looked at one, tapped a few keys on the single keyboard in front of him, looked at another, typed again.

Studious, a scientist, he was planning his next act of mass chaos.

Her stomach lurched; she swallowed back a surge of nausea. This man had tried to rip her mind apart a year ago. This man cared nothing for her. This man was a monster.

The enemy of her enemy was her friend. If she had a place in the world, this was it. She shrugged her jacket partway off, exposing her shoulders.

"Hi," she said.

Not looking up, the Destructor said, "It's the famous Celia West. What do you want?"

She'd practiced this in her mind a hundred times. The way she'd walk, the look in her eyes, calm and cool. She was powerful, in her own way. Step by step, she moved toward him, her heels clicking slowly on the tile floor.

When she got to his table, she half-sat on it, her skirt riding up one thigh. One of the monitors was in the way. She swiveled it aside, so he could see. He looked up.

"I can tell you about the Olympiad. Their headquarters, their computer systems, procedures. Just about anything you want to know."

"And what do you want?"

"A place here. I want to be a part of this."

For a long minute, they regarded one another. If she kept her mind a blank, she wouldn't look away.

He said, "You're only here to aggravate your parents. While I commend the endeavor, I have no use for you."

It occurred to her that if she had a knife right now, she could slit his throat. Wouldn't her parents be shocked and impressed? Except they didn't kill. Eschewed killing as a crime.

She just couldn't win.

He added, "The Olympiad has its headquarters in the penthouse of West Plaza. I know the secret identities of every member of the Olympiad—as you know. I'm naturally immune to Mentis's telepathy. Everything you think you know, I already know."

The worst that could happen, he'd just kill her. Lock her up, torture her, finish her off. And the thing was, she didn't care. At least she could say she tried. If this didn't work, she just didn't care. She had nothing left.

She couldn't let him see that. She only showed him blank. Like Arthur would do.

His lips pressed into a tight, unfeeling smile. "On the other hand, keeping you around might prove amusing."

Set the hook, reel him in. As if she were actually having an impact on him. She'd imagined herself doing this, thinking it would give her some power over him. Imagined how she might possibly win some power for herself in this world, where men flew and women played with fire.

She stalked around the table. It was a long walk, it seemed like. She'd always pictured him in a huge leather executive chair, the kind that dominated a room, massive and luxurious. Like the kind her father had. Instead, he had a simple office chair, flat and dark, with a low back. It didn't even have wheels. He perched at the edge of it, watching her progress.

When she reached his chair, she put her left hand on his desk, her right on the chair back, just behind his thin, dark-suited shoulder. Not touching it. Leaning forward, keeping her eyes open and looking, she kissed him on the lips. It was just a press; he didn't respond. His lips were dry, frozen. She pulled back, waiting for a response.

"Don't do that again," he said. He pointed to a door behind her. So much for her vast powers of seduction.

In the days that followed, she spent a lot of time sitting on tables at the periphery while he plotted, planned, schemed, whatever. She didn't pay much attention. He ignored her. Kept her around because it might be amusing. She fetched coffee sometimes. At his command, all his henchmen ignored her as well. She might have had a *little* fun, otherwise. They all treated her like a kid.

His latest plan—bombs set to destroy government buildings all over the city—was nearing fruition. She could stop this, she occasionally considered. Sabotage the mechanism or call her parents. Redeem herself.

She kind of wanted to see how they stopped it on their own. It would be interesting, watching from the other side.

She perched in the window of the skyscraper where he worked that day, looking down on the canyons of a tiny cardboard city. Cars crawled, people were only specks of dirt shifting around. Everything looked flat.

"I read what the papers say about me. Do you?" The Destructor spoke to her for the first time in weeks. He stood beside her, gazing out the window with her, amusement brightening his features.

"Lots of speculation about why I do what I do. Am I mad? Disturbed? Was I abused as a child? Why am I so bent on destruction? There is so much they don't consider, you know. They don't consider how much worse I could be."

She quirked a smile.

"You've been watching me. I think you've been taking notes. If you wanted to be worse than me, what would you do? What could be worse than mass destruction?"

Mass destruction sounded pretty good to her. It was partly why she was here. She'd never been able to create or save. Maybe she could destroy. Except she didn't seem to be very good at that, either.

"The pundits are wrong about me," he said. "I'm essentially lazy. Mass destruction is for the lazy. It's not difficult. Anyone can crash an airplane. But using an airplane to destroy a cultural icon? That creates despair. That's where the real power lies. In symbols. Money is easy to steal. But a rare gem? A unique painting? These things are truly worthwhile. People will die for them when they will not die for money. So tell me, what can be worse than mass destruction?"

She said, "Specific loss. You choose your target."

He smiled, and she felt as if she'd been rewarded. "How much worse for your parents, to turn you into their next great adversary. Better I had destroyed you last year. How does that sound?"

"Like you're planning to use me to get your own revenge. Again."

"Maybe when the time comes I'll let you push the button," he said.

SEVENTEEN

SHE never got around to ordering dinner. Too much ice cream made her lose her appetite. She didn't even pull herself off the sofa to go to bed. It was much easier to flip channels until she found a decade-old action movie playing on cable. It looked more dated than it should have, and the good bits of dialogue had been edited out. When that movie ended, another one started, and she stared at the TV until she fell asleep.

Halfway through the next morning, her doorbell rang. She flinched to wakefulness and looked at the clock: ten. Sunshine filled the living room. She wanted it to be night again, to get the day over with.

If she stayed quiet, whoever it was would go away. Some kid selling magazine subscriptions or a charity looking for donations. She didn't want to deal with it.

Then the thought burst upon her like a migraine.

—*Celia, it's me. Open the door.*—

Arthur Mentis. Couldn't hide from him.

She looked at her unshowered self, ratty pajamas and all, wondered if she ought to tell him she needed to change clothes. On the other hand, he could read her mind; what did it matter what she was wearing? Running her fingers through her unkempt hair, she reached the door, opened it, and moved aside to let him in. He studied her, his brow raised, and remained standing in the doorway, hands shoved in the pockets of his trench coat.

"If you don't want me here, I can leave," he said.

She sighed. "If you were anyone else I'd never have opened the door in the first place. Come in."

He did, and she closed the door after him. He said, "You weren't at the courthouse yesterday. I tried calling you to check on you, but there wasn't an answer."

"Worried I was getting in trouble?"

"Just worried," he said.

"I had my phone, I would have gotten your call— Wait." The cell phone was still lying on the floor. She retrieved it, checked the display, hit a couple buttons. "I think it's broken. I threw it."

"Did it make you feel better?"

"Not really."

"I see you're not at work."

"I thought everyone would have heard by now. I've been fired. Well, not fired. But almost."

"I see. That's hardly fair."

"That's what I thought. And Mark isn't speaking to me. That's why I threw the phone."

"So when I ask, 'How are you?' the answer is, 'Not good.'"

"I'm fine." She said this through gritted teeth.

"Right. Is there anything I can do?"

She could scream and throw him out. But he was only trying to be nice. It was hard having him around when she didn't want to talk about it. With him, she didn't *have* to talk about it. He just *knew*, and while that was often convenient when she was trying to explain things to her parents, she didn't need that now.

"I'll be okay. I'll let you know if I need anything."

He started to turn, then hesitated. "What's your plan B?"

"Plan B?"

"I don't expect you to stay at home moping."

"What do you expect me to do? My career is ruined. No one

will hire me to pick up trash after this. My friends aren't speaking to me. Maybe I can find a nice dry hole to bury myself in." She rubbed her face, which was warm and flushed. "If I haven't made up for what I did by now, what hope is there? Maybe I should just go be a criminal mastermind myself. Prove everyone right."

"I know you don't mean that." And he did, because he could see it in her mind.

She probably wouldn't make a very good criminal mastermind, either.

"Plan B, huh? What do you recommend?"

He shrugged. "Maybe stop trying to prove to everyone you've reformed, and just do what you think is right."

"The old 'ignore them' ploy? How often does that work?"

"Just because everyone else is looking backward doesn't mean you have to. Call me if you need anything." He closed the door behind him on his way out.

Do what's right, she thought. Maybe that was part of the problem—she was having trouble locating right, at the moment. Her gut was tied up in too many knots right now for her to listen to it.

If she had to work this hard to prove that she had worth, that she wasn't a bad person, maybe that said something about her. If she really were good, she wouldn't have to work so hard. In the end, she hadn't left the Destructor's clutches of her own free will. The only reason she hadn't stayed with him was because he'd abandoned her. Not because, deep down, she was good.

She'd been seventeen and out of her mind. Dr. Mentis said so.

She was still out of her mind.

At any rate, if she wanted more ice cream, she was going to have to leave the apartment.

She considered it a supreme act of will that she managed to put on real clothes and walk herself to the convenience store down the street to pick up ice cream and frozen burritos. Protein—she'd need her strength if she was going to keep eating all that ice cream. In her scruffy state—unbrushed hair, jeans, and a rumpled sweatshirt—she didn't at all resemble the photos from the courtroom that some of the newspapers still had splashed on their front pages, so no one recognized her to give her any trouble.

The headline on *The Commerce Eye* drew her attention. That was what it was designed to do, bordered in red and filling the entire page. It didn't matter how outrageous it was; if it screamed loud enough everyone would have to listen.

"Is the Destructor Controlling Crime Spree from Prison? Mayor Vows to Beef Up Police!"

The recent robberies cum kidnappings—even the Baxter Gang episode, which had the same MO—had all been planned by the same person. It didn't follow that person had to be Simon Sito. But he'd been responsible for most of the crime sprees of the last twenty years. People had trouble pointing the finger in a different direction.

She couldn't get away from the belief that Sito wasn't responsible. If the press and general rumor kept talking about Sito, they deflected attention from who was really doing this.

It occurred to her that just because she didn't have her job didn't mean she couldn't work.

She had real food for lunch and saved the ice cream for later. Microwaved burrito in hand, she fired up her computer.

She approached the problem as if it had been presented to her as part of her job. How do you hide unique, expensive assets? If she were studying the books of someone selling such assets illegally, what would she look for? High-dollar money transfers without claiming assets or deducting depreciation. Someone spending money with nothing overt and legal to show for it.

The Destructor wasn't spending anything; the DA had had all his assets frozen. All the ones they could find, at least. If Sito were smart—and he was, no question there—he wouldn't touch his hidden assets just yet; he wouldn't risk revealing their location. But if he did, would he be buying up unique and priceless cultural artifacts? Or paying someone to do steal them?

It wasn't his MO. He was the Destructor for a reason. He liked blowing things up, taking them apart, and disintegrating them, not collecting them.

Cultural artifacts. That was the pattern. She got online to search the city's events calendar. What else out there would interest a thief who'd already taken rare violins and prize koi?

There it was: The Commerce City History Museum was hosting a philately exhibition: rare stamps, one-of-a-kind printings, unique and priceless to the right collector. The exhibit opened Saturday.

She had to leave the apartment again to replace her cell phone—then hesitated, because she didn't know who to call first. Her parents, came the first impulse. The Olympiad would want to know. They'd be able to stop the theft. They'd even be likely to listen to her. The cops, not so much. Even so, she ought to call them as well. Mark, maybe. The chance of Mark listening to her was microscopic right now. Same with Analise.

Hell, maybe she should call everybody. Then maybe at least one of them would believe her and do something about it.

She called Suzanne's cell. The voice mail picked up.

"Hi, Mom, it's me. This is going to sound weird, but I think I know what the Strad Brothers' next target is. There's a special philately exhibit at the history museum opening Saturday. Rare stamps—it fits their target profile. I suppose we have to assume they'll attempt a kidnapping to go along with any robbery. Anyway, call me so we can talk about it."

Mark and Analise weren't answering their phones, either. With them, however, Celia's paranoia kicked in. Either they were busy, or they saw her name on the caller ID and decided to ignore her. She left messages.

Somebody had to call her back.

She had to make one more call. She looked up the number to police headquarters. "Yes, I'd like to speak to Chief Appleton," she told the receptionist, who asked who was calling.

Celia took a deep breath. "Celia West. And yes, it's important."

She spent time on hold. They didn't even bother putting on bad music for her. Eventually, her name got her through to the chief.

Appleton didn't bother with a greeting. "If you're calling to yell at me about making your record public, I had nothing to do with it. I haven't shown it to anyone. That information got out all on its own, just like I always said it would."

"Hello to you, too," she said. "That's not what I'm calling about."

"I only sealed the record in the first place as a favor to your parents."

"That's not what I'm calling about."

"People deserve to know about you, you know." It was as if he'd been keeping this secret for eight years, and he was damned well going to take advantage of the fact that he could now rant about her as much as he wanted.

"Chief, I think I know what the Strad Brothers' next target is."

The following pause was nerve-shattering. Finally, he said, "And how, may I ask, do you know this?"

"I don't *know* it. It's a guess. They've gone after unique cultural objects, right? The history museum is hosting an exhibit of rare stamps. It seems like this would be just the kind of target they'd go for."

"You don't know this because you're still in the Destructor's pocket?"

God*damn* him, Celia thought. "Sir, I don't think Sito has anything to do with the Strad Brothers. The MOs are completely different, Sito can't organize anything from the asylum—"

"If anyone could organize anything from the asylum, it would be Sito."

Calling him had been a mistake. "I'm sorry to bother you, Chief. But I have this hunch, and in good conscience I had to tell someone about it. I thought you might listen to me."

She hung up on him, because she wasn't brave enough to hear what kind of response he'd give to that.

Suzanne listened to her. The Olympiad had always had the attitude that vigilance never hurt. It wouldn't cost them anything to be on alert. It wasn't too far from their usual routine, after all.

Spark did insist that Celia spend the weekend at the West Plaza penthouse, to secure her against another kidnapping attempt.

Celia couldn't argue. It was only a matter of time before one of these debacles got her hurt. But she could bargain. "I'll stay there if Dad lets me into the West Corp archives."

Her mother hissed out a breath that clearly said, *Now isn't the time for this argument.* All the more reason to have it.

"Celia, this is too serious for you to be playing games like this."

"I've never played games."

"Then here, ask him yourself." The phone rustled as Suzanne handed it over.

Warren's gruff voice came on. "What's going on?"

Suzanne hadn't had a chance to tell him anything, so Celia had to explain it all.

"I've got a guess at the Strad Brothers' next target. Since they'll probably try a kidnapping along with it, Mom wants me to stay at the penthouse. I said I would if you let me into the West Corp archives. So how about it?"

"I don't make deals, Celia—"

"Well, it was worth a try. I'll see you later—"

"Don't hang up!"

She didn't.

He said, tiredly, "Can you just tell me why you want to see those files? Please?"

Enough of a pause preceded the *please* that Celia wondered if Suzanne had prompted him.

It didn't matter. The *please* was enough. "I found evidence that suggests Simon Sito worked for West Corp about fifty years ago. I need to confirm that."

"Simon Sito worked for my father?"

"It was a long time ago. He wasn't crazy then. He wasn't the Destructor."

"If it's true . . . what does it mean?"

She shrugged. "I hope I'll find out when I see those records."

He didn't answer right away. She could hear him breathing, not talking. She could picture him and her mother looking at each other, having one of those silent conversations that longtime couples shared. She probably wouldn't have been able to interpret their looks even if she'd been there, watching them.

Finally, Warren said, "I'll make sure there's a key card for you in the lobby."

That was easier than she thought it would be. She hadn't wanted to bring up Sito. She hadn't known how her father would react. She hadn't expected him to hold his temper. "Thank you."

EIGHTEEN

A S she entered the lobby of West Plaza, she called up to the penthouse. No one answered. The Olympiad was already gone.

Damon Parks smiled a greeting and held up a plastic card to her. "Your father left this for you."

Damn. She'd half-expected him to back out of his part of the agreement.

"You coming to work for him now?" he said.

"Who knows? He might be the only person in town who'll hire me."

"I doubt that. This mess of a trial will blow over soon enough. Especially if this sort of thing keeps up." He held up the front page of the *Eye*, the issue that screamed that the Destructor was controlling the crime spree from prison. Parks clicked his tongue. "Good old Destructor, at it again."

She frowned. "I don't think it's the Destructor. He's in prison, out of commission. Someone else is behind this."

"If the Destructor isn't the mastermind, who is?" He watched her closely, like he was asking a test question and not making small talk.

"If I knew, I'd call the cops." Anonymously, this time. "There's got to be some connection between all these guys—the Baxter

Gang, the Strad Brothers, the guys from the pool. Someone just has to figure out what the link is."

"And that link'll be the mastermind?"

"Or it'll lead us to the mastermind. I don't know, maybe it's just wishful thinking, that the Destructor really is finished."

Parks folded the paper away and smiled. Celia moved on to the elevators.

The records department—a climate-controlled, brightly lit cavern of a room with row after row of steel shelves, located in the skyscraper's basement—was in the process of scanning all the records into digital format. The job was set to take years, because as Warren had said, the company never threw anything away. Only a dozen or so sets of shelves were empty. At a computer workstation, banker's boxes sat on open tables near scanners and high-powered shredders. All was quiet now, but the equipment probably made a hell of a racket during the workweek.

They hadn't yet gotten to the year she was looking for. She wouldn't be able to use a nifty computerized search engine to help her find the file on the Leyden building. The old-fashioned way it was, then. Even with the high-tech air filtration system in a modern facility, the place still smelled like archival storage: old paper, stale manila folders, cardboard, and dust. Libraries and accountants' basements all over the world smelled like this. It was the scent of information waiting to be discovered.

She wondered, if the West Corp people transferring all this paper to the computer had come across the Leyden file, would they have noticed if it mentioned a connection to Sito? Would it have tripped the recognition in their minds that it had in hers? If so, would they have said anything?

She was meant to be here, digging up this data. No one else knew the connections. No one else could find it.

It took her three hours of looking in banker's boxes, scanning the neatly typed labels on hundreds of legal-size manila folders. Real estate deals, stock acquisitions, mergers, sales—every deal possible to make in business was represented. Jacob West had had his fingers in a lot of pies. Oil, telecommunications, entertainment, government contracts. He'd started out importing diamonds, but quickly diversified. Economic downturns had never affected him.

Finally, she found a surprisingly thin folder labeled Leyden Industrial Park.

She filled out the appropriate form needed to take information out of the archives and slipped a card into the folder's place in the box. If she followed procedure, her father wouldn't have any reason to reprimand her. Really, though, she wasn't a West Corp employee. She wasn't entitled to remove files from storage.

She really might break down and ask her father for a job, if no one else hired her.

Feeling a bit like Pandora, she sat at an austere desk in the archives room and opened the folder.

A cover memo addressed to Jacob West outlined experiments in bioengineering. Celia couldn't find a more detailed description than that. These were accounting records, not lab reports. The file included a list of assets, which she hoped might give her some clue as to what the experiments involved. Most of the entries were for machines with complicated names that Celia couldn't guess the purposes of. The ones she recognized—oscillators and autoclaves— were generic, used for all sorts of purposes in every kind of lab. They could be found in dentists' offices.

She set aside that list and turned to the payroll data. Here, she made some progress. West Corp not only owned the building, it had signed the paychecks for the dozen or so people who worked there during that time. She looked for one particular name first, and found it: Dr. Simon Sito was on the West Corp payroll. She was going to have to show this to her father.

The name right above Sito's was Anna Riley. Her position was listed as stenographer. Suzanne's mother's name was Anna Riley. It might have been a different Anna Riley, except her age at the time, twenty-five, was about right.

Celia called her mother's cell. Suzanne didn't answer, which didn't surprise Celia, but she left a message so she wouldn't forget to ask the question later. "Hi, Mom. I have a weird question for you. What did Grandma Riley do for a living? Thanks."

The prickling on the back of her neck grew even stronger when she came across the last name Baker. Analise's last name was Baker. George Baker was listed as a lab technician. But Baker was a common last name, surely no relation.

Celia didn't know if Analise was talking to her or not, so she didn't call.

The last entry in the expenses portion of the trial balance was for a benefits payoff to employees. This cleaned out the account for the Leyden Industrial Park lab project. West Corp abandoned the property to the city, washing its hands of the place utterly.

What had happened there that one of the city's most powerful investment companies didn't try to salvage anything from the aftermath?

This was like trying to identify astronomical bodies by their distant gravitational effects. Celia was circling around the real mystery with no way of seeing it directly. That was usually how her job went. She never caught the bad guys red-handed, and only ever knew they were bad at all by the unlikely amounts of money they shuffled around.

If she'd wanted it any other way, if she'd wanted to be at the center of things, she'd have become a cop.

Somebody somewhere had to have a real lab report, something detailing the actual experiment. Most of the employees on the list had been in their twenties and thirties. A few of them should still be alive. The older ones, maybe not. She copied out the list of employees and found a phone book.

She put a check mark by Sito's name; she knew where he was, and knew the likelihood that he'd tell her anything of use. Anna Riley—if it was the same Anna Riley—had passed away twelve years ago. Celia put a question mark by her name. Then she started at the top of the list and made calls.

"Hi, I'm with the DA's office—" This fib would get her in serious trouble if it got back to Bronson, but what did she have to lose?

"This isn't anything serious, but I'm trying to track down some information. I'm looking for a Harold Kleinbrenner who might have worked as a lab technician about fifty years ago? Is that you?"

No, that was Harold Kleinbrenner Jr.'s father. Harold Senior had died of prostate cancer twenty years ago.

Sorry, wrong Gerald Stowe.

Aaron Masters was dead. So was Lawrence Donaldson.

After an hour of calling wrong numbers and dead ends, Celia had written "dead" by half the names. Four had question marks. They either had unlisted numbers, or no relatives who could vouch for them.

Finally she came to the end of the list. A woman answered the number listed in the phone book.

Celia said, "Is this Janet Travers?"

"Yes?"

"Are you the Janet Travers who worked as a lab tech at a place called the Leyden Industrial Park about fifty years ago?"

The phone line hissed and whispered during a pause. Then the woman said, "Yes."

Celia whispered a prayer of thanks to the data gods. "I'm working with the DA's office tracking down some information. Do you think I could ask you a few questions?"

Her voice was steady, but soft, whispering almost. "About what?"

"What kind of research was being conducted there? What experiments were going on? I haven't been able to find any formal lab reports."

"That was a very long time ago. I don't really remember."

"Nothing at all?"

"I was a bench tech. I processed samples, that's all. I wasn't privy to the overall results, Miss . . . What did you say your name was?"

Celia wanted very much to skip over that part. "Ms. Travers, Simon Sito worked at that lab. Can you tell me anything about—"

Janet Travers hung up.

Well. There was a thread that needed following.

* * *

At the end of the day, she collected her notes, and headed to the penthouse to find out if the museum had been robbed yet.

In the elevator, she ran the key card through the reader authorizing penthouse access. The ride up would take a good long time. Plenty of time to consider her chances on the job market. Maybe there was still time for the trial to produce another scandal that would boot her out of the headlines.

The only thing she had to look at was her reflection in the brushed steel wall across from her: red hair pushed back with a headband, baggy sweatshirt and sweats, sneakers, file folder hugged to her chest, the whole image blurred and warped. She might have been sixteen again, coming home from school. She was grown up now; she just didn't feel like it.

The lights flashed to abrupt darkness and the elevator lurched to a stop. She braced against the wall; an emergency light came on, making the steel walls glow red. Her face looked sunburned in the reflection.

She stood still, frozen, waiting to hear something—a groan of gears restarting, someone forcing a door. Her blood pounded in her ears; all else was sickeningly silent.

The Stradivarius Brothers couldn't possibly infiltrate West Plaza. Impossible. Not with West Corp security, not with the Olympiad's sensors in place. Seconds ticked by, and every one of them dragged.

She was trapped, and they were coming for her.

The intercom crackled on. She flinched.

"Hi, is anyone in there?" A young man spoke. He sounded almost friendly. "If anyone's there, could you pick up the phone behind the panel?"

Under the floor buttons, a panel had a sticker with an image of a phone on it. Celia opened the door and found the receiver.

"Yes? I'm in here." She spoke ever so calmly. Her whole body was clenched tight with nerves, but she made her voice calm.

"Okay, ma'am. I'm Jeff, in maintenance. We were running some routine checks on this part of the building when the power accidentally cut off. We're working on getting the elevators restarted. We should have you out of there real soon, just a few minutes. You okay?"

She almost laughed, but for Jeff's sake, swallowed back the insane cackles. "Yes, I think so. Thanks for telling me."

"I didn't think anyone was working today. You're pretty on the ball, eh?"

She wondered if she should tell him she was Warren West's daughter.

"I just had to pick something up," she said.

"Well, ma'am, you hang tight and we'll get you going any minute now."

She still believed the kidnappers were waiting for her, even after the lights came back on and the elevator resumed its climb. When the car stopped at the penthouse, her heart started racing again. She expected the doors to open and reveal masked gunmen. Even here, even at the Olympiad's secure headquarters.

The doors opened, and Arthur stood before her.

"I could feel your anxiety twenty floors away. I was coming to check on you."

This time she did laugh, slumping against the elevator wall. "I'm just paranoid," she said. "Stupidly, blindly paranoid. The elevator stalled, and I thought . . . I just assumed somebody was about to kidnap me. *Here,* of all places."

Mentis said, "Come out of there. Have a seat and catch your breath, all right?"

The sun was sinking behind skyscrapers outside the wall of windows. She hadn't realized how late it was. He walked with her to the living room, sat her on the sofa, then went to the wet bar in the corner, more of a decorative piece than having any real function, or so Celia thought. She was shocked and pleased when Mentis found a bottle of bourbon and poured a shot into a tumbler.

He brought it to her, and she smiled. "That's exactly what I wanted right now."

"I know."

Simple as that. No questions, no snap judgments.

"Robbie would have tried to feed me hot cocoa, like I'm still twelve."

"I think Robbie misses being the fun uncle. He hasn't quite figured out how to relate to you as an adult."

"You always just treated me like a human being. I preferred that, I think."

He offered a fleeting smile, then indicated the file folder still clutched in her arms. "What have you got there?"

She regarded the folder, which now seemed insignificant, a piece of historical flotsam. "The next trail marker, I hope. I've been tracing some of Sito's assets for the DA. He worked for a laboratory that was housed in a building that West Corp owned fifty years ago. Lucky for me, West Corp doesn't destroy records."

"Still working, even after being laid off?"

"This is plan B," she said.

An alarm sounded—the usual alarm, which meant the usual trouble. Mentis touched a hidden panel in the wall; the piece of wood slid back to reveal a small computer terminal and a comm headset. He typed a few keys, and the alarm shut off, but the computer monitor still flashed red, and Mentis put the earpiece to his head.

Ah, just like old times. Celia waited for the verdict, quietly sipping her bourbon and letting it melt the fear from her nerves.

After a few minutes, Mentis shut down the computer and closed the terminal. When he turned back to her, even he looked somber. She couldn't taste the bourbon anymore.

"That was your mother," he said. "The History Museum's been attacked. They didn't take anything; we were ready for them. They're in custody. But she said Chief Appleton is on his way over here to bring you in for questioning."

She almost asked why, out of reflex. But she knew. She'd guessed right. She'd known what the bad guys were going to do next, and that made her a suspect. If she'd been one of the Olympiad, they'd have been patting her on the back for her insight.

But a former member of Sito's operation? She was a suspect.

"Well. I guess I'll go down to the lobby to meet them," she said, and drained the rest of the bourbon.

NINETEEN

CELIA was leaning against the lobby's security desk when Appleton and an entire squad of uniformed cops entered the building. She crossed her arms and worked hard to stay perfectly relaxed and nonchalant. Appleton wouldn't get the satisfaction of thinking he'd upset her. She was glad for the alcohol seeping warmly through her bloodstream.

Arthur had insisted on coming with her. He stood nearby, hands in his pockets, his face a blank. Damon Parks manned the desk. "I don't have to let them in," he'd actually proposed. "This is private property. I can ask for a warrant, hold them off." He had this look in his eye like he'd do it, too. Stand there all by himself, preparing to do battle. He held himself like he thought he could succeed. That kept Celia from laughing off his suggestion entirely.

"Delay the inevitable?" Celia said. "No. I don't want to piss them off." Frowning, Parks nodded.

Appleton actually had a set of handcuffs out as he approached her. She raised a brow.

"Are you arresting me?"

"That depends. Are you going to argue?"

"I'll cooperate like a good citizen."

He almost seemed disappointed when he handed the cuffs to one of the officers.

When Arthur followed them out to the cars, Appleton turned on him as if to say something. The angry pucker in his expression faded, though, and he only shook his head and stalked off.

At the station, Appleton put her in a holding room and let her have a Styrofoam cup of lukewarm coffee. Arthur went to help interrogate the suspects from the History Museum heist, to skim from their minds what he could. She waited.

Listening to snatches of conversation from the time Appleton picked her up to the time he locked her in the room, she had a vague idea of what had happened. Appleton had ignored Celia's call completely. The Olympiad, on the other hand, set a trap. They didn't tell the museum or police what they were doing. Two of the gang members were disguised as janitors; two more hid in their equipment carts. Just before the exhibit opened, they entered the room containing the display cases. Armed with glass cutters, they prepared to slice into the cases. The Bullet closed and locked all three doors into the hall before the robbers touched the first case. Olympus and Spark knocked them on their asses. It was a classic Olympiad operation, top to bottom. The team still had it.

Later, Breezeway reported a suspicious car parked in front of Celia's apartment. It drove away in a hurry when news of the busted museum heist hit the police radio.

Finally, the door to the holding room opened and Appleton entered, pulling a spare chair from the wall to sit across the table from her. Even more maddening, Mark Paulson followed him and took up a place standing in the corner, his arms crossed sullenly.

"Should I have my lawyer here?" She sounded more bitter than she meant.

"If you'd like." Appleton looked smug.

"What if we ask Dr. Mentis to sit in instead? So that somebody here knows I'm telling the truth."

Appleton nodded at Mark, who went to the door, but it opened before he could touch it, and there stood Arthur. As if she'd called him. Maybe she had.

Scowling, Mark retreated back to his corner.

Arthur said to Appleton, "Would you like this to be a formal interrogation, Chief?"

Appleton looked at Celia. "Do you mind?"

She shook her head. She'd prefer this to be formal, with no ambiguity. It didn't bother her—Arthur was the only person here on her side. He pulled up a chair directly in front of her. Their knees were almost touching.

"Relax," he said. "Just answer the chief's questions. Let your thoughts flow. You know the routine."

Appleton asked simple, straightforward questions, and she answered them rote. How did you know about the robbery attempt at the history museum? She guessed. It seemed like about time for another robbery, and she guessed. What do you know about the Strad Brothers? Nothing. Do you recognize any of these people? He showed her mug shots: the four men arrested at the museum. Two of them she thought she recognized from the symphony gala. Sure enough, he showed her security shots from the Stradivarius robberies. They matched. Beyond that, she didn't know anything. Appleton kept asking, kept looking at Mentis for confirmation, and the telepath only nodded. *She's telling the truth.*

Arthur held her gaze. She only saw his calm blue eyes. It wasn't that she couldn't look away—she was sure she could, if she wanted to. But she didn't want to. His focus, his steadiness urged her to keep looking. Meanwhile, her thoughts ran behind her eyes like a film. Mentis could watch, through her eyes. She felt hollow, invisible. The girl with the see-through skull. It felt strange, but she wasn't afraid. If it had been anyone else but Mentis doing it, though, she would have launched into a screaming fit.

She'd seen that happen when Mentis searched other people like this.

Appleton finally paused. Without breaking eye contact with her, Mentis asked, "Anything else?"

Out of the corner of her eye she saw Appleton shrug. "What the hell—you ever sleep with the Destructor?"

You can't kill him, she told herself. Can't even hurl insults at him. He was *waiting* for an excuse to lock her up. She thought she saw a smile twitch on Mentis's lips, quickly repressed.

"No. I. Did. Not." She broke free of Mentis and looked at Mark, who dropped his gaze.

—*We're finished now. Rest easy.*—Mentis looked away, and a weight lifted. She could breathe again. Briefly, she brushed his hand where it rest on his knee. He gave her hand a quick squeeze in return before turning to the police chief.

"Satisfied?" he said.

"Yeah," Appleton said, obviously disappointed.

"Chief Appleton?" Celia leaned forward in her seat. "You have leaders from both the Strad Brothers and the Baxter Gang in custody now, right? Is there any connection between them?"

"That's what your father keeps asking. He's convinced Sito's masterminding this from prison. We're looking into ways he could possibly be doing that. Maybe that'll keep the Olympiad off our backs—no offense, Doctor."

Mentis waved him away.

But what if the connection wasn't the Destructor?

Appleton kicked them out, apparently satisfied that she wasn't a danger to society. She was hoping Mark would talk to her. She kept waiting for him to apologize. But he walked out of the room without a glance at her.

It was nightfall when she and Mentis stood on the street outside the police station. He looked thoughtfully back at the closed door.

"Your detective is having a very hard time admitting to himself that he was wrong."

"I don't need telepathy to know that."

"No, indeed. Are you all right?"

She checked herself, wondering how much of her tiredness was genuine physical fatigue or overwhelming annoyance. Or traumatic stress.

"I don't know. I guess I don't have to stay at West Plaza anymore, if the robbery's already happened."

"Your mother would probably appreciate you staying for dinner."

He was right, she was sure, but she wanted to run away all the same. "Do my parents think I had anything to do with this because I guessed right?"

"I honestly don't know. I haven't spoken with them since the robbery."

"But they might think it, a little bit."

"Celia, it's amazing how little people control what they think sometimes. I can assure you, though, that your parents love you. Without reservation. They always have."

She chuckled. "Makes me pretty pathetic, doesn't it? Twenty-five years old and still pissed off because I think my parents don't love me."

"Celia, go home. Get some rest. I'll let your parents know you're all right. Mostly."

"Thank you," she murmured, after he'd turned his back and walked away. She had to have faith that even if he hadn't heard her, he'd felt the sentiment.

TWENTY

THIS project rang too many alarm bells in her mind. Far from reaching a conclusion, the clues had branched. She had too many questions, now.

The next morning, attaché and growing collection of notes in hand, she headed back to West Plaza. She was going to do the unthinkable: ask her parents for a crack at the Olympiad mainframe. Maybe their database could make sense of the list of lab equipment, cross reference it with their information about the Destructor. In the afternoon, she planned to knock on Janet Travers's front door. Maybe an eighty-year-old retired lab tech had the inside scoop.

One nice thing about getting fired: she wore jeans and a blouse softened by too much washing. And sneakers. She was the height of comfortable, ratty chic.

She only had two blocks to go between her apartment building to the bus stop and walked that stretch nearly every day without thinking of it because it was a quiet neighborhood, narrow, older streets lined with family grocers and small restaurants.

No reason the sidewalk should open under her feet.

The grating simply dropped. Yelping, she fell with it, she thought into the storm sewer, to concrete and breaking bones. But she landed on something soft, a cushion that protected her—an industrial-size, wheeled laundry hamper, like a hotel would use, filled with foam cushions.

A lid slammed closed over her and the light from above disappeared. A motor started, then movement. Lying on her back, she pushed up on the lid of whatever box she'd been closed in. It rattled but didn't open. She kept pounding on it anyway, and screaming, because what else could she do?

She hadn't been so afraid in a long time. She hadn't been the victim of such an effective kidnapping in a long time.

Movement stopped. She gasped, startled, and then held her breath.

The lid opened.

She sat up, flung herself over the edge of the hamper, and skidded onto the concrete floor, unable to keep her feet.

She'd been brought to a room, pitch-black. She couldn't see the walls, and only knew it was a room by the way her gasps echoed off walls that were too close. The whole journey, from falling through the sidewalk to ending up here had taken less than a minute. Her superhuman guardians—still in place, after all her complaints—would hardly have time to recognize she'd disappeared, much less be able to find her.

A light, white and muted, came to life. A propane lantern sat on a card table. A man, dressed all in black, his face in shadow, also sat on the table.

"Celia West," he said in a flat voice. "You really should vary your route. I thought the daughter of Captain Olympus and Spark would know better."

She clapped her hand over her mouth to keep from laughing hysterically. She waited for the rant to follow—when the villain announced his ominous plan to hold her hostage, to manipulate the Olympiad, to threaten her.

He just watched her.

"You finally got me," she said. "What now?"

"I wasn't behind those other kidnapping attempts," he said. "I'm competent. I succeed on the first try."

This wasn't the Strad Brothers, not by a long shot.

"What—what are you going to do with me?"

"Talk. That's all. Do you know me?"

She stepped a little closer. If he'd lean in, let part of his face show in the aura of the lantern, she might see him. But she didn't want to get close enough for him to touch her, grope her, strangle her—

He set something on the table beside him. He'd kept it hidden behind his back. As he produced it, he leaned forward, and she saw his face: older but fit, frowning but with the wrinkles of laugh lines around his eyes, as if he waited to see how she'd react to a joke.

Her voice almost failed her. "Damon Parks."

The West Plaza security guard.

Beside him, on the table, his hand rested on a leather gauntlet with a silhouette stitched in gold onto the back of the hand: a hawk in flight, wings stretched back, ready to strike. The History Museum's permanent exhibit on vigilante crime fighters had one of those gloves on display.

"Oh my God," she murmured.

"I knew you were smart," he said.

"I don't understand." Her heart raced, making her dizzy. She had to focus on every breath.

"I have some information for you."

"What, me? But why—I mean, you're the Hawk; if you have information, why don't you do something about it?"

"Because I'm retired."

"Then you should give it to my parents, the Olympiad—"

He shook his head. "They won't admit it, but they're not at the top of their game anymore. It's time they pass the job to the younger generation, like I did."

"But I'm not the younger generation. I'm not heir to anything, I don't have any powers—"

"Neither do I."

That came like a punch in her gut. A judgment. Proof positive that not having powers wasn't an excuse for anything. "I can't take on that mantle."

"You've been looking for a connection between these robberies. Between the gang members who committed them."

"Not *really*—"

"And you think there's a connection—maybe even a mastermind—Simon Sito, maybe?"

"I don't know. If it is, he's changed his MO."

"But you've been digging."

Celia didn't have to wonder how much he knew about what; as Damon Parks, working at West Plaza's front desk, he probably saw a hell of a lot more than anybody realized. He'd have seen the logs; he knew she had a key card to the West Corp archives. He was good at his job. Both of them.

"I've been digging into Sito's case, not the current crime wave. If there were a connection between them, somebody should have found something by now."

"Fair enough. So maybe it isn't Sito."

He reached behind him. On the table, in the dark, lay a manila folder. He offered it to her, and she accepted. Inside, she found dozens of newspaper clippings. She'd expected something more high-tech: stolen spreadsheets, classified files. Not data available from vending machines on every corner of the city.

In all of the articles he'd cut out, he'd highlighted names. She recognized a couple, and she was sure if she checked they would belong to gang members arrested during the recent robberies and kidnapping attempts.

"Not quite retired," she said, eyeing him. "You've been busy."

"This is just a hobby," he said.

The headlines of all the articles were some variation of GOVERNOR SNYDER ISSUES PARDONS.

She looked through the clippings again, to be sure she hadn't missed something. "That's the connection? All the gang members were convicted felons who received executive pardons?"

"That's right."

"It's a coincidence. They all got out on the same day and hatched the plan together."

"Everything you've seen, everything you know, do you honestly believe that?"

She didn't, not for a minute. "What are you saying? That Governor Snyder is the mastermind?"

"It's a lead. I thought you'd be interested."

"You're crazy; this is crazy. The Hawk retires, then gets a job working for the next generation of vigilantes as a security guard? You didn't retire, you traded down."

He hopped off the table, fished her attaché case from the laundry hamper, and gave it to her, then picked up the lantern and his glove. He wore a cocky smile, like the afternoon had gone exactly as he'd planned.

She said, "People have been trying to guess who you are, who the Hawk is, for forty years. Why reveal yourself to me?"

"Because I trust you."

She laughed. "Then you're the only person in Commerce City who does."

"Celia, I saw you during those years. I saw what you were going through. I might even understand it. I know Dr. Mentis does. I bet he trusts you, too." He handed her the glove. Absently, she crushed it in her hand.

As the light moved, a passage became visible, an open tunnel that presumably led out. He prepared to walk away.

"Wait—where are you going?"

"Me? I'm retired. I'll go play bocce or something."

"What about me?"

"I'm sure you'll find a way out."

"Why couldn't you fucking *mail* this to me?"

"Maybe I wanted to show you what a real kidnapping looks like."

He and his lantern walked away.

She followed him. She didn't have a choice. When he left, so did the light.

Damon Parks was the Hawk, the city's original hero, who'd kept his secret identity secret for forty years. What could she do with that information? How much would the *Eye* pay for it? Not that she had any proof. Not that anyone would believe her.

Ahead, the circle of white light bobbed along, traveling down the damp, concrete tunnel. Parks turned left, passed the next intersection, then turned left again. Celia kept on twenty or so paces behind him, trying to avoid puddles even though her loafers were already soaked. He had to know she was following him. Maybe he was leading her into another trap. Maybe this was a test. A heroic initiation. Can she survive the maze?

But she already had the folder of information tucked into her attaché, along with the Hawk's glove. Parks didn't care about testing her. He'd just thrown her into the deep end and expected her to swim.

The light faded, and for a moment she was afraid she'd let him get too far ahead. But no, the lantern light faded because a brighter light came in from above—sunlight through a sewer grate. Parks climbed a ladder that went up, jostled loose the grate, and disappeared to the street level.

She hurried after him, climbed the same ladder, awkwardly tucking her attaché under her arm. Just as she reached the top, the grate closed back over her.

"Bastard!" she shouted at him. "Inconsiderate bastard!"

The grate wasn't that tightly set in. A quick push with her shoulder knocked it aside, and she managed to wriggle through to the outside. She was in an alley, hidden behind a garbage Dumpster. No one passing by on the sidewalk even looked twice at her.

She hurried to her feet, quickly moving to the end of the alley and looking down the sidewalk in both directions, but Damon Parks—the Hawk, bane of criminals and one-time guardian of Commerce City—was gone. Of course.

A sudden breeze pushed her, causing her to step back to keep her balance. In the blink of an eye, seeming to appear from no-where, Robbie Denton stood before her. The Bullet, actually, wear-ing his skin suit and mask. He'd run so quickly from wherever he'd been, she hadn't see him approach.

"Hi," she said.

"Celia, where have you been? Breezeway saw you fall through the grate—that wasn't an accident was it? Did you escape? Who did it? What happened?" He was almost dancing in place, arms half-raised and fists clenched, like he wanted to grab her.

She could give Damon Parks away. He had to know that. Did he trust her not to, or was he prepared to have his identity exposed?

Or did he know that she'd keep his secret, because it was one piece of information she had that no one else did? Information was power, and she had so little of it.

"I'm okay," she said, trying to sound reassuring instead of tired. "I don't think I was in any danger."

"Your folks are going to want to hear about this."

Right now? she thought. "Yeah, I bet they will. How about I come over to their place this afternoon?"

He hesitated. He probably had meant right now.

"Really, Robbie, it's okay. It wasn't what you think."

"Okay," he said finally. "This afternoon. I'll let them know."

"Thanks."

He stepped back from her, watching her with that worried frown that had never really gone away since her teenage years. Then, with the gust of a vagrant breeze, he disappeared.

Her mother left three messages on her cell phone. Arthur left one. Everyone knew about the kidnapping, its speed and ruthless-ness, its frightening effectiveness, and its puzzling outcome. It didn't match the Strad Brothers' MO. There hadn't been any rob-beries reported.

She went home and showered. Her subterranean trip made her grubby and cranky. A hot shower cured all woes. Or, most woes. When she returned to the living room, the folder of newspaper clippings still sat on the table, staring at her. What did that psycho expect her to do with this? She wouldn't, *wouldn't* don a mask and start rappelling from the tops of buildings in a quest for justice.

What would she do if this was part of her job? Well, that was easy. She went to the city library.

A true skeptic would question whether the newspaper clippings were even legitimate. They could have been faked—the Hawk might have a grudge against Governor Snyder for some reason and could be trying to frame him. So Celia needed to both verify that the news articles were genuine, and find out if there was a connection between the Hawk and Snyder. That seemed so unlikely as to be ridiculous. The Hawk had retired decades ago, and Snyder had only been in office a year. Not to mention that Snyder had trouble getting through a press conference without offending someone— usually hitting on one of the female reporters—or committing some ludicrous verbal gaff. Celia had trouble seeing him as a criminal mastermind. But maybe that buffoonish politician image was a front. She'd heard weirder theories.

She spent an hour with a microfiche machine and the last two years' worth of the *Commerce City Banner*. She didn't need much time to confirm the articles—Parks had annotated them with dates and page numbers.

She also confirmed what Parks hadn't been able to, double-checking articles listing the names of the men who'd been arrested for the recent crime sprees and cross referencing them to the list of pardons—all of the identified perpetrators of the Baxter Gang and Strad Brother jobs had been pardoned by the governor.

Then she found the photo of Governor Snyder, looking goofy in his pin-striped suit and too-shaggy toupee, shaking hands with Commerce City Mayor Anthony Paulson. It had been taken about eight months earlier and accompanied an article about Paulson negotiating with newly elected Governor Snyder for state funding to help with his epic revitalization program. Paulson had campaigned heavily for Snyder, and apparently called in a ton of favors upon Snyder's election. Among the proposals Mayor Paulson had offered to help pay for the rebuilding of Commerce City's industrial area: furloughs and pardons for a chunk of the state's lesser criminals. Snyder was apparently happy to comply.

That added a new loop to the knot, didn't it?

So the pardons were Mayor Paulson's idea? But why? Was there a reason other than funding? Where was the conspiracy, except in her own mind? And wasn't that healthy?

She called Mark. The phone rang and rang; either he wasn't around, or he was still screening calls from her. She left a message.

"Hi, Mark. It's me, whether or not you want to hear from me. If you've got the time I've got some research for you. I think I have the connection between all your Strad Brothers and Baxter Gang suspects. They all received pardons from Governor Snyder, at the suggestion of Mayor Paulson. Maybe you can figure out what your father was thinking. Look up these articles from the *Banner*." She gave him the dates and references. Mark was a smart guy. Surely he'd give her a reasonable explanation for the so-called coincidence.

When she set off for West Plaza an hour later, she took a cab. It was much later than she'd intended; the research had drawn her in. She'd get lectured for it. Maybe she could distract her parents with the information she'd dug up.

The guard sitting at the front desk was a young man with an earnest expression. She leaned on the granite surface of the desk.

"Can I help you?" the guard said.

"Can you tell me when Damon Parks comes on duty?"

"Who?"

"Damon Parks. The security guard who works the evening shift here."

"Oh, the old guy. I'm sorry, ma'am. He handed in his resignation today. Is there something I can help you with?"

Parks had planned it this way all along.

"Do you have a home phone number for him or something? I really need to get in touch with him."

"I'm not sure I can give out that information—"

He's the Hawk, goddamn it! she wanted to shout, but didn't.

"Celia?"

That reflexive chill she always got at the sound of her father's voice crawled up her spine. She repressed the shiver and turned around. Warren West, looking shockingly normal in a gray business suit, had entered the lobby through the front door and was walking toward her.

The security guy stood at attention. His eagerness cranked up about ten notches, which Celia hardly thought possible.

"Mr. West, sir, welcome back, sir!"

"Thanks, Joe." Warren smiled warmly at the security guard, who seemed to be on the edge of actually swooning. The smile fell when he looked back at Celia. "Robbie says you have a story to tell."

"Um, yeah."

"I'll walk you upstairs."

In silence, they entered the private elevator that went straight to the penthouse. As the elevator began its ascent, she stole sideways glances at her father, who focused his gaze intently on the digital numbers flashing the changing floors.

He wasn't going to believe what had happened. None of them would. Well, Arthur would.

She closed her eyes and calmed herself. Her father chose that moment to speak.

"Are you all right?"

She needed a moment to process the question. She wasn't used to him sounding so genuinely . . . concerned.

"Yeah," she said at last. "It happened so quickly it barely registered."

"Good, I'm glad. I mean, I'm glad you're all right."

"Thanks."

The elevator stopped and opened.

The penthouse doors swung in from the elevator lobby. Warren walked with her into the foyer and around the corner to the kitchen. They were there, the whole Olympiad. All wore civilian clothes. It might have been a casual supper party. Suzanne paced along the edge of the kitchen. Robbie leaned against the counter, his arms crossed. Arthur Mentis sat at the table. He smiled at her.

Suzanne's expression melted when Celia appeared. Celia met her mother halfway and hugged her, before she could burst into tears.

"Celia, we expected you hours ago! Are you all right? Are you hurt? What happened?"

"Shaken, not stirred," Celia said weakly. "I'm fine."

"Have you eaten? I can heat up some lasagna—"

Of course she could. "That sounds great. Thanks."

So the meeting of the Olympiad commenced at the kitchen table, over lasagna.

"I've walked on that grate a hundred times," Celia said. "Who knew it could even move? The whole thing was planned to the second. Even if you'd gotten down to the tunnel, I wasn't there anymore. He moved me into a side room."

"I know," Robbie said. "I *did* get down there."

"Do you know who did it?" Suzanne said.

Celia took a deep breath. "It was the Hawk."

They stared at her.

"Are you crazy?" her father said.

"How do you know it was him?" Suzanne asked.

She produced the gauntlet from her attaché and laid it on the table before them.

Warren picked it up first, studying every inch of the leather, fingering the embroidered hawk. The leather was worn, stained with sweat and age, the stitching around the fingers frayed, and scuffed patches showing around the thumb and pads of the palm. The embroidery was also frayed, loose-colored threads poking up. The glove was old, used.

"Could it be a fake?" Arthur asked.

"It's something the Hawk would have done," Celia said.

"He hasn't been active in twenty years," Warren said.

"I believed him," Celia said. She didn't have to reveal who he was. They'd all assume he'd been in costume, with the mask. "He gave this to me."

She produced the folder with the newspaper clippings. Her parents and Robbie gathered around the open file, sorting through the clippings, their expressions growing more confused as the moments passed. Arthur didn't bother looking; he watched her. He could learn everything he needed to from her roiling thoughts. She tried to stay calm, for his sake.

Celia said, "It's the connection between the robberies we've been looking for."

"But it doesn't go anywhere," Robbie said. "Does it? It's a coincidence. It has to be. Unless you're saying Snyder is the mastermind?" The possibility seemed ludicrous. Governor Snyder came across as being harmless, if ineffectual.

Arthur crossed his arms, which made him look hunched-in and thoughtful. "These names—they're all suspects that have been arrested in connection with the spate of robberies. They have no other prior relationship to each other. They weren't part of the same gang before, they didn't serve prison time together. They're not second cousins. The one commonality are these pardons. The idea of Snyder being involved in this—it's improbable, not impossible. We have to consider it."

"Not Snyder," Celia said, "Paulson." She showed them the last article she'd discovered, and the buried information that Paulson had been the one to suggest the pardons as a way to help balance the budget. But she wondered if he might not also have suggested the names of inmates to be pardoned.

The group needed a moment to process this. Celia waited.

"It might not be him," Suzanne said. "It could be someone associated with his office. Someone else pulling the strings."

"Do we trust the information?" Arthur asked.

"They're newspaper clippings; I verified them all," Celia said. "The Hawk just left the clues, but we're drawing our own conclusions. That's what we have to trust."

"All right, then," Suzanne said. "What do we know about Anthony Paulson?"

"He's got a son on the police force," Celia said, unable to keep the bite out of her voice.

"He's on his second term of office, and is running for a third," Arthur said.

Warren leafed through the clippings. "Arthur, have you ever read anything off him?"

"I've never tried. I can't recall ever being in the same room with him. You three always handle the public appearances."

"Maybe you ought to arrange a meeting."

"I'll see what I can do."

"It's time to pull his file up on the computer," Warren said, indicating the back hallway, which led to the Olympiad's command room. The others agreed and started to move on. Suzanne collected the file folder.

This was in their hands now, and Celia ought to have been happy to wash her own hands of the responsibility. Except she wasn't. She sat in the kitchen chair and grit her teeth, gathering the courage to just stand up and follow them. It shouldn't have been that difficult.

Arthur leaned on the back of her chair and whispered at her ear. "Come on, Celia. You're invited."

The wave of relief she felt shouldn't have been strong enough to start tears pricking in her eyes. She blinked them away and hurried to follow him.

The wood door at the end of the hall looked like every other door they'd passed, the ones leading to bedrooms and bathrooms. But this one had a security keypad by the doorknob. Suzanne punched in a code, and a scanner read her thumbprint. The door slid aside, rather than swinging open.

The Olympiad command room was everything a starry-eyed admirer of superhuman vigilantes could hope for. The cavernous space offered secret elevators and passages to different parts of the building, including the hangar in a warehouse a block over that housed some of the team's vehicles. Computer banks made up an entire wall: keyboards, indicator lights, printers, scanners, and analyzers. One of several screens showed a map of the city, and a radio monitored police frequencies. A gleaming steel table and chairs occupied the middle of the room. This was where the Olympiad had formed hundreds of plans, hunted hundreds of foes. Sparsely lit— only the table and computer banks shone brightly—the place was a den of shadows.

Celia had seen it before, but not for years. Disconcertingly, it hadn't changed at all. There might have been some new equipment, upgraded computers and communications systems, but the hardware blended in with what had been there before. She felt sixteen again. The others walked right in; she stopped and stared.

When she was growing up, if she wanted to find her parents, she checked her father's office first—his normal office, for his job running the normal company. She checked the command room second. She'd been frightened by it. It was slick, steel, all gleaming surfaces and intimidating equipment filled with buttons, dials, screens flashing between a dozen scenes from closed-circuit cameras all over the city. The place hummed with the constant noise of hard drives and cooling fans at work. She'd call them on the intercom, and they'd open the door for her. She'd find her parents leaning over some monitor or printout, piecing together clues from the latest crime spree or tracing the Destructor's whereabouts. Invariably, her question of "Can I make some popcorn?" or "Can you sign this permission slip for school?" seemed to pale beside whatever they were doing.

A couple of times she'd sat at their conference table for a debriefing, telling her side of whatever kidnapping she'd been involved in, recording her story for posterity. She couldn't remember ever sitting at the table as an equal. Or as something resembling an equal—as someone who actually had something to contribute.

Warren said, "Why did the Hawk give this to you and not us?"

"I asked him the same thing," she said. "He said you weren't at the top of your game anymore. That you needed to hand things off to the younger generation."

"How do you like that?" Robbie said with a laugh.

"The younger generation? He didn't mean you, did he?"

Celia's face flushed. She knew this was how this conversation would go. "I would think maybe he meant Typhoon or Breezeway. Block Buster Junior. One of that crowd. I told him I didn't have any powers. Then he said, neither did he."

During another long silence, Celia wished for a moment she was Arthur, so she could know what the others were thinking.

—*Or not.*—

She glanced up and caught him looking back at her. She blushed and quickly looked away. He'd been prying. Or she'd been thinking too loud. He said that happened sometimes.

Suzanne went to the computers. "Let's run the mayor through the database."

The database retrieved and cross-referenced Mayor Anthony Paulson's information, producing the standard biography and a detailed listing of policy decisions and political records. Anthony Paulson was something of a Commerce City folk hero, a hard-luck case made good, an orphaned child adopted into a middle-class family and risen through the ranks of the city's elite through his own hard labor. His policies were moderate, he was fiscally conservative, pro-labor, pro-education, and antisocialization. He was a politician everyone could love, and the greatest buried scandal of his life involved a college liaison with an underage girl—he'd been eighteen, she'd been two days from sixteen. The scandal died a quick death—the girl was Andrea, and the couple married three years later.

"We've got nothing on this guy," Robbie observed. "He's clean as a whistle."

"If we're not entirely wrong," Warren said. "There's got to be another connection. I still think Simon Sito is behind this somehow."

Arthur rubbed his chin, considering. "That's our problem. We have too many explanations that are possible but unlikely."

"Isn't that always the way?" Suzanne said.

A photo of Paulson smiled at them from the monitor. That's

what Mark will look like when he's older, Celia thought. Not a bad-looking man at all. He even had an intriguingly wicked glint in his eye, like he knew very well how to use the power he'd acquired.

Something in his eyes made her stomach go queasy. She'd looked him in the eye before, at the symphony gala, and the dinner at the mansion. But he'd been in a more personable state both times. This photo was from his last campaign; here, he was predatory. Celia recognized the expression. She hadn't noticed it right away because she'd never expected it. Not in this context.

He looked like a young Simon Sito. He had that glint in his eye that the Destructor always showed before he pressed the button.

"Celia, what is it?" Mentis watched her closely.

She'd been hypnotized by that image without realizing it, gazing into that man's eyes and falling back in time, even more so than when she stepped into the command room in the first place. She must have looked lost, staring blank-eyed at the screen.

"I don't know. Just . . . thinking." She couldn't say it out loud. It would sound ridiculous. Sito had nothing to do with this current crime wave. He wasn't masterminding anything anymore.

Paranoia. It was just paranoia.

Fortunately, Mentis was too polite to press the question.

Warren, Captain Olympus, took charge. "Mentis, see if you can get close to Paulson and read anything off him. We need other leads to confirm this. If he's behind the gangs, he has to be paying them. We have to be able to trace the stolen items back to him."

It sounded like accounting to Celia. "I have some sources I might be able to check on."

"I thought you weren't working," said her father.

She was too preoccupied to glare properly. "Public records are public, one way or another."

"You don't have to help. Thanks for bringing us this, but it's not your responsibility."

"I spent a lot of years in college learning how to do this kind of thing. Let me help." She hated begging. She ought to just walk out and go back to her ice cream.

The others waited for Warren's cue. Why couldn't any of them stand up to him? Because he was the Captain. If he didn't want her to help, they wouldn't argue.

"Fine," Warren said at last. Grudging for no other reason than to be grudging.

The planning continued. Robbie appointed himself for surveillance duty. Suzanne would consolidate information from the captured gang members, to try to learn who had hired them.

Celia continued to think, half-distractedly. Anthony Paulson was adopted. Sito couldn't possibly be his biological father. That explanation was so mundane. So simple.

And if it were true, it meant Mark was Simon Sito's grandson. Confirming the relationship should be a simple matter, if she could find Paulson's original adoption records—fifty years old and certainly sealed. A paternity test would also do the job.

"Mom? Does the computer have Sito's DNA on file?"

"Yes, I'm sure. We collected everything we could about him. As much good as it did in the end. Why?"

"No reason. Curiosity."

"Something to do with one of your sources?" Arthur said. He'd be perfectly justified in telling on her. He had to know what she was thinking. Either it was a measure of his trust that he said nothing—or he thought the idea was as outlandish as she did.

"Something like that," she said.

"You'll need access to the computer. You should have access to the computer, if you think it'll help." Suzanne gazed at Celia, bright-eyed and earnest.

She meant the Olympiad computer. As much raw computing power as Warren West's fortune could buy, and the Olympiad database, which held information available from no other source. She meant free access to the command room to use the computer.

Suzanne glanced at Warren, who pursed his lips, and while he didn't nod or give wholehearted assent, he didn't argue. Didn't say no.

"Okay. If you think it's best," Celia said, a little breathlessly.

"You might need something, and if none of us is around—" Her mother smiled. It was like she'd been waiting for years to give Celia access to the command room. To initiate her into the club.

No one was protesting.

Suzanne brought her to the main terminal and had her put her thumb on a scanner, to record her print, to confirm her authorization. The computer accepted her with glowing green lights.

The numeric code for the outer door was Celia's birthday.

Her mother fussed over her some more and wanted to feed her even more lasagna, when what Celia really wanted to do was start pouring data into the mainframe. But she didn't want to do it with everyone hovering over her. Arthur took the cue and excused himself, claiming he had some work to finish up at his psychiatry practice—his office was halfway down the building. So, the group dispersed, and Celia promised she'd get a good night's sleep, and the data crunching would have to wait until tomorrow.

When she left West Plaza for home, she checked her phone and found she'd missed a call. The Olympiad conference room blocked such transmissions.

Mark had left her a message. He sounded angry. "Celia. I got your call and checked up on your information. I don't know what you're implying about my father. You're obviously bored out of your skull to go through this much trouble to dig up this trash. I think your parents' paranoia has rubbed off on you. You're looking for conspiracies that don't exist." He clicked off.

Maybe she could find a few of his hairs on her pillow, to compare against Sito's DNA. She doubted she'd be getting any other kind of genetic material from him any time soon.

TWENTY-ONE

*T*HE *Banner*'s headline the next morning announced in blazing bold letters: "DEFENSE RESTS IN SITO TRIAL. JURY DELIBERATION BEGINS." So, the end was nigh.

In a fit of déjà vu, Celia set out for the bus stop, on her way back to West Plaza to feed her information about Leyden Laboratory into the Olympiad mainframe. She was as giddy as a kid at Christmas about what she might find.

She made a point of walking around the sewer grate by a good margin. No one was going to pull that on her again. When she made it onto the bus, she heaved a sigh of relief.

The baby started crying as soon as the bus left the curb.

It wasn't just a fussy baby. This was a baby who was generally unhappy with the state of the universe and was expressing this with its entire lung capacity. Celia sympathized. The bus's overactive heater had brought the temperature up to about eighty—with everyone on board bundled in winter clothes. It was noisy and smelly, filled with strangers, all of them trapped. The poor mother was doing her best to hush the thing, but her soothing did no good.

Celia was about to give the woman cab fare so she could get off and take her screaming infant home in peace, when the man in the seat in front of her hollered at the driver, "Hey! I wanted that stop! Didn't you see the freakin' light?"

They had zoomed right past the last stop.

The bus was speeding up. Riders started murmuring, shifting restlessly.

Leaning on the seat back in front of her, Celia stood to look.

"Hey, didn't you hear me?" the guy complained again.

The woman sitting behind the driver tapped him on the shoulder. "Excuse me—"

The driver fired a gun into the ceiling of the bus. People screamed, then a sudden hush fell. Except for the baby.

The bus swerved and ran a red light, leaving behind squealing tires and the smashing metal of a collision as cars scattered in its wake.

Celia fell back into her seat and braced, white-knuckled. Runaway bus—the driver was taking the whole bus hostage. He wasn't shooting anyone with the handgun, which was a small blessing. He held it flat to the steering wheel while he glared ahead, oblivious to the chaos he caused.

Then a guy in the second row decided to be a hero. He lunged forward, grabbed the driver's shirt, and pulled, clawing for some kind of purchase on his head or neck, probably hoping to pull him out of the seat. The driver was belted in, lodged firmly in place. He brought the gun to bear without even looking and pulled the trigger. Drops of blood spattered on the windshield, and the guy fell.

Everyone in the front half of the bus pressed back, surging away from the driver as a mass. The bus went faster.

Behind Celia, a screaming woman popped out the emergency window by her seat. The shield of plastic fell away and the woman leaned out. Wind whipped into the bus.

"No!" Celia threw herself over the back of her own seat and grabbed the woman's coat, hauling her away from the opening. The woman, in her thirties and ghostly pale, struggled, slapping at Celia, muttering hysterically, "Got to get out, got to get out." Celia held her wrists, crossed her arms, and pinned her to the seat. "Not that way. You'll smear yourself on the pavement."

The woman snapped back to lucidity and stared wide-eyed at Celia. "We're going to die!"

All the driver had to do was ram the bus into a brick wall and she'd be right. At this speed, a split second was all it would take to shatter everyone on board. Who knew what the hell the driver was thinking, but whatever it was, he'd decided to take a bus full of people with him.

Celia had been face-to-face with the Destructor, not a nose-length apart, and until now she'd never believed that she was going to die. Mom and Dad wouldn't get here in time— Oh, the police alert had probably gone out, they were probably on their way, and she could picture how Captain Olympus might stand in the street and build a cushion of force that would slow the bus to a stop without harming any of them. But there wasn't time. They were four blocks away from the docks and the river. They'd be there in a minute, and the driver wasn't slowing down or turning.

Her hands fell away from the woman, who stayed in her place, trembling. Celia's heart was pounding in her ears, and the world had turned to molasses, thick and slow moving. Around her, people held each other, gripped the seats with clawed hands, and wept. The baby was still screeching.

This wasn't right. This wasn't her time.

"Give me your scarf," she said to the woman. Under her coat, over her black sweater, she wore a floral silk scarf. She blinked, like she hadn't understood, so Celia yanked it away from her. Balling it in one hand, she dived to the aisle floor and crawled, shoving random legs out of the way, pinching when she had to. On hands and knees, out of view of the bus's rearview mirror, she raced.

The first few rows had cleared. Still on the floor, Celia squeezed into the seat behind the driver. Wrapping one end of the scarf in each hand, she twisted it until it became a thin cord. She focused on the driver's head. She only had one chance.

She stood and brought her garrote over the driver's head, across his neck. Dropping, she pulled back.

The man gurgled, choked. He dropped the gun to claw at the cord that was strangling him. The bus swerved wildly, leaning sickeningly, dangerously overbalanced, but Celia held on. Time, this was all about time. Seconds, how many more seconds . . . Then, finally, he stopped struggling.

She climbed on top of him, using him as a seat because there wasn't time to pull him out of the way. She was small, she fit. Steering wheel in hand, she could only try to hold it still, hoping she had the strength to steady the vehicle. She put both her feet on the brake pedal and straightened her legs.

It wasn't going to be enough. Tires screeched, burned—the smell of rubber reeked. They had too much momentum, the whole frame of the bus was shuddering. Ahead, through the windshield, Celia saw water. The road ended at the pier. If they hit the water, their chances of escaping would shrink to nothing.

Celia turned. She grabbed one spot on the wheel with both hands and pulled, not caring which way they ended up, not seeing where she steered to, only wanting to get away from the drop into the river. The bus turned, rocked, tipped—fell.

Celia screamed a denial, echoed by two dozen other screams. The asphalt rushed toward her, the bus was spinning, sparks flying.

And it stopped.

The bus had seemed to be flying at the speed of light, and now it sat still, with no apparent slowing in between. It just stopped. Celia clung to the steering wheel, but flipped over it, her back to the windshield which displayed a lacework of cracks. She stared at the driver, whose face was purple, his eyes bulging and dead.

Police sirens, ambulance sirens, dozens, hundreds of sirens broke the air. She smelled dust, blood, gasoline. That was all she needed now, for the damn thing to explode.

People were piled against the ceiling of the bus, flung over the backs of seats. Some were struggling upright, apparently unhurt. Most were groaning, an agonizing and horrific sound. Celia couldn't think about it. They might have been better off sinking into the river.

Emergency windows popped off, sprung from the outside, and EMTs called into the bus. Celia didn't feel hurt. Numb, but not hurt, so she stayed quiet and let emergency crews help the others. Slowly, she unkinked herself from the dashboard. The lever for the bus door still worked. Hauling on it with both hands, she opened the door. It seemed a long way away, straight up. But she didn't want to sit around staring at the dead driver anymore.

In stages, she found footholds on the railings in front of the seats. She shouldn't be able to do this. She wasn't that strong. But she badly wanted out of that bus.

As soon as her head peered out of the open bus door, like some gopher blinking in the light, a pair of firemen balancing on ladders grabbed her and hauled her away.

Tall, handsome, wonderful firemen, in manly yellow coats and impressive helmets. They set her on the street, and she clung to their arms, even while she insisted, "I'm fine, really, I just need a drink."

"Celia!"

It took her far too long to focus on the sound, especially when she turned and found Arthur Mentis standing right in front of her. She let go of the firemen and fell into his arms, hugging him tightly.

"I thought I was dead. I really thought I was dead this time."

A good sport, he hugged back, patting her shoulder. Finally, she straightened, thinking she ought to recover some sort of dignity—if for no other reason than to help Arthur recover his. She wobbled.

"You should sit down. I think you have a concussion," he said.

"No, I'm fine."

"How many fingers am I holding up?"

She squinted. They kept moving. "Three? Six?"

"Definitely a concussion. Come on."

"My bag—my attaché case, you have to find it, it's got some in-formation about a lab Sito used to work at ages ago. Do you know he worked for West Corp, for my grandfather? I can't lose it, I have to show Dad—"

He gave her an odd look, like he thought it was the concussion talking. "We'll find it, Celia. Don't worry. I'll look for it myself, but you must sit."

She let him lead her to a quiet curb and a blanket. "Where are Mom and Dad?"

"They're helping with the injured. There were forty people on that bus."

The emergency crew was spraying fire retardant foam everywhere, and dozens of stretchers carried away the wounded. So many of them. No one had gotten out of there unscathed.

"They'd all be dead if it weren't for you," Arthur said helpfully.

Celia gripped his arm in a sudden panic. "The baby, is the baby okay? There was this baby, it was screaming, and I think we all wanted to throttle it . . . is it okay?"

He pointed. The mother was sitting on a stretcher while an EMT dabbed at a cut on her forehead. She held the baby in her arms, smiling and cooing at it. It was *still* crying, but the sobs were reduced to tired whimpers.

Celia continued holding Arthur's arm, because it steadied her. The world was still moving at eighty miles an hour. "I killed the driver."

"I know. You did what you had to."

"I'm sorry."

"Don't be. You're a hero."

She started to laugh, but it hurt, so she stopped. "I just didn't want to die."

He gave her a wry smile. "That's good to hear."

She looked down, saw her hand on his sleeve, resting on his arm. "Thanks. You're always there for me when the shit hits the fan, pulling me out of the Destructor's clutches, or just . . . just keeping me sane. So thanks."

"It's my pleasure."

Her gaze focused for a moment, and her breath stopped. He

had blue eyes. She felt them looking back at her, *felt* them, through her eyes and into her mind, and they told her that what he'd said was more than a social nicety.

He never showed emotion. He kept such tight control over himself. But for a moment, that guard dropped, and she saw . . . everything. The look in his eyes left her gut feeling warm.

He glanced away, lips slipping into a frown. He squeezed her hand and stood as an EMT took his place beside her on the curb. Calmly as ever, he walked away to join the rest of the rescue effort.

The medical powers that be wanted to keep her in the hospital overnight for observation. She didn't mind. She lay in bed, between nice clean sheets, and enjoyed the feeling of not moving. They'd even given her a private room. She didn't have to face anything but the walls if she didn't want to.

She had her eyes closed when she heard footsteps approach, then stop in the doorway. Not bothering to lift her head from the pillow, she looked. Blinked, looked again. There he stood, a familiar form in his overcoat, slouching sheepishly. Mark, bringing flowers. He gripped a vase of roses in both hands.

"How are you?" he asked.

"I'm fine."

He didn't look convinced. Probably because of the thick bandage around her forehead. A cut, eight stitches. She hadn't even felt it. She supposed she ought to be milking this for all the sympathy it was worth.

"Can I come in?"

She could tell him off or let it go. Letting it go made her less tired right now. "Sure."

He tried to find a place for the vase of roses, but all the tables were filled, as well as the floor along the wall with the window. He slipped it in between another vase and a teddy bear holding a balloon.

"Popular girl," he said, standing a little ways off from the bed.

A dozen families of passengers on the bus had sent her flowers;

two dozen random people she'd never heard of with no connection to the accident sent her flowers. All because she lacked any compunctions about crawling up to a man with a gun and strangling him from behind. It weirded her out, even more than all the bad press after her testimony. She'd *deserved* the bad press. All the news stations had carried live breaking reports of the bus hijacking. Once her name had come up, the reporters grabbed it and ran record-breaking sprints. The second time in a week she'd made the news, and the only thing reporters liked better than a hero was a hero redeeming a dark past.

"It's a little much," she said.

"They've had a heck of a time trying to figure out what happened, but twenty of the passengers gave sworn affidavits that you single-handedly stopped that bus from going into the harbor. I think you may be up for a medal."

"Don't tell them I was just trying to save my own ass."

He chuckled. Just like a guy to act like there'd never been anything wrong between them.

She mustered the energy to say, "Mark, are you wanting to apologize and be friends again or what?"

He looked at his shoes. "Yeah. I guess I am."

"So all a girl's got to do to earn an apology is save a busload of people from a maniac."

"It wasn't . . . I was going to—" He paused. She watched him visibly collect himself, taking a breath, looking at the ceiling. She waited patiently. This ought to be good. But if he made her cry, she'd never speak to him again. "When I saw your name on the passenger list, but no one knew if you'd been hurt or not, I was useless. I couldn't think, I couldn't focus, or work. I had to find out. I got over here as soon as I could."

As apologies went, he could have done worse. Now she had to decide whether or not she was going to forgive him.

"You should sit down," she said. "You look tired."

Looking relieved, he pulled up a chair. "We've been trying to track down the story on the driver."

"What have you found out?"

"Male, forty-seven, divorced twice. He's got a rap sheet, a half-dozen temper-related reprimands on his work record, and a felony conviction for assault. He'd have been laid off already if the transit authority weren't so short-handed. His supervisor didn't seem surprised when we told him what happened."

Not one of those he-seemed-so-nice testimonials. He'd been boiling and the system hadn't caught it. "He just went postal."

"Looks that way."

Someone knocked on the door, which was already ajar, and didn't wait for an invitation before entering.

"Celia?" Her mother pushed into the room, followed by her father, both in street clothes. Mr. and Mrs. West, now. She hadn't seen them at the accident site. They'd been too busy, and the paramedics had sent her to the hospital with a vanload of walking wounded as soon as they could.

"Hi, Mom."

Suzanne took the invitation to rush to the side of the bed and shower her with maternal attention. She touched Celia's arm, shoulder, cheek, and her eyes teared up. How could a superhero be so *weepy*?

"I can't believe you were on that bus. Are you all right? How do you feel? Do you need anything?"

"Don't worry. They're taking good care of me. Look at all the flowers." She pointed at the wall, a distraction tactic.

"Wow, look at them all." Suzanne acknowledged Mark then, when she was looking right at him. "Hello, Detective Paulson."

"Hello, Mrs. West. Mr. West."

At six-foot-five, Warren loomed over the bed. He nodded formally.

Mark found a couple more chairs. Warren remained standing.

Suzanne said, "You've probably told the story a thousand times already. But what happened?"

Celia had worked out a short version by now. "We were just talking about it," she said, snuggling deeper into the pillow. "It sounds like the driver just snapped. He missed a stop, and when someone argued he pulled out a gun and started shooting. It was clear pretty quick that he planned on driving straight into the river. Someone had to stop him. It probably could have been done cleaner, or better—" If she'd been a superhuman vigilante hero, for example. "—but there wasn't much time."

Beaming, eyes shining, Suzanne looked over her shoulder at Warren as if to say, *Look what she did, isn't it wonderful?*

Shaking his head, Warren said, "It's too simple. There has to be more to it."

"Investigators say no," Mark said.

"Somebody put you in danger to get to us. That's the way it always is," her father said.

Warren's paranoia had been carefully cultivated over a lifetime. Coincidence didn't exist in his world.

"You know, Dad, not everything is about you."

"And you think you just *happened* to be on the one bus that gets hijacked?"

"Stranger things have happened," she muttered.

A knock came on the door frame. Another visitor peered in—a young woman, a purple headband tying back her cornrows. Analise, carrying another bouquet. She must have decided Celia wasn't so bad, too. If she'd only known that all she had to do was stop a runaway bus . . .

"I'm sorry," Analise said. "I can come back later—"

"No, Analise, come in. It's okay. Please," Celia urged her; she wasn't letting her friend get away. Cautiously, Analise stepped into the room, eyeing the Wests.

This was going to get surreal.

Celia made introductions. "Analise, these are my parents, Suzanne and Warren. Mom, Dad, this is my friend, Analise. And this is Mark Paulson."

"Hi, nice to meet you." Analise kept far enough back that she wasn't obliged to shake hands with anyone. Her gaze rested on

Celia. "I just wanted to make sure you were okay. When I saw the news and all . . ."

"I'm fine," Celia said. They couldn't talk now about what they really needed to talk about, not with the others here. So, without a word, Celia accepted the truce that had been offered.

Suzanne was studying her. "Have we met before?"

"We went to school together," Celia said quickly, before Analise had to start making excuses. "You might have met at graduation."

"Ah." Suzanne accepted the explanation, and Celia breathed a sigh. Analise was too composed to react at all, except with an earnest smile.

"Hey, looks like we found the party." Robbie Denton entered, waving at them after knocking on the doorway. Arthur Mentis was with him. The place really was getting crowded.

She wasn't sure she wanted to see Arthur just yet.

The telepath said, "If you'd rather I come back later—"

"No, it's okay, come in. Unless you brought flowers, because I don't think there's any more room for flowers."

"No. I brought your attaché. The police released it from evidence." Arthur lifted her case, and Celia sighed with relief. She didn't want to have to reconstruct all that information. Hell, she didn't know anymore what she was going to *do* with all that information. Her perspective on various recent events seemed to have shifted.

"Thanks," she said.

Robbie stood by Analise. "Hi, I don't think we've met. I'm Robbie. This is Arthur."

"I'm Analise. Celia's friend." Analise looked stricken; she seemed to have realized she was stuck in a room with the entire Olympiad. And Dr. Mentis the telepath had caught her gaze. He studied her a little too closely.

Celia said, rather brightly, "Thanks for coming, all of you. It's really nice of you."

"Of course we'd come visit," Suzanne said. "Did you think we'd just abandon you?"

Mark and Analise both looked away at that one.

A cell phone twittered. Mark and Warren checked their belts. Mark won. He answered his phone with his name and went out into the hallway.

Warren glared after him. "The cops are useless. They can't handle a criminal conspiracy like this."

Celia said, "I'd appreciate it if you not talk about what the cops can't handle around Mark."

"Can't he take a little criticism?"

"It's not criticizing, it's insulting; as bad as that speech the mayor gave."

"I'll keep my mouth shut just as soon as the mayor does."

He was a child. A big, spoiled child. What must Analise think of the great Captain Olympus bickering like this? Maybe she'd be a little more understanding when Celia griped about her family the way other people griped about theirs. "Dad—," she said, the same time Suzanne said, "Warren—"

Analise looked uncomfortable, inching toward the door like she wanted to leave. "Celia, maybe we can get together for coffee when you're back on your feet."

She didn't get away before Mark came back in, phone still in hand, his mouth pulled into a frown.

"They found a pony bottle—an independent air supply for scuba divers—under the front seat on the bus. The driver wasn't supposed to die."

Mentis said, "So it wasn't the work of a random psychotic. It was an assassination."

They all, every last one of them, five of them superhuman, looked at Celia. Her head throbbed viciously. She wondered if the nurse would give her another dose of painkillers.

"There's more," Mark said, his voice growing even more somber, if possible, and Celia wondered what could be worse. "He was granted a pardon for a felony conviction several years ago. Just like the others."

* * *

After Mark's announcement, Analise made a hasty exit, offering
apologies and the excuse that she didn't want to interrupt. Arthur stared after her. He knew about her, Celia didn't doubt. She
wondered if she should say something. She hoped Analise wasn't
cooking up some heroic adventure based on the fragment of information she'd heard. Mark, a grim set to his face, muttered something about needing to be back at the station and followed after
her. Then visiting hours ended, and the Olympiad filed out.

Celia felt like she hadn't gotten to really visit with anyone.

The entire hospital fell quiet after visiting hours. The night shift
of nurses and orderlies came on. Celia got another dose of muscle
relaxant and painkillers. They wanted her to sleep, now that the initial danger from the concussion was over. Once the lights were off,
she was more than willing to do so.

She had to struggle to rouse herself and focus on a figure standing in the doorway. Not a nurse. He was wearing a business suit,
and leaned on the doorjamb, like all he wanted to do was watch
her. Mentis? Had Arthur come back to check on her?

No, it didn't feel like Arthur, which was an odd thing to think.
He was the telepath, not her. She shouldn't have felt anything. When
this man stepped toward her, his movements were menacing. He saw
her stir, and moved out of the glare of the hallway's light into the
darkness of the room.

"Aren't visiting hours over?" she said. Her voice sounded creaky.
She tried to wake up.

"I got special dispensation so I could avoid the crowds when I
came to visit the hero of the hour." It was Mayor Anthony Paulson.
"So. How is the hero?"

The bus hijacking—it *was* an assassination. She'd called Mark
with her suspicions, Mark had told his father—and now he was here.

She wanted to scream. She had to scream. But she just lay
there. *I know what you are, I know what you're doing . . .*

No, she didn't. She had suspicions, and she still couldn't guess
why. Being mayor should have been enough of a power trip.

"I'm fine," she said. Actually, she felt nauseated.

"You don't look so good. A little pale, I think."

"It's the bandages."

He winced, as if in sympathy. "Still, you're lucky. It could have been so much worse."

It was supposed to have been so much worse. "Yeah."

All he'd have to do was put a pillow over her face, or inject something into her, or stab her in the throat with a letter opener. If that was what he was here for, it would only take a moment, and she wasn't strong enough to fight. No one would ever find out until the on-duty nurse made rounds. And no one would suspect Mayor Paulson of any ill deed.

"Mark says you two haven't been getting along. I was sorry to hear that."

"He came to see me earlier," she said. "We have a lot to talk about."

"Yes, I'm sure. I have to say, your testimony at the Sito trial really threw him for a loop. It threw all of us for a loop."

"So I gathered."

"But it's water under the bridge, I'm sure."

"Lots of water."

"You're one of the good guys now. Isn't that right?"

If he was going to kill her, she wished he'd get it over with, since the conversation was making her nervous. Her stomach was churning. She wondered if she could throw up on him.

"I'm just trying to get through the day, like everyone else."

"Ah. Well. So far so good."

She reached to the bedside call button and buzzed for the nurse.

He didn't react, didn't flinch at all. His face was in shadow, his expression distorted. He might have been smiling, wincing, snarling. The tone of it slipped and transformed.

A woman in a nurse's uniform appeared in the doorway. "Ms. West, are you all right?"

"I feel a little dizzy. The doctor said I should call if I feel dizzy."

The nurse turned on the room's light. Paulson's expression was perfectly neutral. Perhaps a little concerned. Maybe he was here for exactly the reason he said, doing his mayoral duty and visiting the hero of the hour.

The nurse said to Paulson, "Sir, I'm sorry, maybe you should come visit another time." She turned to Celia and efficiently embarked on a series of tests, shining lights in her eyes, listening to her heart, taking her temperature.

"Of course," Paulson said. "Once again, Ms. West, on behalf of the city, thank you."

He left, and only then did Celia, slumped back against her pillow, really feel dizzy.

TWENTY-TWO

WHEN Suzanne insisted that Celia stay come stay in West Plaza when she was released from the hospital the next morning, she relented.

The West Corp limo picked her up that morning. Her father rode with her—bodyguard. For the first time in recent memory, she felt safer with him near.

She still couldn't think of anything to say to him, though the information about the Leyden Industrial Park burned a hole in her attaché case. Telling him everything had seemed like a great idea when she was almost dead. Now that she was sitting next to him? Later, she'd tell him later. When she had all the pieces.

Her father's cell phone rang. He answered, then relaxed, which meant it was probably Suzanne calling. "Really? What channel . . . okay."

Warren turned on the TV in the back of the limo.

The scene was the City Hall press room, with its familiar podium and flags in the background. The place was crammed with reporters and TV cameras. Mayor Paulson was just arriving at the podium, looking grim and determined. Beside the network logo in the bottom corner, a graphic announced "Live."

Paulson launched in on his speech. "I have made a pledge to

protect this city. I have pledged to make our streets safe. It is my heartbreaking regret to recognize how far I have to go to make that pledge a reality. Thousands of the city's residents depend on the bus system to carry them to work, to carry them home again. The buses are the arteries that hold the lifeblood of Commerce City. I fear that yesterday's tragedy has eroded confidence in our transportation system, just as other recent events have made people afraid to venture out to our museums, our concert halls, our gardens. We fear that nothing in this city is safe, that nothing is sacred.

"I aim to change that. I aim to once again make our city a place we can be proud of, a place we can feel safe in. It is with that goal in mind that I have taken the drastic step of declaring a state of emergency. Until the masterminds of these plots are taken into custody, until every last member of these gangs is caught, this city is under curfew. All law enforcement officials will be working overtime. All city resources will be directed toward making sure this sort of thing never happens again. Thank you."

For all the chaos that the recent spate of criminal activity had caused, none of the incidents had been deadly. That had changed now. Six people had died on the bus: the driver, the man who'd been shot, and four in the crash. A couple of the injuries were critical, so the number could go up. The police assured Celia that if the bus had gone into the water, that number would have been much higher. They really did want to give her a medal.

Paulson didn't linger to answer questions. An aide stayed behind to announce specific measures involved in the state of emergency declaration: a curfew, a requirement of all residents to carry identification and proof of employment, such as a recent pay stub, while traveling to work. All events where large groups of people would gather were canceled.

The news report continued with talking-heads commentary and man-on-the-street interviews. Public opinion seemed to support the mayor's declaration. News had leaked about the breathing equipment under the front seat, which turned the incident from a random act of violence into a terrorist act. Another mastermind seemed to be laying siege to the city; the Destructor's days of terror had returned.

Warren was a short breath away from a rage when the limo pulled into the West Plaza parking garage. Celia was almost afraid to move.

"Twenty-five years," Warren muttered. "Half my life I've been protecting this city. Do I get any credit at all?"

"I don't think that's what he's saying. It's an election year, he has to sound decisive."

"Are you defending him?"

"No, of course not. This is overreacting. This state-of-emergency thing won't fly for long. People won't put up with it. He—Paulson came to see me last night, after visiting hours."

"Why? What'd he say?"

"Nothing. Small talk. But it felt wrong."

"Are you okay?"

He'd asked her that twice this week. She might get used to it. "Yeah."

He sat back against the seat and sighed. "You have to listen to that. Listen to your gut when it tells you something's wrong. My gut's screaming bloody murder about that guy. No one's going to observe a curfew."

"We still don't have proof that he's behind anything."

"Maybe you could have a look at his credit card statements, see if he's bought any scuba gear." He said it like it was a joke.

She glared. "I'd need a warrant for that."

By then, the limo had stopped near the private elevators. Michael, the chauffeur, opened their door. Warren wasn't so angry that he didn't nod a greeting at the driver. Celia pulled her bag over her shoulder as she climbed out—then Warren took it from her. She resisted an urge to grab it back.

"I can get that, you know," she said. "I'm not an invalid."

He ignored her.

They began another silent elevator ride.

I should say something, Celia thought. She really almost died this time. She should stop being angry at him.

"I'm sorry," she said softly. It was all she could think of.

"For what?" He glanced at her sidelong.

She shook her head and scuffed a shoe on the carpet, feeling like a teenager all over again. "I don't know. For everything."

"Oh. Right." Now he looked down. Was that him scuffing the toe of his Italian leather shoe? "Your testimony the other day . . . I know you took a lot of flak for it. But you did good. You held up. I thought you should know."

She stared. "Why tell me this?"

"Can't I give my daughter a compliment?"

"You never have before."

"Yes, I have."

"When?"

He didn't answer—couldn't. They hadn't had a civil conversation in years.

This clinched it, though. She couldn't accept a compliment any more than he could accept an apology.

"I'm sure I have," he said finally. "I'll ask your mother, she'll know."

The elevator opened up at the penthouse.

Suzanne came to Celia to give her a hug. She drew back to touch the bandage on her forehead. "How are you? Does it still hurt?"

"I'm fine. The doctors gave me some of the good stuff. If it gets bad I'll take a pill and sleep for a while."

"Do you want something to drink? Juice, water?"

"I'm fine, really."

Suzanne looked at her, like all she really wanted was to be able to *do* something for Celia.

Celia repressed a big sigh. "Some breakfast would be nice. I skipped the hospital food."

Suzanne greeted Warren with a kiss, and he bear-hugged her back until she laughed. He didn't ask her about any compliments he'd given Celia.

Over a meal of French toast, Celia's parents gave her the up-dates. Mentis was at City Hall, trying to see the mayor, both to speak to him on behalf of the Olympiad, and to read what he could of his mind. If Paulson really was up to something, Mentis would learn it—assuming the telepath could get close to him. Robbie was trying to find the city's other vigilantes, so they could coordinate their activities. At least she wouldn't be subject to surveillance duty anymore.

Since cultural activities and events in the near future were can-celed, they couldn't guess what the conspirators' next target would be. The Sito trial jury was still deliberating—Paulson couldn't can-cel that. It seemed as likely a target as anything. Warren and Su-zanne would stake out the courthouse, just in case something happened—and to be on hand when a verdict was reached. "I just *smell* trouble," Warren said, more than once.

"Are you sure you'll be okay alone?" Suzanne asked.

Celia nodded. "I'll call security if I need anything, or I don't feel well. You need to be out there."

An hour later, Celia had the place to herself. And she had her own work to do.

She tapped in the code and pressed her thumb to the scanner on the security panel outside the Olympiad's command room. It hummed warmly against her skin, and the door slid open.

The Olympiad's analytical mainframe was almost magical. You poured information in, and patterns emerged. Connections became clear. A mass of raw data became a conspiracy. Like her father, the computer found conspiracies everywhere.

She had gone far past tracking Sito's assets. She wanted to know what had happened at that laboratory. She had questions for the computer, starting with the dead-ends her own inquiries had led her to. First, what could possibly be done with the raw materi-als and equipment listed on the Leyden labs' requisition forms and asset reports?

Second, what had happened to the personnel? Had any of them been involved with Sito and his activities as the Destructor? Could any of them *still* be involved? If Sito was organizing events despite being in custody, and he did have a connection to the outside somehow, this might show how.

One after the other, she lay the pages on the scanner bed, and watched the information transform into glowing pixels. She went to the computer and typed in a search command. It took some doing—the database was immense. The search engine kept asking her to narrow her focus. It finally steered her into a specific category: scientific and inventions.

The search itself took hardly any time at all.

RESULT: 89% (+ or − 4% margin of error) of materials and equipment list entered matches list of materials found at the laboratory of Simon Sito (aka the Destructor) involved in the creation and testing of the machine known as the Psychostasis Device.

When Sito kidnapped her when she was sixteen, he'd tried using the machine on her. They all thought the Psychostasis Device was a new invention. But what if he'd created it fifty years ago? If the computer was right, he'd been experimenting with mental manipulation under her grandfather's sponsorship.

Then there'd been an accident. What had happened?

She scanned in the list of names from the personnel records.

The computer's search results weren't as quick or thorough this time. A few of the names still came up with blanks. The names that hit, though, hit big.

OLYMPIAD PERSONNEL FILES: CLASSIFIED. HISTORIES, NEXT OF KIN, ETC.

Jacob West, President, West Corp: son, Warren West (aka Captain Olympus)

Anna Riley, stenographer, West Corp, Leyden Industrial Park: daughter, Suzanne (Riley) West (aka Spark)

George Denton, machinist, West Corp, Leyden Industrial Park: son, Robert "Robbie" Denton (aka the Bullet)

Emily Newman, technician, West Corp, Leyden Industrial
Park: son, Arthur Mentis. (Note: Emily Newman immi-
grated to London where she met her husband, Nicholas
Mentis. Arthur Mentis came to Commerce City for medical training.)

Four out of twelve of those present at the accident had children
who were superhuman. Then what about Analise's parents? Breezeway's? Barry Quinn's? Any of the other superhumans? Their grand-
parents?

In her father's world, coincidence didn't exist. It couldn't exist.
All that remained then was finding the strands that connected
various parts of the web. One strand showed thick and obvious.

If Simon Sito fathered a child, was that child superhuman?
Was that child Paulson? If so, what could Paulson do? Or was he
like her—a dud?

"I'd have thought you'd be resting." Dr. Mentis stood in the
doorway. "You're still injured, even if you don't want to admit it."

Her face burned in a panicked flush. Quickly, she shut down
the computer file. She hadn't heard Arthur enter the room. She'd
been too wrapped up. Or he moved too quietly. Or he'd convinced
her mind that she didn't hear him. Paranoid, paranoid . . .

Either in response to his suggestion, or her own shock, a headache launched itself through her skull. The stitches on her cut
throbbed; she could feel them.

"I had a couple of things to look up." She had no reason to feel
guilty. She'd been invited here.

"What have you found?"

The source of all your power. "I'm still not sure. I've been digging
into Sito's assets for DA Bronson, but I've opened a couple cans of
worms."

"I'd have thought that would have been old news by now. We
have more urgent questions, don't you think?"

She hesitated to ponder those questions, and how the one connected to the other, when he could see those thoughts laid bare.

"I've been to see Mayor Paulson," he continued. "I came in with the crowd for his press conference this morning. I was hoping to learn what was behind all those snappy sound bites and high ideals he's always spouting off about. Do you know what I found?"

"What?"

He started pacing a long, slow circuit around the room. "Nothing. I found absolutely nothing at all. His mind was blank to me. I couldn't read him."

Just like the Destructor. Like Sito. She now recognized the tension in Arthur's frame—he was afraid. That knowledge tingled across her skin. Dr. Mentis was never afraid. He was never anything.

"Oh my God."

"You know what it means, don't you? You've suspected it for some time."

"I'd rather not talk about it. I still don't know anything for sure."

"That's a bit disingenuous. You know plenty, but you're not saying what."

She wouldn't fall into that trap. She wouldn't say a damn word.

He didn't stop walking. "Celia, what are you trying to hide?"

Nothing, she wanted to say, but didn't. She wondered why she didn't just say it, knowing Arthur could read the thought behind her eyes. *My grandfather and Simon Sito worked together to create superhuman mutations.*

"I'm not trying to hide anything. I just—I just want to be sure before I say it."

"I'm worried."

The fact that he'd admit to an emotion of any kind shook her. "There's a lot to worry about."

"I'm worried about *you*. You worked so hard to get yourself away from all this, and here you are, back in the middle. And you put yourself here. I hope you're not trying to prove something."

And she knew. The thought was simply there, and it wasn't hers. *You are more important to me than anything.*

"So what if I am?" she said, her voice cracking. "You don't have to ask any questions. You just know."

"I try to be polite."

He always said that. But this didn't feel like politeness. It wasn't enough for him to read the answer in her thoughts, he wanted her to say it. This inspired in her a contrary desire to push him. What would she have to say, how mean would she have to be, before he reacted? That was the teenager again, the angry girl Celia had never quite escaped. She shouldn't be like that, not with him. There was a time he'd been her only friend.

"Maybe I'd like to try and keep a few secrets. I don't have much of anything else."

Mentis stopped pacing and laughed softly, as sinister an expression as she'd heard from any criminal. "There are no secrets around me."

"Only the ones *you* keep." *Like the feelings you have for me*— "Why can't you just say it out loud?"

He murmured, "Why can't you, Celia?"

All she had to do was say it. *I love you, too.* But her mouth went dry and the words stuck.

His emotions were palpable. His mind expanded to take in what lay around it, and the people around him felt the impact of it. She could feel him—she wanted to run to him, throw herself at him, pull his arms around her, hold him.

Or was that what he was thinking about her?

She turned away as her tears fell, and covered her mouth to keep the sob from breaking free. Why couldn't she just say the words?

Arthur shoved his hands in his pockets and, shoulders hunched and face returned to its imperturbable mask, left the room.

TWENTY-THREE

HOWEVER much she wanted to, she didn't take one of her pre-scribed painkillers. She needed to be awake. She had work to do. It was a good excuse to distract her from Arthur. So she took a couple of plain aspirin and parked at the kitchen table with a cup of coffee and her cell phone.

"I'd like to speak to the District Attorney, please."

"I'm sorry, he's in a meeting right now, I can take your number and—"

"Tell him it's Celia West."

The woman paused; the click and rustle of office background noise sounded over the line. Then, "Could you hold for a moment?"

As Celia had hoped, her name did hold some weight . . . although what kind of weight remained to be seen, especially now. After the bus incident she'd hoped to have some currency to cash in.

The receptionist came back on the line. "I'm transferring you to his office now."

"Thank you," Celia said, suppressing a sigh of relief.

He came on the line and didn't bother with a greeting. "Celia. You left the hospital before I could check in with you. You're okay? I mean, clearly you're okay."

"A concussion, some cuts and bruises. I'm okay."

"You're a hero, you know."

She might go so far as to claim to be a good citizen. "Does that mean I can ask for a favor?"

Bronson's tone became more guarded. He should have known she had a reason for calling. "That depends on the favor. What do you need?"

Deep breath, and plow on through like this wasn't odd. "I need access to the Department of Vital Statistic's sealed records."

"Why?"

Here she was, thinking this would be easy. "I'm following up a lead on the Sito case. I've got some of that asset information you were looking for."

"Smith and Kurchanski gave you your job back, then?"

She was still waiting for *that* phone call. "Actually, I'm thinking of going into business for myself."

"You've been doing this on your own time, probably throwing my name around like you're still on the case."

"I haven't done anything illegal." Yet . . . much . . .

"And you figured out where Sito's original trust fund came from?"

Give a little to get a little. This was public record, it was just that no one had bothered digging this deep for it before. "It came from a disability settlement he got from West Corp, which he was working for at the time. I didn't need a warrant to get those records. I just asked my dad."

He whistled low. "That's a pretty tangled web. Your dad knows about this?"

"Yes. At least he knows Sito worked for West Corp. I don't think he knows the settlement possibly funded everything Sito did later, as the Destructor."

"Brilliant. And now you want into Vital Statistics. What are you looking for?"

This part, she wasn't sure she wanted to get out. It had the potential of opening an even bigger can of worms than the West Corp connection. "I'd rather not say until I figure out if what I'm looking for is even there."

"And you want me to get you a court order. I can't do that unless you tell me what you want to look at."

"Couldn't you just . . . let me into the records office? Give me a key and no one would ever have to know I'd been there."

"That's crazy. I can't let you do that."

"I didn't say it was an easy favor."

"You think being a hero gives you carte blanche? You think you can run all over town bending all the rules, like your parents and their pals?"

"I'm not anything like my parents."

"I hate to break it to you, but we all turn into our parents."

That pronouncement held a tone of finality that Celia didn't much like.

She said, "And if I could fly or shoot lasers out of my eyes, that might be true for me. This could be important, this could be nothing. I just need a half hour in the records office, no questions asked."

She had other ideas, like developing an ill-advised scheme to break into the office, or forge a court order—that was how badly she wanted this.

She honestly didn't expect Bronson to say, "Can you be at City Hall in an hour?"

"I'll be there."

She asked Michael to drive her in a West Corp sedan, to save time. He seemed happy to do so—like he was pleased that she was finally taking advantage of her birthright. She saw it as giving up freedom; maybe not so much giving up as trading.

Dressed in a skirt and jacket, looking as official as possible with a bandaged forehead, Celia consulted City Hall's building directory and took the elevator to the basement. There, plastic signs with arrows directed her to her destination. She pushed open the door with frosted glass marked with black lettering: VITAL STATISTICS.

The Department of Vital Statistics occupied a corner of the basement of City Hall. The records themselves were processed in any number of departments and offices in the more accessible regions of the building and city government: marriage certificates, birth certificates, divorce settlements, death certificates. Once finalized, they came to live here, in the depths. Most would never see the light of day again.

She entered yet another room with stark fluorescent lighting filled with rows and rows of filing cabinets, shelves with banker's boxes, and file folders, smelling of ripe dust and old paper. It felt like her element. She was at home here and knew what she was looking for.

Before she could get to the files, she had to pass through a reception area and set of desks. Four people worked here, it looked like; there were four desks with nameplates and the usual family photos, sickly houseplants, and odd figurines and detritus that usually occupied office workspaces. The farthest one over stood in front of a closed door labeled with a sign: RESTRICTED. The sealed records section.

No one was here. On the first desk, the receptionist's desk, one of those signs printed with a clock and moveable plastic hands read: OUT TO LUNCH, BACK AT 1:30. She had half an hour. She went to the restricted door and tried the knob—unlocked.

She owed Bronson big time for this.

Inside the room, she turned on the light. Here, folders crammed the shelves. This was a smaller collection than the main part of the department, but still daunting. And old. Dust covered most of the files, and she could mark the difference between various styles and materials used in file folders over the years.

She went to the shelves marked "Adoption Records," then went to the shelves labeled "P."

When the court finalized an adoption, it issued a new birth certificate with the adoptive parents' names in the appropriate boxes. But the original certificate completed at the child's birth remained on file. Anthony Paulson's birth certificate, and independent verification of the identity of his birth parents, should be here.

She muttered, "P . . . p . . . Paneski . . . Parker . . . Pastern . . . Paulson."

There it was, a stiff and aged folder, fifty years old. She opened it; the paper was slick under her fingers. Faded pink cover sheets announced that the material within was sealed by court order, access restricted.

She started searching. They were right on top, the amended birth certificate showing that Anthony Paulson's parents were Claire and Richard Paulson, and under it a birth certificate stamped "Original." Baby Anthony. Father—unknown. The space was left blank. Mother—

Janet Travers. One of the Leyden laboratory technicians.

Celia had ten more minutes. She rushed—calmly, being sure to breathe—back to the front office to make a photocopy, quickly folded it into a pocket, and returned the original to the file, and the file to the shelf. She couldn't think of any way to replace the half-century layer of dust over it. She had to hope it would be another half century before anyone came looking for the file again.

She didn't leave the room. She had a few more minutes left, and a nagging curiosity. The set of shelves in the back labeled "Juvenile" beckoned. Her practiced gaze scanned quickly—and found "West, Celia," stamped "Sealed" in bold letters like all the others.

The file was mercifully thin. One indiscretion. That was all it took.

She slipped the folder into her attaché case and strode out of the room, double-checking to see that the door locked behind her. In the hallway leading to the elevators, she passed a trio of laughing, gossiping women. Celia flashed them a smile and they didn't give her a second glance.

Once the elevator started up, carrying her back to the ground and light, Celia leaned on the wall and sighed. Never mind what she'd discovered about Anthony Paulson. The file she'd stolen burned red-hot where it lay in her case, pressed against her thigh.

She hadn't stolen it; it was *hers*.

Too much to do, but this trumped everything. Back in the company sedan, she told Michael she had to pick up some things at home—her own apartment. She asked him to wait in the car for her. Fifteen minutes, that was all she needed. Inside her apartment, she locked the door, took the battery out of the smoke alarm, and found some matches.

Manic, wide-eyed, breathing too hard, she stood over the kitchen sink, the folder in her hands. Inside she read the pages: the arrest record, fingerprints, the facing and profile mug shots of a sullen teenager with shoulder-length, too-teased red hair, eyeliner blacking her eyes, and the strap of a camisole hanging off her shoulder. God, she looked awful. Mug shots always looked terrible, but this one seemed to draw out the ugliness that had lived inside that girl—a sort of disheveled fatalism. Appleton had arrested her at West Plaza the morning after the incident, threatening her with charges of conspiracy, intent to commit mayhem, and the like. Ultimately not charged, not tried. Released into the custody of Warren and Suzanne West, who promised that this sort of thing wouldn't happen again. As if they'd had the authority to make that promise.

Celia lit a match.

It didn't mean anything. People already knew. Just because the physical file didn't exist anymore, wouldn't make their knowledge disappear.

But this wasn't for other people, this was for her. This was an exorcism.

She touched the match to all four corners of the open folder, then touched it to as many places in the middle as she could before the flame burned to her fingers. She dropped the whole mess into the sink. The crisp, eight-years' aged paper crackled, blackened, and flames swelled over it. The photograph curled and melted.

She opened the windows, turned on a fan. The smoke poured up, black and sour. It flowed out the window above the sink, dissipated, and melted into the sky.

Let it go. Let it all blow away.

TWENTY-FOUR

THE city had become as taut as a drawn bow string, quivering, more than ready for release. People hurried on the streets, waiting for bombs to explode or runaway buses to turn the next corner. Restaurants shut down, no one was shopping. People seemed content to stay indoors, watching TV, waiting for the next big attack.

She couldn't help but think that all these petty little crimes and attacks were merely means to an end, to hold the city in thrall to terror. And here they were. Even the Destructor had never been so calculating.

It was quick work with a phone book and Internet connection to find the location of Janet Travers, the point where the two threads of inquiry Celia had been following matched up.

Travers had an apartment at an assisted living community in a quiet, middle-class neighborhood at the edge of town, the kind with wide, tree-lined streets and signs that warned of children playing. The retirement community had a brick, neocolonial apartment building and scattered bungalows, all enclosed within walled gardens, isolated, quiet and pretty.

Celia signed in with the receptionist. "Let me call up to her room and see if she's taking visitors. Celia, you said?"

"Yes. She won't know me, but it's very important I see her. I have news about her son."

"I didn't know she had a son," the receptionist said as she dialed a number on her phone.

Celia smiled innocently.

The receptionist spoke on the phone for several moments, passing along the message. Celia was sure that Janet would refuse to talk to her.

Then the receptionist covered the mouthpiece with her hand. "Would it be all right if she met you in the atrium?"

"Yes, of course, that'd be fine."

"She'll be down in a few minutes. You can wait for her, it's just at the end of the hallway."

Celia made her way to the atrium. The large glass room was filled with patio furniture, wicker tables, and chairs with big soft cushions. Potted trees and vines flourished, and birdsong chirped here and there. Celia suspected it was a recording. A few people played cards at a table across the way.

She waited long enough to think that Janet had changed her mind. A woman arrived then, her expression taut, frowning. She scanned the room until her gaze found Celia, who was out of place here. Celia smiled in what she hoped was an encouraging manner.

The woman's shoulders were slightly stooped, but she managed to hold herself elegantly, her chin up. Her hair was short, permed, perfectly arranged, and she wore a fashionable blouse and trousers with confidence. She'd have looked at home anywhere. Whatever had happened to this woman in her life, she'd held on to her dignity.

Celia went to her and offered her hand. "Ms. Travers? I'm Celia West. Thank you for meeting with me."

Janet didn't shake her hand. "What do you want with me?"

Celia hadn't expected this to be easy. "I just want to ask a few questions. I don't want to cause any trouble, but I've got a mystery that I really need help solving, and you may be the one to do it."

"Then why bring up a son? Because I don't know anything about that."

Wincing, Celia said, "Can we sit down?" She gestured to a se-cluded set of wicker chairs. Reluctantly, Janet joined her there.

"I originally found your name on a payroll report for West Corp. You worked at the Leyden Industrial Park building. The laboratory there was shut down after an accident. I want to know what happened."

"That was a long time ago."

"Yes. But you must remember something. Simon Sito worked there—"

"I don't want to hear anything about him."

"I know this must be difficult."

"Do you? Then tell me why you mentioned a son. I wouldn't have agreed to talk with you if you hadn't."

She wondered if the old woman realized who Celia was.

"I know who the father was. I assure you, I learned by accident. It's a long story, but I only uncovered the adoption records after I had suspicions."

The tension in Janet's face seemed to melt, as if now that the secret was out, she could stop working so hard to hide it. As if she knew this moment had always been inevitable, but not as terri-ble as she'd envisioned. She rubbed her face with a bony, trembling hand.

"I should have ended the pregnancy," Janet said. "I saw what he turned into, and I just kept thinking how I let his genes loose in the world. That evil—" Celia didn't even have to say the name. Janet knew who she was talking about.

"Did he start out evil? Was he always like he is now? You must have seen something in him, back then."

"No, no. He was . . . it was a long time ago. My memory of him is colored, I'm sure. But he was driven, and I admired him."

A lost love? A quick fling? Celia couldn't guess what they'd been to each other.

"Ms. Travers, I'm not here about your son, or Sito, or your rela-tionship with him. I learned about all that by accident. But you wouldn't talk to me when I called you a few days ago. I'm sorry if I tricked you into talking with me, but I'm running out of leads. What I really want to know is what was going on at the Leyden laboratory. Anything you can remember, no matter how insignificant, would be helpful. I'd appreciate it."

The woman gathered herself, pursing her lips and straightening as much as she could. Her hands lay in her lap, clenched around each other.

"That day, the day of the accident, was the first major test of the equipment."

"Equipment? What kind of equipment?"

Janet shook her head. "The project involved using radiation as a treatment for mental illness. A generator was supposed to create a specific kind of radiation. I'm afraid I don't know any more than that. I was a technician; I prepared tissue samples and microscope slides, that was all.

"The equipment . . . burst, I think. It overheated, or a power surge overloaded it. I don't think anyone ever learned what exactly happened. It was very embarrassing for Dr. Sito, because Mr. West was there observing—"

"Mr. West. Jacob West?"

"Yes— Wait a moment. Celia West. Are you related to him?"

"He was my grandfather," Celia said. She could see the light of recognition in Janet's eyes. Oh, *that* Celia West. Janet must not have recognized her instantly because she didn't watch the news. Probably got out of the habit when the Destructor was featured regularly. As reminders of ex-boyfriends went, that had to have been bad. "Please, go on."

"West Corp financed the whole thing. The only thing worse than failure is failure in front of your investors. But Sito insisted on showing off the experiment. At any rate, instead of focusing the energy in a beam that could be directed at specific targets—such as parts of the brain, for therapy—the entire room got a dose of the radiation. Now, the dose was weak. It was designed to be safe for use on people, of course. I don't think anyone was hurt by it. But Mr. West shut down the project and gave everyone who was there quite generous severance payments. He decided the research was too radical to continue safely. Dr. Sito never recovered from the disappointment.

"He . . . he came to me that night. Drunk out of his mind, despairing. He needed comfort. I suppose I felt sorry for him. That was the night I conceived. By the time I learned I was pregnant, Sito had been institutionalized. I couldn't keep the baby, then. I couldn't raise it alone, with the father in an asylum—" She looked at her hands and flattened them on her legs in an effort to stop wringing them. The tendons stood out.

"I never saw Simon again," she said. "At least, not in person. When he started making the news years later, I didn't recognize him. I've avoided hearing anything about him. I must be the only person in Commerce City not following his trial."

"He doesn't know that he has a child," Celia said. Janet shook her head. "You could probably sell your story to one of the tabloids for a lot of money." She was mostly joking.

"I could," Janet said, her smile thin and bitter. "But can you imagine if the child—*my* child—learned the truth about his parents? If he's still out there—I can't imagine how it would feel, to learn that your father was someone like that."

Maybe a little like having Captain Olympus as a father. It would be different, of course, having a hero to look up to rather than a villain to despise. But somehow, it would also be the same.

How was she going to tell all this to Mark?

"Ms. Travers—I know who your son is. I've met him. Would you like to hear about him?" *He's the mayor, and you have a valiant grandson who's a police detective*—her genes had done pretty well for themselves.

She looked back, stricken. The *yes* sat on the verge of trembling lips. Celia regretted this whole trip. She hadn't wanted to make an old woman cry.

Abruptly, Janet shook her head. "I put that behind me years ago. I've kept it secret for a very long time. If I heard about him, I would want to meet him. I'd want to know if I'm a grandmother, then I might want to *be* a grandmother. No, I don't want to hear any more about it."

"Then I'll leave you alone. Thank you very much for speaking with me." This time when she offered her hand, Janet shook it, lightly, fleetingly.

"You won't tell anyone about me, will you? You'll keep my secret?"

The photocopy of the birth certificate burned in her pocket. No one else had seen it. No one else had to. She'd get rid of it. "I'll keep your secret. Thank you again."

She had one last exorcism to attempt.

Elroy Asylum was one of the places people ended up when they couldn't afford institutions like Greenbriar. Industrial and sadly out of date, the four-story cinder-block monolith had a functional sterility that made it hard not to feel a little sorry for its inhabitants. Except that one wing of the hospital was dedicated to criminals. Technically not criminal, she supposed—they'd been deemed insane. Technically, every one of them stood a chance of being cured and set loose in the world.

But some of them, Celia believed, were simply evil. If evil was a form of insanity, so be it. But those people didn't want to be cured. Knowing what she knew now, she wasn't sure whether Sito was sick or evil. She didn't know if he wanted to be cured.

She only knew she never wanted to see him back in the world of the living.

Scuffed linoleum floor and fluorescent lighting were the prominent features of the asylum's reception area. A man in the white uniform of an orderly occupied the desk and seemed deeply involved in sorting a stack of folders. Celia loomed politely until he looked up.

"Hi, I wondered if it would be possible to visit a patient." She smiled hopefully.

"That depends on the patient's status; let me check that for you. Who do you want to see?"

Deep breath. "Simon Sito."

He stared at her. Her smile froze. All right, so this was rather odd. All she needed now was for him to recognize who she was, and he'd be on the phone to the police.

"I'm sorry, that won't be possible," the receptionist said. "He's under strict security protocols. No visitors."

"No exceptions?"

"I'm afraid not." He couldn't have been any older than she was, but he had the authority of the uniform. She couldn't stare him down.

She didn't have a warrant from the DA. She didn't have permission. She didn't have a reason for being here, except to satisfy her own curiosity.

"What if I said it's really important and the fate of the city could rest on whether or not I see him?"

The guy chuckled. "Fate of the city? Who do you think you are? Captain Olympus?"

That didn't even merit a response. "Well, then. Thanks for your time."

She took a quick look around. The reception area had two doors. The one behind the desk had a security card scanner. Presumably, it was locked. A door to the left had a regular-looking handle.

She turned back to the orderly. "Do you have a public restroom?"

He nodded at the left-hand door. "Through there, third door on the right."

"Thank you."

She was in. Now, she just had to make her way through the maze to the secure section. She tried every door, hoping she'd stumble upon a forgotten back entrance that didn't require a key card. Instead, she found classrooms, offices, the bathroom, and a janitor's closet. She snooped for spare key cards lying around. No luck. But in one classroom, she found an open window looking out on an inner courtyard, hemmed in by tall gray walls. And across the courtyard was another open window.

The windows were aluminum framed, the old-fashioned kind

that swiveled inward, leaving a gap at the top. Thank God she was thin. She stood on the inside sill, stepped through the opening to the outside sill, held her breath, and slid. These kinds of windows were designed to keep elementary-school children from escaping their classrooms. It was definitely a tight fit. Her shirt scooted up; she tried to hold it in place, but she had to hold her arms up to give her torso enough room to slip through. After a bit of contorting, she let her feet drop to the ground and slid the rest of the way through the window.

She stood on a narrow strip of lawn and tugged her clothes back into place.

A couple of people in bathrobes were staring at her.

A young, thin man sat on a park bench near a security-locked doorway. The other, an older man, had presumably been walking a circuit around the courtyard. He'd stopped and, like the young man, watched her, his mouth open. Patients, presumably. The low-risk kind, out for some fresh air.

This could be interesting.

She ignored them and hoped for the best, striding across the lawn like she belonged there, reaching the next open window, and hoisting herself onto the sill. Reversing the process, poking her head in through the window, she squirmed her way into the next room. Her witnesses didn't say a word.

Once again, she straightened her clothes. This new room was a lab, long and narrow, with a workbench holding lots of micro-scopes and other equipment running along one side of it, cabinets and refrigerators on the other side. Fortunately, the place wasn't currently in use. She didn't know how long that would last, though.

She paused long enough to consult a fire-escape floor plan on the back of the door. It even had a helpful YOU ARE HERE star. A label marked the high-security section.

She borrowed a white lab coat off the back of a chair and a clip-board and pen off a desk.

The high-security section had an on-duty guard at a desk station. He monitored the wing via a half-dozen televisions connected to

closed-circuit cameras, which flipped between scenes inside patients'
rooms. The patients showed the whole range of reactions to their
institutionalization: some seemed entirely normal; some huddled
in corners, catatonic; others ranted, screaming at the security cameras, their voices unheard; some paced; one, wearing a safety hel-
met, banged his head against a padded wall, over and over and over
again. Celia didn't recognize Sito among them.

"Can I help you?" the guard asked.

Celia hoped she could brazen this through. "I'm here to check
on Simon Sito for Doctor Steinberg." She remembered the supervising doctor's name from the trial.

Inhale normally, no holding her breath, no sweating.

The guard held a clipboard out to her. "Sign in here." He pointed
to a line with boxes marked DATE, TIME, and NAME. She filled
them out, signed *Celia West*, and handed it back.

The guard didn't even look at the name.

"He's in four-eighty. Six doors down." He pressed a button and
the lock on the door clicked open.

"Thank you."

The corridor beyond the secure door echoed with her footsteps.
The rooms were soundproofed. She didn't hear anything from inside them, no screams, no insane muttering. But she heard something muffled and distant that might have been human voices in
torment. Or she imagined she heard it.

She reached 480. Sito's name was handwritten on a dry-erase
nameplate under a small, round window.

Simon Sito was on suicide watch. His room was small, square,
padded. There were no furnishings, no objects, nothing that could
be picked up, thrown, or manipulated. He wore a T-shirt and sweatpants, and went barefoot. He sat cross-legged in a corner, his hands
resting loosely in his lap, staring straight ahead at nothing. He'd
always been small, but now he seemed shriveled, like he hadn't been
eating. His hair seemed translucent.

She pressed a black intercom button under the speaker by the
door. Close to the intercom's grill, she said, "Dr. Sito?"

"Who is it?"

"It's Celia West."

Sito looked over at the less than face-size window and a faint smile dawned.

"You are constantly drawn to me, aren't you? Like a moth to a flame. I should be flattered."

She waited for a flush of anger, for the defensive stiffening of her back. For the feeling that she was sixteen years old again, and nothing would change. None of that happened. Her skin felt cool. She was on a mission.

She said, "I need to know about the experiment you were running at the Leyden Industrial Park fifty years ago."

He tsked her, shaking his head. "That part of my life is muddled, you know. The psychiatrists did a wonderful job of wiping me clean. *Tabula rasa.*"

"I don't believe that."

"Then I can't help you. You'll believe what you believe."

"I think I know what you and my grandfather were trying to do. I'm only here looking for confirmation. The technical reports from the lab have disappeared. All I know is who was in that room and what happened to them after. Did you ever check up on what happened to them?"

"I told you, that part of my life is murky." He glared at a spot below the window. He wouldn't meet her gaze, though she was desperate to see some sort of recognition in his eyes. Some sort of shock. Any expression at all beside that intense deliberation.

"Most of them had children. Jacob had a son, Warren. Anna Riley had a daughter, Suzanne. Robbie Denton's father was the machinist who helped build the generator. One of your techs moved to England and married a man by the name of Nicholas Mentis. Their son was Arthur. Are you noticing a pattern here? I'm not finished researching the lab personnel, but I bet I could discover a few of the secret identities of Commerce City's heroes by tracing those family trees.

"You and my grandfather were trying to create superhumans,

weren't you? You were trying to induce the physiological anomalies that lead to those powers. When your generator malfunctioned, you dosed everyone in that room. Their genes carried the anomaly to their children and their grandchildren."

He licked his lips, but didn't twitch a muscle otherwise. He might have been frozen in that spot for days. "If you're right, the mutation skips generations, I can't help but notice. *You* probably can't help but notice."

"Yes, as a matter of fact. Not everyone in that room developed a power. Not all their children or grandchildren developed powers. But many did."

Sito's cold gaze struck her hard. She remembered it, searching her, stripping her without him ever laying a hand on her. He'd kidnapped her, strapped her down, would have used his machine—based on that old research—to peel away her mind. He could do it here, just by looking at her.

She refused to flinch.

He stood in a movement so quick it shocked her. She quelled an impulse to step back.

"You're wrong. We weren't trying to create superhumans. I never *tried* to create anything. Anything I created—it was a side effect. Unintended. I should have followed up. Your grandfather might have continued my funding. *That* would be a project worth pursuing: a machine to create superhumans. Or—supervillains?"

He paced, his hands fidgeting, typing on air. She hadn't thought of him as ill until now.

"Why are you here asking these questions?" he said. "Why not your father or that telepath of his?"

She said, "They're busy."

"Is that the reason, or are you afraid dear old Warren won't listen to you?"

"He'll listen to me."

"Like he always did before? I wonder, if I'd had the chance, would I have made a better father than Captain Olympus?"

He continued. "You've had such a terribly hard life, poor little rich Celia West. I read the papers, you know. I saw what happened to you after your testimony. And they think I can't destroy anything from in here. Your life is a tiny little thing to ruin, but it's so wonderful because I can keep ruining it over and over again."

He was on the other side of a locked door. He couldn't hurt her. He was a pitiful old man, taunting her as if they were children in the schoolyard. That was what he was reduced to—childish taunts. She almost smiled.

"Poor little Celia. No one has ever had any faith in you, have they? No one trusts you, no one is proud of you—"

That wasn't true. One person had always had faith in her. One person had stood by her, even at her lowest. She hadn't had the wits to accept that trust.

"Good-bye, Mr. Sito," she said, and turned away.

"I'm not finished!" He pressed himself to the door now, shouting at the window. "I still have plans for you. You have a boyfriend, don't you? The mayor's son. I'll have a go at him next! You'll see! I can still hurt you!"

I could tell him, she thought. *I could tell him everything, about his son, his grandson.* But she didn't.

His voice faded as Celia walked away.

F our years ago, she emerged from the cave where she'd retreated to heal. She celebrated with a graduation. The diplomas were all handed out, tassels turned, and the band played. It was very nearly the happiest day of Celia West's life.

Even if Mom and Dad hadn't come to the ceremony, it would still be the happiest day of her life.

She waited alone by the last row of chairs, thinking they had to see her there, they would come and find her. She had to remind herself that it didn't matter, before that sinking feeling took hold of her chest.

She'd sent her parents a graduation announcement and instantly regretted it. She didn't know what she dreaded more: their showing up and her having to face them, or their not showing up and her admitting her disappointment at them for not showing up. She should have left town. She should have changed her name. They wouldn't want to see her again, not after she'd ignored them for the last four years.

She saw Dr. Mentis first. He wore a trench coat even in the warm spring weather, open to show his tailored suit. He'd finished medical school and set up a psychiatry practice while she was in her cocoon, as she thought of it. He'd called her once, in the middle of her sophomore year, just wanting to see how she was doing, and she'd managed to be polite. That she could be polite to Arthur was how she'd known she was getting better, and that maybe she'd be okay. Halfway through her junior year, she'd called him, to let him know she was doing okay. He'd said he was glad, and didn't ask her to come home, didn't put any pressure on her. Just said he was glad.

Now, he caught her gaze and smiled a wry half smile, as much as he ever smiled, which meant he was as happy to be here as he was ever happy about anything. Her own smile broke wide and unbidden.

Beside him walked Robbie Denton, his wind-burned face grinning. And beside him, arm in arm, walked her parents.

Oh God, they were all here. They'd all made it.

She couldn't help it. As soon as they were within reach, she lunged forward and hugged her mother.

"Thank you, thank you for coming."

"We wouldn't have missed it. Oh, Celia, we're so proud of you."

Warren pressed his lips into something that tried to look like a smile. Awkwardly, he patted her shoulder. She repressed a wince.

"Yeah," he said, his voice muted. "You almost didn't make it this far. I'm glad you did."

It was as much an admission of approval as she was likely to get from him. He made no move to embrace her.

Suzanne kept her arm around her. "Come on, let's go get some lunch."

Robbie tousled her hair like he'd been doing since she was a kid. For a long stretch of time during her teenage years, it had annoyed her into screaming fits, which made Robbie tease her more. But now she laughed.

Arthur Mentis offered his hand. She shook it calmly.

He said, "I always knew you'd turn out all right."

Which nearly made her cry.

When she emerged back into the asylum lobby, the orderly was talking on the phone. He glanced at her, his gaze dark and suspicious.

"Never mind, she's back," he said, and hung up.

Celia didn't wait around for explanations, either his or hers. She flashed him a smile and strolled back into the street.

Michael, bless him, was still waiting with the car. She piled into the front seat.

"Now you're going to say you don't want me telling your parents you were here," he said, starting the engine and preparing to pull into traffic.

"That would just worry them, don't you think?"

"Just tell me you know what you're doing."

She hesitated, which made him glare at her.

"Sure," she said. What the hell? "I know what I'm doing."

"I suppose you're at least making your own trouble now instead of getting wrapped up in somebody else's." That was a kind observation. "We're going back to the Plaza now, right?"

"Yes. Thank you, Michael."

TWENTY-FIVE

THE penthouse was still deserted. "Mom? Dad?" she called out. No answer. They'd been gone all day. The gauze bandage covering her stitches itched, and she felt a raw, gnawing anxiety.

She went to the Olympiad command room. There, she found Robbie—the Bullet, actually, in uniform sans mask—at the communications station, listening to police radio.

"Hey! I thought you'd be in bed asleep," he said.

"I had work to do." He gave her a reprimanding glance. If he offered her hot cocoa, so help her God— "Where is everyone?"

"Your dad's at the courthouse. The jury's taking forever, which has the good Captain worried. Spark's trying to meet with the police chief about coordinating some kind of patrol for the city tonight, but I don't think she's having any luck."

"How's it look out there?"

He shook his head. "It's like the whole city's holding its breath. Something's going to happen but no one knows what. Only thing on the radio is car accidents—people are twitchy, rear-ending each other. I can't find the independent supers; they've all gone to ground, I think. Waiting."

"Has Dr. Mentis been back?"

Robbie shook his head. "Haven't seen him all day. Why?"

"He—" She shook her head. She was worried. She needed to see him. Robbie didn't need to know all that.

"I'd love to know what he found out about Mayor Paulson."

She just bet he would. Arthur ought to be here, and her stomach flipped a little. The Olympiad was in action, and he'd disappeared.

"Have you called his office?" she said.

"If he's there, he's not answering."

"That's not like him."

"Hey, if he's in trouble, he'll find a way to let us know."

He'd speak to their minds across the distance. For his closest friends, space wasn't a barrier for the connection.

Would there come a time when he refused to ask for help?

"I'll see you later," she said, turning to leave.

"You're not going out, are you? I don't think your folks—"

"I won't leave the building, I promise."

"Celia, you're still hurt. You look like you're about to pass out."

"I'm fine. I've got my cell phone. I'll call you if I need help, I promise."

She left before he could say anything else.

She rode the elevator down to the eighteenth floor.

In the heart of the building, the office spaces were efficient and elegant. Gray berber carpeting led down hallways with recessed lighting. Silk plants in brass stands decorated corners. The Plaza hired staff just to keep those plants dusted. Accounting firms, law firms, investment firms, insurance companies—all had offices here, marked by frosted glass fronts with their names painted in neat black letters. Originally, Celia's chief interest in working for Smith and Kurchanski had been that their offices weren't located in West Plaza.

Dr. Arthur Mentis's office was marked only by a brass nameplate on a wood-stained door at the end of a hallway. Not a prime location, but he didn't need much space. He wanted to work here so he'd be close to the Olympiad's headquarters. And Warren gave him the place rent-free.

She knocked.

"Arthur? Are you here? Can I come in?" She knocked again. And again. If something had happened to him, she'd have felt it. She knew she would have.

In much the same way, something told her that he had to be here. "It's Celia. Will you let me in? Arthur!"

At that, the door opened. He might have been waiting just on the other side, debating about whether or not to open it.

She could see why there might be a debate. He looked awful. Face frowning, hair ruffled, he wore his shirt unbuttoned, baring the undershirt. He leaned on the open door and the frame, holding a bottle of scotch. He didn't smell of alcohol; he only looked drunk. The bottle was full and unopened. He was showing some kind of emotion—which one, she couldn't guess.

"You shouldn't be here," he said.

"I was worried about you."

"You shouldn't worry about me."

"Can I come in?"

He stepped aside and swung the door open. When he wandered away, she closed it.

His office suite had two rooms. The front was a calculated, elegant public face, with a soft leather sofa, antique desk, bookshelves, and inoffensive Impressionist artwork on the walls. The back door of this room was open, leading to an inner office. Curious, she walked back there. She expected him to stop her or to intercept her; this felt like an invasion. But he didn't. He kept his back to her.

The back room might have been an office once. There was a desk, some shelves filled with books, a filing cabinet. Now, a pile of clothes lay on the surface of the desk, shirts and trousers waiting to be washed. A foldaway cot, sheets and blankets mussed, sat in a corner. A minifridge with a hot plate and electric kettle sitting on top of it occupied another corner. It looked like a dorm room.

Also on the desk, a half-dozen empty orange prescription bottles clustered together.

"You've been living here," she said.

"Why not? I spend most of my time here. It got so it seemed a waste to go anywhere else."

"It . . . it doesn't seem right, not for you. Not—" Not for someone she admired, looked up to. He'd always seemed so put together. Even she'd managed to build a life for herself. But him?

He was leaning on the door frame, watching her study the odd scraps of his life. He stared at her. He could see it all. All her thoughts were written across her face.

She pointed at the scotch. "Are you going to share that?"

"You can have the whole thing. I got drunk once. Years ago. Pulled everybody in the house with me. First year at university, there were five of us living in a flat in London. They all had hallucinations, screaming fits, and massive hangovers. Even the ones used to drinking a dozen pints in an evening. And it wasn't even that they had hangovers, but their minds convinced them they had. *My* mind convinced them they had. I haven't had a drink since. Can't bring myself to do it now—I really don't know what you see in the stuff. I'd probably tear the whole building down. I've never lost control since that time. I've never done much of anything."

She came to lean on the wall next to him. She took the bottle away, pulled out the cap, and took a swig. Rolled the liquid over her tongue before swallowing. Not the best, but it burned going down, and that was what mattered. It even dulled her headache. She set the bottle down on the desk.

"Mom and Dad think you have a life," she said. "They think you have a psychiatry practice, a home to go to. Hobbies. But you come here, pop a few sleeping pills, and that's it, isn't it?"

"Celia, why are you here?" he said tiredly.

She caught his gaze and invited him to look at the scenes playing behind her eyes. She studied his expression, looking for that flicker of change, hoping to see something in him that might reflect his thoughts. He was too used to keeping that mask on.

But he brought his hand up and traced the line of her jaw. Then the hand dropped, and so did his gaze.

She took his face in her hands, pressing his cheeks, not forcing him to look at her, but drawing herself close to him. She spoke in his ear, so he could hear the words as well as feel her thoughts.

"You are the only person who has never been disappointed in me. It hurts me to see you unhappy."

He gripped her arms. "Celia, you don't understand. I cannot be in love with you. The way I am, it would hurt you, and I refuse to do that, I cannot—"

And she could feel it, the tendrils of his emotions reaching for her, winding themselves around her, binding them together. Like the drunken stupor he shared with his housemates, his emotions, even love, rippled out from him and did damage.

He straightened, pulling away from her. "You see," he said, struggling to keep his voice steady. "I never know if my feelings are returned, or if they're merely my own feelings reflected back at me."

"Arthur. I came here because I wanted to. Because I love you."

In so many ways, so many times, she'd held his example before herself as a model, a way of being to aspire to. But now, she had to make the first move. She had to go to him, and *he* the example. She put one hand in his and squeezed; with the other hand she touched his cheek to turn his face toward her. She was just tall enough to reach for him, draw him toward her, and kiss his lips. Just once, softly, so she could feel his breath on her. His eyes were squeezed shut, bracing.

"You won't hurt me," she whispered. "You've been inside my mind a hundred times. If you weren't with me in mind as well as in body—it wouldn't feel right. Not with you."

His arms closed around her.

She felt his relief wash over her and gave it back to him as bliss.

She was in a dark room, and people were beating her. She couldn't see them, but knew they were there, and couldn't escape. They must have had a thousand hands and feet, punching her, kicking her. Somehow, she knew she ought to be able to make them stop just by thinking it, but her mind wasn't working, her power wasn't—she smelled sage.

She was having his dream.

Just as she was going to shake him awake, he opened his eyes. "Sorry," he said.

They were on his cot, naked, in each other's arms. She snuggled closer in his embrace. He'd always seemed like a slight man, especially next to Robbie and her father. But under his unassuming clothing, his body was solid. He worked out. His strong arms would never let go of her.

"No, it was just weird. Like my body didn't fit. But it wasn't any worse than my dreams."

"Like the one where you're falling, and you hit the pavement, and don't wake up?"

"You know about that one?"

"Hm." He nodded, sighing a breath through her hair. "It used to send a jolt through the whole house when you had it. At least, it did to me."

He politely failed to mention that at the start of the dream, it was her father who tossed her off the roof. "Is it normal to dream about all your bones breaking?"

"It's normal to dream about anything at all. It's not normal to dream someone else's dreams."

She rubbed her cheek against his chest. He had thin, wiry hair growing on it. She remembered when she first met him, in her parents' kitchen, in the middle of a crisis: the young medical student had inadvertently met Captain Olympus and the Bullet, read their minds, and learned all their secrets. Her parents had been a little afraid of him, though they masked it with their usual anger and bravado. But he'd been kind to her. For her, his calmness had always translated to kindness rather than mystery. Then she went away, isolated herself, avoided them; she didn't see him for four years. When she returned, his kindness had been replaced by something else entirely.

"Do you take the pills, isolate yourself, because you're afraid of hurting people with your dreams, or because you're afraid of revealing yourself?" It was a little of both—she could guess by his hesitation, by the thoughtful look in his eyes. "Don't worry about me, Arthur. Don't worry and don't be sorry."

"It's wondrous. You're the only one who isn't afraid of me, at least a little. Even your father takes this extra effort to try and hide his thoughts when I'm around."

They lay still for a time, in the pause the world seemed to have taken just for them. The chaos held its breath for a moment.

It wouldn't last.

"Leyden Industrial Park," Arthur said. Celia hadn't realized she'd been thinking of it, in spite of her intentions. "You think it all goes back to the Leyden Industrial Park."

He cradled her head against his chest. Her mind lay open to him. Maybe he could make sense of the data jumbled there.

"Arthur . . . how much of us is made and how much is born? That Anthony Paulson is Simon Sito's son shouldn't mean anything. It shouldn't add to my suspicions. It's as bad as everyone assuming I ought to be a certain way because of my parents. I have *nothing* in common with my father—"

"Do you really believe that?"

She craned her neck and found him looking back at her, admonishing. Slowly, reluctantly, she shook her head. It would have been easier to get along with her father if they had nothing in common. Not harder.

She said, "Fifty years ago, something happened at the Leyden laboratory. That accident started a pattern that was passed on to the children and grandchildren of those present. It drove Sito mad, and it didn't end. It's been changing the city for fifty years. It's still out there, in you, my parents, Typhoon, Breezeway . . . me. What will my children be like? What will they suffer?"

He ran his fingers along the side of her head, brushing short locks of hair behind her ear. "I'll bet they have red hair. And a bit of a temper. Apart from that, who can say?"

"You're being patronizing."

"A bit, perhaps." He smiled.

"My father will kill us, if he finds out about this."

"Well, he's not going to find out from me."

A familiar chirping beeped from the floor. Celia's phone, tucked in her jacket pocket, was ringing. Arthur moved aside to let her get at it.

At the same moment, his desk phone rang.

Climbing from the cot, he said, "It's Suzanne. Something's wrong."

Do it yourself caller ID.

He answered. "Suzanne? Yes, I'm here; I've been here the whole time. No, I wasn't answering . . . I'm sorry. Would you like to explain what's wrong, please?"

The display on Celia's phone announced the call came from Analise.

Celia answered. "Yes?"

"It's me," said Analise, sounding rushed.

"What's wrong?"

"I'm on the verge of getting arrested, that's what's wrong. Apparently, the cops expect this curfew thing to apply to us, too." Us, meaning the city's superhuman guardians. "It's a goddamn stand-off right now, and I either give in or knock 'em down with a wave and get the hell out of here. Then they *will* have grounds to arrest me. I didn't know who else to call. Have your folks run into this? Do they know anything?"

"I don't know, I've been asleep—"

"Oh my God, you with those stitches and everything, I'm sorry—"

"No, no, it's fine. This is important. Just hold on a second, don't blow anything up." She covered the mouthpiece of her phone. "It's Typhoon. She says the cops are trying to arrest her for breaking curfew."

Arthur covered the mouthpiece of *his* phone. "Suzanne says there's trouble. We'd better get upstairs." Hurriedly, he said back into the phone, "No one, no one, Suzanne. I'll be there in a moment." He hung up and started retrieving clothing and dressing.

Celia turned back to her phone. "Can you rappel out of there or something?"

"They've got a helicopter out," Analise said. Her breathing came fast, and the usually self-assured woman sounded flustered. "But I'll see what I can do."

"Where are you?"

"The corner of Seventieth and Pierson." That was Typhoon's usual patrol haunt, near the harbor, with ready access to plenty of water.

"Hang tight. We'll see what we can do. I'm glad you called."

"See you." The call cut out as if Analise had turned the phone off in a hurry. She shouldn't even have been calling in a situation like this. She must really have been in trouble.

Celia hurried to find her clothes as well. Arthur paused and smiled at her, which made her flush.

"I ought to ask you out for dinner," he said. "Bring you flowers. This hardly seems right, after everything."

Shrugging, she repressed a giggling fit. This was surreal. Pleasantly surreal, but still.

She walked the three steps to his side and touched his cheek. "It's appropriate. It's who we are." She kissed him.

"Thank you," he said with a sigh. "Thank you for coming here."

Her grin turned wry. "Anytime. So tell me—I've always wanted to know why you never wore a costume, a skin-suit uniform, like the others." She indicated his plain shirt and trousers.

"I'm a telepath. A glorified track suit hardly seemed necessary."

Side by side, they went into the hallway and caught the elevator.

Arthur said, "I've found Warren. He knows about Typhoon."

"What can he do?" Celia said. "He's out past curfew, too."

"I'd hope after all this time we've earned some allowances," the telepath said.

"You know what Dad would say about this? He'd say this is a conspiracy to get the supers off the street. To get them out of the way. If the cops say anything about wanting to arrest him, he'll blow up."

She thought it was a joke. At least, when she started she meant it to be a joke. But Arthur wasn't smiling. He didn't even heave the flustered sigh of frustration that the team sighed when Captain Olympus was about to fly off the handle. Instead, the tension around them spiked, as the situation moved from a simple misunderstanding to a crisis.

The mayor had instituted the curfew. He could send an order through the commissioner to the cops, who'd be all too happy with any excuse to go after the superhumans. Again, the mayor.

Arthur said, "Celia, I find it disturbing that you and your father view the world in exactly the same way."

"What, we're both paranoid with severe persecution complexes?"

There, she'd done it again. Made a statement that was far too obvious and true to be funny. He raised a brow as if to indicate, *You said it, not me.*

The elevator doors opened to the penthouse. Businesslike, Arthur strode out, into the West home and to the Olympiad command center. Celia trailed behind a couple of steps, realizing too late what this was going to look like. Arthur's hair was mussed, his shirt rumpled—at least it was mostly tucked in—and he'd forgotten his jacket. Her own hair was usually tousled to some degree, but she'd been sleeping on it. Futilely, she ran her fingers through it to smooth it out. The bandage over her stitches had come off. Her dress suit looked thrown on. She still smelled Arthur's sweat on her.

It was going to be obvious to everyone.

Her phone rang again before she reached the command center—just in time, before she entered the shielded room. She looked at caller ID, and resisted the urge to throw it, to get it to shut up.

"What?" she answered.

"It's Mark. Celia, you need to tell your people to stay off the streets."

That boy had the worst timing. She even felt a thread of guilt at hearing his voice. But the way she saw it, he'd left her first.

"My people? What do you mean, *my* people?"

"Your parents. The other vigilantes."

"They're not *my* people, Mark. And what the hell do you think I can do about it? You think they listen to me?"

"They're your parents. You at least have access to them."

And the police would, too, if they ever bothered to talk to the Olympiad.

"You ever tell your father how to do his job?" she said.

"What they do isn't a job! It's a hobby!"

No, she thought. It's a vocation. A calling.

"Mark, we're already trying. Can't you tell your guys to back off Typhoon? She's not the one trying to start anything."

"The cops at the harbor district have just called for backup," he said.

They were going to spook Analise.

"Mark, please, tell your people to stand down." She wasn't used to begging, but it was a surprisingly easy thing to do when it was the right thing to do, when it might actually help.

He paused, and she thought she was going to scream, waiting for him to answer. When he finally spoke, despair weighted his voice. "I'm not there. I'm listening to it on the radio."

"I'll call Chief Appleton," she said. "Maybe he can do something."

"No, I'll call him. But if there's any way you can get the Olympiad off the street, please try."

"Okay, yes. Thank you, Mark. Thank you for calling."

"Celia, I . . . take care." He clicked off.

They needed to have a nice long talk. God only knew when that would happen.

She entered the command center in time to hear Suzanne say, "Arthur, thank God you're here! And Celia—did you sleep well? Are you feeling better?" she called from her post at the communications terminal. She was in street clothes, though her skin suit showed under the collar of her blouse.

Her mother assumed she'd been in bed—here, in bed—all day. Maybe she and Arthur wouldn't be discovered.

"Mark just called. He wants all you guys off the streets. The cops are ready for a standoff."

Suzanne said, "Arthur, call Warren and Robbie in, we can't risk a confrontation with the police."

"I already contacted Warren. Robbie's with him."

"Are they coming back?"

"I don't think so—" He cocked his head, listening to an unheard voice, sensing something ethereal. "Something's happening."

The city's vigilantes and police force had avoided an outright battle for over twenty years. Forty, if you counted the Hawk's tenure. Surely one wouldn't erupt now.

Suzanne turned a dial that brought the volume up on the police radio. A voice crackled from the speakers.

"Shots have been fired, I repeat, shots have been fired. There's been a flood, a wave of some kind, we have men down—"

TWENTY-SIX

SUZANNE returned from discarding her civilian clothes. She was Spark, now. When the costumes came out, they ceased being her parents and became the four-color heroes of legend.

"Suzanne, what do you possibly think you can do?" Arthur said.

"I don't know." Spark paced back and forth along the computer console. "I have to be ready. They might need me."

The news channels had finally gotten cameras to the harbor area, though the police forced them to keep a wide berth. Pierson Street was completely flooded, as if a tidal wave had crashed in and scoured the place. No one had been killed outright, but two police officers were missing, and feared swept out to the harbor. Typhoon had disappeared during the confusion, and one officer reported seeing the Bullet—briefly.

Reports were mixed as to whether the police had fired at Typhoon before or after she released the tidal wave.

All Celia, Suzanne, and Arthur could do for the moment was watch the jerky, static-laden images from the news cameras, listen to the sensationalist commentary—talk of the superhumans gone rogue, of a new criminal mastermind taking over—and listen for the latest reports on the police radio.

Then Captain Olympus buzzed the Olympiad's emergency line.

The flashing red light made them all flinch; Spark pounded the button to reply.

"Yes, Captain, we're here," she said to the speaker.

"We're coming up from the garage. We have injured." He cut off the line.

Without comment, Spark ran to the back of the room and the elevator that led straight to the subterranean passage, where the Olympiad gained access to its hangar and vehicles. Arthur, more calmly, went to a supply locker hidden behind a secret panel that lay flush with the slick wall and removed a first-aid kit.

Celia waited by the table. She'd only get in the way if she tried to help. The injury couldn't be serious—a graze, a twisted arm. There was only so much they could do with a first-aid kit. She liked to think if the injury were serious, her father would swallow his pride and go to the hospital. Take Robbie to the hospital—no way was Warren the injured party.

The elevator door hissed open. Captain Olympus exited first, as-sisting someone, a woman, her arm over his shoulder. Spark went to her other side to help, bringing her into the light. It was Typhoon, her blue suit damp and shining with water—and blood. The Bullet followed them to the table.

Typhoon was walking under her own power. She just seemed weak. Her taut jaw made her face, or what was visible of it, a pic-ture of grim forbearance.

Stunned, Celia pulled a chair out from the table and offered it to her.

She'd keep her mouth shut. Until Analise said something, she'd keep her mouth entirely shut. She stepped out of the way as her parents helped the young woman into the chair. Then, the bloody gash in her shoulder became visible. It had been bound with a strip of cloth. The wound had mostly clotted, but rivers of blood streaked Typhoon's arm. Not life-threatening, but the shock and blood loss were probably telling on her. She kept shaking her head.

Celia caught Arthur's gaze. *Don't tell*, she thought at him. *Don't tell them who she is.*

He nodded.

"A shot grazed her," Olympus said. "I thought it best to get her to safety."

"I feel so stupid," Typhoon muttered. "They started shooting at me and I just lost it. I never lose it like that when the bad guys are shooting."

Spark said, "It's because you know you're better than the bad guys. The police confused you; they're supposed to be good guys."

"They still are," Arthur said. He knelt by her and got to work, peeling off the makeshift bandage and dabbing at the wound with a gauze pad. "They believe they're following orders and protecting the city, just as we are. Best not forget that. We're all being played, I fear."

"By the Destructor?" Typhoon said. "It's his style."

"That remains to be seen."

"You didn't have to do this. I'd have made it out on my own." She tried standing, as if she really were well enough to walk out of there.

Olympus put his hand on her shoulder and held her in place. No one could argue with that grip, and Typhoon didn't have a body of water nearby to help her. "You're staying."

"I'm not taking my mask off."

"No one told you to," Olympus said.

Typhoon . . . Analise—Celia was getting confused—caught her eye and glared briefly. *Keep quiet.*

So be it.

Celia leaned against the table and watched the news broadcasts. The police had issued a warrant for Typhoon's arrest. The bulletin warned the public that she was dangerous. Not armed and dangerous, Celia noticed.

On one station, helicopters panned searchlights over Pierson Street. Rivers of water ran along gutters to pour back into the harbor. That wave must have been incredible, a wall of water as tall as the buildings sweeping down the street. Red and blue police lights flashed off glistening brick and concrete. Dozens of cops scouted the area; out on the water, divers searched from a police boat. They wouldn't stop until they'd found the two missing officers. Their condition would determine which way this whole business swung.

She turned off the mute key on another monitor, showing a different news station. A woman anchor intoned, ". . . have word that another of the city's superhuman vigilantes has broken the mayor's curfew. This is an exclusive report. Gina, what do you have for us?"

The scene switched to the jerky video from a news helicopter—and why the hell weren't the reporters being hauled in for breaking curfew?—and the rough sound feed filled with background noise.

"Thank you, Paula. Reports say that Breezeway has been sighted in the lower downtown area. A police helicopter has been dispatched. Now, we've been ordered to stay out of the area, but our cameraman thinks we have a good chance of spotting something if we— Hold on. Wait a minute. Yes, there. Can you see that?"

The view zoomed abruptly as the cameraman brought a distant point into focus. The shot was wobbly, vertiginous, but the tableau became visible. A speck, which resolved into a human figure, streaked across the view, flying thirty feet above the tenement rooftops. The camera sped along to keep up with it. Two helicopters approached from opposite directions, apparently hoping to cut off Breezeway's path. They should have known better than to try something like that. Breezeway was setting them up for a spectacular, cinematic head-on collision designed to make them look like idiots.

Reporter Gina continued. "You probably can't hear it, but the police in one of the helicopters are calling over a loudspeaker for Breezeway to turn himself in to avoid charges of resisting arrest."

Gina was right, her microphone didn't pick up the loudspeaker, but Breezeway's form shot ahead, speeding up, a response that would surprise no one. The two police helicopters swung around to follow, one of them climbing in altitude, the other one dropping, as if they could sandwich him between them.

Celia never thought she'd be rooting for Breezeway.

The camera managed to continue tracking the flier. The superhuman had veered left, apparently heading toward the uptown district where he could lose himself among skyscrapers, where the helicopters wouldn't be able to follow. She wondered: If she went to the roof, could she flag him down and offer him a place to hide out? *West Plaza, home to fugitive vigilantes.*

Then, the unexpected. A third police helicopter shot up from a hidden place behind a warehouse, in front of Breezeway, cutting him off. He pulled up, arcing away to avoid the new threat.

But they were ready for him. Something launched from the police helicopter, and suddenly Breezeway was dropping. Even Gina the reporter gasped in shock.

Breezeway didn't keep falling, however. He stopped short, dangling some twenty feet under the helicopter.

"Paula, can we have a replay on that? What just happened?"

Back at the studio, the technicians worked their magic, magnified the image, enhanced it, and replayed it.

The police had fired a net, like something a big-game hunter would use to catch his quarry. Weighted at the ends, it flew at Breezeway and entangled him as soon as it struck. The net remained attached to a rope, which was connected to a winch inside the helicopter. The cops hauled him in as if he was a fish.

Breezeway struggled, swinging under the helicopter until they pulled him inside, but his power was wind and flight, not strength. The net trapped him.

"They got Breezeway," Celia said, amazed, staring at the monitors.

The others joined her, equally entranced by the replay of the cops' triumphant moment. Typhoon stood next to her, her shoulder newly swathed in clean bandages, holding the injured arm to her chest.

"Damn punk," Olympus muttered, but he didn't sound terribly righteous.

Gina ended her report. "We'll be back as soon as we confirm that Breezeway is in police custody, and if they decide to reveal his secret identity. Back to you, Paula."

Arthur said, "Celia, turn to the other station. That one, yes."

Celia switched the sound over to the station that was covering the search in the harbor district.

". . . missing officers have been found."

Celia's stomach clenched. She looked at Arthur, who watched the screen and gnawed at his lower lip.

"One of the officers was found clinging to the base of a pier a hundred yards from where he'd disappeared, with minor injuries. Unfortunately, the second officer was not so lucky. The body of Officer Douglas Grady was pulled from the river moments ago. Reports from the scene confirmed he drowned when a tidal wave swept him into the harbor. The police have issued a statement that Typhoon is now wanted for murder. . . ."

Typhoon turned away from the monitors and found the nearest chair. Lowering herself into it, moving in slow motion, she murmured, "It was an accident. I swear to God it was an accident."

Arthur moved to her side. "We know, my dear. Look at me." She closed her eyes and shook her head, until Arthur took hold of her chin and directed her. "Look at me."

With the weight of his power behind the words, she couldn't help but obey. Trapping her gaze in his, he murmured, "Sleep. Very good."

She slumped into his arms without so much as a sigh.

"You didn't have to do that," Celia said, too tired to sound as irate as she wanted.

"Perhaps not," Arthur said, easing Typhoon back. "But with the evening's shocks, she's emotionally ill-equipped to deal with this new information."

"Who are you to decide that?"

"Would you rather have her lose control and burst the building's water pipes?"

"She wouldn't do that."

"You can't guarantee that."

And she couldn't.

Spark said, "We can put her in one of the guest rooms until she wakes up."

"She's going to be pissed off," Celia said.

Olympus crossed his arms. "This wasn't her fault. They can't pin this on her."

Arthur said, "Technically, it was. Maybe not murder, but they'll want to charge her with manslaughter, maybe negligent homicide."

"This was rigged. This is exactly the kind of bad press Paulson wants to pin on us to get us out of the way," the Captain said.

"But why?" Spark asked.

"Does it matter?"

Ultimately, a universe filled with conspiracies was so simple, so elegant, a series of interlacing clockworks.

"We're in a world of trouble, my friends," the Bullet said.

"No more so than usual," Olympus replied with false cheer as he gently picked Analise up and carried her in his arms.

Suzanne led him out, to show him which guest room to use. The Bullet followed.

"Sleeping out the night isn't going to make things any easier for her," Celia said to Arthur, who remained behind. "You just made it easier on the rest of us, not having to deal with her right now." She hugged herself tightly and watched the monitors, which showed replays of Breezeway's capture, of the police boat in the harbor, of a file photo of Officer Douglas Grady in uniform, proud and smiling.

"Perhaps," Arthur said. He walked over to her, tentatively touched her shoulder. She wanted him to. She had begun to wonder if their time together that evening had happened at all—they both reverted to their rigid selves so quickly, so firmly.

Then, he squeezed her shoulder, put his arms around her. She leaned into his embrace, and he kissed the top of her head. How could he have been so afraid of emotion? His feelings for her wrapped her in a warm cocoon. She'd never have to wonder if he loved her.

He pulled away abruptly. She started to complain, but a moment later the others returned to the command room. She was sure she blushed as red as her hair. Arthur quietly watched the monitors. He'd had much more practice maintaining that mask of calm.

Suzanne and Warren had pulled street clothes—shirts and trousers—on over their skin suits. Suzanne had pinned her hair into a bun.

"Warren and I are going to try to post bail for Breezeway. If we're lucky, maybe we can talk Chief Appleton into releasing him into our custody."

Warren, the Captain, added, "Robbie, Arthur, I want you to stay here and monitor the situation. Don't go out, unless it's an emergency. We don't want to give the cops an excuse to start shooting."

Arthur said, "It begs the question: After all this, what constitutes an emergency?"

"The Destructor breaks out of the asylum?" Warren said, offering a cocky grin. He put his arm around Suzanne's shoulders and the two of them left, side by side. Like they were just going to bail their kid out of jail or something.

Arthur huffed. "As if I'd be able to do anything about that."

Nobody told Celia what she was supposed to do.

"Perhaps you could keep an eye on Typhoon," Arthur said softly.

She nodded. She wanted to kiss him before she left, but Robbie was right there. Maybe if she imagined it, filled her mind with the thought of it, he'd read it there. He'd know.

—*Later.*— Was the thought he returned.

Thoughts weren't enough for her, she decided.

She looked in on Analise, sleeping in one of the guest rooms down the hall. Her parents had honored her request and left her mask on. It must have been uncomfortable, but Analise was out cold and didn't seem to notice. She lay on her back, arms folded over her stomach, head tilted slightly. She breathed deeply and seemed fine, for now.

Celia went to the living room to stare out the windows.

It was the same city. It couldn't have been, though. The city she looked out on had turned hostile. A half-dozen police helicopters circled over various neighborhoods, at various heights, shining lights down on the streets. Where one of them focused a light on one spot, then circled around that spot, the craft looked like a toy spinning on an illuminated wire. She listened for the pounding beat of helicopter engines, but heard nothing.

She was lucky to be here, lucky to be safe within these walls, protected by the city's heroes. Not out there, restricted by curfew, holed up, alone and afraid.

It was a different world, where she could return to her parents' home and feel safe.

Absently, she rubbed her forehead. She ought to bandage it again. The throbbing of the stitches had been increasing all evening.

"You ought to sleep. You ought to have been asleep all day." She turned. Arthur came toward her, hands in his pockets, his expression sheepish. "I couldn't stay away. Robbie can watch the monitors by himself."

In another step they came together, body to body, arms wrapped around each other.

"Don't worry about the city. It'll come out right. It always does. There's nothing you can do just now."

"I've got all these puzzle pieces," she said, her voice tight, on the verge of tears. It was just stress—she wasn't weak, she wasn't breaking down. "I should be able to figure it out. I should be able to pin something on Paulson by now."

Arthur guided her to the sofa, made her sit, then sat with her and eased her back until she was cradled on his lap.

She sat up abruptly. "You're not going to make me sleep, are you?"

"That wouldn't help you get rid of the headache, would it? No, Celia. Not like that anyway. Please rest, though. I'll watch over you."

He didn't crawl inside her mind to shut it down, not like he did when he commanded sleep. He just held her, stroked her hair. When he said he'd keep her safe, she believed him. She slept.

TWENTY-SEVEN

W HAT the hell is this?"

"Warren, keep your voice down. This is the first she's slept all day."

That was Arthur speaking. His chest rumbled under her cheek with the words.

"Then she didn't spend the day in bed? What was she doing?" That was Suzanne, sounding as irate as Warren, or at least sounding as irate as she ever sounded.

Arthur sighed. "Trust me, you don't want to know."

"Am I to understand that you've . . . been spending time together. Or something?" her mother asked.

Celia imagined her mother's arms were crossed. Suzanne's voice made it sound like she'd crossed her arms. She supposed she ought to open her eyes and look. She shouldn't leave Arthur to deal with this by himself.

"That isn't any of your business," Arthur said matter-of-factly.

Warren exploded. Not literally, though close to it. "You took advantage of her. She looked to you for protection and you—"

"Dad." Celia emitted a dramatic-sounding groan as she sat up. "Stop it."

"Celia, what the hell are you *thinking*!" He was on the verge of smashing something. Maybe he'd show a little more restraint in his own house.

The room was awash with a faint, chill light of early morning. She was still half sprawled on Arthur's lap. Her parents must have walked in on them—embarrassing at any age. Arthur hadn't woken her. He'd let her sleep. Or he didn't care anymore if her parents knew. She met his gaze. He smiled thinly. Again, and always, she felt warm and safe.

Suzanne was, in fact, crossing her arms. Her gaze was worried, her brow furrowed and confused. "This . . . this isn't so bad, maybe. You remember some of the boys she brought home in high school? This'll take some getting used to, but at least we can trust Arthur—"

"Would someone we trust seduce our daughter, a girl he vowed to protect—"

Celia sat up straighter. "Actually, I think it was me."

"What?" Warren said.

"I think it was me who seduced him." Arthur's hand rested on her back. She hoped he kept it there.

Warren sputtered a moment, then said, "Then he shouldn't have let himself get seduced!"

"Warren, please stop shouting," Arthur said. Celia couldn't tell if he'd wrapped any power in the command. Mostly, he sounded tired.

"I'm not shouting! Mentis, this is . . . outrageous! She's my *daughter.*"

This was him finding her in the Destructor's lair all over again. Small comfort that he wasn't actually yelling at *her.* She wondered: had he not been as upset at the thought of her joining his enemy as he had been at the thought of her sleeping with his enemy?

"Warren—," Suzanne said tiredly, rubbing her forehead like she had a headache.

Arthur said, "She's also an adult, or hadn't you noticed? I certainly have."

That sent a warm and pleasant rush through her gut.

Her father, however, roared. They all knew him well enough to recognize what came next: he cocked his arms back, preparing to launch a wall of force that would knock his enemies aside. Except this time his "enemies" were in his own living room.

Warren's attention focused on Arthur, but Celia was caught between them. She let out a short scream and huddled forward, arms protecting her head.

"Stop!" Arthur called out, reaching forward with a hand. The single word shook the room, rattled through their minds.

Warren made a choking gasp of pain and clutched his head. He stumbled back, but didn't quite fall.

"Will you two stop it!" Suzanne put herself between the two men, pointing an arm at each of them as if ready to let out a blowtorch. Celia looked up, hesitating—surely her mother wouldn't lose it, too.

Arthur put his arm protectively around Celia's shoulders and glared at Warren, who was straightening, muscles trembling with tension.

If she had known she'd cause this much trouble, she'd have let the bus carry her into the river.

She peeled herself from Arthur's grasp. "Look, I'm sorry. This shouldn't be such a huge, end-of-the-world deal, but apparently it is. I'm sorry."

She started to leave, to stomp back to her room and take a painkiller.

"Celia, wait," Suzanne said. Celia waited. "This is about us, not you."

She indicated the three of them. The three grown-ups, Celia thought, even now reverting to the old way of looking at them. It didn't matter that most people, seeing Celia and Arthur walking hand in hand down the street, wouldn't look twice at them. In a different world, they might have met in college. They might have met when she did his tax returns. In a different world, this would have been normal. But Warren and Suzanne saw something different.

Celia crossed her arms and wished she could hide while the three of them exchanged glares.

Suzanne suddenly pointed at Arthur. "Don't you go trying to convince me this is all right!"

"Wouldn't dream of it," Arthur said softly. He looked at Celia.

They could run away, she thought, staring back at him. Flee the city. If her parents couldn't handle it, then they could leave Commerce City altogether.

—And what of the city?—

He was one of its protectors. He couldn't leave. Neither could she, or she'd have done it already.

Suzanne continued. "It's just . . . it's just going to take some getting used to."

"I understand," Arthur said. "What if we promise not to get caught snogging on the sofa like a couple of teenagers?"

Warren sputtered; Suzanne hiccupped. She put her hand over her mouth. Then, she was giggling, and she wiped tears from her eyes.

"Okay," Suzanne said finally, recovering to a point.

"Bah!" Warren rolled his eyes and stalked out of the room.

Celia couldn't have hoped for better than that, really.

Arthur had known what to say to calm them down, or at least to diffuse the situation a touch. He said to Suzanne, "Did you have any luck with Breezeway?"

"No. The police are charging him with breaking curfew. No bail's been set."

"Damn. That means the rest of us are targets."

"Not until nightfall. I'm going to make some breakfast." She crossed her arms as she left, as if she were still holding something back.

Arthur let out a sigh. "That went well."

Celia giggled, and returned to the sofa and his arms, giddy with . . . something.

JUSTIN RAYLEN IS BREEZEWAY!" shouted the front page of the morning paper, alongside a mug shot of a surly man in his twenties, with a flop of sandy hair above a slim face. Celia recognized that face, but only if she imagined a mask over the top half of it, and a broad, cocky grin. In the mug-shot photo, he still had some of that brash air. But he glared like he wanted to hit someone. Like maybe the person standing behind the camera.

The police had released his secret identity, apparently out of spite. She imagined the scene at the police station. How many officers had it taken to hold him down before they could take off his mask? How much weight did they hang on him to keep him from going airborne? Had his winds scoured the police station, sending papers and debris flying? Had anyone gotten hurt, so they could lay those charges on him as well? So far, the police had charged him with breaking curfew and resisting arrest.

The morning news shows were worse. They'd tracked down Justin Raylen's girlfriend, Marjorie Adams, a waitress at a downtown diner—Analise's favorite diner, in fact, and wasn't it a small world? Cameras chased her—a familiar scene that gave Celia a dose of déjà vu—as she fled to what looked like an apartment. They focused intrusively on her tear-streaked face; over and over again, she told them she had no comment, she didn't want to talk to anyone, just leave her alone.

One intrepid reporter found Marjorie's mother. "No, she had no idea what he was. He always told her he worked nights, that he was on call at his job, and that was why he disappeared all the time. She never guessed he was Breezeway. How could she?"

Celia had an urge to call Marjorie, to tell her it wasn't so bad having a superhero in your life. She wasn't sure the young woman would appreciate it.

She found herself hoping her parents would sit this one out. Maybe they'd take to heart what happened to Breezeway and Typhoon, and not get involved this time. But they wouldn't stop. They'd been doing this for long enough; that ought to at least reassure her that they knew what they were doing.

After the newspaper and a cup of coffee, and after changing into jeans and a sweater, Celia went to the guest room where Analise slept. She knocked, listened, heard nothing. Softly, she opened the door. Inside, the lights were off, the curtains drawn.

She crept into the room, opened the curtains, and put a chair by the bed, to sit and wait.

Once the room grew light, Analise turned, stretched, and hissed in pain. She touched her bandaged shoulder and opened her eyes.

"Hi," Celia said.

Analise rubbed her face, then pulled off her mask and threw it aside. She lay back on the pillows, staring past Celia's shoulder to the far wall.

Celia could sit there all day, watching her friend, waiting for her to say something, but Analise didn't look like she was ready to talk.

"I brought you some clothes to change into. There's coffee and bagels in the kitchen," Celia said. "I can clear the place out, if you don't want to see anyone. Or you can sleep all day. Or something."

Analise was stubborn. She was just as capable of lying there, silent, as Celia was of sitting there. More than anything, though, Celia hadn't wanted her to wake up alone in a strange place after all that had happened. Typhoon didn't have a team like the Olympiad to back her up, or to pick up the pieces.

"Mentis," Analise said finally. "I could feel him in my mind, shutting me down."

"He thought it was best. He didn't want you to panic."

"He had no right."

"No, he didn't."

Analise bit her lip and rolled to her side, so that Celia had even less chance of looking her in the eyes. *She's going to crawl into a hole and never come out.*

"He knows who I am. What am I going to do, Celia?"

Two rooms over, some eight years ago, Celia had woken up in her bed the morning after the Destructor had abandoned her, after her throw-down, screaming argument with her father. She wouldn't let either of her parents approach her, and Celia remembered the profound look of hurt on Suzanne's face, the reddening that meant tears were on the way. Celia couldn't have hurt her mother more if she'd stabbed her in the gut and wrenched the knife. Mentis and Robbie had had to corner her, calm her down, and take her home themselves, where the telepath had finally made her sleep.

Convenient, being able to knock out anybody you had a problem with at the moment.

She'd woken up and asked herself, *What am I going to do?*

After Appleton arrested, then released her, she'd ended up packing a duffel bag and going to a homeless shelter.

To Analise she said, "You take it one day at a time. You move on."

"But what I did—"

"One day at a time, Analise. My parents will probably let you stay here as long as you need to. This is all part of something bigger. We're trying to clear it up."

"We? You a hero now? You going to help save the world?" She smirked bitterly.

"I'll be in the kitchen if you need anything. It's down the hall."

Analise stared at the wall, eyes closed, hand on her forehead.

Her mother was alone at the table when Celia returned to the kitchen. She held a mug of coffee in both hands and pretended to read the paper.

"How long? You and Arthur, I mean," Suzanne said.

Slowly, Celia took a seat and tried to catch her mother's gaze, but Suzanne wasn't looking up.

"Not long," she said. It wasn't her mother's business. It wasn't anyone's business. She resented the need to defend this. If he had been anyone else, some stranger she could have invited over for dinner, Suzanne would have been ecstatic.

"I know you're both consenting adults, and I shouldn't say anything, but . . . but it's very strange. He's known you since you were young."

"I know," Celia said, looking away. She hadn't realized how securely she'd locked her old life away, that it took effort to dredge up those memories now. That it was like she'd died and become someone else. "After I went away, though . . . I came back, and everything was different. Everything." That was all she could think to say. Her only explanation.

Finally, Suzanne looked up. She was smiling. "I still see the little girl in braids and a white dress. I'm sorry, I always will." She quickly brushed away tears.

Celia's throat closed up. God, now Suzanne had her doing it. If she opened her mouth, she might burst. So she came around the table to Suzanne, knelt by her, and gathered her into a hug. Suzanne needed it, and it didn't cost Celia anything.

"He's the only person who sees me for what I am, Mom," Celia whispered. Suzanne squeezed harder.

Someone cleared her throat.

Analise stood in the kitchen, her gaze on her feet. She wore the T-shirt and sweatpants borrowed from Celia and carried a wadded-up mess of blue fabric in her hands—her costume and mask.

"Oh!" Suzanne said, recognition dawning. "Oh my—can I get you some coffee? Analise, isn't it?"

Analise nodded. "Yeah. Thanks."

Celia pulled out a chair and made her friend sit. "You decided to get out of bed."

"Had to sometime."

"Without the mask."

"I don't think I can do that anymore." She dropped the costume on the table and grimaced at it.

She's going to give it up, Celia realized. The idea of it seemed wrong, out of alignment with the rest of the universe. She couldn't give it up; she was the next generation the Hawk was talking about. Wasn't she?

"Celia, you knew all along, didn't you? That Typhoon, and she—"

"Yeah," Celia said.

Handing Analise a cup of coffee, Suzanne said, "I have to ask: How on earth did you two meet?"

"By accident," Celia said. "It turns out I have a knack for recognizing supers without their masks. God knows how that happened."

Analise gripped her mug with both hands, as if it were an anchor. "Are you going to hand me over to the cops?"

"No," Suzanne said. "I might think about talking you into turning yourself in. But not right now. Not until everyone calms down."

"You've done this for how long, and you never killed anyone in all that time," Analise said, low and tired, so unlike her. "And here I am—"

"Oh, I've killed," Suzanne said. "We all have."

"Bad guys, sure." As if that made a difference. "In self-defense. What am I going to do?"

"You're going to wait here," Suzanne said calmly. "We're going to let things settle and make sure you get a fair hearing."

Analise frowned, making her whole face pucker. She wasn't used to taking orders or listening to advice. She wasn't used to waiting. But she nodded now, no wind left in her sails. She was broken. Celia hated seeing her like that.

The men had retreated to the command room, waiting for the next crisis. Celia didn't think anything would happen during the day. The explosions always came at night. She wondered how Arthur and her father were getting along. Probably ignoring it, pretending like nothing had happened.

Robbie suddenly appeared in the kitchen. He'd run from the command room, followed by his trademark wind, which ruffled the women's hair. To them, however, he just appeared.

"The Strad Brothers aren't finished yet. Or maybe not the Strad Brothers. It's a new MO. It could be somebody brand-new. It isn't robberies this time—it's bombs."

Celia stood. Suzanne was already on her feet, but she stepped forward, an intent look on her face.

Leaving another breeze behind him, Robbie disappeared, back to the command room.

"It is the Destructor," Suzanne said softly. "We should have known, no jail can hold him—"

But Celia knew that wasn't right. She'd seen the Destructor,

Simon Sito, a shriveled old man ranting in his cell. The three women followed Robbie to the command room.

On the view screens in the darkened room, Celia saw the nightmare her parents had always dreaded, the vision of what would happen if they failed to stop the Destructor or any of the other ultraambitious villains who'd come along: fires burning, the city in ruins. *Their* city, her home.

One screen showed a map of the city. A half-dozen flashing red dots marked trouble spots. They lay scattered all over the city: one by the harbor, another by the university, a couple in the south end—one of them only a few blocks from her apartment. None of them was in the downtown area, near West Plaza. And none of them was in the northeast warehouse district. Those areas showed dark.

The other screens flashed between images captured on security cameras or broadcast by news teams. Fires burned everywhere. Flames engulfing buildings filled up the screens. Firefighters ran, lugging hoses. Water and fire retardant sprayed and arced toward the blazes, seemingly futile. The liquid droplets were so tiny.

"The bombs went off simultaneously," Robbie explained, his voice steady and somber. "Incendiary, rather than explosive. Like whoever did this wanted to set half the city on fire, to keep us fighting all day rather than causing one round of damage and letting us pick up the pieces. This is about chaos."

"We'll help," Warren said. "Suzanne, do you think—"

Her lips turned up wryly. "Fighting fire with fire? Maybe. Find out where the flames are spreading fastest and I can try to create firebreaks."

"Me, too," Robbie said. "Scare up a little wind, steer the flames back on themselves."

Warren turned to Arthur. "Doctor?"

"I'm sure I can think of something."

Typhoon stared at the screens without blinking. "I should go. This was made for me—"

Suzanne touched her shoulder. "No. You're hurt, and you're

wanted by the police. Stay here, monitor the situation, stay by the radio. If we need your help, we'll call you."

Celia was shocked when, instead of arguing, Analise nodded and sank into the chair by the computer.

Warren had already marched to the hangar elevator.

Suzanne quickly smoothed back Celia's hair. "Hopefully this won't take too long."

"Just be careful," Celia said.

Suzanne and Robbie—no, Spark and the Bullet—joined her father, Captain Olympus.

Arthur hesitated. Without a word—without even a thought for once—he gripped the back of Celia's neck and kissed her on the lips, quick and heartfelt. He drew away quickly, looking in her eyes before he turned to join the others.

The Bullet was sputtering. "Hey—what? What the hell was that—"

The elevator doors closed on the quartet before Celia heard the others' response.

Her lips were still tingling.

"What happened to the cop?" Analise said.

"I don't know," Celia said, and she didn't. At the moment, Mark was out in the city somewhere, dealing with the bombings, with the fires and chaos. Saving the city. "Are you okay? I mean, really okay. I know you want to be out there—"

"No," Analise said. "I should. I should want to, but . . . Do you have a glass of water? Is there a glass of water somewhere?"

"The kitchen."

Analise stood and ran from the command room. Celia followed more slowly. She still had a headache.

When she arrived in the kitchen, Analise was filling a glass from the faucet. When it was full, she set it on the counter by the sink and glared at it. Both hands braced on the edge of the counter, her back bent, her face puckered in concentration, she watched the glass like she expected it to get up and dance.

"I can't do it anymore," Analise said, with a strange calm. "I ought to be able to make that water jump out of there. I ought to be able to soak the whole kitchen with it. I can't do it."

Celia didn't know what to say. She managed to choke out, "You're just tired. You've had a shock. You'll get it back."

"What if I don't want it back, Celia?"

Would Analise be Analise without the part of her that was also Typhoon?

Analise picked up the glass and drank all the water out of it. She finished, wiped her mouth, and gave Celia a bitter smile. "Guess I'd better keep an ear on the radio like your parents asked."

Head bent, she went back to the hallway that led to the command room.

Celia didn't know what to think.

She went to the living room and the windows. From here, she could see the smoke rising from three of the fires. The two on the south end were close together, the harbor fire a ways off to the right. Pillars of black rose into the washed-out sky, pulsing as they grew and shrank, as new flames fed them or other flames were put out. A gray haze filtered the sun, bathing the city in pale orange light. News and police helicopters swarmed like moths.

The whole city could burn to the ground in hours, if no one was there to fight it.

Her phone rang.

"Hello?"

"Celia? It's Mark. I don't know who else to go to. You're in the middle of this as much as I am. You seem to know more about it than I do."

He sounded panicked, as if the Destructor was breaking down his door then and there. "Mark, what is it? What's wrong?"

"This is all a distraction, isn't it? Like the kidnapping plots, like all the crime sprees. Something else is at the heart of it. I think I've found it. There's a place, a building, the Leyden Industrial Park."

Celia's nerves stretched, as if they all waited to snap at once. She stared out at the burning city.

Mark continued. "The place was supposedly mothballed fifty

years ago, turned over to the city for urban development. It was slated to be demolished for the highway plan, but that got held up. Celia, the place is active. My father's been channeling money out of his office. Embezzling."

Embezzling. That spoke to her line of work, and the professional side of her interrupted him. "Mark, how do you know? What evidence—"

He kept talking, like he had to get it all out at once before he lost his nerve. "Phony payroll, phony contracts, grant money to nonprofits that don't exist." All rote stuff, downright mundane. Paulson deflected attention from such activity with smoke and mirrors—with an orchestrated crime wave. "There's more. I found evidence of payoffs to all the robbery suspects, and the bus hijacker. The rest of the money is going to this Leyden Industrial Park."

Pieces snapped into place, almost too neatly. If Mark had all this evidence, he could serve his father up on a platter.

If he could turn in his own father.

"Mark, we shouldn't be talking about this on the phone."

"I'm going there, to the Leyden building. I have to see for myself."

"No, you should call the police." But he *was* the police. "Call for backup. You don't know what he's doing, he could have an army in there—"

"Will you meet me there, Celia? I need to talk to you. I need your help."

"Yes, of course," she said without thinking.

"Meet me there in an hour."

"Mark, hold on, you shouldn't—"

He hung up. She growled at the phone. He was being an idiot. He only had half the pieces and couldn't see the whole picture. He probably thought his father was running some sort of gambling or drug ring. He probably thought he could talk to Paulson, make him see reason, convince him to turn himself in. He wouldn't be able to stand up to Paulson and arrest the guy.

If she got there first, maybe she could talk him out of it. Maybe his call to her was a suicide's cry for help. She ran to the foyer, then hesitated, thinking of Analise in the Olympiad command room. No, her parents might need Analise where she was, able to survey the entire city and monitor police activity. They might need her more than Celia did.

Celia entered the elevator. Inside, she punched the button for the parking garage. Going down.

TWENTY-EIGHT

ON the elevator ride down, she thought about calling Arthur's cell and leaving a message. Then realized he must already know what she was thinking, what she had planned, even across the city. The thought was both ominous and comforting. There was a time when all she wanted to was to be alone. But if she got in trouble, Arthur would know.

Michael was on-call, but not in the valet office when she reached the basement parking garage. She wasn't about to ask him for a ride anyway.

The key card her father had given her worked on the West Corp valet office, where the keys to the fleet cars were kept. Not that she'd driven at all since Michael taught her how when she was sixteen. Assuming she found an inconspicuous car, and assuming she could drive it, and assuming she didn't get pulled over by hyper police—

She found a dark blue sedan, automatic transmission, and matched the license plate to the keychain. Settling into the driver's seat, she reacquainted herself with the controls and dials. She could do this, she could do this. Key in ignition, turn, shift gears, press gas pedal.

The engine revved, but the car didn't move.

Then she remembered to release the parking brake.

So slowly the speedometer barely registered, she pulled out of the parking space and up the ramp leading to street level. Once on the street, she pressed the gas a little harder—if she drove five miles an hour the whole way, she'd take all day to get there. She sat leaning forward, her back rigid and away from the seat, clinging to the steering wheel and peering fervently through the windshield.

Fortunately, with the city blowing up around them, not too many other people were on the road. She had little traffic to contend with, and the cops were all in areas of the city where bombs had gone off.

Carefully, she drove northeast.

The warehouse district was an area of wide streets and cavernous buildings. This was a whole other city, the opposite of the one she looked down on from her parents' living room. Here, she was an ant staring up at concrete walls that went on in all directions. She was trapped at the bottom of a canyon.

Slowing down, she looked for street signs, made out address placards bolted to the sides of buildings—some of them rusted and illegible. She found the right street and was afraid she'd spend the afternoon driving back and forth along its length, looking for the right building.

She shouldn't have worried.

A shroud of smoke covered the city, along with a smell like a furnace, making the sky like dusk, dark enough that she could see her destination lit up like a storm cloud. Crackling electrical lights glowed through clerestory windows like faint bursts of lightning. Something was happening inside a building that was supposed to be abandoned and crumbling to ruin. That had to be the place.

It had taken her too long to get here. Mark would be here any minute. She couldn't let him face down his father. No one should have to do that, no matter how great they were or how great their father was. She drove around the block and when she didn't see his car, she parked, got out, and waited on the corner.

Twenty minutes later, twenty minutes of pacing the sidewalk

and wondering about the crackling electric hisses that occasionally whispered from the warehouse, and wondering if maybe she shouldn't be standing in plain sight, Celia began to think she'd been too late after all. Mark had been smart enough to not park right in front of the building and hid his car on one of the side streets.

Maybe he'd already gone inside.

Maybe she should try to talk to Paulson herself. And say what? *You're a jerk, just like your father?*

Actually, that had its appeal.

She could just sneak in and take a look. If she saw Mark in there, if he was in trouble, she'd call Arthur, the police, and Analise at Olympiad HQ and get help. If they weren't too busy keeping the city from burning down.

Celia approached the front door. Glancing nervously at the windows high on the warehouse walls, she hoped no one was watching. They looked too frosted to see out of.

What she took to be the front doors, double steel slabs that swung open, had chains looped through the handles, secured with a padlock. Just what she'd expect to find on a shut-up building. She walked around. In the back she found a loading dock, and a sliding steel door that was not only unlocked, but open a crack. She climbed up on the ledge and squeezed through.

She entered a dark receiving area, a block of bare concrete, cold and musty, with an air of abandonment. Continuing through it, she stepped softly, aware of the numbers and depth of the shadows, and how much danger might be waiting for her.

She reached the door in the back of the warehouse area. Standard size, simple knob, unlocked. It led to a hallway. She passed a few doorways with frosted windows showing dark interiors. Ahead, though, a light with a bluish tinge showed. Voices murmured. Mark, was Mark in there?

The rectangle of light before her beckoned. Pressing close to the wall, she crept forward until she reached the frame, where she could peer into the main room.

This was it. This was the lab where Sito performed his great experiment, where the accident happened, where a dose of radiation bathed a dozen technicians and instigated mutations that no one had expected or understood.

And now, Anthony Paulson was trying to re-create it.

She looked into the cavernous heart of the building. The ceiling reached up three stories, and the tile floor stretched fifty yards across. Most of the space was empty. All activity congregated in the middle, in an area that could have fit in any of the rooms she'd passed. She expected dust, the stale smell of air that had been locked behind walls. But the air was fresh—the hum of fans and filters edged the background noise. Floodlights blazed down on a clean room, spotless lab benches, cabinets, tables, monitoring equipment. In the center of it all stood a device mounted on a wheeled pedestal. A hundred wires looped from point to point, from a box underneath that might have been a battery or a power relay, to bolts protruding from steel rings looped around a cylinder that made up its bulk. The thing looked like a cannon, tapered at one end, where a series of glass or crystal nodes reached out, aimable and threatening. Toward the back, coils of copper wire glowed, like the interior of a toaster grown too hot.

A half-dozen people worked, some of them studying equipment, making adjustments and scribbling observations onto clipboards. Another half-dozen, burly men wearing dark clothing and brooding expressions, stood at the periphery, armed with machine guns. She recognized Paulson's ubiquitous aides and bodyguards among them. More pardoned convicts? Loyal henchmen?

She found nothing unexpected here. Nothing particularly impressive. Nothing she hadn't seen before. Like father like son. This might as well have been the Destructor's Psychostasis room.

Or this might have been a scene from fifty years ago. She could almost see it, in the black and white of newsreel footage. Her imperious, bearded grandfather standing to the side, cane in hand, observing; a young Simon Sito bustling around the equipment, perhaps rubbing his hands together in anticipation; and a dozen scientists and techs, innocent, just doing their jobs—George Denton, Anna Riley, Emily Newman, Janet Travers. Young faces from personnel files, come to life in Celia's imagination. History changed here, and none of them ever knew it.

She didn't see Mark.

"Ah, at last. Ms. West, I've been expecting you." His voice echoed, a rich tenor used to giving speeches to filled auditoriums. Anthony Paulson emerged from behind a bank of computer servers and strolled toward Celia. The sleeves of his dress shirt were rolled up, the collar undone, tie missing. A couple of the lab people glanced up, frowning.

Celia blinked, stunned, a deer staring down the barrel of a hunter's rifle. She'd been quiet, she'd stayed hidden, she hadn't made a sound—Paulson must have been watching the door. He'd left that loading dock door open just for her, and made sure she found her way down exactly that hallway.

She turned to run. Behind her, two gunmen stepped out of formerly shut rooms, barring her escape. They moved toward her, threatening with their weapons, herding her through the door and into the warehouse, into the glaring lights.

Flanked by her captors, she approached Paulson.

Mark told him he'd called her. Mark told him she was coming, that was the only way he could have known to look for her. Still, she said, cautiously, "How?" She couldn't think of anything else to say.

Paulson raised his hand, showing her the mini digital player he held. He touched a button, and Mark's voice played back at her:

"Celia? It's Mark. I don't know who else to go to. You're in the middle of this as much as I am. You seem to know more about it than I do . . . This is all a distraction, isn't it? Like the kidnapping plots . . ."

God*damn* it! She fell for that stupid, idiotic trick *again*. She stamped her foot and growled, rolling her eyes to the ceiling and mentally beating herself up.

Paulson said, "I've been recording Mark's phone calls for some time now. He made this one to Chief Appleton an hour or so ago. I had my people doctor it up a little for you. Fortunately—for me—the good chief has his hands full with other business right now and can't spare anyone to send over here."

Celia shut down her emotions and recalled the bitter teenager who would have sought out this situation. People like Paulson, like Sito, expected people like her to be cowed by their power and intelligence. They expected that a bright-eyed young woman would want everything they had to give—or that she could be frightened into putting herself in their control.

They expected her to care.

That was the trick: be blasé enough that nothing they did affected her. She crossed her arms, turned her back to the gunmen, and faced Paulson. She locked a careless smirk on her face and raised an eyebrow. She watched him like this was all some silly joke. Stayed quiet, because she couldn't think of anything witty to say.

She kept herself from looking at the gunmen. They weren't going to kill her. Paulson needed her or he'd have had her killed already. One of them reached for her shoulder. She sensed him approach, timed it, and stepped forward before he could touch her. Heart racing, stomach knotting, she walked toward the lab area and the machinery.

"What are you going to do with me?" She wanted to laugh. Almost, she let herself laugh.

"Nothing special," Paulson said. "Human shield. Keep your parents out of my way."

The usual reason, which meant he wasn't any different than the others. She was only ever a tool to them. Which was a good thing—no one ever expected a tool to fight back.

"Huh," she said, like she thought this was an interesting but irrelevant conversation, and turned her attention to the tower of glass, wires, and steel. "So this is it? Sito's machine?" she said, gazing at the device as if it were a piece of incomprehensible art in a museum. "You know what it does, right?"

Paulson said, "Do *you* know what it does? Exactly how much do you know?"

"I have a guess. Did you have to rebuild it, or was it intact?"

"It had been stored—wrapped in plastic and shoved in a closet. The place hadn't been touched. It's like someone expected to come back to it."

But no one ever had. Sito's depression and madness consumed him, the other techs had signed nondisclosure agreements. Had her grandfather saved the lab? Had he suspected how the device had worked?

"Hmm," she murmured, by way of polite observation.

"Ms. West, I'm curious. What do you think this does?" He watched her, gaze sharp, smile amused. His intensity burned; she felt like a mouse to his cat.

Calm, stay calm. "You know, I could make the argument that all this really belongs to me, as Jacob West's direct descendant."

"I heard that your father disinherited you. Or that you disinherited yourself."

She gave a noncommittal shrug. "People hear lots of things."

"Be that as it may, I claim salvage rights on behalf of the city."

"You're not doing this for the city."

"Oh? Really?"

She tested her range, strolling a couple more steps toward the machine, moving partway around it, looking it up and down, purely out of curiosity. The gunmen didn't move to stop her. All three men watched her closely, but she might as well have been a bug in a jar for their lack of apparent concern.

No one was afraid of her; she didn't have any powers. But she wouldn't flinch. That was her talent. That, and recognizing people under their masks.

"No one ever does anything like this except for themselves." She offered him a sad smile, full of condescension.

"You sound so sure."

"You've killed people to get what you want. The good guys don't do that." She made it an observation of fact, not a judgment call. Like she didn't care that he'd killed.

"Weber, hand me that folder. Yes, that's the one."

One of the people in a lab coat brought Paulson a thick file from the top of a filing cabinet. The brown pressboard folder looked familiar; Celia had been looking through similar folders all week. The texture of files from that era was distinct.

Paulson passed the folder to her. "Take a look at this."

She opened the file, balancing the spine in her left hand. Stacks of pages were fastened to both sides. She flipped through, taking in random lines and data. Charts, graphs, diagrams, rows of jagged lines labeled with numbers, black-and white-photographs.

The top page of text read, "Use of Directed Radiation to Induce Neurophysiological Responses, with the Intent of Encouraging Specified Emotional Traits in Human Subjects."

The early West Corp logo, before the last couple of redesigns— the crescent moon as the arc of a bow and an arrow tipped with a star preparing to launch—was printed on the bottom of the page.

West Corp didn't have a medical research division. At least, it didn't now.

"This is the original lab report," Celia said. "I found the financial statements, but not the research notes."

"Because I found them here months ago. One of my aides uncovered this place during a survey of the area. This is what I put the highway plan on hold for. Go on, keep reading."

Sito, a psychologist with an interest in how the physical structures of the brain contributed to the development of personality and psyche, had been experimenting with methods of altering the brain physically to treat mental illness, as an alternative to medication or shock therapies. Other potential applications had presented themselves.

In a memo to Jacob West in which he urged secrecy, Simon Sito outlined the potential applications of his procedure. Some of the most promising involved nonlethal crowd control: draining aggression from people at the touch of a button, or pacifying prison populations to prevent riots. The process could curb the socio-pathic tendencies of habitual criminals.

Initially, Sito planned on concentrating his efforts on one emo-tion, one simple but particularly useful personality trait: loyalty. With a press of a button and a dose of mild radiation, the test subject would become instantly loyal to the chosen ideal or person. Convicted criminals could finally be made into useful citizens. And more—the military and police forces would have nothing but intensely loyal soldiers and officers in their ranks. No more treason, no more bad cops.

Sito had identified the characteristic that he believed held soci-ety together, and he wanted to learn to manipulate it. This was the same technique he would later use to develop the Psychostasis de-vice, which used radiation to erase his victims' basic sense of self and individuality. Like the rest of his psyche, he'd gone from want-ing to alter—to improve—to wanting to destroy.

"I don't understand," she said, not because she didn't, but be-cause she didn't believe it. She didn't believe she could possibly understand what she was reading. The conclusion refused to allow comprehension.

The superhuman mutation was a side effect. Completely unin-tentional and unobserved by everyone involved in the experiment. It was crazy. But it wasn't. It was all right here. She couldn't let her shock show. She had to be vaguely interested. Not appalled.

Paulson said, "If it had worked, West Corp would have had a monopoly on the human spirit. Too bad for you it didn't. Your father might have been the mayor now."

Now that was an appalling thought. But he was missing some-thing. He didn't know about the superhuman connection.

"You know there was an accident, right? You may have the lab report, but I've seen the accounting files. The employees were paid off." The lab file didn't have anything about the accident, as if no one had thought to update the information after that. The report was frozen in time.

"Nothing happened," Paulson said. "The device released a benign dose of undirected radiation. It had no effect."

So she did have something to hold over him. She had a lot of cards, in fact. *Play them one at a time.* Let him think she was giving him something.

"Would you like to hear some of the names of people who worked here at that time? The people who were present during the accident? Jacob West, father of Warren West, also known as Captain Olympus. Anna Riley, who went on to have a daughter, Suzanne, who became Spark. George Denton, father of Robbie Denton, the Bullet. Emily Newman was the mother of Arthur Mentis. I'm not through tracking everyone down. But I think you get the idea."

She let him consider that. The look of wonder growing on his face was rewarding.

"Really?" he exclaimed finally. "Sito accidentally created the superhumans? That's kind of ironic, isn't it? It almost makes me wish we hadn't fixed the thing. Oh well."

He didn't want superhumans. He wanted a troop of undyingly loyal supporters. He didn't want anyone stronger than he was getting in the way. That was why he'd worked so hard keeping the Olympiad busy, wearing them down, distracting them from the real danger.

She stopped her slow pacing around the machine and looked at Paulson across the radiation emitter.

"Have you considered something?" he said. "The device must have worked partially, even when it malfunctioned. Why do you think the superhumans have all become crime fighters and not circus freaks? Something inside them drives them to it. They're loyal to this city over everything else in their lives. You know that better than anyone."

She'd asked Arthur if people were born or made. Maybe they were both. She could be forgiven for feeling that her entire life had brought her with purpose to this point.

But the process wasn't perfect. Janet Travers should have passed along the mutation to Anthony Paulson—and she had, Celia supposed. The man had become mayor, after all. But he'd inherited Sito's megalomania as well. For every person Paulson successfully converted, how many would he push into insanity? Did he, in the end, think he was doing this for the good of the city? Then again, maybe the loyalty experiment *had* been passed on untainted to Janet's grandson, Mark, the dedicated cop.

And what of Jacob West's granddaughter, who had spent half her life standing on the cusp between success and disaster?

In a low voice she said, "You think you can make the experiment work."

"I have."

He had a room full of loyal scientists and bodyguards here to prove it. And more—

"You tested this on Andrea." Instead of a sullen woman who'd grown tired of politics, he now had the eternal publicity photo standing by his side.

He just smiled.

Nothing frightened her anymore. She had to remind herself of that. Otherwise, her hand would shake. She closed the file and set it on a nearby table. One of Paulson's technicians glared at her and shoved it away from where he'd been working.

"Great. Now what?"

"Ah. This is where I make an unlikely speech revealing all my plans, thereby giving you a chance to thwart me. That doesn't happen in the real world."

"Who says I'm trying to thwart you? You know my history. Maybe you've shown me where the cards are falling. Maybe I want to ask you for a job."

"I'm curious, what exactly do you think you can offer me and my operation? What did you bring to the Destructor's operation when you joined him?"

"Nothing," she said. "Absolutely nothing."

"Figures. Too bad I'm not in need of a staff accountant."

The evil masterminds never were, more's the pity. Accountants knew when to shred the documents.

"Then what can I do for you, Mr. Paulson?"

"Sit quietly in the corner like a good little hostage." He smiled.

At some unseen cue, the two henchmen took a step toward her, preparing to herd her off again. As soon as they moved, she jumped.

"Don't shoot, you'll hit the machine!"

They'd raised their weapons; Paulson had stopped them. At least something had played out in her favor.

She jumped onto the lab table. If she'd thought about it, she wouldn't have done it. It was too far, too crazy. But she didn't think. She jumped again—toward the radiation emitter.

She only had to knock some of the cables off, or break the glass focal points, assuming they were breakable, or throw it out of alignment. Mysterious devices always had alignments they could be thrown out of. Her heart was beating too hard, her blood rushing too fast for her to worry about what would happen to her *after* she crashed into the thing.

She landed awkwardly, scrabbling at narrow handholds, kicking to keep her balance. For all its bulk, the machine was delicate, spindly almost, balanced on a single-wheeled column. The column spun, the whole thing rolled, and cables came unplugged in her hands, emitting sparks and crackles. Lab workers scattered, and Celia managed to slide to the floor, stumbling but keeping her feet and clutching the machine for balance. It gave a few more sickly sputters for good measure. Static prickled along her arms. She let go, brushing her hands and wincing.

That would delay the plan. Probably even long enough for those with experience in battling evil masterminds to get here.

She assumed the Olympiad would show up. They always did, somehow.

Please, Arthur. Get here quick. God only knew if he'd pick up on her thought. Could he hear her across the city? Only if he was listening?

Or would her thoughts pull at him like a fish hook? After they'd slept together, did her thoughts feel any different to him?

The two henchmen tackled her. She went limp and let them, offered no resistance, gave them no reason to start pounding her with the butts of their weapons. Or start shooting. They each took a shoulder and shoved her to the floor, facedown, then pried her arms back. It felt like they used duct tape to bind her wrists together. When they'd finished, they hoisted her to her feet.

"You do have a death wish," the mayor observed. "You weren't lying when you testified at Sito's trial."

Nobody trusted her. Not even the bad guys. She didn't glare. She wasn't even angry. She'd accomplished something: She'd learned what Paulson was planning, and she'd delayed him. Apart from that, let him think she was crazy. That was easy enough for most people to do.

She gave him a great, smug grin, like she didn't care, like she thought he was an ass. And on one level she didn't care, because this wasn't about her. It had never been about her. When she was seventeen and thought everything *should* have been about her, that was when she grew angry. But now, she knew better. Commerce City ran on the blood of all its people.

His frown grew deeper, emphasizing the lines of his face, making his cheekbones hollower, and for a moment she saw in him his father, Simon Sito. She saw a bitter old man bent on chaos. Paulson's rhetoric about the greater good aside, whatever he did would result in chaos. And she'd stopped him.

"Put her over there." He pointed to a chair, out of the way by a bank of computers. The henchmen pulled her off her feet, dragged her over, and slammed her into it, jamming her bound arms behind the back. Her shoulders ached. Paulson regarded her with a sense of smug triumph. "Good thing I have an updated model."

He shoved the now-broken model—a mere prototype?—out of the way.

"This is the wide area broadcast version." He pointed up, to the end of the warehouse, where a similar device but newer looking—

sleek, modern—was mounted on a platform, suspended from the roof. Instead of the focusing materials on the narrow end, however, it had a parabolic dish that would beam out radiation to as great an area as possible.

One of the lab people pulled a large knife switch on the wall. A panel in the roof slid open and, with a mechanical whine, the platform rose. Cables trailed from it, along the ceiling, secured to the wall, and leading finally to the computer banks.

He wasn't going to use the machine on his underlings, or his political opponents, or the prisons. That wasn't his plan.

"You're going to use it on everyone. The whole city."

"Think of it: every citizen working for the common good. Everybody feeling a deep emotional connection to every other citizen. There'd be no more crime, no more selfishness—"

The communist ideal obtained through the wonders of modern technology.

"What about free will?"

"What about it? What has free will done for you in your life, except brought you trouble and heartache? Commerce City doesn't need free will, it needs direction."

"Your direction," she said.

"Of course. Who else has the vision to lead this city? Your grandfather might have had it, once. But your father surely doesn't."

The place, the situation he described, was no longer Commerce City. Celia could act like she didn't care—that holdover from her teenage personality filled her so easily. Maybe she hadn't changed so much after all. But in the end, she did care about at least one thing. There was a reason she'd never moved away.

"You just did it, you know," she said.

"Did what?"

"Told me your plan."

"So what? You're tied up."

Celia couldn't pretend not to be appalled. She had run out of tricks, and she'd run out of attitude. "My parents will stop you. The Olympiad will stop you."

"Oh, they will? Because they always stop the villain? They may try, and they might even believe they're doing the right thing. But they'll have to realize that I'm the one working for the greater good here. And they'll have to get through you to get to me."

"That's never worked for anyone else."

"I'm not anyone else, am I?"

She wriggled her hands, strained her arms, but the tape held tight, pinching her skin in the process. This was wrong, all wrong, like some kind of tabloid headline gone astray. The son of the Destructor and the daughter of Captain Olympus—but Paulson didn't know. She had to assume that the mayor had never learned who his father was. He was as wrapped up in the history of this experiment as she was.

She shook her head. "You're just like everyone else. I've heard this all before. I've seen it all before. No one who's ever tried to destroy Commerce City like this has ever succeeded."

"I'm not trying to destroy the city—"

"But you might succeed anyway. Your father would be so proud. He was always trying the direct approach."

"What are you talking about?"

"Your biological mother was a technician in this lab fifty years ago. She was present when the accident happened. Your father, Simon Sito, was also present. It begs the question: What mutation did their genes pass on to you?"

He laughed nervously. "I think you've just crossed the line into madness."

"I looked up the adoption records."

He stopped his pacing, his gloating over his accomplishment, and stared at her. She might have played the card too early. Distracted him at the wrong moment. But she had to buy time. She had to trust that someone would come get her. Her lack of fear, all the times she'd been in situations like this and been able to hide her fear—it hadn't been out of indifference, or boredom.

She'd always believed her family would rescue her.

Nothing to do but keep on. "Haven't you ever wondered about

your real parents? Haven't you ever wanted to find the records? You're the mayor, you could have seen the files whenever you wanted." When he didn't reply, she kept on. "You're like me. You inherited the mutation from both sides of the family. But what did it do to you? You have to ask yourself that now, don't you? What has the mutation done to Mark?"

He went to the table, found the roll of duct tape, and cut off a piece. Returning to her, he slapped it over her mouth. Didn't bother securing it all the way. It didn't matter—she couldn't open her mouth at all.

She couldn't gasp through her nose; she tried catch her breath and to stay calm. Maybe she could scoot the chair over to the electrical outlet and pull the cord out with her feet.

Her cell phone rang. It was still in her front pocket. She hadn't turned it off. She'd done stupider things in her life, she supposed.

Everyone in the room—except Paulson—checked pockets and belts. Paulson looked at her, then came over. Checked her out, found the pocket. Moving to stand behind the chair, he reached forward, almost embracing her, and worked his hand into that pocket. He didn't bother trying to be quick about it, or gentle. He moved slowly, searching, kneading along her hip. If her phone hadn't been in the way, he'd have done more, reaching as far as the pocket would allow. Her skin crawled. She looked over her shoulder at him. Glared, trying to catch his gaze. The bastard was groping her and wouldn't even look her in the eye.

He finally pulled out the phone, with enough time to answer before the ringing stopped.

"Hello? Who is this? Mark, hi! This is your father. Yes, she's here, but she's a little tied up at the moment."

Why did people think that was funny?

Celia wished she could hear Mark's reply. He wasn't shouting, which was probably good. Was he here? Outside the building? Had he found the car, traced it to West Corp, and guessed it was hers?

Paulson continued his side of the conversation. "No, I haven't hurt her, except maybe her pride. Hopefully the situation will stay that way—"

He lowered the phone, regarded it thoughtfully for a moment, then clicked it off and tossed it on a nearby table. "Oh well. Weber, how close are we?"

"I'm still not sure we can draw enough power—"

"You've been working on that problem for weeks."

"Yes, I know sir, and I swear we've done everything we can—"

"It'll have to be enough, won't it? We'll probably have some unwelcome visitors shortly. We have to do this now."

Now. *Now* the Olympiad would crash through the doors, flames bursting and a wind buffeting in their wake. Her mother would come to her first, rip off the duct tape, and start crying.

The mechanical grinding of a generator motor started. The computers whined, ramping to a higher level of activity. The flood-lights overhead flickered and dimmed.

Above them, the device started a low, electrical throbbing. It threw off a shower of sparks. This sent the technicians into some-thing of a frenzy, running to monitors and checking cables.

"Weber?" Paulson asked.

"Systems nominal, sir."

The device sat just below the roofline, visible over the lip of the platform. The parabolic dish, the emitter, protruded above the roof at an angle, westward, toward the center of Commerce City.

Paulson watched her staring at it. "The dish will emit a pulse of low-grade radiation. Not harmful in any way. But it's designed to leave people disoriented, open to suggestion. Ready to be led. Ready to be loyal. Then, as the dutiful mayor, I'll step forward and offer my guidance."

His voice had to compete with an increasing volume of noise. The generator was screaming now. The device crackled, and more sparks arced away from it. Some of its cables glowed white.

One of the computers in the work area caught fire. A henchman rushed forward brandishing an extinguisher. The odor of chemicals and burning plastic became overwhelming.

"What's happening, Weber?" Paulson said.

"A circuit breaker's malfunctioned. We can't regulate the flow of power."

"But the device will still work?"

"Yes. I mean, I think so. It may work a little too well—"

Celia wasn't strapped directly to the chair. Theoretically, she could get up and . . . throw herself at something. Kick a computer or knock Paulson over, maybe. Before somebody shot her.

"Weber!" Paulson had stormed forward to grab the scientist by the collar of his lab coat. He hauled Weber around and held him so they were face-to-face. Weber was pale, bloodless, just a shade lighter than his coat. His eyes were wide and shocked. The man was trembling in Paulson's grip. "What's happening, Weber?"

"It's out of control! We were having trouble finding enough power, but I think we overcompensated, reducing the resistance in the fuses . . . it's caused an overload, but the device is still online, it's still—"

"What are you saying? Will it work? That's all I care about."

"That's what I'm trying to tell you, we're using the circuit breakers from the original equipment—fifty-year-old equipment—and they can't handle this kind of power. The surge has overwhelmed them all. The emitter still works, but the power flowing into it is completely unregulated. The radiation burst will be equivalent to that produced by a hydrogen bomb."

"The radiation. Not the explosion?"

"Yes, nothing will be destroyed, but the people—"

A hydrogen bomb going off in the middle of the city. Millions affected. Radiation poisoning would burn them all. He'd stop it, the mayor would stop it, now that he knew it wouldn't work. Celia worked her mouth, trying to loosen the duct tape so she could shout at him. Her fingers were tingling; she'd cut off circulation in her hands in her struggles.

"Can we stop it?" Paulson asked.

Weber shook his head. "Not in time. The building's circuit breakers are shot, we'd have to get the power company to shut down the entire grid in this area. The emitter's cycle has already started. It'll launch the radiation burst in minutes!"

At the roof, the device hummed, like a continuous spark of static. Many of its parts were glowing now, including the parabolic dish. It was spliced directly into the building's electrical wiring. There wasn't a cord to unplug.

Paulson stared at it a moment. At this stage, the criminal masterminds, the ones like Sito, would rant about their imminent failure, scream about how close they'd come, carry on about the general unfairness of the universe, then they'd escape through whatever back door they'd made for themselves. Had Paulson built himself a back door?

He said, "We'll have to get underground. That should protect us, shouldn't it?"

"Yes, yes," Weber said. "But the city—"

"The city will need a steady hand at the helm after a disaster of this magnitude. I'll have to make sure it has one, won't I?" He raised his hand and signaled to the rest of his technicians and henchmen. They gathered and followed Paulson as he marched out of the room, to the corridor that led to the loading dock. Presumably the building had a basement. Presumably it would protect them from the blast.

No one even looked at her as they left.

She threw herself sideways, tipping herself and the chair over. Kicking the chair away, she extricated her arms from around the back. Partially free. With a bit of contorting, she tucked her legs up and pulled her arms under them, so her hands were now bound in front. She ripped the duct tape off her mouth and took several deep, heaving breaths. She could breathe again. She'd thought she was going to faint.

Lying on her back, she stared up at the roof, at Paulson's doomsday device. The thing glowed white-hot, searing her eyes as the rest of the room's lights flickered. No cord to unplug, no way to shut down the power. No way to get up there and break it. No way to throw herself on that grenade. She couldn't fly, she couldn't send a lightning bolt to destroy it.

Maybe she could audit it to death.

Then again maybe, just maybe, she could limit the danger. Contain it. Save something. Hope Mark put the pieces together and brought his father to justice. What a mess. And how terrible that she had time to think about it. To consider. To decide.

Her life had brought her to this moment. She had practiced for it. She didn't hesitate.

Hands still bound, tucked to her chest, she ran to the knife switch that controlled the platform. With her luck, the power to it would be fried, sucked into the radiation emitter. Maybe it was on a different circuit.

How much time did she have? Minutes, seconds—

Holding her breath, forgetting to inhale, she reached the wall, crashing into it because she hadn't thought to slow down—it would take too long, slowing down. She grabbed the switch with both hands, got under it, shoved it *up*.

Another spark flashed, a hiss like the circuit was failing— then gears creaked. The platform mechanism groaned to life. Slowly, the device sank below the roof, and the steel roof panel slid closed. The device, now enclosed inside the metal and concrete warehouse, glowed like a sun.

Next, she went to the computers. She'd fight it; right to the last moment when she didn't have any time left, she'd try to stop it. Because if the radiation could penetrate walls, she hadn't saved anything. At random, she toggled switches, hit keys, pulled cords.

The emitter's noise changed, the whine rising in pitch. The light faded to orange—the color of something overheating, not the color of deadly energy. A shower of sparks flew, raining down on her like burning snow.

She laughed. She didn't know if what she'd done would help anything. But she'd done something. Maybe it had helped. She'd tried, and that had to count for something. So she laughed, because the weight of something she couldn't quite identify lifted from her. Elation made her lighter than air.

This was what her parents felt every time they saved the city, every time they battled evil and won. It was a high, addictive, they couldn't stop. Something like that thrill she got when she found a lost piece of data, but so much more. Infinitely greater. As big as the world. Superhuman.

"Celia!"

Captain Olympus stood in the doorway that led to the loading dock. His fists were clenched, arms bent in his fighting pose.

"Dad!"

He ran to her. He wasn't fast, not like the Bullet. He seemed to take forever to cross the distance. She wanted to meet him halfway, but her legs had turned to butter. She was melting in place. The room was getting hotter.

Then, he was right in front of her. He ripped the tape off her hands, gripped her shoulders, so full of intensity she could barely look at him.

"We have to get out of here, the thing's going to blow up, Paulson said it's radiation, going to kill everyone. I tried to stop it—"

"Shh, Celia, it's okay, you did okay."

The ambient noise shaking the room—electrical, mechanical, vibrational, pervasive—increased in pitch again, sliding upward in anticipation.

There wasn't time to do anything.

"Get down!" Her father pulled her to the floor, hunched over her, gripped her in a rib-crushing embrace. She curled up like a little child, fetal, as small as she could make herself, huddled in the shelter of his body.

A boom rocked the building, the steel girders, sheet metal, and concrete. The pulse lasted only a second, but the vibrations continued. The trembling of the floor traveled to the marrow of her bones. The sound, like an electric shock, but larger, slower, lingered in her ears. Her whole body shook.

The air smelled of ozone. Of burning.

A weight pressed down on her, like something had fallen on her. She was hurt, all her skin tingling—part of what was burning. Pushing up, she struggled to get out from under what trapped her.

Her father fell over.

He was burned. The invincible Captain Olympus had lost most of the hair on the back of his head. The scalp underneath was blistered. Most of his uniform had melted away. Strands of it melded into blackened skin.

Around her, the whole room was black, scorched. The platform, which had sunk halfway to the floor, had disappeared. The struts that had held it swung, flames trailing up their length. The device itself had fallen to the floor, and was now melted to an unrecognizable lump. The computers and equipment were smashed and burning, weak yellow flames licking and spitting from crumpled plastic and steel. The walls were scorched, the floor was black with soot—except for a circle around her, a body-size shape where she had been sheltered by her father. The fire had only reached her extremities: the bottom half of her jeans were blackened and torn, the skin underneath red and tender; her arms had also burned to a cooked lobster shade; her hair had singed. She was hurt, but she was alive, and she could move.

Her father wasn't moving.

"Dad," she whispered.

Wincing, he shifted, a flinch moving through his arm. His face was intact, the whole front of his body looked unhurt. But how deep inside him did the damage reach? She started to roll him over, but he cried out. She couldn't touch him without hurting him.

"Daddy, what do I do? I don't know what to do."

He opened his eyes, reached for her, found her hand by touch. Squeezed it hard, but not as hard as he was capable of. Not Captain Olympus hard. Could he see? Was he even seeing at her?

He whispered, "You're safe—"

He died with his eyes open, looking at her.

She pulled his limp body onto her lap, cradled him as if it would help, as if it would comfort him somehow. As if it would comfort her. But it didn't, because the skin on his shoulders came off in her hands.

Captain Olympus hadn't died saving Commerce City, as he'd always vowed to do, as everyone thought he might. He'd died saving her. Just her.

Twenty-three years ago:
"Suzanne, that's not normal, is it? A two-year-old shouldn't be able to lift that much weight."

The weight in question was an oversize pillow from the sofa. The lifting was nominal at best. Celia had managed to stand the thing upright and was valiantly maneuvering it so she could leverage it over her head, for some arcane toddler purpose. She'd get it off the ground an inch before the weight overbalanced and the whole thing slid out of her hands. Determinedly, she bent over and tried again.

Suzanne stood in the doorway to the kitchen, drying a plate. "Actually, I think that's pretty normal."

"Look at that," Warren said. "Persistence. *That's* a good trait."

"Yes, it is."

"Celia!" Celia looked at her father and grinned at the wide-eyed hopeful expression he wore. "Come here, Celia. Come on!" She ran to where he sat a few feet away—jerky, toddler running steps—and jumped at him. Laughing, he caught her. "You're going to be a runner, aren't you? Fastest girl in Commerce City."

"Warren, her powers might not manifest until she's a teenager, like it did with me. Ten more years at least."

He was tickling Celia now, and she was squealing happily. "I know, I just can't *wait* to see what she's going to do! You know—" He pointed excitedly at Suzanne. "I'll bet she flies."

She rolled her eyes. "So help me God if you throw her off the roof to see if she can fly, I'll *roast* you." Suzanne could do it, too.

"I wouldn't do that."

She smirked at him like she had her doubts.

Celia squirmed and laughed, oblivious.

* * *

She was still on the floor, holding her father half sprawled on her lap, pietà-like, when the others arrived. She heard footsteps echo, then more footsteps—too many. She looked up, through squinting eyes. The rest of the Olympiad was there. Robbie, Arthur, her mother.

She ought to say something. They'd expect her to say something. She opened her mouth, intending to apologize. She choked on a sob instead. Tears fell.

"Oh, Celia." That was Arthur, because of course he took one look at her, took one glimpse inside of her, and saw it all.

Robbie touched Suzanne's arm, but she moved away from him, stepping toward her husband and daughter. Maybe she'd been expecting this moment for a long time. Maybe she'd never believed it would happen. Celia didn't know, and she'd never ask.

Suzanne knelt by Warren's body, touched his chest, looked on him with such tenderness that Celia held her breath. This will kill her mother. She'd watch her mother die in front of her as well.

Suzanne looked at her and smiled. She cupped Celia's cheek in her hand, leaned forward, and kissed the top of her head, as if she were a child who'd skinned her knee.

Then she stood and walked away.

When Arthur came to her and touched her shoulder, all strength left her. She let him fold her into his arms and take care of her.

Robbie looked after Suzanne. Not that Suzanne needed looking after—she appeared elegant and stoic, regarding the proceedings with the cool detachment of a goddess. But he'd look after her anyway. Just in case.

Celia left the building, gingerly holding on to Arthur around the middle while he carefully gripped her across the shoulders. Eventually, she'd go the hospital for the burns on her arms and legs. In the meantime, they fit together and she wasn't going to leave him.

People would tell her later that there was nothing she could have done, that she had succeeded in saving the city, the building had contained the explosion, and her father knew the risks of the role he'd taken on. Every hero, even an invincible one, had a weakness, and subjected to a high dose of the radiation that had a part in his creation proved too much for the great Captain Olympus. People told her this over and over, trying to be helpful, not understanding that Celia had accepted her own death, and now had to accept the death of another instead, which was somehow harder.

Appleton was there, supervising the throng of cops sent to clean up the mess. He stopped her.

"We're okay," he said, pointing at her like this was another accusation. The look in his eyes, though, was pleading. "From now on, you and me, we're okay. Right?"

She only nodded.

Anthony Paulson and his scientists had been found hiding in a basement storeroom. Mark himself put the handcuffs on his father. He spotted Celia, and his eyes lit, then darkened when he saw her nestled against Arthur.

After Mark had secured his father in the backseat of a patrol car, Celia detached herself from Arthur to go talk to the detective.

"What were you even doing here? I know you suspected my father, but you should have come to me—," he said.

"He set a trap, and I fell for it." She shrugged. That moment seemed a long time ago, now.

He laughed, a stifled, bitter chuckle. "You always complain about having superheroes for parents. I'm guessing that's nothing compared to having a supervillain for one."

He looked to the backseat of the patrol car. Around the glare on the window, Paulson stared back. Both men's expressions were taut and unhappy, the family resemblance reflected back at one another. Celia and her father spent much of their own lives looking at one another like that. At least she'd had the excuse of foolish youth. At least she'd been able to make some repairs to that bridge. A few patches.

The mutual bitterness before her was palpable.

She looked away. "Mark, there's something you need to know.

I looked up your father's adoption records. I talked to some people. You probably ought to do a paternity test to confirm it, but I'm pretty sure your father's birth father was Simon Sito. I don't know what it means, if anything. But you should know." Not just the son of a criminal mastermind, but the grandson of one, too. How did *that* feel?

Might as well tell him he was the king of Prussia, as blank as his expression showed. No, not blank. Scarred. The vacant stare of a disaster survivor. He couldn't take another blow. He was done processing. It would have to wait.

He said, "I think I'll want to do that paternity test. To confirm that."

"Of course."

"I'm sorry about your father."

She didn't really believe it herself. That would have to wait until morning. "Thanks."

"What happens now?" He looked pointedly at Arthur Mentis, who was watching them.

"A funeral. Another trial." In which she would have to testify again. The cycle continued.

"What about us?"

The question evoked no emotion in her.

She shook her head. "I'm sorry, Mark. I . . . I'm just sorry."

TWENTY-NINE

SUZANNE West wore red to her husband's funeral. It was the talk of the society pages, as was the fact that she brought Spark's costume and threw it into the grave, along with what was left of Captain Olympus's. That was all she did to announce her retirement. The Olympiad was finished.

Damon Parks attended the service. So did Analise Baker, Justin Raylen, and a few others Celia recognized when she imagined them wearing masks. Like the middle-aged man with his arm over the shoulders of a skinny young punk—the Block Busters. Father and son, clearly. Junior looked as shell-shocked as she felt—maybe imagining his own crime-fighting father in that grave. She almost went to give him a hug.

Everyone was very polite and said wonderful things about Warren West and his service to the city. Celia and Suzanne held one another's arms. Celia thanked everyone. Suzanne remained silent.

The four Stradivarius instruments, along with the prize koi—alive, barely, in a fifty-gallon aquarium—were found in the basement of the mayor's mansion. Andrea Paulson threw herself across the door, refusing to let the authorities in, sobbing, vowing to stay loyal to her husband no matter what. She recovered from her nervous breakdown at Greenbriar, then filed for a divorce.

The day after Captain Olympus's death, Breezeway—Justin Raylen—was released, all charges dropped. With his identity revealed, he did more charity fund-raising events than crime-fighting.

The Bullet and Dr. Mentis continued the work, doing what they could, as anonymously as they could. Without the team, they returned to their early days of running down muggers and trapping burglars. Crime rates stabilized, with nothing more sensational than the usual examples of urban malfeasance to combat.

It was as if the whole city was exhausted.

Typhoon never reemerged. The warrant for her arrest remained outstanding. The tabloids had a field day with the mystery of what had happened to her and offered rewards for the revelation of her secret identity. Many young women came forward claiming to be Typhoon, even in the face of the arrest warrant. Of course, none of them could so much as tip over a cup of water. Books came out retreading the mystery, offering vague solutions, defending the hero, vilifying her.

Analise collected the books, the papers. But she never came forward. She became manager of the record store where she worked, and volunteered at the rec center teaching inner-city kids how to swim.

Apart from a trust set up for Suzanne, Celia inherited everything.

For a long time after the company lawyer left their first meeting, Celia sat behind the desk in Warren's penthouse office, the new owner of West Corp. The sleek, mahogany piece was a museum-quality example of high modernist design purchased by her grandfather. The thing was aerodynamic. Her fingertips skittered along the surface, smooth even after fifty years of constant use. Her father had left it in a state of disarray, pens scattered, file folders stacked in every corner, laptop computer still running. She'd have to clean it up, piece together what he'd been doing. She could do that.

The desk was her grandfather's, but the chair had been Warren's: large, leather, generously padded. Celia sank into it and felt lost. It had her father's shape to it. She'd get a new one. Something more modest, unassuming. She'd move this one to . . . somewhere.

Suzanne appeared and leaned on the doorway. Celia blinked back at her, feeling about five years old and in over her head.

"I always assumed he wrote me out of the will," she said starkly.

Her mother smiled. "He did, for a while. But he wrote you back in when you finished college. The West family is a dynasty. It's up to you to continue it."

Celia had spent the two weeks since the funeral bursting into tears at unexpected moments. She felt tears about to start, which wasn't fair, because she hadn't had a chance to talk to her mother in all that time. Suzanne had spent the weeks alone, looking at pictures, reading letters, with an attitude—clear in her hunched shoulders and bowed head—that said to keep away. If she started crying now, Suzanne might come over to comfort her—might start crying herself, and they'd comfort each other. But they wouldn't talk.

"If he'd asked me to come work for West Corp, for him . . . if he'd ever just *asked*—"

"He'd never ask," she said. "Neither would you. You are the two most stubborn people I have ever known."

She turned and walked away. For dinner that night, she made lasagna, the first time she'd cooked anything since he'd died.

The Sito trial jury returned a verdict of not guilty by reason of insanity. Sito was remanded to the care of the Elroy Asylum. The trial might as well have not happened.

A year later, Anthony Paulson was tried and also found not guilty by reason of insanity. He'd been diagnosed with narcissistic megalomania. Like father like son, although that connection was never made public. He agreed to undergo treatment at the Elroy

Asylum. Celia had a talk with the hospital's management and convinced them that under no circumstances should Anthony Paulson and Simon Sito ever be brought anywhere near each other. They shouldn't have known each other by sight, but Celia didn't want to take chances. Coincidence didn't exist in her father's world, or in hers. Better to prevent the opportunity for fate to take a hand in events.

Mark Paulson visited his father once a month. Celia learned that he also visited Simon Sito once. Soon after, Sito suffered a heart attack. A second heart attack a month later killed him. It was a peaceful death that he didn't deserve.

The detective worked like he thought he had to make up for both his father's and grandfather's misdeeds. Double shifts, countless hours of overtime. No number of promotions and commendations was enough, and he received many. At age thirty-five, he suffered a stress-related cardiac infarction.

Celia visited him at the hospital. It was déjà vu with a twist.

He couldn't look her in the eye. He kept an embarrassed smirk on his face, like he knew he'd done something stupid.

Celia crossed her arms and glowered. "You really need to stop trying to prove you aren't your father. I mean, look what happened when I did that."

He chuckled painfully and spoke softly because of the oxygen tubes in his nose. "You turned out all right."

"In case you haven't noticed, so did you. You inherited the untainted mutation, the loyalty trait. You'd do anything to keep this city safe, and the city needs that. You have to keep yourself alive because of that."

The smirk relaxed into a true smile and he sighed a breath of acquiescence.

"It's really good to see you, Celia. I'm glad we stayed friends."

"Me, too. We superhumans have to stick together."

Two years after her father's death, Celia West and Arthur Mentis had a daughter, Anna.

Celia lay on her side in the hospital bed. The baby lay nested on a pillow, sheltered within the curve of Celia's body. Anna had a round red face, scrunched-up eyes, and a fine fuzz of coppery hair.

Arthur sat by the bed, leaning on the mattress, his chin on his hands, watching the baby and wearing an odd half smile.

"What's she thinking?" Celia asked.

"It's very strange," he said. "She thinks in feelings. She doesn't have colors or sounds or images yet. But she has 'warm' and 'cold' and 'hungry' and 'sleepy.' She's a little of all of them at once, like she can't sort it all out. Right this minute, though, I look at her and feel 'safe.' I've never really looked at babies before." He was staring at her like she was an interesting scientific oddity.

Celia could see it now: Anna's teenage years were going to be hell with a telepath for a father.

Celia puckered her face to keep from crying. She'd spent far too much of the last nine months crying.

"What have we done?" she said. "What's she inherited? I'm going to be watching her every minute to see if she flies, or shoots lightning, or talks to animals. If she has a power . . . what are we going to do? What do we tell her? I'm so scared for her."

"I think that's normal for any parent."

"I want her to be normal."

"You don't get to make that choice."

She looked at Arthur. "You want her to have powers."

"Celia. I want her to be happy."

Anna stirred, opening her toothless mouth in a wide, wet yawn that made both parents smile.

Celia couldn't stop the tears this time, and her voice cracked. "I keep thinking he'd have been such a good grandfather."

"Perhaps."

The baby slept, for now.